Marriage Material

Sathnam Sanghera was born in 1976. He is an award-winning writer for *The Times*. His first book, *The Boy with the Topknot: A Memoir of Love, Secrets and Lies in Wolverhampton*, was shortlisted for the 2008 Costa Biography Award and the 2009 PEN/Ackerley Prize and named 2009 Mind Book of the Year. *Marriage Material* is his first novel, and has been shortlisted for the 2014 South Bank Sky Arts Award for Literature and the 2013 Costa First Novel Award.

D0321506

Praise for *Marriage Material*

'Sathnam Sanghera is busy carving out his own literary niche – in the multicultural British Midlands – which he explores with incredible grace, generosity and humour, while also locating himself cannily in a solid tradition of English provincial writing that includes Arnold Bennett among others. Definitely a man to watch.'

Jonathan Coe, *GQ*

'A stunning novel . . . touching and funny and feels so fresh . . . it just leaps off the page. I adored it.'

Deborah Moggach

'Adroitly updating Arnold Bennett's Edwardian masterpiece, *The Old Wives' Tale*, this engaging novel portrays three generations of a Sikh family who run a newsagent's shop in Wolverhampton from the 1960s to the present day ... As ruefully funny as it is keenly observant, the book is warm, affecting and enormously enjoyable.'

Sunday Times, Books of the Year

'Well-observed . . . *Marriage Material* rises far above cliché, not least thanks to its sharp prose and at times laugh-out-loud humour, which peppers the text even in the darker scenes . . . *Marriage Material* triumphs.'

The Times

'A satirical masterpiece . . . A razor-sharp disquisition on the trials of being an Asian newsagent . . . Handled with a poignancy that makes it hurt to read. But those tears are soon replaced by ones of laughter . . . Sanghera is such an engaging and versatile writer that the pages fly by in a flurry of pathos, politics and paratha with extra butter.'

Sunday Telegraph

'Smart, funny and melancholy, Sanghera's debut novel goes straight to the heart of family life.'   *Marie Claire*

'Sathnam Sanghera's impressive first novel is filled with incidents . . . in which moral confusions, personal insecurities and impossible situations jostle furiously with one another until they give way to bathetic humour . . . Sanghera's choice of Bennett as a model is in itself clever and amusing . . . a fascinatingly detailed portrait of immigration and integration during the 60s and 70s . . . He blends the historical with the personal extremely well . . . he is adept at wiggling out humour without sacrificing seriousness.'

Alex Clark, *Guardian*

'Subtle and often very funny prose . . . What lifts this novel far above cliché is Sanghera's deft sense of irony and self-awareness regarding his subject matter . . . The family's unfolding history is beautifully counterpointed by real-life events in the local political landscape . . . Sanghera's tender and funny book is a cracking and pacy read.'

Meera Syal, *Observer*

'An entertaining story . . . Playful wit infuses the novel . . . But behind the humour and the plot twists, is an important novel that explores an often overlooked part of this country's history.'

Independent

'Enormously enjoyable . . . Sanghera's forte is wry comedy tinged with pathos . . . There is a concluding twist that has all the poisonous horror of finding a cobra coiled around boxes of confectionary in a corner shop . . . [A] warm, keenly observant and immensely appealing novel.'

Peter Kemp, *Sunday Times*

'A smart, funny tale of immigrant life in the UK . . . smartly crafted.'

Fatima Bhutto, *Financial Times*

'A hugely enjoyable read, packed with plot twists and laugh out loud set pieces but it is also tender and insightful . . . Sanghera deftly sets out the conflicting demands of family, culture, religion and individuality in this ambitious story.'

Sunday Express

'What marks this as an uncommonly accomplished debut novel is the warmth Sanghera lavishes on his characters.'

Metro

'*Marriage Material* has humour, cultural relevance . . . I'd heartily recommend *Marriage Material* to anyone who needs a little push to reconnect to where they've come from.'

Stylist

'A funny and insightful first novel . . . A thoughtful examination of the complexities of modern Britain . . . An engrossing, entertaining and rewarding read.'

Daily Mail

'A novel that ingeniously "shoplifts" (his word) characters and elements of plot from Arnold Bennett's *The Old Wives' Tale* . . . This dangerous material is handled with a darkly comic lightness of touch, and an impassively detached ironic tone that may owe something to Bennett – like Bennett, Sanghera makes good use of local newspaper cuttings, letters to the editor, and contemporary fashion magazine material, which gives an unobtrusively authentic period flavour to each passing phase. This book is so well researched you hardly notice the work that's gone into it

... The mix of comedy, satire, realism and optimism is nicely judged.'

Margaret Drabble, *Spectator*

'It is very good and has many of the qualities found in Bennett's masterpiece: acute observation of society and societal change, thoroughly imagined and well depicted characters, mastery of naturalistic detail, and generosity of tone. It is very enjoyable ... It is acute about human frailty, but also understanding of this. It is often funny and its great merit is its humanity. It's a worthy homage to Arnold Bennett.'

Scotsman

'Important issues aired with humour ... in this gem of a multi-generational novel ... a funny and touching read ... Brilliant ... A superbly updated version of Arnold Bennett's *The Old Wives' Tale*. At its heart, this is a simple story of family ... yet, all this is handled throughout with the lightest of touches, so that on reaching the end, you want to begin again to pick up the subtle nuances of this book.'

Psychologies

'This is gorgeous, grand-scale storytelling.'

Sainsbury's Magazine

'A comic feast, full of delectable matter. It does what only the best comic fiction can do: it robes important social subjects in laughter ... This is a splendid debut.'

Lisa Appignanesi

'A wonderfully engaging book, full of heart and wit. Its exploration of what it means to feel torn is rich and subtle. Its characters stay with you. Its jokes make you laugh in the night.'

Susie Boyt

Marriage Material

S ATHNAM S ANGHERA

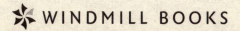
WINDMILL BOOKS

Published by Windmill Books 2014

2 4 6 8 10 9 7 5 3 1

First published in Great Britain in 2013 by William Heinemann

Windmill Books
The Random House Group Limited
20 Vauxhall Bridge Road, London SW1V 2SA

Addresses for companies within The Random House Group Limited
can be found at: www.randomhouse.co.uk/offices.htm

The Random House Group Limited Reg. No. 954009

www.randomhouse.co.uk

A CIP catalogue record for this book
is available from the British Library

ISBN 9780099558675

The Random House Group Limited supports the Forest Stewardship
Council® (FSC®), the leading international forest-certification organisation.
Our books carrying the FSC label are printed on FSC®-certified paper.
FSC is the only forest-certification scheme supported by the leading
environmental organisations, including Greenpeace. Our paper procurement
policy can be found at: www.randomhouse.co.uk/environment

Typeset in Fournier MT by Palimpsest Book Production Limited,
Falkirk, Stirlingshire
Printed and bound by CPI Group (UK) Ltd, Croydon, CR0 4YY

For Jasveen and Simran

'The West Indian or Asian does not, by being born in England, become an Englishman. In law he becomes a United Kingdom citizen by birth; in fact he is a West Indian or an Asian still . . . he will by the very nature of things have lost one country without gaining another, lost one nationality without acquiring a new one. Time is running out against us and them. With the lapse of a generation or so we shall at last have succeeded – to the benefit of nobody – in reproducing "in England's green and pleasant land" the haunting tragedy of the United States.'

Enoch Powell, Member of Parliament for
Wolverhampton South West, November 1968

'They dream in courtship, but in wedlock wake.'

Alexander Pope

CONTENTS

You learn to expect certain questions in this business. Like 'Are you on the phone?' And 'Do you have any bags?' And 'Where are the eggs?' And 'Why are you always on the phone?' And 'Could I have a bag for the eggs when you're off the phone?'

But there is one query that comes up more often than any other: 'Are you open?' A pet irritation for many shop owners, given that they probably wouldn't choose to wake up at 4 a.m. seven days a week to stand in front of a fag stand unless they were *actually trading*. But in the case of Bains Stores, it's a valid query. An advert in the window for a discontinued chocolate bar suggests the shop may have closed in 1994. The security shutters are often stuck a quarter open, adding to the general air of dilapidation. A push or kick of the door triggers something which is more 'grating alarm' than 'tinkling shop bell'.

We could, frankly, make more of an effort. But, believe me, your entrepreneurial spirit would also be blunted if the tower block opposite your shop had been demolished to make way for an estate of eco-homes that failed, continually, to be built. If a long-standing non-compete arrangement with Buy Express, a nearby Indian superstore, meant you could not stock alcohol, lottery tickets, or other material which might make Bains Stores a financially viable concern. If you had to spend fifteen hours a day being patronised ('You. Speak. EXCELLENT. English'); having your name mutilated ('Ar-jan, is it? Mind if I call you Andy?'); dealing with people paying for Mars bars with £20 notes; giving detailed directions to surly motorists who buy nothing in return; dishing out copies of *Asian Babes* to shameless septuagenarians; smiling serenely as locals openly refer to your establishment as 'the Paki shop'; serving people who turn up in their slippers and pyjamas and sometimes even less; being told you're 'posh' because you pronounce 'crips' as 'crisps'; being called a 'smelly Paki' by people reeking of booze and wee; and dealing with seemingly endless chit-chat.

My God, the chit-chat. 'Ow bin ya? Bostin day, ay it? It ay stop raining in yonks. Weren't the Blues good yesterday? Soz, yow must be a Wolves man. I'd kill for a kipper tie. Bostin' carrier bags, these. Tararabit, cocka, see yow tomorra.'

It seems that while war may be 90 per cent waiting around, retail is 90 per cent mindless small talk. And despite what the term may imply, there is nothing minor about the long-term effects. If you spend your waking hours talking to people who get their news from the *Daily Star* and talkSPORT, pass most of your day discussing nothing more substantial than the weather and the price of things (which, let's face it, is all customers over a certain age want to talk about), you slowly begin to feel like you don't exist. Your local Asian shopkeeper will, whether he wants to or not, work out so much about you – which way you vote (from your news-paper); whether you might get lucky tonight (from those emergency condoms) – but I bet you can relate nothing of his biography in return.

At least nothing beyond the eye-rolling clichés of a man arriving in Britain with just £5 in his pocket, who sets up shop to avoid the racial prejudice of the job market, and builds a business through the Asian predilection for family slave labour and tax avoidance. One of the most onerous things about my father's passing was that when the local newspaper he sold and delivered for nearly five decades devoted some column inches to his death, it couldn't come up with much beyond 'hard-working immigrant' and 'self-made'. 'Everyone on the Victoria Road in Blakenfields seemed to have a tale about their newsagent,' claimed the journalist, before singularly failing to produce any tales whatsoever.

He could have been anyone. Or no one. And that's the thing, if you're Asian and happen to run a shop, you are anyone. Or no one. There are few more stereotypical things you can do as an Asian man, few more profound ways of wiping out your character and individuality, short of becoming a doctor, that is. Or fixing computers for a living. Or writing a book about arranged marriages.

I struggle with these generalisations. On the one hand, they clearly apply to lots of Asians, and they are a useful way of highlighting broad truths. But on the other, they are reductive and sap us of any hope of personality or individuality. To stand behind the counter of a shop as an Indian man is to face a barrage of expectations and assumptions, with people assuming you are richer than you are ('Bet you'll be a millionaire soon'); more ambitious than you are (the plural is misleading: there has never been more than one Bains Stores); or cleverer than you are ('Guess you'd be a doctor back home').

It goes the other way too, of course. To some of my customers, sometimes those on benefits, I am a parasite, somehow sapping British resources and bleeding the public dry. To others, often Indian ones, I am a physical illustration to their children of what will happen if they don't work hard enough at school ('You wanna end up loik that?'). Then there are the ones for whom I am a raghead who wants to impose sharia law on Britain, and who, in his spare time, grooms white girls for exploitation.

The sexual predator thing is a recent development and I didn't, at first, make a connection between the insults occasionally hurled in my direction and the headlines passing over my counter. After all, the gangs reportedly grooming young white girls are based in the north, and I am in the West Midlands; most of the offenders are Pakistani, and I am of Punjabi Indian heritage; and while some of the perpetrators run takeaway and taxi firms, I run a newsagent. To be honest, I barely blinked the first time I was called 'a dirty Paki pervert' – if memory serves, by a teenager who had just tried to buy a pornographic magazine. You get used to being called all sorts of things in this business and one tends not to dwell on the semi-coherent rantings of people so dim that they are seemingly unaware of the existence of the internet, which offers mountains of free porn.

Moreover, it's difficult to tally shop life with sex, in any way whatsoever. There are certain places that bristle with sexual tension: libraries, Tube carriages on hot days. But your Asian corner shop, reserved for the purchase of emergency milk and Rizlas, is not one of them. Occasionally some gross individual will make a sexual remark to my mother while buying bread ('Nice baps') or when paying by credit card ('Want me to push it in, eh?'), but, in general, the sexual invisibility is just another aspect of the overall invisibility of the Asian shopkeeper.

The penny only really dropped the morning I found graffiti declaring 'TALEBAN PEEDO' on our semi-functioning shutters. The realisation wasn't a cheerful one. We Asian blokes have never exactly been at an advantage in the sex game, our undesirability reflected in statistics from dating websites which show that, along with black women, Indian men are among the least popular demographic groups, no doubt a victim of the endless, though obviously entirely groundless, insinuations about penis size.

I remember once talking to an Aussie girl in a nightclub in Bombay, her surveying the crowded dancefloor and moaning at length about the seediness and lecherousness of Indian men, seemingly oblivious to the fact that I was one too. In the end, I pointed it out. Her response? 'You international Indians are different.' But are we? I'm not so sure. Reading the papers, it sometimes feels as if the world sees all brown men as perverts. It's enough to make you miss the days when we were just invisible. Enough, even, to make you want to give up selling the newspapers that plant and perpetuate the stereotypes in the first place.

Indeed, sometimes, given that we are for many customers the only interaction they have with multiculturalism, I think the Asian shopkeepers of Britain should cut out the middle man and present themselves to be questioned directly by the great British public. To spend, perhaps, a day or an afternoon a year answering not queries about the location of eggs and the quality of plastic bags, but serious questions about our religion and culture.

At least, I would welcome the opportunity to explain that a Sikh is not the same thing as a Muslim. That while I did once sign up for medical school, I was until recently working as a graphic designer in London. That while I have a white girlfriend, Freya, my fiancée, she is an adult, and we met in the most boring, conventional way possible, through work.

For what it's worth, the life of the Indian man who originally set up this newsagent was not a cliché either. Admittedly, Mr Bains came to Britain with no more than a shilling in his pocket. But he wasn't, as was often the case with Asian entrepreneurs, driven into retail by racism. When he arrived in Wolverhampton in 1955, aged forty-nine, an Asian immigrant was a relatively rare thing, and if a white person ever accosted him on the street, it was usually to ask if they could stroke his luxuriant beard.

The sole survivor of a family butchered during Partition, he regarded Britain, if anything, as a haven of racial tolerance, and when in 1958 he took over number 64, Victoria Road, he did not do the predictable thing and start catering to his own people. He took it over determined to run it as it had been run for more than thirty years by Geoffrey Walker. A place where brown paper and string was used for wrapping produce. Where fresh bread was flogged over a marble counter, and where customers could rely on being served by someone who knew their name and would, on occasion, let them buy something on tick. By far the best thing you could have said to him was that walking into his store felt like stepping back in time.

As it happens, my father's life was not as clichéd as it may first seem either. In his way, he fought to be an individual, to be seen for who he was. And I know the post-mortem report says it was a heart attack that sent him plummeting on to the shop floor that evening, that he died of 'natural causes', with people of South Asian origin being statistically susceptible to heart disease, a certain proportion being afflicted by a particular gene mutation which almost guarantees heart problems. But not everything can be explained by demographics and generalities.

Wolverhampton stood in the county of Staffordshire in the 1960s, not in the West Midlands. It was a town, rather than a city. And Victoria Road, cutting from the centre of Wolvo, or Wolves, into what was then open countryside, was more commonly known as 'Wog Row' by locals, owing to an experiment in mass immigration which, while it had not yet led to Asian men being feared and ridiculed as paedophiles, had nevertheless resulted in white residents forming associations to exclude black and Asian syndicates from buying houses in certain areas, and election leaflets openly drawing 'links' between the arrival of immigrants and cases of leprosy.

Mr Bains had, in short, been proved wrong about the appetite of Wulfrunians for racial tolerance. He had also slowly accepted that running a grocer's as Mr Walker had done, using paper and string for wrapping things, selling bacon and even biscuits in terms of weight, was a mistake. The format was outdated. The fact was Walker had sold up at just the right time, with several nearby light engineering factories closing down and the abolition of resale price maintenance, which had protected margins.

Though these calamities would pale into insignificance with the emergence of illness – the initial symptoms so slight that not even Mr Bains noticed them. His young wife in India, who penned long letters begging for money and protesting about having been abandoned with two young daughters among a hostile extended family in Delhi, began to complain that the handwriting in his short responses was getting smaller and smaller – to the point of illegibility. He became so softly spoken that he had to routinely repeat what he had said, a process that led to him castigating his 39-year-old assistant for being hard of hearing.

Bill Hinton, whom Bains had inherited with the shop along with a large quantity of unsellable Wellington boots, and the idea of flogging butter and flour under his own label, did not take the criticism well. Which was quite something, given that he was routinely stealing from his boss. The sweets that he chomped upon all day, which Mr Bains had assumed were treatment for some kind of gastric disorder, were actually a symptom of his dishonesty. He was under-ringing, routinely charging customers the full price for products, registering a lower price on the till, each empty sweet wrapper representing a unit of cash. The overall contents of his pockets served as a physical reminder of how much money to remove from the till when his boss wasn't looking.

The revelation, when it came, was almost as devastating for Bains as the diagnosis, and when he reported Hinton's thieving to the police, and they let him off without even a warning, he sank into a depression. He was not a young man any more, had squandered all the money he had made during three years of foundry work, and now, just as his body began packing up, having missed out on his daughters' childhoods, he had nothing to show for it.

Little did he know, as he complained to Patwant Dhanda, a local foundry worker and activist, who had turned up in his shop and offered to raise the issue with the relevant police commissioner on behalf of the Indian Workers' Association, that his luck was about to change. Accounts vary about what happened, but at some point during this meeting, as Dhanda snacked on horseradishes plucked from the shop's indoor wire rack without suggestion of payment, and as he attempted to bond with Bains over their common experience of Partition, Bains took on this impetuous

25-year-old man, who was less than half his age and twice his size, as his assistant. And together, they transformed the shop into a newsagent.

The basic idea was that doing so would give them reason to open longer hours, and they did, serving many of the area's immigrant workers as late as 11 p.m., opening every day, resolutely ignoring the garage owner next door, who was fond of remarking, 'The Lord made the Earth in six days, you won't make a fortune in seven.' They also thought that stocking a wide range of publications, everything from *Birds* to *Penthouse*, would expand the range of their customers, and they installed a hatch into the front of the shop to attract passing factory workers, so they could pick up their papers on the way to work. At the same time they fitted an outdoor wood rack for fruit and vegetables, delivered groceries when necessary, changed everything short of succumbing to modern notions of self-service (Bains believed in the personal touch) or promotion (there was no sign out front, his thinking being that it would be called the 'ration-wallah' by his compatriots, or the 'Paki shop' by non-compatriots, whatever the frontispiece declared).

It worked. By the time we join him in early 1968, Bains is running the most successful retail outlet on the road; he has helped Dhanda set up a shop nearby, on condition that they will not compete in the same specialist trades; he has hired a new assistant, Tanvir Banga, a 27-year-old Chamar boy whose family has worked for his wife's family for decades; and he has finally been able to pay for his wife and daughters to join him in England. Though the slow and reduced movements, the muscular stiffness, the loss of balance, and the tremor are so debilitating at sixty-two that Mr Bains is confined to bed, unable to feed or dress himself, and reduced to running the shop by barking directions down the stairwell.

The task of looking after him normally falls to his family or to Baljit Kaur, a diminutive pensioner from down the street, and from down the road in Mrs Bains' home village in the Punjab, who provides the service in exchange for her weekly groceries. But tonight, as he does twice a week, Dhanda has charged himself with his care. Sitting next to his friend and mentor, he massages his legs, feeds him a few crumbs of each ladoo he chomps through, informs him about trade at his new drapery store, reads out headlines from various Punjabi newspapers, and brings Mr Bains up to date with the activities of the ever-expanding Indian Workers' Association, which is currently preoccupied with the case of Tarsem Singh Sandhu, a Wolverhampton bus driver fired for returning to work from a three-week illness in a beard and turban.

'We're planning a march,' he says, oblivious to the irony of a clean-shaven, un-turbanned Sikh taking up the cause. 'We're billing it as a general appeal for religious freedom. Local Council of Churches might join us. Could be the biggest march in town since World War II. Six thousand people.'

Downstairs, as Wolverhampton's answer to Malcolm X continues to brief Mr Bains, in what would be the front room if number 64 were a private residence like the other 250 terraced houses on the road, Mrs Bains, a thin, pale-skinned woman of about forty-five, is cleaning up after a busy day in the shop. She straightens goods which customers have picked up and thrown back untidily, wipes down surfaces inked with the paw prints of schoolchildren popping in for crisps and lemonade, the coloured glass bangles on her wrists tinkling as she dusts the wooden box she needs to stand on in order to operate the bacon slicer. Small pox scars dot her face, her prematurely thinning black hair is tied back in a bun, and, as she gets down on to the floor to sweep it with a dustpan and brush, her breasts squeeze between her knees, threatening to tumble out.

Her modesty would normally be protected by a chuni, but she has just used it to mop up a spillage, while her green apron has been requisitioned tonight by her eldest daughter Kamaljit, who is standing over a stove in the kitchen cooking keema. The lamb comes from the butcher on a nearby corner; the greens have come from the front of the shop; the salwar kameez Kamaljit is wearing underneath the apron has been made from material purchased from Mr Dhanda's drapery shop; and the concoction on the gas stove simmers, as does the chef. The evening meal used to be a task she split with her sister, but ever since she left school, the housework, to her resentment, has become entirely her responsibility, while her pampered, spoilt, precocious, baby sister . . .

. . . well, her baby sister would normally be catching up on homework, or making new suits and dresses for Mr Dhanda, or, in her capacity as the most literate person in the shop, filling in forms or going over paperwork. But tonight she is standing in the living room, which the family call the 'baithak', located between the shopfront and the kitchen, playing a role in an unusual scene. Tanvir is sitting in a chair, old newspapers laid out at his bare feet, a bath towel tucked into his shirt collar, while Surinder, in an adaptation of her school uniform (she changes from a skirt into trousers for the journey to and from school), hovers behind him, brandishing her mother's sewing scissors in one hand, some handwritten notes in the other, her lips pursed in concentration.

Tanvir has proved himself so indispensable in the shop that he now has a bedroom in the house, or, at least, a bedroom full of all the excess stock for which there isn't room in the basement, with a corner cleared for a mattress on the floor. And after five years in England he no longer has the fresh immigrant's tendency of comparing everything to life back home. But there are still some Indian habits he can't shed – such as overuse of the '-ing' form ('I am working in shop') and the farmer's disinclination to spend money on anything that doesn't serve a clear practical purpose. The things he considers an extravagance include: shoes (he prefers to walk barefoot or in chappals); toothbrushes (he cleans his teeth with the same tree bark he would use for the task in the Punjab); and, when he learns that Surinder trims her father's hair, barbers too.

Surinder recoils at the suggestion. The idea of being in close physical proximity to Tanvir's shoulders, fingering his greasy hair, making chit-chat in his painfully bad English, is about as appetising as plunging a hand down the bowl of the outside loo. But the request plays on her mind. She has never had her own hair cut – being obliged to keep it long, trailing behind her in a ponytail – but her favourite pastime as a girl, during her heady pre-pubescent days of freedom, was hanging out at Maureen's hairdressing salon next door. Cutting her father's hair is the only aspect of his nursing that she actually enjoys, and she has in recent months become a devoted, albeit surreptitious, reader of the *Hairdressers' Journal*.

Magazines are, as far as Surinder is concerned, the only perk of growing up in a shop. Her schoolmates imagine her gorging each night on slabs of Dairy Milk. But the sweets which line the walls of the shop, and the chocolates displayed in the glass cabinet counter, are just as much of a treat for her as for most girls, owing to her mother's obsession with her girls staying slim for their future husbands. Surinder does, however, get to intersperse library books with *Bunty*, and in recent months she has moved on to more adult fare, chief among which is the professional journal delivered once a fortnight for the salon next door.

The news pages are of no interest. Surinder doesn't care, for instance, that the National Hairdressers' Federation is considering banning the press from its annual general meeting. But she loves the full-colour adverts and the long feature articles on how to make yourself resemble celebrities. She must have read the item about Elizabeth Taylor forty times before giving the magazine up. Just holding the *Hairdressers' Journal* makes her feel sophisticated and metropolitan, and soon after Tanvir made his request she notices that the magazine also featured regular step-by-step guides to men's hairstyles.

One week, for instance, there is an extensive item on a hairstyle called 'the Wentworth', which she, in spite of herself, pictures on Tanvir, but dismisses on the grounds that it is aimed, judging by the headline, at a 'mature' man of about forty, and 'men of higher status'. Tanvir is twenty-seven and, being a lower-caste Chamar, is certainly no man of status. Conversely, the following week she discounts an article on a hairstyle aimed at 'the Young Male Client', on the grounds that Tanvir isn't young, will probably never 'work in a large office', and doesn't, as the piece expounds, 'like pop records, dancing and generally having fun'. Tanvir works in a shop and the only time he seems to be having fun is when he's stocktaking.

But then she spots an article entitled 'How a Continental Master Styles a Head', a step-by-step guide to how 'one of Germany's top stylists, Heinz Krethen of Cologne' achieves a new kind of cut aimed at twenty-something young men, so when Tanvir, sporting a lopsided bouffant, once again whines about the tedium and expense of haircuts ('I am not having time to do all this work, as well as going to barbers in town'), she finds herself offering to help him out. She has made salwar kameezes and English dresses for payment from Mr Dhanda, designing her own patterns, becoming a master at estimating yardage and box-pleated bodices. Surely a new hairstyle couldn't be much different?

Surinder approaches the enterprise with high precision. She copies out the instructions from the magazine by hand, so as to minimise the chance of Maureen complaining that her subscription has been rifled through. She lays used newspapers on the floor, to protect the plastic Dandycord mat, and puts out her tools on the foldaway dining table. Among them: a pot of Brylcreem and two plastic combs, which are normally to be found in the letter rack underneath the mirror in the hallway upstairs, permanently clogged with long black hairs.

She begins, as instructed, by 'examining the general growth style' (wild), and 'special features of the hairline and crown' (receding). Then, having combed his fringe flat on to his forehead, avoiding the patches of acne, she snips a quarter of an inch off the edge. The texture of his hair surprises her: her father's is wispy and feathery and white. But Tanvir's is thick and black. She wonders briefly what her hair would feel like to someone running their fingers through it, but then remembers who she is with and flinches. Tanvir flinches in response.

'Keep still,' she snaps in Punjabi. Tanvir is older than Surinder, but she cannot help being brusque with him. 'Do you want me to have your ear off?'

She reads the next set of instructions out to herself, under her breath, and follows them to the letter. She starts cutting at the nape in order to get the basic shape of the back. She makes sectional partings across the head, cutting each section individually to reduce bulk and length, and is congratulating herself on how well it's going when she realises she doesn't understand a single sentence of what comes next, under the heading of 'stage eight'.

'Attend to the neckline with the hair-cutting machine; taper out.'

She doesn't have a machine but can improvise, but what on earth does 'taper out' mean? Does it involve a measuring tape?

'Using the dryer, apply the air stream against the natural root-growth tendency.'

There is no hairdryer in the house, owing to Mrs Bains' conviction that, like drinking unsweetened tea, or doing embroidery in the evenings, they induce illness and disease. But *natural root-growth tendency*? Tanvir's thick hair seems to grow in every direction.

'Brush movement, applied all over the head, will give the desired amount of lift.'

Lift? Brush movement? What? Like copying down maths equations from a blackboard, she has somehow managed to transcribe it all without taking any of it in. She skips stage eight for stage nine. Which she then skips for stage ten. Soon she is hacking at Tanvir's hair in the manner her mother occasionally employs when tackling the privet hedge in the back garden. Then, suddenly, she is confronted by a patch of bare scalp on the crown of Tanvir's head. The sight of it makes her gasp, and freeze, like her father sometimes does when being guided out of bed towards the bathroom.

'Teek taak?' asks Tanvir.

She coughs. Has the patch always been there? Or has she created it? She steps across the room to consult the original magazine, hoping for advice or guidance. But all she discovers is the unhelpful news that 'the square Bob in Vidal Sassoon's salon this spring will have the back hair falling short and the sides about one-and-a-half inches longer than the back'.

Her voice wobbles. 'Just finishing up.'

This 'finishing up' takes the form of Surinder attempting to comb hair over the bald spot, and, when this fails, cutting all of Tanvir's hair short – her feverish logic being that if the overall length is reduced, the spot won't be so visible. It doesn't work.

The final paragraph of the article read: 'When Heinz has finished treating a head, there is not a hair out of place.' But Tanvir looks like he has just undergone electro-convulsive therapy, his hair having fallen out at the points the electrodes were attached. In silhouette he resembles a kind of startled owl. And then suddenly Kamaljit walks into the room. Her eyes are watering from chopping onions, her apron is padded with flour. She looks horrified.

'Kiddha?' smiles Tanvir. And then in cringy English: 'How does it looking?'

Standing opposite each other, you wouldn't think the girls were

15

related. Aged eighteen and fifteen, they have both been in England now for four years, but while Surinder is fair and slim, Kamaljit is dark and stout. While the elder sister wears prescription spectacles, the younger surveys the scene with bright clear eyes. Struggling to stay composed, blaming her tears of mirth on the onion fumes drifting in from the kitchen, Surinder removes the towel from Tanvir's shoulders, hands over a comb and instructs him to inspect the results of her handiwork in the upstairs mirror. As he trots off to do so, she remarks, half to herself, half to Kamaljit, 'Well, Tanvir might need a shit down when he sees that.'

The remark is a reference to one of Tanvir's famous malapropisms, which form much of the banter between Surinder and the paper boys, others including 'Both of you three over there'; and 'Let's go see the backside.' But Kamaljit refuses to be amused.

'When did you become such a witch?' she asks in Punjabi.

Surinder laughs in reply, and only registers Kamaljit's seriousness when she is met with a glare. It wasn't long ago that they would tease Tanvir together. In a home where the stock is out of bounds, where they have to take turns to open the shop at 4 a.m., are expected to conceal the existence of secondary sexual characteristics with baggy salwar kameezes and chunis draped around arms and shoulders, it is the only thing that comes close to amusement. But Kamaljit has recently been suffering from an extended bout of humourlessness.

She continues in Punjabi. 'Do you even know what day it is?'

It takes a moment or two for Surinder to work out that she is referring to their mother's belief that it is bad luck to wash, let alone cut, hair on Tuesdays. Mrs Bains was full of such superstitions. Never leave one shoe lying on another; lamps should be extinguished with a wave of the hand, not blown out; cooked food that is unused during a solar eclipse should be given away or thrown out, because it has become impure. But this is the first time she has heard Kamaljit utter such words and it earns her a dismissive tut. It feels like it was only yesterday that the sisters were making models and castles out of mud, playing in the courtyard of their family's Delhi home. Now she is bossing her around like an auntie.

Kamaljit continues sanctimoniously. 'Do you know how hard he works for us? We are the closest thing he has to family in Bilyat and all you ever do is mock him. You just think you're better than everyone else, don't you?'

Mrs Bains had given Surinder a version of the same speech when she had overheard her daughter address Tanvir without a respectful 'ji'. That time Surinder, while chewing the end of her hair, apologised. But she isn't going to take the same from her sister.

'You are not my mother.' Surinder stiffens. Her large brown eyes narrow, and she straightens up in a way that highlights that she is taller than her sister, despite being younger. 'Do you think Mum doesn't know I was cutting his hair?'

A yelp from upstairs.

'You've not got away with this,' warns Kamaljit as she runs up to assist Tanvir. 'You've gone too far this time.'

The sisters had shared a bedroom since arriving from India. The mahogany wardrobe they inherited was so old that you almost expected a gas mask to fall out when you opened the doors, and, with suitcases and bits of stock taking up so much space, there was room for just one bed. But after Delhi, where the girls had lived, eaten and slept with their mother in a single room, it had felt like a palace.

It was through this window, directly above the shopfront, that they had whiled away hours watching customers come and go during their first few months in Britain. And it was in this room that the sisters would stretch long loops of elastic between the bed legs and wardrobe stand, jumping over the parallel lines, turning round, crossing their legs, raising the height of the elastic until it became too hard, or until they got told off for disrupting the customers in the shop below with their thudding. At night they snuggled up against each other for warmth, telling each other stories, sometimes waking up in each other's arms.

However, by 1968, these were just memories and the room was sharply regimented. They shared a kitchen side table, which had been customised to vaguely resemble a dressing table, but the girls now had a single bed each and both had a suitcase for storage. Both of their sides of the room were identical in size and shape, except for the fact that while Kamaljit's area was pristine, Surinder's was a mess. The elder girl kept her space free to perform nightly prayers cross-legged on the floor. Surinder could manage only the first four lines of the Japji Sahib in the original Gurmukhi, and would add the Lord's Prayer on to the end of it by way of compensation and apology, but Kamaljit knew the whole of it off by heart. Surinder's space, meanwhile, was littered with unwashed clothes, draft dress and salwar designs, cut-out-and-keep posters she was not allowed to put up on her wall, library books and various magazines she had squirrelled away from the shop downstairs.

It was a constant source of mystery and bemusement to everyone who knew Surinder that someone who was so physically composed could be so untidy. Kamaljit had learnt to live with it, just as Surinder had learnt to cope with Kamaljit's snoring. But by the time Kamaljit came upstairs that evening she was still so annoyed with her sister that on entering she pronounced, 'This room is a rubbish tip,' grabbed a school skirt from the floor and shoved it into the cupboard.

Surinder, half looking up from her novel, moaned under her breath. Tanvir had turned up to dinner in a turban that Kamaljit had helped him tie: less the immaculate contraption Mr Bains wore in the portraits displayed around the house, and more the untidy length of cloth Gandhi famously refused to remove during legal assignment in South Africa. Surinder might have risen above the comedy of the scene had Mrs Bains not picked up on his appearance and launched into one of her monologues, telling everyone about how handsome Mr Bains had looked in his turban when she first met him on his wedding day in 1949, how her late father, the becharar, preferred a loose-style turban not dissimilar to Tanvir's, how the worst thing about her husband's escape from what became Pakistan was that he had to cut his hair short and trim his beard, Muslim style, for safety. Getting into her stride, she bemoaned that the most upsetting thing about Mr Bains' illness was that he had to have his hair cut again, this time for reasons of hygiene, bewailed the fact that Sikh men arriving in the Midlands were chopping off their kes, getting rid of their turbans in order to get jobs in factories and the bus department, and exclaimed how thrilling it was, in turn, that some Sikhs like Mr Dhanda were fighting for the right to practise their religion in Britain. How much she wished, she concluded, her thali of food now totally cold, that she had time to join the pro-turban march that Dhanda was organising.

Throughout, Tanvir stared into the middle distance. Kamaljit glared at her sister, and Surinder fought to contain her giggles – overt laughter, or 'showing your teeth' as her mother put it, not being allowed, along with make-up, unsupervised contact with male strangers and, for some reason, leaving home at a quarter to the hour.

However, there was no trace of a smile an hour later when, upstairs, Kamaljit did the unthinkable and, crossing the invisible line dividing the room, began tidying away some of Surinder's other belongings. The younger sister watched in disbelief as Kamaljit picked up a pair of her used socks and put them into a laundry basket, started making a pile of used newspapers, stacked her Brontë on to her library editions of Austen and held up a copy of *Jackie* with the words: 'Have you taken this from the shop?'

'I'm going to put it back,' said Surinder, feeling a hint of embarrassment that the cover featured a topless sunbathing man. 'I always put everything back.'

Kamaljit ignored her and continued shuffling through the detritus on the floor. Next, she brandished a copy of *Woman*. 'And this?' She put it under her arm. Then, a copy of *Vogue*. 'I'm taking them back down.'

Before Surinder could even think of what to say, Kamaljit was storming out of the room. The younger girl had slipped out of bed and was primed for confrontation by the time she returned, but Surinder barely managed a word of protest before Kamaljit pronounced, 'By the way, you'll be leaving school in the summer.' Turning her back to her little sister, Kamaljit began removing her glass bangles in preparation for bed. 'Straight after your exams. I heard Mum and Dad talking and they are looking for boys. For *both* of us.'

The oddest thing was that I was braced for it. I had anticipated the phone call, imagined the late-night drive back, even pictured the scene when I got home: the phone ringing in the hallway and no one picking it up; women I didn't recognise brewing tea in our kitchen. But it was my mother I was preparing to grieve, not my father. She was the one who had suffered bowel cancer and when strangers began arriving to offer their condolences for my father, it was hard to comprehend.

The delay with the funeral, as my father's death was briefly deemed officially 'suspicious', added to the sense of unreality. The shop was sealed off for the gathering of forensic and non-forensic evidence, door-to-door inquiries conducted. A newspaper report speculated a youth might have been spotted running out of the shop that Friday evening, and we argued with the authorities about when the body might be released.

But no evidence transpired. The post-mortem concluded that my father had died of a heart attack, so-called 'natural causes'. His body was released for cremation. And a week later my mother was approaching me with her mouth muffled with the damp end of a white chuni, her voice hoarse from going over it all. 'You need to go to town this afternoon, son,' she muttered. 'Get your father some new clothes. It is traditional to clothe the deceased in fresh garments before cremation.'

I've noticed that as she gets older, and frailer, my mother becomes increasingly reliant on custom. A fortnight before my father died, and more than half a year before my planned wedding, she had suddenly insisted I have a traditional Sikh engagement ceremony. The closest Freya's 69-year-old father, a retired quantity surveyor from Sussex, had ever got to India was a visit to his local curry house, but suddenly he was standing in our living room presenting me with eleven baskets (apparently, it has to be an odd number) of fresh and dried fruit (consisting of an odd number of ingredients), and £51 in cash. He looked ridiculous with a garland over his shoulders, the surreality of it all accentuated by the fact that Freya wasn't even there, the prospective bride not, traditionally, playing a role in the ritual.

I remember feeling frustrated at the level of detail Mum insisted upon, wondering where she got it all from, suspecting that she was making it up as she went along. Our religion, after all, was founded as a reaction to the pedantry of many established Indian faiths. And when it comes to death, we are meant to approach everything with equability. We do not, for instance, obsess about the day someone is cremated, or make sure a body is pointing in a certain direction when buried.

But whatever you say about any culture, you can usually say the opposite too, and another strange thing about my father's sudden passing was that I found myself clinging on to ritual. It was when there was no guidance, when I wasn't being told what to do, that I began to feel unnerved. And so, dismissing the suggestion of popping over to Wolverhampton city centre – I wanted, for one afternoon, to avoid going over what had happened – I got into my father's Escort van, helped myself to one of the extra-strong mints he kept in the ashtray, and drove further afield to the Merry Hill Shopping Centre with a sense of purpose.

Only for this sense of purpose to dissipate on arrival. When did shopping become such a chore? I remember a time when I used to actually walk around department stores in London for fun, fantasising about a time I might be able to afford luxury without worrying about the cost. But when the time came, I found myself unable to look beyond the snooty shop assistants, or the fact that my waist size and age had been interchangeable since 2004. And at Merry Hill, walking around the 210 stores, taking advantage of one of the 10,000 free car-parking spaces, this aversion combined with indecision.

My father always wore a blazer and tie in the shop he ran, sometimes, on cold days, a waistcoat too. But another thing about Sikh funerals is that we do not wear suits, smart clothes being associated with celebration. Did this dress code apply to the deceased? And if I did get a suit, what colour should it be? The Indian colour of mourning is white. But did that extend to the corpse? I wasn't sure I wanted my father going out looking like a member of Boyz II Men. Also, what would be the right amount to spend? I couldn't recall the last time I'd spent less than £500 on a suit. But my father objected to expense; every time I looked at something more than a few hundred pounds, I could hear him protesting, feigning a heart attack as he did the time he discovered I'd paid £80 for a T-shirt.

In the end, after two coffee stops, I drifted towards a supermarket 'designer' range, and found myself looking at something modern, priced at £300 and sky blue, not too dark, not too light, not cheap, but not expensive either. A compromise. For some reason, I held it up against the light. An attentive shop assistant, an Asian teenager with bright red lipstick and an LA smile, congratulated me on my choice.

'You'll find the fitting rooms at the back of the store.' She gestured behind me, like an air stewardess pointing out the exit doors. Her prettiness made me self-conscious about not having shaved in a week.

'Actually, it's not for me.'

'No problem, sir.' The smile widened. 'You have the measurements with you?'

I did. That morning I had visited the room upstairs my father referred to as his 'study' and my mother called 'the office', which sometimes functioned, like every room in the house, as a stock-room. It was out of bounds to me as a child, and as I stumbled over a stack of nappies and toilet paper, I couldn't quite banish the feeling I was trespassing. The shelves which lined two of the walls were heaving under the weight of books by Jeffrey Archer and Stephen King and rows of box files marked with labels like 'gas bills' and 'personal tax'.

The sight of the mobile phone on his desk, which had been briefly requisitioned by the police as 'evidence', and which he, to my annoyance, rarely switched on, reminded me of the last time we'd talked over it. I had rung him and shouted 'Happy Father's Day!!' down the line, with Freya whooping congratulations in the background. His reply? 'I'll just get your mother.' He wasn't a great conversationalist. And I didn't, though it killed me to admit it, put enough effort into our relationship. But the memory made me laugh and, wondering whether his voicemail was still working, I made the mistake of calling his number on my phone. The sound of his voice made me crumble.

It was some time later before I finally got to the point of the excursion: his wardrobe, which stood in the corner of the room, a flat-pack contraption from MFI I'd helped him assemble as a ten-year-old, but that was now collapsing in on itself, none of the doors closing or opening properly. It was infused with the nostalgia of his cologne, and as I put my head against one of his corduroy jackets to breathe it in, I wondered if anyone would notice or mind if I crawled in and spent the day asleep inside.

'Chest 40.' Smaller than me. 'Waist 30.' Thinner than me. 'Inside l . . .' Suddenly, a difficult thought: did corpses bloat? 'Actually, make it chest 42, waist 34.'

'Inside leg?'

'Doesn't matter.'

'We have a tailoring service. Could have it turned up and ready for collection in an hour.'

'No need.' A pause. 'My mum's a seamstress.' Sometimes a lie, or in this case a half-lie, is easier than the truth. Even now I sometimes find myself telling people, when they ask, that my father is on holiday. I picked a shirt and a tie to go with the suit and thought briefly about haggling over the price. It was what my dad would have wanted. There was nothing he wouldn't barter over – TV sets, utility bills – tutting as he did so, looking offended when declined, launching into speeches about non-existent grasping mother-in-laws. But in the end I couldn't face the prospect of banter, and as the assistant talked me through her company's refund policy at the till, informing me that if I wasn't completely satisfied with my purchase I could simply return the goods within fourteen days of receipt, I thought of where the suit might be in a fortnight. Burnt, rippling in the tiniest fragments, through one of the five rivers that gave the Punjab its name.

I returned home to find that someone had taken the parking space for the van, and succumbed to a bout of sweary rage that was less to do with the hassle of having to park a few hundred yards away, in the car park of Buy Express, the ever-expanding Asian superstore nearby, than it was to do with the guilt I was forced to confront in doing so. My father was seventy years old, had diabetes and heart problems, the bathroom had to be fitted with handles so that he could get into and out of the shower more easily, and yet he was still dragging heavy boxes up and down this stretch of Victoria Road. I should have stopped him. I should have saved some money, paid for his retirement. Yet I had spent my twenties and early thirties gallivanting around London being 'creative'.

There was little to improve my mood on the short walk to the shop. A youth I vaguely recognised was kicking the top of the zebra crossing light down a pavement. The old working man's club had been transformed into Singhfellows, an imposing and off-putting desi pub. A new firm of solicitors had been established, seemingly to cater for the increasing number of illegal immigrants and criminals residing in the locality. And then, bleakest of all, next door to Bains Stores, the sight of Ranjit Dhanda, who ran Buy Express with his dad, in his large 4x4, taking advantage of the £3 'full valet' offered by Polish Polish, the hand car wash.

The scene depressed me in a thousand different ways at once. The garage that used to be on the site had once been my playground – when I was a a child, the owners would let me get behind the steering wheel of the cars they were fixing. But it was now home to yet another of the low-cost car washes which scatter the Black Country in the way fried-chicken outlets scatter South London. One of the few growth industries around, they epitomise everything that has gone wrong with this once-mighty conurbation, and the meagre ambitions of its residents. After all, this is all Wulfrunians truly desire nowadays: to earn enough to buy a second-hand Audi Q7, to be left alone to drive it as fast as they want, to get it washed for almost nothing by someone from Eastern Europe and then to reserve the right to rant about parasitical immigrants after they have done so.

As for Ranjit, well, I hated the way he did not turn off his engine, which meant the washers had to work with fumes being blown into their faces. I hated the fact that he didn't turn off the stereo, which meant the washers had to work while being subjected to the bassline of a succession of Malkit Singh tracks. And I struggled to remember what I had even liked about the guy. We had grown up together, were childhood friends, but nowadays he was insufferable, forever trying to flog me a dodgy Sky box, rebranding himself 'Jay' (a nickname I just couldn't bring myself to use), insisting on calling me 'professor' in return because I had gone to university, driving a car that looked like it had been designed by a four-year-old boy, spewing conversational gambits that rarely went beyond 'Have a smoke' and 'Call me Jay, not Ranjit', his interests not extending beyond bodybuilding and smoking weed, and banging on about movies starring Steven Seagal (any film was either 'better than *Under Siege*' or 'not as good as *Under Siege*'). I hated the fact I would, inevitably, find myself having to make polite chit-chat with this man later in the day. A man whose first remark on seeing me, after I had rushed back to Wolverhampton on hearing about the death of my father, grabbing my girlfriend's car, was 'Those your wheels, or did you hire it?'

Entering the shop through the private entrance next to the shopfront, into the kitchen that my father had built in an extension, the scene was not much more cheering than the one outside: a gaggle of strangers, arranged around my mother, sitting on the floor, crying. The weeping is another one of those contradictions. Officially, we Sikhs should rival the English when it comes to the stiff upper lip. The scriptures state that relatives should not indulge in wailing during times of mourning. Hymns that inspire detachment are sung on the way to the crematorium to aid the family in hiding their grief. But in reality the tears are endless.

I could even recall my mother telling me as a child that they were compulsory. One could not enter a house in mourning with dry eyes, she said. At the time I was impressed by the theatre of it. I couldn't switch on the waterworks at will, even when I thought of the saddest thing that had ever happened to me, which at that time was probably the failure to receive a bicycle that Ranjit already owned. And if, years later, you'd asked me if the tears were healthy, I would have replied, 'Yes.' I would have said that such is the effect of the ceaseless sobbing that by the end of the two-to-five-week mourning period, you're totally cried out, aching to return to the banality of the *EastEnders* omnibus and the commute to work – surely a healthier approach to death than the British stiff upper lip.

27

The only English funeral I'd attended, for Freya's grandfather, had, with the endless clinking of wine glasses and chat about the weather, been a surreal experience. I went to offer his widow my condolences, only to be asked in return about how I'd found the drive down the A4040. But three weeks of dealing with weeping strangers remarking that my father had 'had a good innings' (he hadn't, but I didn't want to go over this again, so I agreed) and 'He would have been proud of you' (I doubted it, but whatever), turning up whenever they wanted, being unable to ask them when they might leave, made me appreciate the point of the stiff upper lip.

Certainly I was in no mood to hang out with them on the day before the funeral, so, having placed my father's last suit in his wardrobe, I busied myself with chores: increasing from two to three the number of coaches taking mourners from the crematorium to the temple; and clearing some of the bouquets placed on the pavement in front of the shop, reading some of the messages as I did so ('Tanvir, I'll miss your smile').

That evening, there was another instruction from my mother, albeit one with a get-out clause. 'It is traditional for the body of the deceased Sikh to be bathed before it is dressed in clean clothing. But it's all right if you don't want to, if you want to remember him as he was. I didn't with Mataji.'

Mataji. My grandmother. Her funeral was one of my earliest memories. I must have been three or four. I remember being held up by my father to sprinkle almonds and sweets into the open coffin and my mother's tear-strewn face surveying me as I did so. The coffin must have been standing in the front room of the house in Southall. But I couldn't exactly recall where it was. Or what the corpse looked like. Which was perhaps why I agreed to wash my father. That plus the fact that my mother and I had been prevented from getting close to my father's body during the arduous process of identification, the officer informing us in a monotone that the body was 'property of the crown' and could not be touched in case forensic evidence was 'contaminated'.

I guess if I had imagined anything, I had probably thought of the ceremonial application of a sponge to a head of an otherwise concealed corpse. However, what followed, at six the next morning, when I was ushered with two of my mother's male relations from Southall, Ranjit and Mr Dhanda, Ranjit's 78-year-old busybody father, through the back door of a funeral home, was far from ceremonial: an undertaker, not yet shaven, without his tie, informing us that it would be advisable, in the interests of health and safety, to wear plastic gloves as the fluid applied to the corpse could damage our skin; the sight of my father in the morgue, lying on a stainless-steel trolley, his head lolling about at one end; and then, suddenly, the sheets being whipped away, and the undertaker, smelling of fags, asking if we wanted the post-mortem bandages removed.

I didn't get to respond. As I stared at his distorted corpse, at his purple lips, which made him look as if he'd just been sucking an ice lolly, Mr Dhanda informed the undertaker from his wheel-chair that the bandages should be removed, and my father was dragged towards a shower console on the other side of the room for the washing procedure. It turns out that we Sikhs are not the only people who indulge in this ritual: Judaism and Islam also advocate the washing of bodies. But while they do so according to strict rules – with some Muslims, for instance, insisting that the body be washed three times, or an odd number of times up to seven; and some Jews insisting the corpse should be cleansed care-fully, including the ears and fingers, with nails pared and hair combed, so that the corpse can be laid to rest in the manner that the person had visited the synagogue during life – there seemed to be no system behind the way we did it at all.

One person washed a leg with soap. There was an argument about whether the few strands of hair on father's head should be combed before the turban was retied. At one point my father's body was turned over, and various bodily and embalming fluids leaked out of his mouth. I remember the removal of the bandages, revealing stitched-up post-mortem wounds beneath. I remember the crack of an arm as it was forced into the suit.

I guess, in theory, the washing of a corpse could be a positive experience. It could emphasise the circularity of life: we are washed as babies, when we are brought into the world, and then when we die. It could symbolise the washing away of sins, a return to the state of perfection we experience in the womb. Maybe there is some comfort to be found in seeing someone beyond pain. But for me the whole thing felt like a massive invasion.

Unlike my mother, my father was always a private man, so coy that I'd never seen him naked. I hadn't even realised he was so bald until that moment: he kept his turban on at home, at least when I was visiting. And while Dhanda and his son had been part of our lives for so long, appearing in our home without warning, the way Punjabis do, my father never seemed particularly comfortable with them around. But here he was in his final moments on earth, naked, being manhandled, not only by strangers, but by people he disliked, with a radio in another room playing Dido.

It was awful for him. Though for me, the most terrible thing was the smell. You see, the problem with washing a corpse that has been frozen for a few weeks is that the body begins to decompose very quickly and suddenly when put in water. The stench had me throwing up in a corridor. I could smell it when I returned home and had the obligatory bath that my mother had already run for me. I could smell it when my father's coffin stood in our overly warm front room for an hour, mourners filing past.

I was still retching as my fiancée's family arrived en masse, getting it all wrong: Freya's mother dressed in black instead of white, her father in a suit and tie instead of casuals, struggling to cross his legs in the temple, Freya in a skirt, being given a blanket in the temple to cover her long tanned legs, clearly worried that the headscarf was going to ruin her hairdo, saying sorry when we don't say sorry, sitting with her feet pointing at the Holy Book, when we don't point our feet at the Holy Book, reaching out to hug me when we don't do public displays of physical affection. A few weeks earlier I had been so grateful for their patience and efforts during the engagement ceremony. But that day, with everyone staring, I felt embarrassed.

Later, when the visitors had left, the emptiness and quietness of the house felt so unbearable that I went and slept on my mother's bedroom floor. There was a moment's stand-off when she offered her bed – the urge to self-sacrifice, years of putting her son and husband first, was profound. But eventually she relented, and we spent the night talking about Dad. We had had weeks of nostalgia and reminiscence, of course. But not alone. We ended up talking half the night, telling our favourite stories about Dad, Mum recalling, among other things, the time he took an air rifle to the backyard and shot a pigeon, with the intention of flogging pigeon meat in the shop. I can't imagine there would have been much demand for game in inner-city Wolverhampton, but the smell of the resulting flesh in the shed was such that my vegetarian mother wouldn't let him back in the house until he had got rid of it. In return, I remembered how he would always buy a family pack of popcorn when we went to the cinema, find three smaller cartons and then stand in the corridor dividing it all. At the time I found it mortifying, lived in fear of being seen by a schoolmate, but telling the story, I found it touching, and not for the first time that week, fell to sleep on a damp pillow.

The next morning, I woke and found Mum was already downstairs. I assumed she was up to pray. But then: the sound of ringing. Not the ringing emitted by my iPhone, or by our landline, or the ding-dong that came when people pulled the iron pull mounted next to the private entrance into the house. It was the grating ring of the shop's door-mounted alarm, which buzzed every time someone entered or left. The alarm that interrupted every episode of *Neighbours* I had watched as a teenager, every dinner we sat down as a family to eat. I initially half thought it might be a feature of the vivid dreams I'd been having since I had come back home. But when I got up, slumped down the stairs and followed the noise, which merged with the sound of prayers burbling from Mum's cassette player in the hallway, through the green satin curtain that separated the house from the shop, there was another explanation. Mum was selling Amy Wilson a packet of cigarettes.

I'd only been in the shop once since my father's death: to open it up for a cleaning company. One of the onerous discoveries about a suspected homicide was finding out that the families of victims are left with the task of cleaning up the crime scene after the police have removed the evidence. But the shopfront had been more than cleaned up, it had been transformed. The shutter was up, at least as far as it could go. The chilled section had been stocked with milk; a pile of nappies had been stacked near the door; and, behind the counter, near the spot which had a few weeks earlier been marked out with yellow plastic tags indicating findings of significance, stood my mother.

'All roit, cocka,' proffered Mrs Wilson in my direction, smiling broadly. 'Fancied a lie-in, did yow?'

I ran a hand self-consciously through my hair and tightened the cord on my dressing gown. And then, as my eyes grew accustomed to the light, I took in a few more details: a medicine shelf stocked with goods bought in tiny quantities from Poundland (they were cheaper there than at the cash and carry), and a microwave that my father had recently installed for customers' use.

The question of what would happen to the shop after a parental bereavement was something, again, I had given some thought to, but only from the point of view of my mother's passing. I knew my father would want to carry on running the shop: it was his life. But my mother? No. We hadn't discussed the future since Dad's death, but I had just assumed that the next stage would be a trip to India, to consign my father's ashes to Kiratpur Sahib, as seemed to be the fashion nowadays. Maybe some travelling afterwards: she had not, after all, returned to the subcontinent since childhood. Then some kind of retirement. But she clearly had other ideas.

'Thank you, £4,' she informed Amy, before turning to address me in Punjabi. 'Some tea and paronthas in the kitchen. Get me a cup. And if you could call the newspaper people, we can get them started tomorrow.'

Surinder didn't sleep that night. She spent it tossing and turning, feeling alternatively too hot then too cold, mentally rehearsing how she would tackle her mother in the morning. But with people hurrying past on the way to the local factories and foundries, grabbing papers before they were even handed over through the hatch, she didn't get the chance. The following night she slept still worse. But again, she couldn't seem to find the right moment. In the end a whole weekend had passed and Tanvir had almost grown a convincing beard to match his new turban before she got to the point, blurting out her feelings at five to five in the morning, as she helped her mother drag a crate of milk into the shop.

'Mataji,' she intoned. 'I'd like to carry on at school next year. Carry on into the sixth form.'

In Punjabi this came out harsher than intended. She had been eleven when she left India to join her father in Britain, and Punjabi was her mother tongue, but the better she became at English, the less dexterous she seemed to become in Punjabi. She needn't, however, have fretted. Mrs Bains hadn't even registered her daughter's pronouncement. The newspapers had just landed on the doorstep. There was no time for a cup of tea, let alone conversation.

Surinder persisted as she helped her mother lift the stack of *Daily Mirror*s from the doorstep on to the counter behind the hatch.

'Mum . . .' Her voice trembled. 'I don't want to leave school.'

Maybe a question would be better than a declaration. 'I was wondering if I could stay on to do my A levels? Then maybe go on to nursing college? I want to be a nurse.'

In the years that followed, Surinder would not be able to recall where this desire to be a nurse came from, given that she knew no nurses, let alone Asian ones, had never been in hospital and was squeamish about blood. It actually came, like Tanvir's haircut, from a magazine. Almost every girls' title in the 1960s, from *Bunty* to *Girls' Crystal*, seemed to feature a nursing-themed cartoon strip, with titles like 'District Nurse Angela Ford' and 'Katy O'Connor: Ship's Nurse' outlining the limits of female professional ambition. There was even one strip called 'I Want to be a Nurse'.

But the choice of profession was not the point. The point was that Surinder was defying her prescribed destiny, one drilled into her from the youngest age: to develop vital domestic skills and then to be married off into a good Sikh family. She may as well have suggested that she wanted to play spoons in a folk band. And when Mrs Bains finally registered what her daughter was going on about, she reacted as such, nipping the end of her index finger with the scissors she was using to open the stack of papers.

'Hai!' she yelped, sucking the incision. Her daughter ran to assist, but was pushed away. 'What is this nonsense you're spouting, Surinder?' She examined her hand for blood. 'Your poor father is lying sick in bed, his body broken from trying to provide for us. I'm trying to open the shop, keep things going, your sister is working twenty-five hours a day making sure there is food on the table, and all you can do is stand there blurting nonsense about college.'

Surinder began chewing the end of her ponytail before switching to her thumbnail, as she always did when being castigated, averting her eyes to a newspaper headline, which bellowed, 'SACK FOR POWELL IN TORY RACE ROW'. Just as instinctively, her mother, who had resorted to tying chillies around her daughter's thumb to encourage her out of the habit as a toddler, pushed her hand away from her mouth.

'Stop that. How old are you now?' This was one of her mother's favourite rhetorical questions, along with 'Do you want a tight slap?' and 'What will your future mother-in-law think?' She didn't want an answer, just wanted to follow it up with 'Sixteen?', even though Surinder was actually fifteen. But this was how Punjabis measured age: if you were fifteen, it was said that you had 'begun your sixteenth year', this being yet another way, Surinder thought, of making children behave older than they were. Her mother continued. 'Too old, anyway, for such childishness. I don't know where you get such ideas from. From those stupid books and magazines you read?'

Now it was Mrs Bains turn to feel she could have been more subtle. It was true that she came from a part of the world where a woman with no sons is considered not only unlucky but a carrier of bad luck, but she had refused to be cowed by fate. At least, when the girls were young, she had defied the warnings of her husband's malevolent and grasping extended family – even the advice of her elder sister in England, who had whipped her children out of school as soon as possible – and lavished them with love and freedom, sending them to school to be educated like boys. Besides, she had not really come to terms with her husband's recently mooted idea of marrying the girls off jointly. She had barely slept since he had mentioned it.

Surinder resumed her plea. 'But Seema stayed on to do her A levels. She is studying to become a doctor and has not become bad.'

'*Seema?* The *Hindu* girl at your school? Whose parents are lawyers from *Bombay*? Leh. Next you'll be telling me you want to live like a gori and drink and wear miniskirts and cut your hair and have boyfriends and go dancing in nightclubs.' Surinder blushed. 'Good Sikh girls do not become nurses. We have your izzat to consider.'

Surinder moaned inwardly at the mention of *izzat*, the invisible force that dictated everything she could and could not do. It was the reason she had been stopped from playing with the boy at the garage next door when she was younger, why she could no longer pop into the hairdresser's next door for a chat with Maureen. Sometimes she thought they might as well be still living in an Indian village. Sometimes she wondered why her parents didn't just throw her into the local canal and have done with it. And she was considering saying so when they were interrupted by the sound of knocking on the front hatch. It was Mr Andrews, his ginger hair and black coat furred with rain. He worked at a nearby copper tubing plant and was a stickler for timing. If he didn't have his paper by 5.01 a.m., he would start kicking the front door down.

'One minute,' shouted Mrs Bains at the hatch, pronouncing it 'one ment', waving her uninjured hand in his direction.

She turned back to her daughter and peered through bleary eyes. Even with her bottom lip sagging in self-pity, her uncombed hair forming an absurd frizzy halo around her head, her daughter was impossibly pretty. There was a time when this beauty had thrilled her, but now it just made her anxious. She took a deep breath and tried to sound reasonable. 'Look, your father will not allow you to stay on at school. Too much education makes it difficult to adjust. And we are not like Seema's family. We are simple people. We need your help in the shop. If you are lucky, God willing, maybe you will marry a doctor.' She beamed at the thought, stroked her daughter's face. 'So stop this nonsense now, putt. And open the hatch before this bloody gora kicks it down.'

'But Mataji . . .'

'Bas.' Two raised hands. 'I haven't got time for this. No more discussion!'

Inevitably, there was more discussion, just twelve hours later when Surinder returned from school, and was sent up to her father's bedroom to relieve Baljit Kaur of her duties. Some children grow up with the threat of 'Wait till your dad gets home', but with Kamaljit and Surinder the warning had long been 'Behave or you will be sent up to talk to your father.' Not that they were allowed to complain about it, or in any way acknowledge it as a punishment or chore. Like being sent to do seva at the temple on the morning of one's birthday, they were required to look upon the task of caring for their father as a privilege, a blessing.

There were other parallels between visiting the temple and visiting her father's bedroom: both places smelt strongly of feet; it was compulsory, on entering, to cover one's head as a mark of respect; one generally arrived with offerings of food and drink; and both were places where tradition and myth were reinforced. At least, having no recollection of her father as a healthy adult, Surinder felt that the tale of how Mr Bains lost his family in the West Punjab, travelled to Delhi, and then to England without his family and with just a shilling ('shleng') in his pocket and had gone on to build a thriving business was as intangible to her as ancient tales about Sants making pilgrimages to Indian jungles and living for decades on nothing but the leaves that had fallen from trees.

On opening the door, she was confronted with the dispiriting sight of her father's bedside commode, kept to allow voiding at night. It sat on a cold wooden floor covered in lino, the durris and rugs removed to prevent tripping, next to a bed which had had its wooden legs cut down to make transfers easier. There was a mattress in the corner of the room, where her mother slept because Mr Bains had begun thrashing around so forcefully at night while acting out dreams and nightmares that he had recently given her a black eye. This afternoon her father was lying still on his side, however, pillows placed between his knees and ankles and arms.

Surinder put the sandwich and tea she had brought on the

dressing table which functioned as a medicine cabinet, and began the task of sitting her father up. He was moved around several times a day, to reduce the chances of bed sores, and was propped up vertically at mealtimes so that saliva would collect in the back of his throat which might, in turn, stimulate a swallow. A year ago he was still able to feed himself, though the food had to be cut into small pieces. A year before that he could use cutlery, though the knife and fork had to be extra sharp so they required less effort, and plates and bowls had to have high sides to make scooping easier. But now, though his tremor was less marked, he needed to be fed each meal, sandwiches being dunked into tea for ease of mastication.

Surinder watched as he struggled with his first bite. His scalp was dry and his facial expression was frozen, impossible to read. After his third bite, he lifted his hand – a signal which Surinder had learnt meant 'stop' – and made a noise which Surinder had learnt was an attempt to say her name. Unlike her mother, he spoke to Surinder in English, but she had to concentrate as he did so. The days he could bark instructions from his bed into the shop were now gone. He tended to mumble in a muffled monotone, his sentences petering out to the point of whisper.

'Here, putt,' he said, patting the bed next to him.

She placed the plate on the floor, moved from the chair to the bed, held his hand and waited for him to speak.

'Your mother tells me. You want. College.'

She could not tell whether he was making a statement or asking a question, the ability to inflect being yet another skill that had been eroded by disease. But she corrected him anyway.

'No, not college. Sixth form. My school has a sixth form, for A levels. My teachers think I could do well.' Thinking she should get all her arguments in while she had a chance, she added, 'It is a girl's school.'

'Your mother tells me. You want. Be nurse.' He spoke good

English but pronounced 'nurse' in an Indian accent, perhaps to emphasise the ridiculousness of the idea. And then laughed raspily. After a long pause: 'What kind of job is that?'

Surinder could have pointed out that it was the kind of job that kept him alive. That he would be nowhere if it wasn't for the army of people who nursed him. She could have also pointed out that he was once a believer in his children's education, agreeing with his wife that they attend school in Delhi (when most girls didn't), or at least not caring enough to object. But all that seemed to have gone with his health. Suddenly there appeared to be limits to what women could learn, and she maintained the obligatory respectful silence as Mr Bains, his bloodshot eyes dry and itchy, his forehead glistening with sweat that ran down his face despite the unseasonable chill in the air, emitted a series of short statements which, when added up, amounted to: 'How on earth can you be thinking about working in a British hospital with white people when things are so bad out there?'

Once more, there was a gap between Surinder's dutiful silence and what she actually thought. She suspected she knew rather more about what was going on 'out there' than her bedridden father. No doubt Dhanda had told him about the speech that local Tory MP Enoch Powell had made, attacking the government's immigration policy, saying it was like watching a nation busily engaged in heaping up its own funeral pyre, calling for repatriation and warning that as he looked to the future he was filled with a sense of foreboding and 'like the Roman' could 'see the River Tiber foaming with much blood'.

No doubt he had heard on his radio that Conservative leader Edward Heath had sacked Powell as shadow defence spokesman and that subsequently thousands of dockers, factory workers, brewery workers and meat porters across the country had walked out in protest at what they termed Powell's victimisation, carrying placards demanding 'Back Britain, not Black Britain'; that Powell had got tens of thousands of letters of support. And Mrs Bains had doubtless informed him that several windows and door panels of a nearby Sikh temple had been broken, that Indian workers leaving a foundry had been stoned by white youths, that Indians were having their cars wrecked and daubed with graffiti declaring 'Enoch'.

But he didn't know from his bed what it was like to be spat upon by children in the street. To hear her schoolmates talk unembarrassedly about how coloured people were pigs, that they wanted burning. To endure, as she had that day, a white teacher at her school refer to a West Indian girl as a little monkey.

Mr Bains grabbed her arm so hard that she could feel it bruise. 'No college, no nursing,' he spat. 'OK?' He relaxed his grip and continued. 'We are looking for boys for you and Kamaljit. Dhanda has ideas. One family with two brothers. Shop family. Nice to be married into the same family as your sister?' She thought it sounded sick. 'You will have good life, my dear. Good life. We will get you settled.' Surinder waited for the inevitable sign-off – 'Baapu di izzhat samalni, beti da sabh to badda dharam ne', one of her father's favourite sayings, which translated as 'A daughter's main religion should be to uphold her father's and family's honour.' But, instead, he made an attempt at empathy: 'I too did not want to get married. Waited too long. You know how old I was?'

She knew all too well; he was forty-three, her mother was twenty-six. It was 1950. Her mother had been widowed young, after just a few years of marriage, and was facing a life of poverty and childlessness. He had fled the West Punjab for India during Partition, his family had remained and been wiped out, and also facing a life of loneliness, poverty and childlessness, he worked where he could, living with an extended family who treated him like a servant. And so on.

'Marrying your mother, best thing I did,' he remarked. 'You will feel the same.'

Surinder wept, but lowered her head while doing so, making it look like she was meekly presenting herself for parental blessing. Mr Bains obliged, patting her with his palm and declaring, 'Shabbassh.'

Surinder recovered enough to suggest some exercise. It was the doctor's recommendation that Mr Bains have his limbs moved as much as possible, to stretch the muscles and maintain joint function. She must have done it hundreds of times, but this evening, as she lifted his arms and then his legs up and down, she omitted to put a hand against his joints for support, and pushed so hard at one stage that Mr Bains yelped out in pain.

The conventional modes of protest were not open to Surinder when it came to expressing upset. Argument and sulking were not tolerated in the Bains household. But she nevertheless made her feelings felt. If her parents wanted her to be a good little village girl, then that, she decided, was exactly what she would be. She started addressing Tanvir as 'paji' at every opportunity, to his not inconsiderable distress, and called Kamaljit 'pehnji' whenever their mother was in earshot, to her not inconsiderable confusion. She refused the weekly treat of fish and chips for the vegetable sabzi she insisted on making even though it was not her turn to do so, and declined invitations to the cinema. In short, the most frivolous person in the household suddenly became the most sombre. Her misery spread through the house like damp. And then, one evening, Surinder came home from school bearing a green envelope.

Mrs Bains recognised it as one of several discipline strategies employed at North Park High. Minor offences resulted in detention or lines. More serious offences got instant punishment in the form of slaps or swishes of a ruler against hands and legs. But in cases of severe transgression, girls got the 'green 'un' – a note to take home to their parents for signature, the idea being that punishment at home would be more severe than anything that the school could dream up. Mrs Bains had previously been sent one when Tanvir had fallen sick and she had been forced to keep Surinder at home for a week to work in the shop. Her daughter handed it over as she walked into the back of the shop, with the kind of nonchalance she would reserve for passing on a leaflet or bill. Her mother handed it straight back for translation. She could get by with English customers with a vocabulary of 'morning', 'hello', 'evening' and 'shilling', and an ability to tell the difference between the *Express* and *The Times*, but struggled at anything more expansive.

Surinder read it to herself, although she was already aware of its contents.

Dear Mr Bains,

I am writing in relation to an important matter concerning your daughter Surinder. I was hoping you could pop in for a brief conversation with me at school one day soon. Please contact my secretary Susan on the number below to make an appointment at your convenience.

Yours sincerely, Mrs Flanagan.

Surinder telescoped the note in translation to: 'My headteacher wants to talk to you about something.'

'About what?'

'I don't know.' She shrugged.

'What have you been up to?'

'Nothing.'

'*Have you been going to school?*'

Surinder gestured at her uniform and began biting her thumbnail. 'What does it look like?'

'Don't take that tone with me.' Mrs Bains pushed her daughter's hand from her mouth. 'Have you been doing your work?'

43

'What's the point if I'm leaving?' Surinder responded bitterly.

If Mrs Bains had spoken to her own mother like that at fifteen, she would have been dragged by her hair out of the house. It took considerable self-control to resist hitting the girl. But she realised Surinder had her in a bind. 'I didn't mean you should give up entirely.' Mrs Bains sighed. 'We will have to go to see this dadni teacher of yours. I thought, as you girls got older, you would help me, provide me with support, but you just seem determined to make life even more difficult.'

With Surinder sitting an O-level exam, translating duties that Friday afternoon fell to Kamaljit. And while time spent alone with her mother was normally something Kamaljit treasured, the prospect of accompanying her to North Park High filled her with dread. Her little sister was a mystery in many ways. She didn't understand how she could be taller and yet younger, fairer and yet have spent her entire childhood playing out in the sun. But the thing she found most bewildering, even more than her obsession with magazines and her ability to identify any brand of clothing at a glance, was Surinder's fondness for school.

The sisters had never attended the same educational establishment in England, owing to the local council's policy of randomly transporting immigrant children from school to school to achieve an arbitrary balancing figure of 'the black problem'. But for her, school had been a daily torment of being teased about the smelliness of Indian food, sarcastic teachers asking, 'Don't you understand English? Or are you just stupid'?, dismal academic failure and being addressed as 'Camel-shit'.

Not that her attendance had really been daily. She had been fourteen when they moved to England, sixteen when she left school, and had found the whole thing so bewildering that she had skived whenever possible. She had left school with no friends – the white pupils in her class would look away if they saw her on the street – no qualifications, able to vaguely follow basic English, but unable to speak it very well. Which rather added to the stress of translating this afternoon.

They arrived to find the school full of students, but eerily silent, everyone huddled away in classrooms or exam halls. The central building smelt strongly of coffee and freshly mown grass, aromas Kamaljit would always, along with fags, associate with white people, and on arriving she couldn't shake the feeling that she was the one about to be castigated. There was no solace to be found in glancing at her mother. In the shop, Mrs Bains was a tower of strength. But out of context, in her purple salwar kameez, surreptitiously snuffling boiled sweets from one of the shop's paper bags, the paper bag stowed away in undergarments, she looked vulnerable and incongruous, decked out like a Christmas tree in the middle of June.

Eventually Mrs Flanagan, the headmistress, appeared, the authority of her smart suit undermined by her girlish blonde curls and high-pitched squeaky voice. She greeted Mrs Bains with a smile and a welcoming handshake. 'Ah, thank you for coming, I was expecting Mr Bains, but this, in some ways, is better.' Mrs Bains smiled back, blankly. 'I find that things are easier, not only when you cut out the middle man, but men in general.' She laughed at her own joke and noticed Kamaljit. 'Were you one of ours? No? Course not. Never forget a face. Follow me, please!'

They plunged down a sequence of corridors at a pace that betrayed the fact that Mrs Flanagan still taught Games three times a week, ending up in a study which felt larger than the entirety of Bains Stores. It was furnished with a green leather sofa the size of a double bed, and three leather armchairs, each the size of a settee. Despite this, it still somehow felt empty, and Mrs Flanagan's squeal echoed around the chamber as she noticed Mrs Bains glancing at a children's magazine on her enormous oak desk.

'Good edition, that!' She picked it up and held it out for her visitors' benefit. The cover featured a picture of a Viking warrior under the headline 'Who are the British?' 'Makes the point that immigrants have been entering the country for hundreds of years. Did you know there are nearly two million people living in Britain who were born outside the country?'

Kamaljit froze in her seat. Suddenly, she was fifteen again and being shouted at in a classroom. She could tell from the inflexion in the headteacher's voice that she was asking a question, and gambled on a response. 'Yes?'

'Quite!' squeaked Mrs Flanagan, pacing around and sitting on the edge of her desk. 'Exactly!' Kamaljit breathed out in relief: it was the right answer. 'A sister of Surinder's was always going to know that! But did you also know that in the mid nineteenth century Wolverhampton had 6,000 Irish people in a population of nearly 50,000? That's over 10 per cent! They worked in the factories and coalfields and lived in a slum known as Caribee Island! Seems funny now, doesn't it?'

Kamaljit stared absently at a pen on the desk and then risked another gamble, less tentatively this time. 'Yes.'

'Yes!' Mrs Flanagan scratched the back of her hand. 'My point simply being that in the nineteenth century Wolverhampton saw much immigration following the Irish Potato Famine. And that I was once an immigrant too – at least my grandfather was among them. There have always been foreigners in this town. The problem with Enoch Powell, of course, is that, unlike us, he has no historical awareness. No historical awareness! Eh?'

A long pause ensued. Mrs Bains nudged her daughter to say something. Blushing, avoiding eye contact, she coughed. 'Sorry, miss,' she whispered eventually, uttering one of the phrases she recalled from school. Even these words felt unnatural to utter. 'My mother. No English.'

Mrs Flanagan, who by this stage had marched across the room and was standing at the grand marble mantelpiece which dominated one side of the room, turned on her heels. 'Oh!' she yelped, lamenting inwardly that she was succumbing to the vice that seemed to claim all headteachers eventually: pomposity. She walked back to the leather chair behind her desk, sat down and began addressing Mrs Bains in a loud but slow squeal, as if her visitor were deaf and stupid. 'Anyway, I just wanted to discuss your daughter Surinder. SURINDER. Talk about her plans. The question of her future. FUTURE.'

She waited for Kamaljit to translate. 'I think she wants to talk to us about Surinder.'

'I consider your daughter a highly accomplished student. SHE IS VERY GOOD.'

Translation: 'She's good at school.'

'She has GREAT POT-ENTIAL.'

Translation: 'She's particularly good at cookery.'

'She is the most diligent girl I have known – here 8 a.m. every day.'

Translation: 'She is also good at maths.'

'She is probably the brightest girl I have come across in twenty years of teaching. You get girls who are good at languages or cookery or maths or English, but very rarely do you get a girl who is accomplished across the board. I wouldn't be surprised if she gets top grades in nine or ten of her O levels. Nice girl too, gets on with everyone, knows her mind, doesn't assume politics is the domain of the adult and the male. And her English, well, it shames her classmates, in truth.'

Translation: 'She will do well in her exams.'

'Given this, it would be a great shame if she didn't stay on for A levels.'

And so on. This exchange went on for some time. The more Mrs Flanagan raved about Surinder, the shorter were her sister's translations. It was, the teacher thought, the conversational equivalent of mining for gold – excavating tonnes of earth for very little in return. Exhausting. And typical of so many of her encounters with immigrant families.

Though Mrs Flanagan would have conceded she was having a rather good war in this respect. At the age of forty-eight, having never worked outside Wolverhampton, or lived outside it, she had found herself at the centre of things, teaching in a town that was enjoying five minutes of fame as Britain's equivalent of Harlem. Pinpointed as the county borough with the highest proportion of coloured immigrants in the country, barely a week passed without education in Wolverhampton making the national papers, whether it was Powell claiming that there was a class in Wolverhampton in which there was only one white child, or white parents claiming that their children, besieged, were 'becoming fluent in Punjabi'. Running a school where one in three pupils were black, she had become sought after for her expertise. There had been an op-ed piece in the *Times Educational Supplement*, appearances on the TV news.

But there were also downsides to the whole thing: emotional outbursts from the National Front and the Indian Workers' Association, both as unreasonable as each other. Children arriving at the age of eleven, or even fifteen, who couldn't speak English and didn't even seem to want to – children not unlike the girl before her. And parents like this Mrs Bains, who did not value education and whose plans for their daughters extended only to trotting them off to India or Pakistan at the age of seventeen to sell to the highest bidder.

Nevertheless, she believed in being proactive, making a difference one child at a time, and when Surinder had alluded to her parents' medieval intentions, Mrs Flanagan knew she had to try to do what she could. Just the other day she had read in the *Guardian* about a Sikh Punjabi family who had imprisoned their eldest daughter, chained her to a bed for four days because she refused to marry the man of their choice.

But ten minutes into it, it was obvious from the faraway look in the mother's eyes, from the terseness and physical rigidity of the elder sister, that she was getting nowhere. The meeting was going the way of her attempt to incorporate Indian food in the home economics syllabus, which had almost resulted in a riot; or the even more misjudged interview she had given to the local paper when she had inadvertently implied that her experience teaching retarded children was relevant when it came to teaching English to Punjabi students.

But as she half-heartedly handed Mrs Bains a leaflet entitled 'Careers in Nursing and Other Hospital Professions', which featured a sketch of a busy hospital ward on the cover, and outlined the educational options for girls like Surinder who wanted to nurse, she heard Mrs Bains emit a sound which sounded suspiciously like the word 'yes'.

'Sorry?'

'Jes. Surinder . . . stay.'

She sat forward. 'Mrs Bains. Are you saying that you are fine with Surinder staying on at school for her A levels?'

Kamaljit intervened, alarmed. 'Mum, I don't think she wants an answer now, she just wants you to think about it.'

Mrs Bains repeated herself, addressing Mrs Flanagan directly. 'Jes, Surinder stay. Good girls, good girls.' She patted Kamaljit on the lap to emphasise the point. 'She good cooking.' She mimed Surinder reading a book. 'Surinder always read. Always newspapers. This girl, always cook. My girls, good girls.'

Neither Kamaljit nor Mrs Flanagan could quite believe what they were hearing, and both wondered if Mrs Bains had followed what had been said and if she knew what she was doing. The fact was that she hadn't entirely got the gist, gathering only that Surinder was being complimented, and feeling vaguely flattered that she was. But what Mrs Bains did see in Mrs Flanagan's argument was a neat way out of her husband's plan to marry off her two daughters at the same time. A plan which had been troubling her since its inception.

She understood and sympathised with her husband's thinking, of course. She, like all Punjabi mothers, had taught her daughters from the youngest age that parting was inevitable, regarded marrying them off as a near-religious duty. But even more intense than this feeling was her memory of the poverty she had endured, first as a young widow, when neither her husband's parents nor her own had wanted her, and then when Mr Bains had parted for Britain and left her in Delhi with his insufferable extended family. For thirteen long years, when she drank water instead of milk, used mustard oil instead of ghee, she had looked forward to the day when she would be mistress of her own courtyard, and now that she had the shop, and it was trading well, she had no intention of giving it up.

And this was the essential problem with the idea of marrying both girls off at once. It would devastate the shop. Tanvir's English was improving, but Surinder still did most of the paperwork and translation, while Kamaljit more or less ran the household. With both girls suddenly gone, they would have to take on new staff, or even close, and as tired as she felt sometimes, she wasn't ready to retire. It was all right for her husband, it was not like he had long to live but she was not checking out anytime soon and had no intention of returning to the days when she had to wash dishes in an outside gully, when the few animals she owned went hungry and kept the household awake with their groaning. Doubtless her husband would be annoyed that she had overruled him. But given everything she had done for him, holding on to her daughters for a year or two longer was not much to ask for. Besides, what could he, ultimately, do about it? The days when he could make his point with the back of his hands were long gone.

'That is excellent news, Mrs Bains,' said Mrs Flanagan, coming

over to her visitors and shaking them vigorously by their hands.
'EXCELLENT. News.'

Conscious of the uneasiness many immigrants felt at the moral
values of white people, and sensing wariness in their uncertain
handshake, she found herself adding, 'Now then, you need not
worry about Surinder here, Mrs Bains. There are no boys at this
school.' For some reason she mimed an action representing 'boy',
which involved flexing her biceps. 'I will keep my eye on her.' At
that moment Mrs Flanagan could have performed celebratory
bhangra around her office. And Kamaljit would have looked no
more astonished had she done so.

I can't say my parents and Freya's parents ever had much in common. Except maybe the fact that my father and her mother, a retired civil servant, were both, inexplicably, fans of *Midsomer Murders*. And then, of course, the fact that my mother and her father both struggled to conceal their disapproval at our match.

In Freya's father's case this disapproval mainly took the form of mispronunciations of my name ('So, Tarzan . . .'), and endless fussing about my dietary requirements. 'You allowed to eat this?' he once asked while handing over some *asparagus* during dinner at their Sussex home, making me explain yet again that I ate pretty much everything, except beef, and that for cultural rather than religious reasons.

Bill Tunstall was prejudiced, and out of touch, but I put up with it, in part because my Indian upbringing had, ironically, made me instinctively respectful of the elderly, and he was nearly seventy. But mainly because Freya had, in turn, quite a lot to put up with from my mother. Though Mum's disapproval was rarely so direct. Take, for instance, the only visit my parents had paid us in London, on a Sunday a year before my father died. Mum went into the bathroom as soon as she arrived and didn't come out for half an hour. It turned out she was cleaning. When she finally reappeared, she went straight into the kitchen and started washing and mopping up. The criticism was implicit: your white girlfriend is filthy and does not know how to look after you.

There followed an excruciating meal in an Indian restaurant in

East London where my father nearly passed out at the sight of the prices, even though he wasn't paying, and my mother almost passed out at the idea that the chefs handling her food might also be handling meat, and refused to eat anything but a naan bread with yoghurt. And then a strained visit to Madame Tussauds, where Mum failed to recognise any of the waxworks except for Tony Blair and Indira Gandhi and took umbrage at Freya's suggestion that she have a photo taken with the latter. 'Does your girlfriend know what that woman did to us? How she wanted to exterminate the Sikhs?' She probably didn't. But then what did my mother know of World War I, World War II, the ongoing situation in Iraq, or any other geopolitical dispute that didn't involve Punjabis? She lived in a bubble.

Talking of which, in Wolverhampton, Mum's passive-aggressive disapproval of Freya mainly took the form of regaling me endlessly with stories which reflected the most excessive aspects of the lives of white customers. She did this with Asians too – sometimes it seemed she continued shopkeeping only for the gossip-mongering auntie conferences which convened several times a week. But there was a definite uptick in the intensity of the former sort of stories after my engagement. And when, the morning after my father's funeral, I went downstairs in my dressing gown, found she had opened the shop and was serving Amy Wilson, then returned, dressed, and asked, 'Mum, when did you decide to reopen the shop?', she ignored the question entirely and instead continued updating me on Amy Wilson, whose life she followed like other people followed *EastEnders*.

'You know she has five children? And they say it is we Asians who have big families. By three men as well. Her latest bloke is a tattoo artist, apparently. Practises on the kids. No shortage of space there of course.'

I stood, swaying on the spot, wielding two cups of tea, stunned momentarily by my mother's ability to absorb such gossip and information, despite her refusal to speak English (a quality that caused me endless confusion and distress as an adolescent), and Amy Wilson's desire to share such information despite the lack of meaningful feedback. Then again, maybe this was the appeal.

'Mum, I didn't know you were going to reopen the shop.'

'She calls him her boyfriend. A *boyfriend* at her age,' she continued. 'Can you believe it? But then again, she *is* old enough to be his mother.' A pause. 'What did you say?' There was a short hiatus as I noticed that a picture of my father had been put up behind the counter. I repeated myself. Her eventual response: 'You never asked.'

This, admittedly, was true. I hadn't got my head around 'What happened?' yet, let alone 'What next?'

'And this is what you want to do? To run the shop?'

'Why not?'

A million reasons flashed through my mind: trade was anaemic; she was in remission but not exactly in peak health; running a shop on Victoria Road was not the safest thing for a widow of sixty-one to be doing alone; I didn't want to give up my life in London to help my mother run a shop in Wolverhampton. But all I managed was: 'Mum, you're not well enough.'

'Leh. I'm doing all right this morning, aren't I? If I need help, there's Ranjit.'

I tensed up. Ranjit. Who with his arranged marriage to a girl from India and two kids and decision to stay in Wolverhampton to run the family business was another weapon my mother used to provoke guilt.

'Ranjit has his own shop to run. I know he's being helpful at the moment, but he can't be here all the time. And even he had trouble last year. Remember?'

The attack was currently one of Ranjit's favourite stories, and I had heard several versions of it over the preceding fortnight. He had apparently refused to serve an underage Polish/Romanian/

West Indian boy some booze, and the said boy returned with five illegal immigrants/gangsters with metal bars/machetes, who left him with a cut on his neck which needed seven/twelve/eighteen stitches, the account of what happened varying according to how much weed he had had, and which Steven Seagal movie he had watched the night before.

My mother added, 'You mustn't worry. What will be will be.'

The antagonism deepened. There comes a point in an argument with any Indian parent when they try to kill the conversation with: 'Don't worry, what will be, will be' or the karmic variant, 'Chaloo koi gaal nahi'. Sometimes, I envied my mother for this approach to life: it helped her cope with her illness and Dad's death. But sometimes, like now, it enraged me. I was torn between emitting a despairing 'Naaaaaaheee!' in the style of a Bollywood hero, and explaining calmly that we have choices, free will. But in the end, in spite of myself, I blurted, 'Mum, it's not safe.'

'I can look after myself. And you mustn't worry about what the police said.'

I wasn't worried! No one had been more sceptical than me when the police briefly classed Dad's death as unexplained, and I was not at all surprised when the post-mortem provided a straight answer. But even though I was now thirty-five, Mum still felt the need to coddle and reassure me as if I were a child. I found myself adding, in an adolescent whine, 'Mum, I can't leave my job to help you run the shop.'

'I'm not asking you to give up your job,' she snapped back. 'Have I asked you to? Tell me, what would I do if I didn't work in the shop? Why don't you go back to London . . .' She didn't say it, would never have done, but in my head, I finished the sentence for her. '. . . to your white girlfriend.'

I recoiled. The tension between us, her bitterness that I had left Wolverhampton and got engaged to a girl who wasn't Sikh, my father's annoyance that I hadn't become a doctor or a lawyer, and in turn, my annoyance at being compared unfavourably to Ranjit, at how my parents valued making money over professional or educational development, convenience over romantic fulfilment, their refusal to be impressed by Freya's charm, all the tensions we had put aside since Dad's death, and, for that matter, since her diagnosis, threatened, momentarily, to reappear. I did the sensible thing, and retreated.

The morning after that argument with Mum, I was up at four to open the shop, spent six hours standing at the counter as she rested and caught up with housework, and visited the cash and carry to restock. I did a version of the same over two days at the weekend. But on Sunday evening I had no choice but to go back, to return to East London and the life I'd abandoned weeks earlier.

Freya was delighted to have me back, had laid on dinner and, judging from the prominence of the pile of 'save the date' cards on the living-room table, which we had been intending to fill out when the news about my father came through, was hoping to carry on where we had left off. But the conversation was stilted, I had little appetite, got up to call Mum during the meal, felt too tired for wedding admin and couldn't face TV. I thought an early night might help with re-acclimatising, but then I couldn't sleep. And at 3 a.m. I was padding around the flat I co-owned, trying to relearn the basics of my former life like a stroke victim learning to talk again.

The framed Bollywood poster in the hallway, a souvenir from Goa, though I disliked Goa and have never liked Bollywood. The square blackboard we had painted in the kitchen, bickering as we did so – Freya anal about getting the lines perfect; me, less so. It was covered in slightly self-conscious messages and a picture of a dog she wanted but we had no space for. Meanwhile, in the living room, above the reclaimed period fireplace, a bright abstract picture. A bright abstract picture painted by *me* and which had, in effect, brought Freya and I together.

She was working for a private equity firm at the time, had specialised in finding promising new technology companies to invest in, but as part of her accelerated promotion she had been tasked with revamping the company logo and marketing material, a task which she made clear from the moment she walked into my agency's offices she considered an exercise in banality. It was far from a case of love at first sight. Not least because we were both dating other people: her, an earnest Canadian academic; me, a cheerful Asian corporate lawyer, who was just my type – pretty, out of my league. I remember complaining to her about Freya. Specifically, the way Freya made out that she didn't care about the project, was happy for me to take the lead, but then, when presented with the designs, had a thousand and one comments to make about everything from the font to the way white space was used.

However, after the assignment, she turned up, with her boyfriend, at an exhibition I was having for a bunch of pictures I had painted during a trip to India. I couldn't recall telling her about it, though she claims that I did. I remember feeling embarrassed that she was there: the set-up, a disused shop with barely whitewashed walls, was unprofessional, to say the least. The pictures weren't even framed. I also remember she looked very different that night, in a Whistles dress and ankle boots, instead of the suit I had got used to seeing her in. She apologised for being difficult at work. She had a nightmare boss, was just passing on the grief. Then she told me I was talented, that I should give up graphic design for painting, and she bought this picture entitled, if memory serves, something painfully pretentious like *Jodhpur Luminescence #9*.

The story goes that the Canadian academic never liked it. He said it was like 'something you might see in a mid-priced Indian restaurant'. But she got the Nietzschean subtext, said it reminded her of Rothko and of the heat and colour of India, and in return, I sent her web links to my work in case she had friends who might like my stuff too. There followed an intense email and text exchange. Though it wasn't the intimacy which was intense – most of the time the content was banal – links to new music, pictures, and so on. It was just the sheer amount of it. Twenty to thirty messages a day. I didn't think there was anything wrong with it, even when I found myself going online and checking out her boyfriend's books, 'liking' all the one-star reviews he had received, and deleting our message exchange on my phone in case my girl-friend discovered it.

But then we met, purportedly for coffee. The afternoon began in the tone of our messages: we agreed that *Barry Lyndon* was Stanley Kubrick's finest moment; argued about the merits of Phil Collins' back catalogue. As we moved on to food, deciding on an early supper, I discovered she had a grandparent who was Jewish, and we bonded over the parallels with Punjabi culture, listing all the similarities together: the workaholism, the large overbearing families, the value placed on education, the tendency for migra-tion, the emphasis on integration, the pressure to get married within the community, the massive inter-community variance in religious interpretation, the guilt, the emotional blackmail, the belief in property as an investment, the emotional hysteria, the inability to be laid-back, the noisiness, the studiousness, the self-sufficiency, the obsession with the healing properties of chicken soup/lentil dal, the propensity for beards, the incompetence in the field of sport, the talkativeness, the degrees in law, accountancy, medicine and finance, and the mothers who with their meddling, intrusive-ness, inability to recognise boundaries, nagging, protection, nourishment and self-sacrifice kept everything going.

I'm not sure if it was the thought of my mother or our second bottle of wine that made things turn maudlin, but soon Freya was confessing to regretting giving up a promising career in academia for cash, and I was admitting to occasionally regretting giving up medicine for art, and giving up art for graphic design. Inevitably, I found myself saying my girlfriend didn't really approve of my career choice, painting her in a worse light than she deserved, confessing in the process that I was stuck in a sequence of three-month-long relationships, which seemed to be the amount of time it took to get excited by someone and bored by them again. It had the response I must have hoped for: Freya said my girlfriend didn't deserve me, that my problem was that I hadn't met the right person yet. And when she complained about her boyfriend's narcissism, that she thought her relationship was on the rocks, I inevitably returned the compliment, saying that he was lucky to have her.

There was an uncomfortable moment when we finally kissed, when something like dread passed across her face and she said, 'You don't kiss like my boyfriend.' But actually that was the beginning and the end of awkwardness. Lying on a hotel bed that night, our limbs entwined, I imagined our whole relationship unfolding in the form of a storyboard. And that was pretty much how things unfurled. The shared flat in Dalston. Saturday mornings at a farmer's market, Freya in an oversized cashmere jumper and leggings, me in jeans and jacket and a scarf tied in one of those neat knots. Lunch with friends in artfully dishevelled pubs. Yoga holidays to India. We had got everything we wanted, except perhaps the dog in Freya's case, and, for now, the beautiful inter-racial children I'd imagined, with self-conscious ethnic names like India and Kashmir ('And maybe, if we have a third child we could call it Bangladesh,' Freya had added archly, when I confessed to the fantasy).

They say people don't fall in love with people, they fall in love with a quality they want to possess. I hope this isn't true because I think the thing I loved most about Freya was the intensity with which she adored me. I could do no wrong, in her eyes. And the picture above our fireplace epitomised this adoration. When I'd painted it, I'd imagined I was scorching the canvas with a radical evocation of the deserts of Rajasthan. But the ex-boyfriend had a point – it was derivative. Where Mark Rothko feathered his brushstrokes across the picture field, blending tones with a whispery subtlety, my marks were crude. But it was touching that Freya loved it so much, that she believed so much in an artistic ambition I had abandoned. I went back to bed, and, my cold hands against Freya's warm skin, we made love.

However, the unsettled feeling was back the next day at work. Everyone was sweet. There were cards and hugs from my sensitive colleagues. But I found concentrating difficult for more than a minute or two. It took physical effort to stop myself from saying 'Shut up' when clients called and said things like, 'I will know what I want when I see it' and 'Could you jazz it up a little?' Meanwhile, I fretted endlessly about my mother, working alone in the shop. I must have called home three times by lunchtime. Mum insisted she was fine, but that evening I did something no one had ever done in the history of my agency and left work at 5 p.m., cancelling my evening with Freya.

The following morning I was up at 4 a.m. to help Mum open the shop, then arranged the installation of a new CCTV system and drove back to London. There was a birthday dinner in Soho that evening for one of my closest and oldest friends, Matt Metcalfe, whom I had met at school in Wolverhampton, but who was now running a technology company in London. I was too tired to attend, and Freya went alone, apologising for my absence. I promised I would have lunch with her the next day, to bash out that list of wedding invitations, but I never made that either. That morning, when my mother didn't pick up the phone when I rang twice, I panicked, rang the police and immediately hired a car to drive home. It turned out it had been quiet in the shop and she had been tidying the kitchen. That evening, I got an email from my agency's managing director, asking for a 'chat'. Which was followed five minutes later by an email from Freya asking if we could 'chat soon'.

The breeziness of what the word 'chat' implies, in my experience, invariably belies the gravity of the discussion that lies ahead. As it happens, I had had a 'chat' at the beginning of it all, amid the shellshock, with my employer's head of HR, who had called, expressed sympathy and then prattled on about 'statutory right of employees to unpaid bereavement leave in the event of a parent, spouse or dependant passing away', how our company went further than most in offering 'five days' paid leave for any family bereavement' as long as the entitlement was not used more than once a year, but how in my extenuating circumstances they were willing to be 'flexible'. At the time, the idea of official bereavement leave as a perk struck me as odd. But I was nevertheless grateful for their 'flexibility', given that it basically seemed to amount to unlimited unpaid leave.

Sitting in a room opposite my boss, who had hired me a decade earlier, with the words 'I like Indians, they work hard', it became clear that things had changed. He was as generous as his laconic demeanour allowed, enquiring after my mother, listening as I outlined my predicament with the shop, but then, in conclusion, he pointed out that my work performance was not up to my 'usual high standard', and politely suggested that I either get a grip or take some time off and come back once I had got a grip. 'We can't, realistically, hold your position open longer than, say, the New Year, and we wouldn't be able to pay you while you're off. But we would hate to lose you.' From the reflection in his designer glasses, I could see that he was following a football match on his computer monitor. 'Why don't you have a chat with your fiancée and get back to me? Within the next week or so? I hope she's being supportive?'

Of course she was being supportive. You could say that her

response to my father's death was textbook. Literally. That morning, I was looking for a pair of trainers for a run, when I spotted, under the desk in the spare room, a book entitled *How to Help Your Spouse Deal with Grief*, and inside it an article from one of her favourite women's magazines which was headlined 'Life after Loss'. This was typical of Freya, the trained economist. If there was a problem, she threw a book at it. She'd given me endless reading material about bowel cancer when Mum got sick, and in the build-up to our engagement she had feasted on books about the Sikh faith.

We'd be at dinner at a friend's house, or she'd be on the phone to a friend, and I'd hear her reciting bits verbatim, informing the person on the other end of the line that Sikhism was a modern, liberal, open, democratic, monotheistic religion, established in the late fifteenth century by Guru Nanak, that one of the founding principles was opposition to Hinduism's oppressive caste system, that Sikhs didn't worship human beings, that the Gurus declared men and women to be equal, that Sikhs didn't drink, that it was the only major world religion to acknowledge that other religions were a valid way of reaching God. 'I'm not going to convert,' I heard her say more than once. 'But if I had to choose a religion . . .'

What she didn't realise was these books were useless. The theory of the religion tells you little about the etiquette of Punjabi life or the actuality of Punjabi *culture*, which is rarely written about, because one of the defining things about it is that it is defiantly un-self-examining. In practice, Sikh society often runs counter to the principles of the religion, being, for one thing, highly patriarchal. Some believers risk being disowned for marrying outside of the religion – we were struggling to find a temple which would allow us to have a mixed wedding. The world's fifth-largest organised religion has a caste system of its own, certain Sikh sects believe in living human gurus, some mainstream Sikh families revere spiritual figures and ancestors, and though officially Sikhs don't drink, and some people like my mother don't even allow booze to be stored in their houses, the Sikhs of the Punjab have one of the highest alcohol consumption rates in the world.

At the time I loved Freya for making an effort. It was the thought that counted. But in 2011 these morbid texts had a different effect. I bristled at the idea that there might be some kind of formula to my grief, and they amplified the self-consciousness I had been feeling about our relationship. Freya would suggest a Woody Allen film and I'd think, 'Page 23, tip four: "Make sure you keep doing fun and pleasurable things together, such as catching a flick."' She'd hug me and I'd think, 'Page 52, tip seven: "It is important not to withdraw from giving one another physical affection."' It was odd that none of the books gave the most basic advice: do not at any point let your spouse discover that you are reading these books.

The 'chat' with Freya took place that evening, during the night in I had endlessly postponed in order to go back home. I had picked a science DVD to watch. By this point I could just about cope with TV as long as it remained factual. And the presenter of the documentary in question was standing on the top of a mountain, banging on about how the universe was a 'billion billion billion billion billion billion' times larger than anything we could conceive, making my problems feel a little less significant in the process of doing so, when I told her about my day.

'I don't understand. Are they offering you a sabbatical or are they suspending you?' Freya asked.

'Fine line, I guess.'

'How long for?'

'He said they will keep my job open until the New Year. Which gives me, what?'

As the man on TV pointed out that the Sun would run out of fuel in about five billion years, Freya did the instant mental arithmetic. 'Five months.' Behind her brown eyes, which were partly concealed behind a straight brown fringe, I could almost see a sign flashing with the words: 'We are meant to get married in December. How long will this take?' But she was too sensitive to say such a thing. 'So what's the plan with your mum and the shop?'

I pressed the mute button on the TV remote. 'I need Mum to give up the shop. I've got to sit her down and have a chat. A proper chat. I will do it this weekend. Promise.' I kissed her. 'Look, I know we need to sort out the wedding, send out the invites. You've been incredible. Just give me a week.'

She clasped my hands and I thought, 'Page 87, tip four: "Express affection. Make eye contact and hold hands as your partner articulates their feelings."' 'I'm not worried about the wedding, I'm worried about you.' And then she opened her handbag and produced something which wrecked the mood entirely: a brochure for Saffron House, an old people's home for Asian people in Birmingham.

I was shocked. Of all the complaints my mother had made about the goras over the years – the bland food; the lack of manners; the chaotic nature of their family life; the absurd obsession with front lawns and tea; the insistence on concealing TV sets in cupboards; the divorces; the selfishness; the irreligiosity; the sexual immorality; the custom of baths, sitting in their own dirt; the refusal to wash their bottoms with water after going to the loo; and so on – the one thing that came up most often was their attitude towards their elderly relatives. 'No respect,' she would complain. 'Do you hear how they speak to their parents? I wouldn't speak to my dog like that. But the parents are as bad – what do they expect when they charge their own children rent? When they throw them out as soon as they can?'

'What's wrong?' asked Freya.

'Just stunned, to be honest.'

'What?'

'An *old people's home*?'

'It's not an old people's home. It's "culturally specific care". Sheltered housing.'

I continued regardless. 'My mum is a widow. She had cancer last year.'

'Why don't you actually look at the brochure before you start banging on.'

'Her husband has just died,' I banged on. 'I'm her only son, the only family she has. I can't put her in an old people's home. She's not even old, for God's sake. And we just don't do that.'

It was only a two-letter word. 'We'. But it was the worst thing I could have said to her, harsher than the four-letter word she hurled back in response.

'Oh, do fuck off, Arjan.' She had moved away from me and was sitting bolt upright, her hands on her lap. 'Just listen for a second. I wouldn't put my own parents in a home. But it's an extra-care scheme – flats, where people can get care if they need it.'

No. I couldn't get past the phrase 'old people's home'. The evening was ruined. By the time she apologised for swearing I was already up and storming out in disgust. I aimed for the pub, but on the way there I rang Mum and told her not to switch the new alarm on. I would be getting the last train from London to Wolverhampton.

It was a Saturday morning in the spring of 1969, Surinder was in the lower sixth and had the weekend to complete a 2,000-word essay on *Tess of the d'Urbervilles* and revise for a biology exam. But wherever she sat down in the house, she found herself distracted. At the kitchen table, there was the problem of Kamaljit banging away on the saucepans. In the bedroom, she found the griping of her father next door intolerable and could hear Tanvir downstairs making mindless, cringe-inducing chit-chat with customers with a view to improving his English. And she had just settled down at the dining table in the living room, which also served as the shop's office desk and family ironing board, when she was interrupted by the sound of her mother bellowing from the shopfront, in between serving customers.

'Surinder, are you sure you don't want to come?!' This was how Mrs Bains communicated: shouting from wherever she was, knowing that the shop was small enough and she was loud enough to be heard by anyone in any part of the house. 'Dhanda says he needs as many people to come along as possible! We could call Baljit Kaur over to look after your dad, and close the shop for lunch!'

Surinder glanced up from trying to memorise a five-part diagram for cell structure. Irritation at being disturbed coalesced with annoyance at the ultimate source of the disturbance: that fatso Dhanda, and his inane obsession with turbans on Wolverhampton buses. There had been a time when it looked like the Sikh activists' dispute with Wolverhampton Transport Department might fade away. The issue which had arguably helped trigger Enoch Powell's 'Rivers of Blood' speech the previous April, or at least made the response to it so explosive, had faded as Powell's star rose. It may have inspired the biggest march since World War II in Wolverhampton before Powell spoke, but just a few weeks afterwards a second pro-turban march in London drew just 350 supporters.

However, the topic had recently returned not only to local but to international prominence, in melodramatic fashion, when Sohan Singh Jolly, a physically unassuming resident of Southall with a penchant for snow-white turbans, who had arrived in Britain four years earlier from Kenya, where he had worked as a police inspector and lost an arm while fighting Kikuyu during the Mau Mau revolt, declared the turban ban 'a monstrous crime', denounced Wolverhampton Transport Committee as 'the worst racialists in the world', and pronounced that he would burn himself alive on 13 April, the Sikh New Year, if the ban was not overturned.

The response, you could say, was mixed. The mayor of Wolverhampton accused the 65-year-old of blackmail, and someone high up in the new Supreme Council of Sikhs in the UK worried out loud that Jolly's actions would lead to 'the worsening of community harmony', and dismissed Jolly's campaign as excessive and hysterical. Meanwhile, Mr Billy Wilson, a 31-year-old Wolverhampton hairdresser and father of three, threatened to burn himself alive if Wolverhampton Transport Committee gave way. 'I am very serious about this,' he informed a reporter. 'Somebody has to stand up against these people.'

At the same time Jarman Singh Parmar, the editor of the *Indian Observer*, an obscure London-based Punjabi newspaper, was so inspired that he vowed to burn himself alive fifteen days after Mr Jolly died, unless the ban was lifted, and suggested other men would follow the example at fifteen-day intervals until the 'racialist policy' was reversed. And it goes without saying that Dhanda also embraced the cause as if it were the last samosa in the kitchen, insinuating in vague terms that he would join in the chain of suicides, and also organising a pro-Jolly rally at the town hall which Surinder's mother had declared the family would, at Mr Dhanda's request, join.

The whole thing was ridiculous. Though when it came to religion and politics, Surinder had long learnt that it was best to keep your mouth shut.

'No!' she shouted from her desk. 'I told you! I've got to study for my biology exam!'

'Kee?'

'I'VE GOT MY BIOLOGY EXAM NEXT WEEK!'

'Leh,' Mrs Bains continued, now addressing Kamaljit and Tanvir, who were restocking shelves in the front of the shop. 'Did you hear that? Maharani Surinder is too busy to come along with us.'

Surinder imagined Kamaljit and Tanvir giggling along at the remark, and felt a fresh twinge of irritation. Her sister, embittered about the extension of Surinder's education, or at least about still having to shoulder the lion's share of housework, had recruited Tanvir in her campaign to paint her as spoilt and aloof. And while she could forgive Kamaljit and her mother for responding to Dhanda's invitation, given their functional illiteracy and essentially unexamined approach to life, she couldn't be so understanding of Tanvir. He had, after all, started wearing a turban only after she had botched his haircut. He continued to wear a turban, she suspected, only because he was balding. And he was now reading two newspapers a day, taking notes and learning new words as he did so.

But what was the point of Tanvir reading, of understanding English, if he was not going to digest the meaning of anything?

He, of all people, must have been aware how the turban dispute was poisoning race relations in their town, how associating themselves with such a campaign at a time when Indians were being beaten up by thugs shouting 'We want Enoch!' was suicidal. People like Jolly and Dhanda were painting Sikhs just as their enemies wanted to portray them – namely, as medieval peasants. They were illustrating Powell's specific complaint in *that* speech that the Sikhs, in 'claiming special communal privileges', were producing a 'dangerous fragmentation within society'. At a time when the enemies of immigration were talking about repatriation, supporting Jolly was insanity, the political equivalent of buying the community a one-way ticket back to India. Even Dhanda's once-beloved Indian Workers' Association thought Jolly's threat was too much to support.

It took more self-control than Surinder was capable of to conceal her annoyance when, a few minutes later, Tanvir crept into the living room and, making the march sound like an outing to the park or to the cinema, asked if she would mind manning the shop if he joined her mother and her sister on the rally. 'So this stupid protest is important enough to close the shop, but my work is not?' Tanvir looked abashed. 'I haven't even got *started* on my revision.'

Her mother, proving as capable at hearing as broadcasting, interrupted from two rooms away.

'Surinder!' she snapped. 'Your paji will be coming with us!' The 'ji' was her way of letting her daughter know that she had registered her disrespectful tone to Tanvir. 'If you can't be bothered to join us because of your *test*, then at the very least look after the shop! Just move your books to the counter! Make sure you pop in to look at your father! Make sure you do the dishes! They have been sitting there since this morning! And the kitchen floor needs mopping! Do you hear me?'

'Hahnji,' responded Surinder in return, biting her tongue, bristling at the mocking tone at which her mother had referred to her 'test'. She had been allowed to stay on at school but she felt no concessions had been made when it came to chores or housework. 'I'll get it done.' She slumped at the table in defeat.

As the protestors departed, a heavy silence descended upon the shop, a silence which, for Surinder, merely served as a reminder of the racket she normally had to study through. She moved her books and notes to the front of the shop and, settling on the chair behind the counter, spent some time flicking alternately through her Thomas Hardy novel and studying a diagram of the human liver. But eventually, unable to focus, she did what no teenager can resist doing when left home alone: she had a nose around.

She went up to her bedroom and lay on her elder sister's bed, concluding with some self-satisfaction that, yes, her side of the room was warmer. She peered into Tanvir's bedroom: the mountains of excess stock had been pushed to the far end of the room, blocking out the daylight, but the near side was pleasant, with a mattress on the floor, a bedside cabinet improvised from used newspapers, and a neat pile of letters and books. And she was in the kitchen trying but failing to find something resembling pop music on the radio that was normally out of bounds, when she heard the shop bell tinkle.

She ran to the counter to find a man standing in the middle of the shop, smiling broadly and bearing a large briefcase. A sales rep. One of the balding, itinerant, middle-aged white men in shiny suits, hyping goods under the pretence of retail 'advice' who were a blight upon shop life. But this rep was not typical. He was young – about twenty-one. He was dressed in a long polo coat, tied at the waist with a sash. His extravagant blond hairdo must have required the use of a dryer and hairspray that morning, and when he spoke, he did not do so in a Black Country drawl, but in a sing-song Irish lilt.

'All right, love. James O'Connor.' He held out his hand. 'Call me Jim. What's yer name?'

Actually, what he said, as a result of a slight stutter, was, 'All right love. James O'Connor. Call me Jim. What's yer n-name?'

Surinder, unused to unsupervised contact with male strangers, resisted eye contact and whispered a reply.

'Sue-rinder, did you say?' he asked, his fringe flopping above his blue eyes. 'That's a nice name.'

Was it? She had never thought about it, beyond being grateful that she had not been named 'Kamaljit'. She blushed and felt self-conscious about her lack of make-up, her unbrushed hair, her Indian clothes.

'I've got an appointment to see Mr Bains at 1.20.'

He meant Tanvir Banga. But the mistake was so common that even Mrs Bains didn't bother correcting it any more.

'I'm sorry,' replied Surinder, her chuni slipping down the back of her head and down her neck. 'They've all gone out for a while. Should be back soon.' She glanced at the electric clock above the front door, its second hand rotating smoothly around its face, the one thing in the house that moved without making a racket. 'In about an hour.'

'They involved in the havoc up the road? Quite a crowd, TV cameras and everything. It's like the Queen is visiting or something.'

The analogy was a good one. The last time there had been such mayhem in Blakenfields it had been sparked by a passing visit from the Duke of Edinburgh. But while her mother's enthusiasm to join the crowds was joked away that time, with her husband teasing Mrs Bains that she clearly identified with the Queen, and Surinder amusing the household by pointing out the other parallels between royal and Punjabi life (the predisposition to living as an extended family in a house together, the cohabitation with parents after marriage, the preference for arranged marriages, etc.), this was insane.

Surinder rolled her eyes and explained, suddenly finding an

outlet for her frustration. She intended to make just one point: that the whole thing was pointless given that the Transport Committee was only running the buses on a caretaker basis until the new West Midlands Passenger Authority formally took over. But after she had mentioned this, she thought she might as well emphasise the hypocrisy of the fact that Dhanda, the man in charge of the protest, did not even wear a turban. Then she pointed out that Mr Dhanda and Mr Jolly were more interested in how the dispute played in the Punjab than in Britain, regardless of the consequences for Sikhs living in Britain; that 90 per cent of the male Sikh community were clean-shaven and had given up the turban, and Sikh women didn't wear turbans at all, so it could hardly be said, as was being claimed, to be a community or a human rights issue; and that the turban was actually, in her view, the least relevant tenets of the Sikh faith.

'Basically, they're reducing a whole religion to a dress code,' she concluded.

O'Connor looked taken aback, and when he laughed, Surinder realised she might have overdone it. 'I'm guessin' you're not on their side then?' He put a hand on the counter. 'I don't see why they shouldn't just let people wear what they want. Where I come from, everyone looks the same. Never know who is going to be behind the door here.' He looked at her in a way she had not been looked at before. 'Sometimes you get some pleasant surprises.'

Surinder was not sure what she was more taken aback by — the idea of a white person supporting the turban campaign, that he had ignored her arguments entirely, or the compliment. As she reeled, he launched into a frankly circuitous account of how he had ended up in the town. The story went that he had been hired by his employer some six months earlier, as a sales rep, beating some 500 applicants for one of five jobs; he wanted to work in London, where he lived and where there was real money to be made, but before being given a patch he had to spend several months working across the company, including standing in as a relief rep in various parts of the country; he had spent the previous week in Birmingham and returned home at the weekend only to be told he had to get on the train again to spend this week in Wolverhampton.

'Sorry, going on, ain't I? It's being on the road all by yourself so long.'

Surinder nodded sympathetically, feeling better about her own turban digression, but in the process triggered another lengthy speech, this time about Black Country nightspots, in particular the Catacombs nightclub, which he had visited the night before, and where the music and dancing was taken so seriously that for the most part men and women ignored each other.

'You been?'

'Not my kind of place,' Surinder replied, failing to add that nothing was her kind of place unless it was the shop, the temple or, at a push, school.

O'Connor finally recalled the point of his visit.

'Don't suppose Mr Bains left a cheque? He's due a payment. Or left any empty tins for collection?'

Surinder glanced at the sheaf of papers lying next to the till, at least fifty sheets thick, containing an assortment of letters and bills, organised according to a system comprehended only by Tanvir. There was no chance of finding anything in it, but she offered to search around for the used sweet tins. On returning with three, having taken the opportunity to fix her hair in front of a mirror while doing so, she found that O'Connor had let himself behind the counter and was rearranging the sweets and chocolates in the glass cabinet. This was something all the reps tried to do – they called it 'merchandising', rearranging displays to give their products prominence and thereby boosting potential commission. But most weren't so brazen.

'Ahem,' she coughed.

'Just tidying up,' he laughed.

'You'd better put everything back exactly as you found it.' She imitated her mother's tone of voice. 'I will never hear the end of it.'

O'Connor did as he was told, thanking Surinder sheepishly for the tins, remarking on the layout of the shop as he did so, saying they really should consider altering it, selling newspapers through a window hatch was very old-fashioned, there was no logic to the confectionary displays at all; and then, back on the other side of the counter, he lifted up his briefcase, plonked it on to the counter, unclicked the locks and turned it around so that Surinder could examine the contents.

It was a surprise to find it contained not a single file or document or piece of foolscap. Instead, rows and stacks of neatly arranged chocolate. On one side, bars and brands she recognised. On the other, samples wrapped in anonymous coloured foil. The whole thing was lined with silk and reminded her of the chocolate boxes she had played with as a child. She was rarely allowed at the contents, but if you ran your fingers across the insides, and drew in the aromas, you could almost replicate the experience of eating chocolate. O'Connor pulled out two small bars wrapped in red foil and waved them at Surinder.

'Want to try our new brand? This stuff is still in d-development. You'll be among the first in the world to taste it.'

Surinder arched an eyebrow, sceptically, and glanced at the shop door. She fancied the chocolate, but felt uneasy at the same time. It didn't take much to become talked about on Victoria Road. Smiling when giving a member of the opposite sex directions, or not covering your head as you served a male customer, was enough to be viewed as evidence of an affair. Nowadays her mother didn't even stand for her talking to the paper boys. Besides, these reps, spending week nights in local hotels, partaking of too many cafe lunches, were famed for their ability to get shop owners to order stock they didn't need. Tanvir was forever complaining that if you ordered fifteen of something they would encourage you to take twenty; if twenty-five, they would suggest thirty. It was the reason Bains Stores was still flogging Christmas boxes of chocolate even though it was Easter.

'Like I said, I'm not in charge here. You'll have to come back.'

'I'd worked that out, love. Just need to practise my sales patter, don't I? How will I ever get better if I don't practise?'

She glanced at the clock. 'All right, but be quick.' She wanted to add, 'before someone comes in'. But instead, gesturing at her textbooks, she said, 'I've got to get back to my work.'

Jim handed over one of the chocolate bars. 'Now, let me get this right.' It was unclear whether he was addressing her or talking to himself. 'The thing is, I am not meant to give the customer the chocolate immediately. It is important to create a sense of theatre. So if you were a customer . . .'

'. . . which I'm not . . .'

'. . . which we have established you are not, I would say, "I want you to try my chocolate", and then I would unpeel the chocolate like this.' He unwrapped the foil in one smooth movement, not leaving any of the paper stuck on the bar. It was a neat trick. Unlike the chocolate in the jars that lined the walls of the shop, it was smooth and unblemished. No sign of dustiness or ashy-whiteness. 'And then I would cut off a piece with this.' He produced a small knife from another compartment of the briefcase. 'And then I would present the whole thing to you on one of these tiles with a flourish.' He put on a theatrical voice. 'Would you like to try my new chocolate, young lady?'

'Yes please, Mr O'Connor,' repeated Surinder, playing along at shop.

'BUT,' he said. 'You are not meant to eat it straight away. You see, taste isn't actually the only sense that matters when it comes to flavour. Do you know which other sense is important?'

'Smell,' responded Surinder immediately, reciting a passage from the book she had been memorising the day before. '*As you chew, you're forcing air through your nasal passages, carrying the smell of masticated food along with it. Without the interplay of taste and smell, humans wouldn't be able to grasp complex flavours.*'

'Proper swot, ain't we?'

He looked impressed, broke off the corner of his piece of chocolate, rubbed it between his thumb and index finger until it softened and held his finger under her nose. Surinder closed her eyes and drew in the rich aromas of vanilla and cinnamon. Behind them, the scent of O'Connor's citrusy cologne. Taking another piece of chocolate, and putting it into her mouth, she pushed the melting chocolate around with her tongue.

'Mmmm,' she hummed in appreciation. 'Are those raisins?'

'Yes. And can you work out what the raisins taste of?'

She took another bite, rolled the chocolate around until it coated her tongue, and after a while guessed, 'Coke?'

'Not quite. It's something people sometimes have with Coke though. No? You should also be able to taste rum. You're sampling our next brand, Old Kingston, a special blend of milk and plain chocolate with rum-flavoured raisins.' He put on a Jamaican accent and sang an excerpt of a song which was going to be part of a forthcoming advertising campaign, but as he did so Surinder spat the chocolate she had been enjoying out into her hand.

'Was my singing that b-bad?' he laughed, offering a handkerchief.

'I'm not allowed to drink,' explained Surinder, between coughs.

'Hahaha. Don't worry, you won't get drunk.'

Surinder hacked into the handkerchief. 'It's against my religion to drink.'

'Oh.' He handed her an information sheet which showed the

ingredients. 'Actually, it doesn't really contain rum. Just flavourings. Look.' He handed her the wrapping and as Surinder examined the list of ingredients he launched into yet another rambling story, this time about a club in Blackpool which apparently hosted fantastic Northern Soul nights, despite having a policy of serving no alcohol whatsoever. 'I take it I have failed in my sales pitch then?'

Surinder wiped the corners of her mouth, feeling intense embarrassment. 'Yeah. You get two out of ten.'

'TWO!'

He looked crestfallen. Or he pretended to.

Not looking her in the eye, he added, 'That's a shame because I'd give you nine. *At least.*'

The remark hung between them, and then the shop bell tinkled.

Surinder's tone and posture changed in an instant. 'Tanvir will want to see written proof of the order before he agrees to payment,' she pronounced formally, making eye contact with the customer who had just entered.

O'Connor seemed unsettled for a moment, but got the message. 'Of course,' he said as Surinder busied herself with fetching some Cheddar for Mrs Gill. 'If you could let Mr Bains know to send money by post it would be appreciated.'

As Jim shut the door behind him, a draught shot through the house and made it slam loudly against the frame. Surinder fretted briefly that the noise might have woken her father. But there was no need to worry. He couldn't have been more oblivious. Having heard his daughter laughing and joking with a male stranger, he had tried to get up out of bed to make his presence felt, and in the process of doing so had tripped and smashed his head against the floor.

Mr Bains wasn't to the forefront of anyone's mind when Tanvir, Kamaljit and Mrs Bains returned from the rally. There were more pertinent matters to discuss and dissect, such as the fact that the local paper had sent a photographer and a reporter, and that a television documentary camera crew had appeared to film the entire thing. The journalists were mainly interested in Mr Jolly, but the photographer had taken pictures of the Bains Stores contingent, and Tanvir had, in his beard and turban, been approached to give his views, to Dhanda's visible irritation.

'And what did they ask you, Tanvir?' asked Surinder, still high from her encounter with O'Connor. 'I do hope you told them about your lifelong devotion to the religious symbol of the turban.'

Tanvir noted the change in Surinder's mood – she was being as playful as she had been prickly before – but missed the sarcasm. 'They wanted to know what the Transport Department should do if other groups made similar demands to the Sikhs. You know . . .' Tanvir made an attempt at his interviewer's BBC English. 'What should the Transport Department do if a Turkish member of staff decided he suddenly wanted to wear a fez to work?'

'Was he Welsh?' teased Surinder, mocking Tanvir's impression. 'What?'

'Just joking. And what did you say?'

'I said, "well, what is a fez?"' Laughter. 'And then I said, "The turban is more than hat. For Sikhs, it is who they is. In the last Two World War, thousands of turban-Sikhs fight, with no other protection but turban. It is impotent to them. Very impotent."' Surinder suppressed a giggle. Kamaljit, only half following the account, beamed with something resembling pride. Tanvir continued. 'They said I was very good. Very artic-ka-lute.'

Tanvir smiled, although he had made a mental note to look up 'artic-ka-lute' in his dictionary later and he was still grinning as he took his position behind the counter. And it was after he had re-enacted his TV interview for half a dozen customers, and after Mrs Bains had wondered out loud for the third time if the picture would make that evening's newspaper, that she went to check on

Mr Bains. And it was only after her scream had ricocheted around the shop, after Surinder had called an ambulance, and after Kamaljit had accompanied her parents to the hospital, that Surinder was asked if she had checked on her father.

'Did you go up to look?' enquired Tanvir as they sat in silence in the kitchen together. The evening paper had arrived, but no one had bothered to check it for Tanvir's appearance. The saucepan of tea Surinder had brewed, more out of a need to do something with her hands than for reasons of thirst, remained undrunk.

'Yes,' lied Surinder, aware that for the previous two years Mr Bains had not been left alone for more than twenty minutes, and yet, distracted by O'Connor, and then daydreaming about it afterwards, she had not checked on him for nearly an hour. 'Of course I did. I looked in on him three or four times. He was fast asleep. Do you think he'll be OK?'

Tanvir evaluated the little evidence that was available. Namely, the diligence with which the ambulance attendant had wiped his feet on the mat as he entered, and the leisureliness with which Mr Bains was taken into the ambulance, encased in ambulance-service blankets. There were no sirens as the ambulance left. It all suggested the medics were not in a rush, which implied, in turn, that Mr Bains couldn't have been too unwell. 'I think they would have been in more of a hurry if he was in trouble.'

'Yes. They would have used the siren, right?' Surinder felt reassured. And guilty about having teased Tanvir earlier. And sick at the idea that her father might contradict her when he returned.

'He'll be fine.'

'Yes, he'll be *fine*.'

A long pause. The house had never been so quiet.

He wasn't fine.

There was no shortage of surreal things about the English riots of 2011. The sudden but complete collapse of law and order. Scenes in London not witnessed since the Blitz. The strange way events seemed to confirm everyone's view of the world, whether it was that the police forces of Great Britain had become emasculated as a result of political correctness, or that the underclass, for too long ignored and sidelined, had decided to take revenge on mainstream society.

But the thing I remember most clearly was the geographical dislocation of it all. I was in Wolverhampton when rioting broke out in London that weekend, helping Mum with the shop, completely failing to get around to the 'chat' I had promised to have about her future, and I remember watching images of a bus on fire on a London street. Our flat was miles away from the scene, and Freya and I still hadn't made up, but my instinctive reaction was to call her to check she was OK.

I proffered a kind of apology for my tantrum as I did so, promised I would be back soon, but having once again failed to have that 'chat', I extended my stay in Wolverhampton by a couple more days, telling myself I could not return to London until I had resolved my mother's situation. Then as the trouble in the capital subsided, copycat rioting broke out in Leicester, West Bromwich and Wolverhampton, and, as a precautionary measure, the police advised retailers on Victoria Road to close up.

We Sikhs are meant to be good in these kinds of situations. We are by tradition warriors and soldiers, renowned for our daredevil courage. But the closest thing I had come to a fight was on a PlayStation. So I was forced to seek outside help, from the closest thing I knew to a Sikh warrior: Ranjit. He couldn't have been more pleased to hear from me, having been continually suggesting that we hang out since my father's death, texting me invitations that went along the lines of:

'Kidaa. a ha ha you Salaa, nex time you in da endz, come round benchod.'

And: 'How its going any ways chitterface – when you coming for a glassie at Singhfellows? Innit.'

Besides, I was asking for emergency self-defence advice, which was his specialist subject. His whole life, or at least a lifetime of repeatedly watching *Under Siege*, seemed to have been building up to these riots. By the time I arrived, the police having advised all the shops in the area to shut early, he had arranged for a vigilante group of fifteen to patrol Victoria Road to guard the two temples and surrounding businesses.

At Buy Express, he greeted me with a mournful solemnity that was more than a little reminiscent of Mr Miyagi, the karate master in *The Karate Kid*, and guided me in near silence through his family's superstore, past the massive stacks of nappies and lentils and chapatti flour, the new greengrocery concession that had been built in a stand-alone extension, the butchery, the post office, the Asian cooked food stand, the chair where his father liked to sit and bark semi-coherent instructions at his long-suffering staff.

I'd not been in the shop for years and was impressed. My father always put the Dhandas' success down to good fortune, and they had certainly lucked out in having a shop near the temple, where people would proffer gifts of groceries, and in owning a freehold property which could be expanded in every direction. But I realised now they had also proved better retailers than us: expanding heavily into Asian groceries; opening almost twenty-four hours a day; selling alcohol; setting up greengrocer's and butcher's sections; and, recently, developing a line in ethnic goods for the Eastern Europeans moving into the area. The post office concession was particularly inspired: half of Blakenfields cashed their giros there, only to immediately spend the money on National Lottery tickets and booze.

There was a delay in the kitchen as Ranjit's mother and wife would not let us leave until we had partaken of a handful of pakoras, but we eventually made it into the garden, which had been paved over since I last visited, and, finally, into an outbuilding. I used to come here as a teenager with Ranjit, before he gave up cycling and pretty much everything else for marijuana. It was a garage then, containing his bikes and occasionally an actual car, in which we would sit and reconstruct entire episodes of *Knight Rider*. But like most things in Ranjit's life, it had since been pimped up. A pool table had been installed at one end. The walls had been plastered and painted black, with a sixty-inch flat-screen TV hung on one side. This was plugged into an Xbox and faced a black leather sofa. As we walked through it, I also spotted a Kelly Brook calendar opened on the wrong month of the year, a silver fridge, a stash of martial arts DVDs and magazines, and, as is always the case with Ranjit, several ashtrays littered with the stubs of spliffs. He may have been thirty-six, the father of two, but this was a fourteen-year-old boy's idea of heaven. Except, that is, for the washing machine in a corner, which, it turned out, was there at his mother's instigation – 'Gotta respect your elders, innit' – and a shiny black cupboard in another.

It was this black cupboard that I was guided towards, and as we approached it I had no idea what it might contain. Some of the thousands of tight black T-shirts that Ranjit favoured for how they flattered his biceps and highlighted his tattoos? Cans of the endless protein shakes he consumed? In the end, it turned out to be something more sinister. It was an armoury. Home to a terrifying array of weapons.

'Jesus Christ, Ranjit,' I gasped, at the sight of some knuckle-dusters and a spear. 'Is this legal?'

'Innit,' he smiled, stroking the blade of one of the swords. 'It's Jay now, seen. But bare mans call me Jizz.'

I stifled laughter. He continued. 'When it comes to family, man, ain't no laws, ya get me? That bredrin Guru Gobind Singh, he was the geeza who's saying we carry kirpans. You don't want to defend your yard? I'd rather die that watch mans abduct my gyals, innit.'

The speech sounded as practised as the MC Hammer dance moves and special *Street Fighter II* combo moves that I still remembered Ranjit for, and did not contain factual inaccuracies, as such. But he wasn't a baptised Sikh. He shaved his head and smoked. Moreover, while some people had died during the riots in London, nobody had been 'abducted'; people were attacking shops for flat-screen TVs, not women or 'gyals', and the police instruction to shut up shop on Victoria Road was, like my hunt for self-defence assistance, purely precautionary.

'Dude.' There was no way I was going to call him Jay. 'I don't see any kirpans here. And isn't most of this stuff Japanese?'

A pause. 'Chinese, Japanese, whatever, still Asian, innit.' He pulled out a samurai sword – a curved, slender, single-edged blade with a long grip to accommodate two hands. 'Anyways. Here's a ting for you. This bredrin's called a katana, innit.' He presented it to me with a bow. 'You may have heard of the five ks. This is number six, innit. Careful though. That shit'll cut your hand off.'

It was heavier than it looked. I passed it back. 'Actually, I think I'm looking for something more . . . discreet.'

'More what?'

'Discreet. Something smaller.'

Ranjit sucked his teeth.

'Look at this bre'er parring me with big words.'

He scanned the armoury.

'How 'bout this then?' He picked out something that looked like a deformed crutch, stroking the short perpendicular handle while doing so. 'The tonfa. You know, from *G.I. Joe: The Rise of Cobra*. Or maybes . . .' He pulled open a drawer which was originally designed to house underwear. '. . . some nunchucks? Awesome in a sword attack. As featured in Bruce Lee's *Fist of Fury. Way of the Dragon. Enter the Dragon*.'

'*Teenage Mutant Ninja Turtles*,' I interrupted.

Something flashed in Ranjit's eyes. Clearly, this weaponry, like respecting one's elders, and the musical output of Malkit Singh, was a subject that he considered beyond mockery. 'Sorry.' I noticed something on the floor, leaning against the cupboard – something stubby and mean-looking. 'How about that? What's that called?'

'*That?*'

'Yeah.'

'Serious?'

I nodded.

'My mum's mop handle.' He smiled broadly, as if acknowledging a secret, revealing whitened teeth while doing so, patted me manfully on my shoulder and attempted a fist bump, which I responded to with a kind of handshake. Anyone walking in would have thought we were playing Rock, Paper, Scissors. As Ranjit recoiled, I noticed that he had started plucking his eyebrows since I'd last had a proper look. Everything about him, from his sideburns to his pecs, was sculpted to precision, the once-weedy kid with a monobrow gone. 'Old school. You wanna go dark on a bredda.' He tapped his nonce. 'A *dhanda* from Dhanda.' His surname translated as 'stick', and as it was also a euphemism for 'penis' I braced myself for what was coming next. 'Ain't the size what counts, innit.' He shut the wardrobe doors and lapsed, briefly, into coherent English. 'But you'd better ask my mum first. She goes mental if anyone messes with her shit.'

I walked down Victoria Road, back to Bains Stores, the mop handle wrapped in a black plastic bag, with mixed feelings. On the one hand, Ranjit was a moron, and I felt I'd lowered myself by indulging him his puerile martial-arts fantasies; but on the other, I was grateful for his assistance, if not with weaponry, then at least when it came to organising a patrol that evening. The civil disobedience that was afflicting parts of the country was scary, but maybe a spot of rioting was exactly what I needed to make my mother appreciate the insanity of her plan to continue running the shop.

This discombobulation continued into the evening. Before taking my seat outside the shop, brandishing a mop handle, thinking about how exactly I would tackle my mother on the question of her future, I had finally done some research into Saffron House, the 'old people's home' that Freya had mentioned and, to my mortification, discovered she was actually right. It turned out it really wasn't an old people's home, after all. It was a block of modern flats, in a suburb of Birmingham, where nursing support was available if necessary, and where a central social area linked the individual homes, should the residents feel like hanging out.

Looking at the website I'd been surprised by quite how much there was to like about it: the way the managers encouraged 'culturally specific' leisure activities such as watching Zee TV; the way they ran IT classes introducing residents to Google and Skype and online shopping. The whole thing was also run by a portly, friendly-looking turbanned bloke. Maybe it wasn't such a crazy idea after all. I emailed an apology to Freya, promised again I would be returning home soon, that things were coming to a head in the shop, and then, as I sat clutching a stubby mop handle on a kitchen chair on the pavement outside, Mum watching B4U inside, refusing to pay heed to the fuss, saying that she had been through it all before with the Handsworth riots of 1980, when she and father had boarded up the shop for, as it turned out, no reason at all, I began to feel relaxed for the first time in weeks.

This was, of course, due in part to the fact that my mother was right: the little trouble that had been reported was in the centre of town and there was a distinct carnival atmosphere among 'the looters' drifting down towards the city centre, who, far from being a braying mob, seemed to be a friendly bunch, mostly just heading into town to see what was happening. I was also cheered by the fact that with all the shop owners on the road standing outside their shops – the 55-year-old West Indian grandmother-of-five next door brandishing a hammer outside her hairdressing salon, shouting 'Get away from my shop' at anyone who passed; and the owner of Polish Polish, babbling away (in what turned out to be Romanian) – Victoria Road suddenly felt like a community. But, more fundamentally, this was exactly what I'd wanted to do since my mother had reopened the shop. I realised that if I could stand outside Bains Stores with a mop handle in my hands, with an army of vigilante Sikh warriors passing every ten minutes, I felt safe. If things were always like this, I could even see a future for our family business.

Though I guess you should be careful what you wish for. A couple of hours into it all, with most of the other shop owners gone to bed – a little bit of me holding out for some kind of disturbance, so that I had a scare story for my mother, while at the same time prepared to strike out at anyone who did cause any kind of disturbance – a white Vauxhall Astra came roaring past the shop, performed a U-turn at the traffic lights a hundred yards away and returned, coming to a sudden halt outside the shop. It didn't have the friendliest air: the number plate had been removed from the back of the car; there were boxes of what looked like loot on the back seats. But I only really started to worry when a window was wound down and one of the two kids in the front, his face obscured by a baseball cap and scarf, shouted, 'Got a light?'

In my extensive experience of being mugged and assaulted as a youth in the West Midlands, almost all violent exchanges begin with this question, or the close variant, 'Have you got the time?' What it actually means is: 'Please get close enough to me so that I can hold a knife to your throat, or put an arm under your chin and rifle through your pockets for valuables.' It's why I don't wear a watch or carry a light. 'No,' I said. Looking down the street there was no sign of witnesses or help. 'Try the garage on Dudley Road.'

He wasn't, it turned out, keen on taking this advice. Instead, he opened the car door of the car and came towards me. In doing so, the scarf dropped enough for me to recognise him as Nick Wilson, one of Amy's boys. Her children shared few identifying features, but you could usually identify them from the wonky Wolves logos, the misspelt declarations of love that their latest stepdad had tattooed incompetently on to their hands and limbs. This boy, who had an unsymmetrical lightning bolt tattooed on his right forearm, had been in the shop at the weekend and taken it badly when I'd asked for ID when he had tried to buy some cigarettes, despite being visibly underage. And sure enough, this was what he was after tonight.

'You got any fags then?'

I stood up and stepped back as he got closer, leaving the mop handle on the floor but picking up the chair.

'You'll have to come back when we're open, mate.'

'I don't have Pakis as mates,' he replied, grabbing the legs of the chair I was now holding up towards his chest.

His claim was not actually true. When he was young and sweeter, Nick would sometimes get locked out of his home because his bad dreams annoyed his mother's boyfriend, and one time, when Mum saw him scavenging in bins for food, she'd asked him into the house and fed him dal and roti. My father, meanwhile, generally had no time for kids but, under Mum's influence, would occasionally let him flick through the astronomy magazines the shop stocked. But this all seemed to have been forgotten.

The driver of the car revved the engine and shouted at him: 'Hurry up, man.'

'Just a sec. Gotta teach this Paki a lesson.' He turned back to me. 'Ain't yow heard that Wolvo is a twenty-four-hour city tonight?'

Now, I know I said that I was no warrior. And experience has also taught me that the best thing to do in these kinds of situations is to be passive. If someone grabs your bag, let it go. If some bloke accuses you of looking at his girlfriend, just apologise and say that she looked like someone you used to know. Call the police. This, after all, was a version of the advice I had been giving my mother three or four times a day. But the police weren't going to come tonight. There was no sign of any witnesses. And maybe I have inherited the warrior gene after all. Because before I knew it, I was swinging the chair at him, aiming at his jaw, but somehow connecting with his shin.

Chaos followed. If you read martial-arts magazines, they will tell you that when fighting it is important to 'assume a stance with your feet about one foot apart', and to 'conserve your energy'. I broke all these rules. The chair ended up in the road and I ran around. Instead of punching, I scratched, grappled, shouted for help and at one point inexplicably screamed, 'Fire!' One of the few direct punches I landed was on the top of Nick's forehead, which, it turns out, is not the best place to punch someone. It hurt me more than it hurt him. And I was bent over in pain, clutching my shattered knuckle, bracing myself for a kick or punch, for his friend to join in too, when I heard my assailant yelp. I dared to glance up and saw him writhing on the floor, for some reason clutching his leg, and by the time I had straightened up he was being dragged into the car by his mate. Then, to the right, the sight of a figure running towards us. Ranjit. He was dressed all in black and, despite the dark, was sporting mirror-effect aviator sunglasses. The car pulled away as he reached us, but that didn't stop Ranjit from pulling out a truncheon and smashing the rear windscreen in one smooth move.

'You all right, bruv?' he enquired eventually. 'Impressive display there, Pataka.'

This was Ranjit's old nickname for me — it meant 'firework' and derived from 'Banga', my surname. I saw fresh drops of blood on the pavement, examined my hand and realised Ranjit had cut himself as he smashed the windscreen. 'Think I should be asking you.'

'Oh, that ain't nuffink.' He pulled out a handkerchief. 'What happened wid you?'

Dazed, I gave an account. And then asked: 'Was that you? Who made him fall down like that?'

Ranjit beamed, took off his sunglasses, removed his rucksack, unzipped it and pulled out a glass jar. It turned out to contain what I recognised from my youth as ninja stars.

'Shuriken,' he elaborated, putting on a Japanese accent. 'A traditional Japanese concealed weapon. Innit.' I was impressed. But, as is often the case with Ranjit, this feeling didn't last long. He leant down towards the pavement and retrieved the weapon he had fired, before lifting the jar in the direction of my nose with the words, 'Take a sniff of that.' I didn't need to. I could tell from two feet away that it contained human faeces. 'Back in the day, ninjas buried their shuriken in animal shit and shit like that so they gave enemies a tetanus infection.' A look of nostalgia passed over his face. 'Those was the days, blud.' He picked up a ninja star from the pavement, put it back into the jar, and pulled out some antibacterial handwash. 'Anyway, he won't be feeling too good tonight, the fucking bhenchod gora pakora piece of shit.'

'Yeah,' I said, still clutching my hand. 'Bhenchod gora.'

I didn't really sleep that night, a thousand questions rattling through my mind. Should I report what had happened to the police? Had the CCTV I had installed in the shop caught the encounter? Would I be able to report it without mentioning my violence and Ranjit's illegal weaponry?

The thought of legal repercussions was sobering. If Nick had no visible injuries I could possibly be done for common assault. With bruising it could be actual bodily harm. But even more troubling was my own behaviour. Where had my anger and violence come from? What on earth had possessed me to say 'bhenchod gora', a phrase roughly translating as 'sister-fucking white man'?

I hadn't quite pulled off the racial epithet. My tone was timid compared to Ranjit's. I screwed up the pronunciation. Still, it was a racist remark. The first racist remark I ever recall making. Which had, perhaps even more than the street fight, left me feeling shaken. After all, my whole adult life had been built upon the belief that races could get along. I was engaged to a white woman. My experience of 'racism' in the workplace amounted to little more than being mistaken for the IT person. When I thought of the West Midlands, I thought of pop bands like UB40, the army of turbanned supporters of Wolverhampton Wanderers.

Of course, in recent weeks I had found myself having rather basic conversations with school kids explaining why the BNP was wrong and how as a Sikh I was not expected to marry my cousin or join al-Qaeda. And I'd seen a kid running into the shop just to shout 'Paki' at my mum before running out again, a depressing urban version of Knock Down Ginger. But the former was just a consequence of bad education, a question of class rather than race; the latter was unusual. Yet that evening I'd said the words 'bhenchod gora' out loud, meant them in the moment. What the hell had happened?

The only comfort, I suppose, was that I now had a real scare story for my mother, something she would have to acknowledge. Guarding the shop with a mop handle wasn't a realistic way forward for the business. I would have it out with her the following morning. The battle was over. She would have to give up the shop. I could get on with my life.

However, the next day, after I'd woken late, gone for a run to get my head straight, washed and dressed and had lunch, it became apparent that this might not be the case. It turned out that while I was out that morning, planning my speech, a reporter from the local rag had turned up in the shop. The same reporter who had appeared in the aftermath of my father's death – not old enough seemingly even to have developed facial hair, wielding his notebook, mispronouncing our names, asking a load of questions and extrapolating massively from Mum's monosyllabic answers delivered in broken English.

If you've ever had to deal with the press, you won't be surprised to learn that the resulting report of my father's death was full of mistakes. The ages were off. My cited profession was incorrect. The headline was, at best, reductive and sensationalist, the claim of 'exclusivity' ridiculous. But the report that appeared in the middle of the paper's riots coverage that afternoon, amid the news about how an electrical repair shop had been destroyed, how the entire frontage of a shoe shop had crashed to the pavement in the city centre during the disturbances, was even more annoying.

Tragic Death Shop Defies Rioters

The widow of a tragic shopkeeper who recently died of a heart attack in his Wolverhampton store has vowed that rioters will not stop her trading.

Speaking exclusively to this newspaper, Mr Singh's widow, Kamaljit Banga, 61, revealed that the shop had been inundated with offers of support after last night's disturbances.

'People have been very kind,' she said. 'The owner of the shop down the road helped keep guard last night. The community has really come together.'

Just hours after rioters left cars and buildings burning and streets strewn with shop-window glass, thousands of volunteers from across the Black Country arrived with brooms to reclaim their streets. Around 50 volunteers who formed a group called RiotCleanUp turned up at Queen Square to assist the council.

Tanvir Singh Banga, 70, died at Bains Stores in Blakenfields in July. His death was initially deemed suspicious, but a post-mortem cited 'natural causes' and no arrests or charges have been made.

This morning the prime minister praised members of the Sikh community for volunteering to stand guard at various temples and businesses across the country. 'My husband would have been very proud,' added Mrs Banga. 'It will take more than a few idiots to close us down.'

The week that followed was one of high tension for the town as the deadline approached for Mr Sohan Singh Jolly's threat to burn himself. Thousands of Sikhs marched on the British High Commission in New Delhi in protest at Wolverhampton Transport Committee's ban on Sikh busmen wearing turbans and beards. Mr Arthur Bottomley, the chairman of the Parliamentary Select Committee on Race Relations and Immigration, which was taking evidence in Wolverhampton, told *The Times* that he thought Mr Jolly was serious about suicide, 'and it would not be an isolated case', while a member of the Transport Committee added, 'I have heard nothing yet to make me change my mind. Mr Jolly has his way of life and we have ours, and that is all there is to it.'

Meanwhile, grief tore through Bains Stores, as it succumbed to mourning. Mr Bains had suffered a stroke after falling to his bedroom floor. In hospital he had experienced a second, fatal one. Within an hour of Mrs Bains returning home from the hospital with Kamaljit, the living-room furniture was being moved upstairs to make space for the grief-stricken, and Surinder, shellshocked, was putting together mourning clothes from white cotton bought from Dhanda's drapery store.

The shop continued to open at dawn to sell newspapers, but it closed for general trade at nine, to accommodate the mourners arriving in tens and twenties through the house door, their expressions of grief and sympathy being dictated by their sex. The women, for their part, sat on the floor on one side of the living room, under the window, around Mrs Bains and her daughters, the most traditional and most devastated wailing and beating their breasts, the less traditional dabbing tears with the hems of their Punjabi suits, each new visitor taking a turn to envelop Mrs Bains in a tearful embrace.

Stationed in the opposite corner across the room, the men were led in grief by Mrs Bains' brother-in-law from Southall, a thin man in his fifties whose naturally doleful expression made him perfectly suited to the task. In contrast to the women, the men wept quietly, interspersing tears with religious reflection and rational asides. They dwelled soberly upon the deceased's qualities and achievements, remarking that the only real tragedy of the noble man's life was that he had not lived to see his daughters married off, pointing out that the body was just a shell, and Mr Bains' soul was now blending with the divine, like a river rippling into the sea.

At least, this was the idea. In reality, there being no separate room for the men to sit, both sexes found themselves grieving and reminiscing together, and Dhanda, who more or less moved into Bains Stores during the mourning period, appearing suddenly in a snow-white turban which just happened to resemble the one sported by Mr Jolly, at times gave the women a run for their money. So as Mrs Bains used her white chuni to wipe away a stream of tears and opined 'Why couldn't it have been me first?' for hours on end when it was plain to everyone that, being seventeen years younger, she was never going to be first, Mr Dhanda transformed every belch and fart into a howl of grief, pawing at anyone who would let him, his overbearing hugs and flatulence driving visitors to the furthest recesses of the ground floor.

Though his preferred mode of grieving took the form of hysterical nostalgia. Sitting cross-legged against the wall with a bag of crisps he had taken, without asking, from the shop, stroking a beard which, despite the white turban, he hadn't actually grown,

he would hold forth on how sad it was that his dearest friend Mr
Bains would never again see the golden fields of the Punjab, on
the agony of their common experience of leaving the homeland
and, among other things, on how they had met in Britain.

The way he told the tale, Mr Bains was on his knees when he
turned up one day in the shop, canvassing support for the Indian
Workers' Association, or the local Socialist Party, or whichever
activist organisation he was obsessed with at the time. The old
man, abandoned by fickle white customers, betrayed by his gora
assistant and the police, had lost all the money he had saved in
three years of foundry work, and, on top of potential financial
ruin, was facing a devastating medical diagnosis. The story went
that Mr Dhanda, feeling sorry for Bains, gave the old man some
advice. He reminded him that he was a Jat, a caste renowned for
producing good ploughmen and never feeling downtrodden, and
that he was from a part of India know as the 'Sword Arm of
India'. He also reminded the old man that they had both been
through much worse in 1947. And then, he offered to quit his
job to help him resurrect the shop. The way he told the tale, things
had improved the instant he moved in and they converted the
shop into a newsagent. And obviously it was *all* his idea.

'That man is too much,' complained Mrs Bains' sister to a fellow
mourner. 'Too, too much. You would think that he was the one
who saved paji, and not the other way round. He was nothing but
a pendu factory worker before he got given that job.'

'He makes it sound like he was doing it for charity,' muttered
Tanvir to Kamaljit in the kitchen. 'I heard he asked to be paid
double what your father was paying that thieving gora. *Double*.
But at least when he is wailing like a bullock he is not eating. He
will have wiped out all the shop's stock before the end of the
week.'

One person who didn't mind Mr Dhanda's shop stories so much
was Surinder. For when he was reminiscing about Mr Bains,

dominating the conversation, it at least brought relief from the endless group speculation upon Mr Bains' final moments. Everyone seemed to have a theory on why and how he had ended up on the bedroom floor that afternoon and seemed to want to share it. Mrs Bains was keen on the romantic notion that Mr Bains heard the rallying call from the turban protest down the road, decided he wanted to join the protestors, and fell, symbolically at least, in defence of his faith. Mrs Bains' sister, the girls' massi, meanwhile, considered it nothing less than a miracle: she had always thought there was something saintly about her brother-in-law, had heard stories about the crippled suddenly being able to walk when overcome by the holy spirit, and pronounced him something bordering on a saint.

As for Dhanda, his contribution to the topic normally took the form of firing questions across the room at Surinder like a police inspector. 'Which way was he sleeping when you checked? How many customers had you served?' But, fortunately for Surinder, Dhanda was often asked to restrain himself during these inquisitions; his fellow mourners reminding him that death and life were merely stages in the progress of the soul on its journey to God, so why dwell on the details of one's passing? It was also useful that it was acceptable at such times for Surinder to be overcome by emotion, to cry and pray for her father's soul. Which is not to suggest that her prayers were in any way insincere. For while she did fret about being found out, about Tanvir noticing that the chocolate tins had been collected that afternoon, her bereavement was as deep as her mother's and sister's. Indeed, another reason she didn't mind Dhanda's stories was that the gap between his recollections and others echoed her own dislocation about her father. If it was shocking that someone could be remembered so differently by different people, it was even more so that one person could change her mind so completely about someone upon their passing.

Before her father had died, she had considered his biography the most tedious topic in the world, right up there with Tanvir's interest in the variable price of sprouts. To her, Mr Bains was a stern man without any sense of fun, interested only in money and appearances. She saw his opposition to 'ostentation', to the point of even refusing to put up a sign on the shop, as symptomatic of his meanness and joylessness. If she ever thought about the essential facts of his biography, not that she ever really did, they merely confirmed her view of him as passive. The way she saw it, almost all of his major life decisions had been forced upon him. He left the West Punjab during Partition because his family, who all perished, had decided to send a member of the family to India, just in case. He left Delhi for London because his extended family there had made life so difficult, and, she suspected, because he found being a husband and father tedious.

But spending day and night in the living room listening to all sorts of people reminisce about him – the girls had given up their room to the visitors – she realised that not only had she never known her father, but she had also never given him the benefit of the doubt. She had judged him through the prism of one fact: the fact that he used to hit her mother. But she had never witnessed this herself. Maybe she had exaggerated the importance of it. Perhaps there was a kind of nobility to his lack of ostentation after all. She was certainly moved when Baljit Kaur recalled something her father had said when trade finally started to pick up and Mr Dhanda was encouraging him to expand quickly. 'Some men open a shop and in the first fortnight make profit of £60. They tell themselves that if they had two shops it would be £120 and expand. But I would rather work harder with one and aim for £70.'

Then there were all the stories of how hard he toiled to revive the shop. The way she had seen it, he started a shop because factory shifts were too much like hard work. And she had dismissed the stories about this time as attempts to emotionally blackmail her into obedience. But now she had to tally this view with the moving image of him working through the night on the books, tying his long hair to the wall so that he could not physically nod off. Delivering groceries as far afield as Dudley, carrying the produce on buses and trams when the van broke down, serving people even in the middle of the night when they knocked on the door asking for ham or cheese or emergency loans.

Even more affecting were the stories of her father's escape from the West Punjab during Partition. This was part of her father's life that she had never really heard acknowledged before, a topic, like her mother's first marriage, which was largely taboo. But that week, some of the strangers who visited came with haunting stories and images from this prehistoric era. The Bains family sitting holed up in their family home in a village in a Muslim-majority district, not unlike how they were sitting now, hearing stories of how nearby villages were being wiped out, corpses of young Sikh children being found hanging from trees. A debate among the men about whether they should slaughter their own daughters so that they would at least be protected from defilement at the hands of rapacious males. The agonising decision to send the eldest son to Delhi, so that the family had someone in India, in case they needed to flee later. After this, her father's long journey, his hair cut short, Muslim style, on the back of a truck with some other families from the village, all the family gold stolen from him within twenty miles, the young girls picked out within thirty miles. Surinder would have nightmares for months, disturbed by descriptions of murdered refugees, earlobes and noses cut away to get at jewellery more easily. Her father dipping his hands into the wounds of his dying neighbours, smearing blood over his face so attackers might leave him for dead.

Of course, it was impossible, as Tanvir pointed out, to tell how much of this was fact. Dhanda was egging on those recollecting, taking any opportunity to emphasise his own grisly experience, though rumour had it that his family, who lived only a few miles from the border, had bribed themselves into India in an army truck and had quickly arrived unscathed in Jallandar. But the fact was that her father *had* fled Partition, he *had* been the only member of his family to survive, and he had nevertheless built a successful life for his new family. And how had Surinder repaid him? She had forgotten to look in on him, while flirting with a white boy. Her shame was intense. So intense that she sometimes hoped Jim O'Connor would reappear and she would get the punishment she deserved.

As Surinder tortured herself, the turban dispute ground to a resolution four days before Mr Jolly's deadline. Ernest Fernyhough, the Parliamentary Undersecretary for Employment and Productivity, suggested to the Wolverhampton Transport Committee that it would be unfortunate if Mr Jolly were to carry out his threat; that his martyrdom would be seen throughout the coloured world as the result of British racialism. And eventually, the eight members of the Transport Committee met for two and a half hours and announced they had eventually agreed to change the rule on turbans.

Reaction was, once again, mixed. *The Times* said that 'the decision by the transport committee in the face of government and other pressures' had saved Wolverhampton 'from a macabre experience', but the committee chairman expressed little joy in arriving at the conclusion, remarking that 'the ordinary man in the street feels that this is an encroachment on his way of life'. Meanwhile, an editorial in the *Express & Star* complained that the conclusion was 'hardly a victory for anyone' given the dispute had 'made Wolverhampton a sad byword for racial injustice and intolerance in many parts of the world', and the secretary of a Wolverhampton temple, speaking of how the episode had seen the Sikhs of the town portrayed, remarked sadly that 'a small piece of bread with the respect of one's fellows is better than a whole loaf without it.'

Nevertheless, Jolly and his supporters were jubilant, Mr Dhanda finding it in himself to overcome his grief for a few hours to join hundreds gathered at a local gurdwara to thank Sohan Singh Jolly for his campaign and to present him with a congratulatory ceremonial snow-white turban. A day later, he was back as part of a smaller congregation gathered at the same temple following Mr Bains' cremation, the older women lining up to wash their hands and faces in the sinks at the end of it all, a tradition brought from India, where the ashes of the deceased sometimes rained upon the bereaved. Kamaljit and Surinder copied their elders, finding solace in the ritual.

The visitors began to peel away quietly that afternoon, and Bains Stores started to return to normality. Kamaljit, still in her white suit, started cleaning the house. Tanvir began making a tally of the stock that had to be reordered from the cash and carry. However, one visitor remained: Mr Dhanda. He hung around the house, walking around listlessly, staring mournfully at random items on shelves and on walls, shaking his head, talking distractedly about how sad it was that there was no turban ceremony for Mr Bains, when it was customary for relatives to bring turban lengths to the eldest son of the deceased. Then, in the living room, failing to help Mrs Bains fold away the white sheets that had been spread across the living-room floor, shuffling weight from one leg to the other, he made a suggestion: that he cook a meal for the family.

It was a bizarre offer. In India, there is a tradition for mourners to feed the bereaved family after a funeral, but the Bains, as was customary in England, had instead arranged a meal at the temple, gaggles of mourners gathering around Mrs Bains and her daughters to encourage them to eat, reminding them that self-neglect was not going to bring back their loved one. Also, Dhanda had not once offered to cook before. Even during his time working in the store with Mr Bains he was renowned for preferring the produce of the local chippy to toiling over a stove.

As it happens, Mrs Bains might have normally indulged the offer, however surreal – the rules of hospitality forbidding her from asking him to leave – but after a week of visitors, she ached for peace and found herself being more direct than usual. 'Listen, Patwant, please feel free to cook for yourself, what is ours is yours, as it always was and always will be, but I think we're just going to have the food from yesterday, and actually I think I am going to go to bed soon. I am very tired.'

At this point, Dhanda began behaving even more strangely. Watching him, Mrs Bains was reminded in part of the shoplifters who had recently been caught in the store, one of them making transparently aimless chit-chat with Tanvir in order to distract him from what his friend was doing at the biscuit shelves. She was also reminded of watching the panchayat in her village as a girl – the group of senior residents to whom disputes were taken for resolution. The defendants had a certain posture, their hands resting on their fat stomachs, and a certain way of speaking, mixing flattery with digressions, it being considered inelegant to voice grievance too soon. They would only very gradually come to their point. As did Dhanda. In the end. He offered to buy the shop.

Though he didn't put the offer in such direct terms. He said that Mrs Bains had worked hard. She deserved some peace and relaxation. She should be taking it easy after all the shocks she had endured, turn her mind to God. With his money Mrs Bains could pay for her daughters' respective weddings and still afford to retire respectably in India. 'Besides,' he added in conclusion, 'a shop is not really something a woman can manage on her own.'

This last remark was Dhanda's real mistake. Surrounded by a circle of female mourners, she had been spared his excesses over the preceding week, and aware of her husband's affection for the man, their shared history, she had felt instinctively benign towards him, even enduring his lecture with relative calm. But

101

with that remark, she thought of how she had effectively run the shop alone for years, defying her husband's reciting of old sayings that 'gut picche mat' ('women lack wisdom'), and that 'women are like an old coat or shoes and you can replace them when you want'. She remembered how, before that, she had herself taken on her husband's family to send her girls to school in India, and how, before even that, she had been taught Punjabi, Hindi and arithmetic by her mother in defiance of social norms at the time.

This then led to deeper, even more stirring thoughts on how her religion had put men and women on an equal level, condemning practices such as purdah and, unlike many other religions, allowed widows like her to remarry. And, having folded the white sheet she was handling so tightly that it was almost the size of a napkin, she thought of how Sikh teachings gave women full equality to participate in religious performances, remembered how her own mother had been a pioneer in her way, the first in her village to wear a modern salwar, and recalled how one evening when Surinder was a baby and about to topple out of her cot on to a brick courtyard in Delhi, one of Mr Bains' malevolent aunts had remarked, 'Let her fall, she is only a girl.' She snapped.

'Listen here, Patwant, this shop may not have my husband's name on the front of it, but every single shelf, every nook and cranny, is stained with his toil and sweat. My girls and I will run it in his name, in his honour and I will make a better job of it than you or any man could.'

Her sister had joked earlier that week that Dhanda's white turban made him look like he had a nappy on his head. In that moment Mrs Bains could have tipped the contents of one all over him. The intensity of her response surprised them both.

'Yes, pehnji,' said Dhanda, withdrawing meekly. 'Yes.' Dhanda walked backwards, taking an apple from the fruit bowl on the table as he did so. She snatched it back. 'If you ever need any help, I am at your service, as I was for your precious husband, who was like a father to me. And a brother. A brother and a father.'

After he left, Mrs Bains found herself standing in the centre of the living room, shaking and sobbing into the sheet she was still clutching. She had been crying all week, but these were not the theatrical self-conscious tears you weep when you know you are being watched. They were tears of the snotty and uncontrolled variety, her chuni slipping and exposing the patch of alopecia that had appeared on the back of her head since her husband had died.

She was not, it turns out, the only one weeping in the house at that moment. In the cellar downstairs, the week's events had caught up with Kamaljit, and cleaning the stockroom, she had felt overwhelmed. On seeing her, Tanvir had done the thing he had wanted to for days, if not months, beforehand: he had held her in his arms and stroked her hair. Meanwhile, upstairs, Surinder was weeping into a textbook. On hearing her mother's sobbing, she ran down and gave Mrs Bains what she needed most – a hug. She apologised tearfully as she did so, for not being the dutiful daughter her mother deserved, and, keeping her end of the bargain she had struck during her week of fevered prayers, she promised to be more useful around the shop and, if her mother so desired, to quit her studies and prepare for marriage.

Mrs Bains was deeply touched by the consideration of her dear, beautiful daughter. She replied that there was no need for her to quit school, she could stay on another year, finish her A levels, but she could do with more help in the shop and Surinder should start fasting on Mondays, in order to ensure she got a good husband. For she realised now that when their father, a man who was worth his own weight in gold, had suggested a double marriage, it came out of the feeling that he was not long for this earth; the guilt that she had deprived him of the basic paternal satisfaction of seeing his daughters married was a torture, the most painful aspect of his passing. And yes, their aunt was right, it was dangerous for young women to be fatherless and unmarried at their age, and the call for boys would soon go out, her request being that the men be of Jat extraction, tall, in the retail trade, turbanned, British residents and modern in outlook. At least, modern enough to appreciate that Surinder needed to finish her schooling before marriage, to understand that the recent loss of a father meant unextravagant nuptials, and to appreciate that the girls would have to approve of the match.

It would be agony to lose her daughters, but amid all this misery it was some consolation that Surinder was on her side. Knowing that would take the sting out of losing her two beloved daughters at the same time.

8 – HARPERS WINE & SPIRIT
TRADES REVIEW

There was no shortage of challenges during those initial long months of full-time shopkeeping. The brutally early mornings. Balancing the politics of allowing certain trusted customers credit while denying it to others. But the single most difficult and disconcerting thing? The slow but gradual realisation that Ranjit was right.

Not about everything, of course. Steven Seagal is not a good actor. There is no dignity in consuming drugs in your mid thirties. But take, for instance, his approach to education. Ranjit had always looked down on the life of the mind, preferring to make money than to read books. He left college at seventeen, halfway through a BTEC, for which I had looked down on him in return.

But which one of us had ended up with the better life? The phrase 'graphic designer' may trigger images of attractive men in ponytails being alternative and creative in fashionable offices, but most are badly paid, frustrated artists who spend dehumanising hours working in front of computer screens for projects commissioned by big business. In contrast, Ranjit was his own boss, spent more time in the gym and smoking weed than working, drove a car worth almost as much as my share of the London flat, owned, with his father, some nineteen buy-to-let properties, including a penthouse apartment in Birmingham which he kept for his own use, and had never had to endure a conversation with an HR department.

Then there was Ranjit's antagonistic attitude to the police, or 'the Feds', which, if I had thought about it at all, I had dismissed as cartoonish, another consequence of all the hip hop he listened to, along with his faux Jamaican accent, and his insistence on being called 'Jay' or 'Jizz'. But what were the summer riots if not a direct result of a failure in policing? And while I didn't, in the end, report Nick Wilson, thinking that I wouldn't really be able to explain Ranjit's involvement without getting him into trouble, and because the kid got arrested anyway for his involvement in a raid on a sportswear shop that night, when his friends began taking revenge through random acts of abuse and vandalism, the police failed to do anything about it. Ranjit was right: the Feds were incompetent, lazy, self-interested, ineffectual and most likely racist too.

Another matter on which I reluctantly realised Ranjit had a point: his approach to relationships. If you can call having an arranged marriage at the age of twenty-five to a teenager from India, and having extramarital sex at every opportunity in that Birmingham penthouse flat, an 'approach to relationships'. It was morally repulsive, obviously. And I do not, in general, buy into the myth of the arranged marriage. Families are the last people who should be entrusted with the task of finding you a spouse, given that they are incapable of appreciating that you may have changed since the age of twelve. As for the high 'success' rate of arranged marriages relative to their Western counterparts – it is in large part attributable to the fact that the Indian youths in question are so limited in their encounters with the opposite sex that, when they are married off at random, they have nothing to measure the relationship against and endure behaviour others wouldn't consider reasonable over a single evening, let alone a lifetime.

But then again, where had my pursuit of romance got me? Freya and I were living more than a hundred miles apart, talking and seeing each other when we could on weekends, but we were drifting apart emotionally. The tone of our weekly meetings was all over the place, hovering as they did between a prison visit and a play date between estranged parent and child. Meanwhile, Ranjit had security, the support of his parents, the devotion, seemingly, of his spouse and children (who were oblivious to his extramarital activities), a relationship which didn't require the constant explanation of cultural differences, and also sexual adventure. In his heart of hearts, which man wouldn't enjoy such a set-up? The more I hung out with him, the more I envied him. Not that I exactly *rushed* into hanging out with him. Before I would even consider doing *that* I would have to, over the course of two hard months, become truly desperate.

Looking back, that early period of full-time shopkeeping might not have been so arduous if Bains Stores enjoyed either less or more custom than it did. In the former case, it would have meant I could have invested my energies elsewhere, or at least spent longer on YouTube, while in the latter I might have been too busy to notice it all. But Bains Stores had just enough customers to ensure that you could never really relax or really get lost in the work.

Equally, the boredom that came from returning to a town which all my school friends had abandoned a decade earlier, and a social life curtailed by the shop's punishing 5 a.m. to 8 p.m. opening hours, might not have been so crushing if there had been an end in sight. But the fact was that my return had backfired in terms of getting my mother to reconsider her future plans. If I'd left her to it, the impracticality of running the shop alone might have become apparent, but as I'd returned, she had an excuse to avoid the subject entirely.

Things became too comfortable too quickly: I'd wake up at half four and open the shop and man the till until 9 a.m.; Mum would wake up at 8 a.m. and, having had breakfast and done her prayers, would take over the till for the duration of the morning. I'd go for a jog and when I returned Mum would have run a bath for me and I'd take over the till again at lunchtime; Mum would be back looking after the shop between two and four, then I would take over until closing time.

It wasn't always onerous. I enjoyed talking to the newspaper boys and girls, telling them for instance, why the *p* and *n* words were unacceptable, and how 'electric' should not be pronounced as 'elecytrick'. There was a certain satisfaction in helping aunties and uncles with filling out forms. But the long days were exhausting. I used to resent my father's implication that office work was not real work. He saw sitting at a desk as leisure. Now I realised he had a point. Standing around for more than twelve hours is shattering.

Even worse than the exhaustion: the intense boredom. At one point the desire for intelligent conversation, or at least the need to talk to someone about something other than the weather or the quality of plastic bags, became so profound that I asked my old schoolmate's parents out for a drink. We spent two hours in a pub on the other side of town discussing Matt Metcalfe's stellar career and success, although I hadn't seen him in four months, before moving on to the problems his dad was having with his prostate. Next, I approached the victim support volunteer we had been assigned during the brief time my father's death was deemed suspicious, my suggestion of a drink being met with a lengthy silence, and then a polite refusal over text, in which she addressed me as 'Mr Banga', a classic distancing device. But even this humiliation was not enough for me to reply to one of Ranjit's regular text invitations for a drink. I would have to plumb further depths, and did so in my seventh week back.

On the Monday morning I caught two kids trying to pilfer stock from the drinks chiller. On Tuesday three of our five newspaper boys didn't turn up, two citing illness, one oversleeping, and the van got a puncture while I delivered the papers. By Wednesday two customers had complained about their newspaper deliveries, one coming in to cancel his order in person, saying his paper had arrived late, that the sections hadn't been separated and that it was torn (actually it must have got ripped when he dragged it through his letterbox), and that from now on he was going to pick up his papers himself from the Tesco's in town. On Thursday a sweet-looking girl of about ten buying some crisps on the way to school asked, casually, 'What religion are you?'

'Why?'

'Because I'm EDL and you're a fucking Paki.'

'Right.' I gave her change from a pound coin. 'You realise that racial abuse is against the law and you're being filmed on CCTV?'

'Good for you. You can have something to wank over later.' She turned out to be one of Amy Wilson's grandchildren.

That afternoon a man I'd not seen before asked for three packets of Marlboro Lights and some medication, all items from behind the counter, and I was just wondering why they didn't rename 'Imodium' 'Imodi-bum', given that is what everyone called it anyway, when I turned around and saw that he had made off with the fags I'd placed on the counter. I'm not sure what was more annoying: the fact that I'd fallen for one of the oldest tricks in the book, or that I hadn't spotted he had asked for medication for both diarrhoea and constipation.

Then on Friday morning I woke to graffiti, painted in gloss white paint, no doubt by Wilson or one his mates, all over the shutters, pronouncing, 'TALEBAN PEEDO'.

It came as a shock. Vandalism is an occupational hazard in an inner city. But I could only recall one other instance of racist graffiti, when I was about seven and someone had scrawled a massive 'KKK' on to our house door. I remember asking Dad what the letters meant and him replying that they must be the initials of the miscreant in question. I eyed a classmate at my infants school going by the name of Kuljit Kaur Kalirai with suspicion for months afterwards. But in 2011, it was my turn to protect my mother from the truth.

'Ah ki hai?' she asked as she examined the damage on the pavement.

'Well . . .'

I didn't have the Punjabi for 'paedophile', let alone the vocabulary to explain the laboured connection between us and the gangs reportedly grooming young white girls in the north. It's strange how the first thing you learn in most languages is the smutty words, but with my entire Punjabi vocabulary coming from my parents, I struggled to explain anything that ventured on the sexual.

'It's just a swear word, Mum.'

'Pee?' She muttered the words under her breath. 'As in pe-shab?'

'Kind of.'

'Leh, it's these goras who smell of piss, not us.'

The racism was casual. But this was one of my mother's most common complaints about the goras – she even kept a can of deodorant behind the till to spray liberally when particularly stinky customers visited.

Getting rid of the graffiti turned out to be more difficult than it looked. The gloss paint had dried and got stuck. Bits had gone through the mesh on to the glass underneath. It took an hour of scrubbing, and mockery from passing schoolchildren, to get rid of the 'O'. At which point I realised I should have started with the 'P', because the graffiti now proclaimed, 'TALEBAN PEED'. In the end, getting nowhere, I figured the only thing to do was add the letter 'S' before the 'P', and it was at this point, having made Bains Stores look like it had started flogging a range of Islamic amphetamines, that a passing child threw a half-empty can of Sprite at my head. When I got yet another invite for a drink from Ranjit a few minutes later, feeling a sudden and keen need to offload, to get blind drunk, I agreed to meet him at eight o'clock.

Needless to say, at eight we were nowhere near having a drink. And this is the thing, or at least one of the things, about hanging out with Ranjit: you have to revise your notions and expectations of 'time'. If you have a conventional social life, like I once did, it probably involves making an arrangement, arriving within ten minutes of the prearranged appointment and then departing after a few hours. However, with Ranjit, if you arrange to meet him for a drink and food at, say, eight, you know he will ring you at eight to say, 'Hey, just getting into the shower, bare missions today innit, link me at half eight.' You will then get to his place for a quarter to nine, because you suspect from his spaced-out tone that he will be running later than claimed, at which point he will prob- ably just be getting out of the shower, and you will have to spend an hour or so killing time variously walking around his shop or listening to his father opine upon the good old days, watching Ranjit eat (even if you are supposedly going out to eat), regaling you with the benefits of chicken as he does so ('Man needs bare protein if he wanna get hench'), being told to take up weights ('Girls like guys who are hench'), watching him smoke a spliff ('Just gonna bun dis spliff'), and finally, two, maybe three, hours after originally arranged, any complaints along the way being met with the remarks 'Leeeave it, bruv' and 'Man needs to do these bare missions', you will find yourself being driven in his massive German 4x4 for a pint in Singhfellows.

Which brings me to the other thing you need to revise when socialising with Ranjit: your notion of what constitutes 'fun'. If you have a conventional social life, like I once did, socialising probably involves a combination of eating, drinking and animated debates about Simon Cowell's sexuality in critically acclaimed establishments. But 'bare jokes', as Ranjit would put it, will almost always also involve: (a) driving around in his German 4x4, hollering at girls; (b) driving around in his German 4x4 to find alleyways and playing fields in which to smoke weed; (c) driving around in his German 4x4 and listening to bhangra and hip hop, nodding along in time; and (d) hanging out at Singhfellows.

Each of these pastimes takes some adjusting to. I've never really understood the logistics of trying to seduce the opposite sex in cars, given that when you're driving you are usually moving at speed, whereas the mythical girlies you are supposedly attracting are stationary, usually nothing more than a blur in your window or wing mirror, which surely limits the possibility of seduction. The idea of driving around circuitously to Singhfellows, when it is just a short walk from our respective homes, is also a struggle: I didn't enjoy standing around getting high in alleyways and on school playing fields the first time round, when I was an adolescent. As for bhangra music with its repetitive beats, occasional cries of 'Balle Shera' and 'Chak de Phate', and lyrics fetishising fair-skinned women raised on milk and butter who look like peacocks and walk like deer – it has always left me cold. Then, the challenge of Singhfellows itself.

My God, Singhfellows. Carved out of the remnants of a once-proud working man's club, with a banqueting suite around the back providing catering facilities for weddings, it defines itself by a religion that, officially, rejects drinking. This is odd – only a range of pork pies named after the Prophet would be more strange. But even weirder is how we can as a community continue to have one of the highest rates of alcohol-related disease in Britain when so much of the drinking is done in desi pubs like these. You'd think it would put you off booze for life. The lighting is fluorescent and of the unremitting kind you might see in a hospital operating theatre. The tables resemble the kind you might see in an abattoir or butchery, the menu offers nothing more than chicken and samosas, the wine list extends to two varieties (red or white), and the staff and clientele are indistinguishable – overweight Asian men displaying absolutely no pleasure in what they're doing.

Taking a seat with Ranjit, I was momentarily impressed when

someone brought over a pint of lager and a basket of tandoori chicken without him even placing an order. But I have since realised that this is often what you get, whatever you try to order. He began motoring his way through the food, even though he had demolished half a dozen drumsticks only an hour earlier, and before Ranjit had even asked, I began to offload my troubles. I complained about my customers, who had turned out to be much ruder than I remembered. About the abuse and graffiti and falling fag orders. About my mother's need to endlessly feed me and her tendency to start hoovering the living room just as a TV drama approached a dramatic conclusion. About how newspaper deliveries were more hassle than they were worth.

'If they're not complaining that their papers are late, or that the sections haven't been separated, they are moaning that you didn't pop into their kitchen, make them a cup of tea and read out the headlines over breakfast.'

I assumed, as I talked, that Ranjit was nodding in acknowledgement of my woes, but it turned out he was actually nodding in time to the Bollywood soundtrack playing on a flat-screen TV above us. The screens were, like the Monet prints and the framed football programmes, hung absurdly high up on the walls – almost as if they didn't trust customers not to try to pull them down.

The lack of empathy shouldn't, I suppose, have come as a surprise. This, after all, was a man whose condolences on the day of my father's death amounted to a text saying: 'Il have a fat smoke now in the honour of your pops. RIP innit.' More generally, sympathy just is not a Punjabi trait. I remember reading an account of a visit to a Punjabi village by an English woman called Sarah Lloyd, in which she complained that her hosts didn't even seem to understand the word 'sympathy'. 'I had certainly never heard anyone use it. If I was ill I would be diligently looked after as far as food was concerned, but . . . the stock phrase, whether one was suffering from a slight headache or a burst appendix was,

"Never mind, you'll soon be all right." Spoken in a standard indifferent matter.'

Having said that, Ranjit did manage something resembling sympathy when I got on to the topic of the graffiti. He sucked in his cheeks, narrowed his eyes and, while it is hard to do his speech justice, spat out something along the lines of: 'Swear down, I bet it was one of those fucking bhenchod Wilson boys. These breddas don't know the difference between Muslims and Sikhs. That these fucking Musselmen have been trying to nail Sikh girls for centuries? One brown-faced person is another brown-faced person innit to them, like all Chinese people look the same to us. Racist sala kuttas. Don't bother with the Feds, man. They just par you. We know where they live. We should pay them a fucking visit. Ya get me? Time you stopped being a pussy man. There's a reason we never get anyone messin' in our shop. They know to leaaaave it, yeah?'

This continued for some time, with Ranjit expounding at length what he would do to the culprits – 'I'd chop their fuckin' heads off and then fuck 'em in the neck' – speculation about how Wilson and his mates might have been involved with my dad's death, and what he did the last time he caught a kid graffitiing his store ('I made the dickless brainless khota clean it up. And then the next time his dad came in for bread I switched the packet for one I jizzed into. Innit'). I dismissed Ranjit's speculation about my father without even thinking about it – years of drug abuse had made him paranoid, and he was forever seeing threats and conspiracies where none existed. But I wouldn't have put masturbating into packets of Hovis past him. As a youth, I remember seeing him wipe fresh snot onto vegetable produce just for amusement. It was gross behaviour, but tonight, a spot of anger and solidarity, in whatever form, was just what I needed. It made me laugh, and I was struck again by another thing that Ranjit had turned out to be right about.

For years I had dismissed the man as a bigot. It was one of the main reasons we had drifted apart. I hated the way he hated the goras (prefaced usually with an apology to my fiancée), the Muslims (he called the mosque down the road, the 'mushque', a Punjabi word translating as 'smell', and referred to a local taxi firm as 'Al-Qaeda Cabs'), the Eastern Europeans (though several worked for him, and they formed an increasing proportion of our customers) and the blacks (though he listened and identified with rap and hip hop). But maybe he had a point after all. At least, it is one thing to be colour blind in liberal, middle-class East London, but quite another when you regularly get called 'Sama (Osama Bin Laden) or curry muncher by youths running in and out of your shop.

After the riots, when a historian went on TV to feverishly blame the riots on 'a violent, destructive and nihilistic' black culture and, after citing Enoch Powell's 1968 'Rivers of Blood' speech, complained that the problem was that 'whites have become black', I had gone through the intellectual motions of rage. If you reread that speech, I told Freya, one of Powell's targets was the policy of 'integration', which he described as a dangerous delusion, unacceptable even to immigrants such as the Sikhs, who were campaigning at the time for the right to wear turbans and beards while working on the town's buses. But these Sikhs were the same Sikhs who in 2011 were praised for reacting so visibly and force-fully to protect several British communities from rioters. The same Sikhs behind Sangat Television, a community TV station based in Birmingham, which was praised after one of its presenters helped the police to chase and arrest suspected rioters. Even the Tory MP representing what had been Enoch Powell's constituency, who greeted the prime minister on his tour of riot-battered Wolverhampton, was now a Sikh.

Intellectually, I appreciated that my community and my home town, not least my own life, stood as a testament to the fact that

Enoch Powell was not right. But the longer I spent in the shop, the harder it became to hold on to this thesis. In my heart of hearts, I couldn't forget that the only Asians on the streets of Wolverhampton that night were shop owners, or people trying to protect the shop owners. All the looters I'd seen that night were black and white. And once I had accepted this, started seeing the world in monochrome, embraced casual racism, I felt liberated. Political correctness, thinking about what you say, is the hard thing.

Ranjit drained his pint and, physically deflated after his rant, continued, 'Anyway, how's bhua-ji? With the shop and everyfink.'

A flash of déjà vu. I had, as it happened, sat in exactly the same seat a few weeks earlier and been asked the same question by Freya, albeit in better English.

'So, got anywhere with your mum?' she'd asked, not even pretending to drink her pint, taking up about a quarter of the space Ranjit would occupy. 'Got to say, she's looking better than she has in ages.'

It had been both the first time I had brought Freya to Singhfellows, and the first time I had been there myself, and though I felt uneasy with all the Indian men staring at us, I still felt more relaxed than I had in the country pubs we had visited over the preceding weekends. We would drive miles and miles to find the kind of gastropub we might consider passable in London, and I would feel self-conscious about being the only brown person in the room, and Freya would say I was being oversensitive, that in the countryside people stared at anyone who wasn't from the village ('You've got racial Tourette's – not everything comes down to skin colour, you know'), and she would tiptoe around the subject of my possible return to London in the way that I tiptoed around my mother and the awkward matter that I had stopped contributing towards our joint mortgage. It was strange how in London I never thought of how we looked together. Just took it for granted that we were part of the furniture. But in the

Midlands, it was always on my mind, whether it was in country pubs assuming that people were thinking 'What is she doing with him?', or, in Singhfellows, assuming everyone was thinking the opposite.

Freya played with her ear lobe, something she always did when she was anxious. 'Have you managed to talk to her about her plans?' she asked.

My reply to both Freya and Ranjit was the same: that my plan to persuade my mother to give up the shop, to find some way for her to move on, wasn't working out. In my first few weeks of running the shop I had only come close to discussing the issue twice. The first time, I had tentatively suggested my mother join a local community group, the basic thinking being that a small change of scene might be a small step towards a more fundamental change of scene and lifestyle. She dismissed the idea with the words: 'I won't be comfortable. Even when I go to the temple, I feel as though they are all saying, "There's that woman whose husband has died."' Meanwhile, the suggestion of a trip to India, to scatter my father's ashes, produced the response: 'Your father saw England as his home. And someone needs to look after the shop.' The question 'What next?' quickly became taboo, yet another thing that we didn't discuss as a family, along with my relationship with Freya; what happened to Dad; Mum's illness; sex; politics. At the same time, the problems we were having with sporadic abuse and violence made leaving Mum alone in the shop even more unthinkable.

Needless to say, Ranjit's and Freya's reactions to my admission of paralysis did differ somewhat. Ranjit, distracted now by the fact that someone had put twenty pence into the jukebox, had emitted a triumphant 'brauhhaa' and began singing along and performing sedantry bhangra to Malkit Singh's 'Aj Bhangra Paun Nu Ji Karda'. Meanwhile, Freya said, 'Why don't you ask your mum to move in with us?'

It was an insane suggestion. There was barely room in our flat for two of us, let alone three. My mother would never have agreed. But it was also a sign of how desperate Freya was becoming. It was September and we still hadn't sent out our wedding invitations. I realised I had to do something.

'It's really kind of you to suggest it, Freya. *Really* kind. But I don't think my mum is a London person.' I cleared my throat. 'Look, she can't carry on with the shop, it's ridiculous. *I* can't carry on. But it's just going to take some time to sort out. And I have been thinking about the wedding. Christmas isn't that far off. Do you think that maybe it would be best if we postponed it?' A long silence ensued. Freya stared into the distance, stunned. When she still hadn't said anything after half a minute, I added, 'I think it was always going to be ambitious, what with Dad dying and everything.'

Freya looked pale. Even paler than she had coming off the train from London, which, with its tilting, and her insistence on reading all the way, made her nauseous. Eventually she spoke. 'Look, Arjan, if you're having second thoughts, I would rather know now, rather than prolong the pain.'

I reassured her earnestly that I wasn't having doubts, that I needed her, which I did, that the whole thing was just a question of timing and that I would pay back the mortgage payments I had missed; and though she was upset and sad, she seemed to accept the argument. Ranjit was, however, less than understanding when, in the same spot some weeks later, I told him about Freya's tearfulness.

'Oh, man, she can fuck right off.' I bristled at his aggression but then it made sense that Ranjit, who still lived with his elderly father, would be horrified. 'Does she not get that family comes first? I ain't disrespecting you, blud, but are you sure you want to be with this girl? I mean, English girls are good for a bit of fun. But you need to marry a desi girl.'

'Like you, you mean, and keep shagging on the side?'

'Who says I shag around?'

'You do.'

'Swear down, it don't count if it's in the mouth.'

I winced.

'Point is. Best to stick to your own.' He finished his pint and waved at the barman for another, pulled out some hand cream from a trouser pocket, squirted some into a palm and rubbed it over his meaty fists. 'Anyway, you looked into selling the shop?'

I had. This had been another of the lowering events that month. I had taken it for granted that a sale would provide enough proceeds to give Mum options. But when I did something constructive and, at Freya's gentle suggestion, invited a business broker over to value the place, our financial predicament turned out to be complicated. The agent had arrived in his BMW 3 series, his jacket hanging from a hook in the back, a Bluetooth earpiece fixed to his ear, a tattoo just visible behind the collar of his shirt. He had barely registered the physical aspects of the shop. Instead, he asked for some ID ('Due to money laundering regulations, and the Proceeds of Crime Act 2002, we are obliged to check') and then asked if he could see the accounts. I had pointed him up to my father's study, explaining shamefacedly that I hadn't got my head around them yet. He raised an eyebrow. Ran a hand through his hair. Did everything short of rolling his eyes. I guess I probably wasn't the most professional business person he'd met that week. And then I told him he had to be gone by three.

'My mum will be back from the doctor's by then and she doesn't know I'm thinking about selling the shop.'

Just half an hour later he was striding down the stairs, seemingly determined to escape while I was busy serving a customer. But I managed to get to his car before he drove off. And after he had emitted a series of phrases ranging from 'streamlining processes', 'market conditions', 'performance benchmark signals' and 'CTN market value is usually 1.25 to 1.35 times the adjusted net profit', he hit me with the news that our family business, after fifty-three years of ownership and development, was worth £25,000. £472 for every year of work. £9.08 a week.

'The accommodation has been done up nice,' he said, speaking through a gap in a window. 'But this is a leasehold property. Even if it were freehold, doing up the back would be a waste of money. The Indian and Turkish families who take over these kinds of shops nowadays are not very interested in living accommodation. They are interested in making money. And you can't really let out the living quarters separately.' He shrugged and touched a spot on his satellite navigation screen. 'I'm sorry.'

Looking back, none of this should have come as a shock. Finance wasn't a strength of mine, but I knew Bains Stores was a leasehold. I had heard my father complain about the rent often enough, and it puzzled me that he had spent so much time improving property he didn't own. I also knew the shop was doing badly. When you wake up at 4 a.m. every day, you cannot help but keep a mental tab of how little you are selling. By eight that morning the takings had amounted to £41, which given the average profit margin of 20 per cent meant I was working for a wage below the minimum wage. I had joked to a customer that day that we should rename the shop 'Ten items or less' given how few things people bought. Ranjit was not surprised either, when I told him.

'That shop is waste. You need to get out of it.'

'I know! That's why I've come back. But how do I do that when my mother doesn't want to quit?'

'Why don't you ask your massi to help.'

'Massi?'

'Your mum's li'l sister, innit.'

I looked into his pupils to check he wasn't stoned. Or rather, to check he wasn't more stoned than usual.

'The one who died in a car accident, you mean?'

'Not what I heard.' He sipped his drink. 'Might be around still.'

With that he burped out loud, glanced at my thin arms and made another point that was beginning to make sense to me. 'You really should think about doing some weights. Get hench, man. Truss.'

The mop handle, on reflection, probably has more in tune with the prosaic nature of shop defence than the ninja star or the samurai sword. At least, Tanvir's self-defence weapon of choice, in his early days of shopkeeping, was a pound of keys on a heavy chain. Meanwhile, when, one evening in the winter of 1969, a young man in a cream raincoat and blue velvet trousers ran into the shop, slipped in his snakeskin shoes and went sliding across the floor into the crisps rack, Mrs Bains reached, instinctively, for a bottle of Stanley's Oven Cleaner.

'No!' protested Jim O'Connor, holding his left hand up in semi-surrender. 'Not in my face!' He was bleeding, but it was difficult to tell where he was bleeding from. 'Boys. Breaking into your car. Your van. Outside shop.' He made a gesture which was meant to mimic steering but actually made him look like he was pulling a toilet chain. 'I saved your van!'

Mrs Bains got the gist from his hand actions. It took a certain amount of imaginative effort to get your head around the notion of a gora defending an Asian property, but the story was in all other respects commonplace. Paki-bashing was becoming such a casual pastime for white youths that Dhanda was encouraging the Indian Workers' Association, or the Wolverhampton Council for Racial Harmony, or whichever activist organisation he was currently courting, to form vigilante groups and self-defence committees in response. The shop's van had been vandalised so often that the garage owner next door would joke that they may as well leave it with him permanently.

'You're putting the van into vandalised,' he would laugh when he saw Tanvir getting behind the wheel.

'Haha,' Tanvir would laugh back. 'Jes. The van into vandalised.'

Mrs Bains kneeled over the injured salesman, emitted a plaintive 'hai' and, muttering out loud about how human civilisation was degenerating and entering the age of kaliyug, she took her ever-versatile chuni and began wrapping it around his injured hand. She hollered out for Tanvir as she did so. 'Bangooo! Oi, Bangooooooooooo!'

Tanvir Banga heard the call. In truth, there were people in parts of West Bromwich who probably heard it. He pulled out those aforementioned keys on a chain, and as he came running up from the stockroom in the basement, instinctively grabbed something else that might work as a weapon: a large cooking spoon. But he dropped both on seeing O'Connor on the floor, working out from his suit, briefcase and demeanour who he was and what might have just happened.

'Police,' he shouted. 'I will call police.'

'No, p-please,' responded O'Connor from the floor.

'Yes, police, I call now.'

'No. I said "please".' He waved the hand that was now wrapped in turquoise chiffon. 'No real damage.'

It was not a point that Tanvir was keen to argue. Everyone knew if you were black or Asian you could not trust the authorities to take your side. However, Mrs Bains insisted something had to be done for this brave gora, and, with several customers now waiting to be served and several others gawping on, she suspended her instinctive distrust of the whites, and her habitual concern in shielding her daughters from unsupervised contact with young unmarried men, and insisted the two girls, who were preparing pakoras in the kitchen for the occasion of Tanvir's birthday, look after him. Mr O'Connor would not be able to leave without first being cleaned up and fed; a friend of the shop was a friend of the family; one never knew when God was visiting in disguise; etc.

As for Kamaljit and Surinder, they would not have been more startled if their mother had walked into the kitchen with a Shetland pony. Kamaljit simply because she could not ever recall seeing a white person, let alone a white man, in the family's living quarters before. Surinder, meanwhile, had wiped O'Connor from her head and from her heart, out of a combination of shame and guilt, after her father's death. His reappearance more than six months later triggered a maelstrom of emotions: squeamishness at the sight of his visible injuries (so much for the career in nursing); panic at the idea that he might betray that they had previously met and, more pertinently, when they had met; confusion over the fact that he seemed much taller and paler than she remembered; desire at the sight of those blue eyes; and then acute self-consciousness at the possibility of conveying any of these feelings. She didn't know what to say or what to do, even whether she should cover her head as she did with Indian men.

'Don't just stand there like donkeys,' bellowed Mrs Bains. 'Can't you see this poor man has been injured? He took on half a dozen boys outside the shop by himself!' The story was already being amplified out of all proportion and recognition. 'Get him some tea and food, get his hand cleaned up and sort out his coat. I've got to get back to the shop.' She clapped twice. 'Jaldi jaldi!'

The girls got to it, Kamaljit preparing food and drink, Surinder removing her apron and retrieving something that resembled a first-aid box from next to the TV in the living room. She returned to the kitchen, where she helped him remove his raincoat, unravelled her mother's impromptu bandage at the kitchen table and applied antiseptic to his cuts and grazes. O'Connor explained what had happened as she toiled. He was doing his rounds, walking down Victoria Road, making his way to Bains Stores, his sixth meeting of the day, when he spotted some youths hacking at the tyres of the Bains' van. He remonstrated. They swore at him. And when he returned the volley of abuse, one came up and punched him in the face.

Surinder gasped, and translated the most dramatic elements of the story for her sister's benefit. But Jim reassured his audience that he had retaliated immediately, connecting on his first attempt. If it had been one or two of them, he could have had them. But it was three versus one, and before he knew it, he had been tripped over, falling over awkwardly on his hand, and by the time he got up, the youths had, after hurling various remarks too offensive to repeat to young women, legged it.

Surinder's heart beat hard in appreciation and, in spite of herself, an entire relationship with Jim flashed past her eyes in the form of a *Jackie* magazine cartoon strip. Here they were skating together, her saying 'Oh, I'm going to fall' and Jim responding 'No, you won't, I'm holding you.' Here they were in straw hats at the seaside, Jim saying 'THAT HAT SUITS YOU!', Surinder replying 'SO DOES YOURS!' The pleasure of the fantasy interspersed with a hundred pleasurable questions. Was he in town as a relief rep? Was he back in Wolverhampton for good? But all she could actually manage to say was 'Does it hurt?'

'I think it's fine. It will just be annoying if I can't pick up my briefcase, or write.'

'Oh,' replied Surinder, struggling not to gush. 'Do you write?'

'For work. Poetry and prose when I get time. But, you know, when you read a great writer like, say, Thomas Hardy, you just want to sling everything you've done in a fire.'

A-level study had rather put her off Hardy, but Surinder often felt the same about her creative efforts in relation to writers like George Eliot and Arnold Bennett, and if her sister hadn't been there, she might have exclaimed in delight. Instead, she concentrated as hard as possible on fastening Jim's bandage with a safety pin. He squirmed as she did so, and squirmed even more when Kamaljit, holding a cup up to his lips, encouraged him to take a sip of hot tea.

'Too hot?' asked Surinder.

O'Connor shook his head.

'Too milky?' asked Surinder. Everyone knew the goras boiled their tea in water rather than milk.

O'Connor indicated no again, struggling to swallow.

'Ah, it will be the saunf then.' Both girls laughed at the memory of being force-fed the concoction as children. They grew up dreading it more than illness itself. 'It's a mixture of herbs added to tea,' explained Surinder, playing along at nurse. 'I'm not sure what you call it in English. Cardamom? Fennel?' For some reason she glanced at Kamaljit for an answer. None came. 'Anyway, it will make you feel better.'

The pakoras weren't such a struggle: Kamaljit threw several fresh ones into the pan of oil and O'Connor polished off two in quick succession. And as Surinder started brushing his raincoat clean of mud, discovering a paperback edition of *The Mayor of Casterbridge* in the inside pocket as she did so, he regaled the girls with an account of his morning before it was ruined by thugs, acting out bits for Kamaljit's benefit. He had visited a sweet shop in the town centre which also functioned as a bicycle accessories shop, and where bars of chocolates were displayed alongside canisters of 3-in-One Oil; an old lady on the other side of town, who bought branded chocolate in large quantities, only to unwrap it all, break it up and sell it in jars, insisting it tasted better that way; and then an Italian who couldn't pronounce any brand names and was almost impossible to make any sense of. O'Connor did an impression of the man, gesticulating wildly, getting overemotional as he talked about 'da family' and the glory of his homeland. 'Zis chocolate eees good. But zee chocolate in Italia is fackin' great!'

The girls giggled along giddily, Surinder at the accent and the risqué cursing, Kamaljit at the slapstick actions.

'Some characters in this town,' Jim continued. 'Though I hope all my days here are not going to be so eventful.'

Surinder suppressed another gasp. So, he was going to be around for a while! And O'Connor was just remarking on what a nice laugh the sisters shared, how pretty they both were, making sure not to compliment one more than the other, when Tanvir strode into the room. He appeared with his hands clasped behind his back, like a member of royalty inspecting a line of foot guards, bolt upright, as if he had Mrs Bains' umbrella stuck down the back of his shirt. His pristine turban, which he spent half an hour tying each morning, using a knitting needle to push stray hairs underneath the material, and beard, which he smoothed down with mustard oil, were by now the wonder of Victoria Road.

'Kamaljit,' he said in English. 'Come, come. We need hand in shop.'

Surinder cringed at his English and his accent. Her pet hate at the moment was the way he greeted male customers with the remark 'Good morning, gentleman,' when it was often the afternoon, and when he actually meant 'sir'.

'Oh,' responded Kamaljit. 'Give me a minute.'

She cleared up the food and the tea and dishes and left Surinder and Jim in the kitchen together. There followed two short conversations in two parts of the shop between the two men and two women, which, even if you ran them end to end, would amount to no more than a minute, and which, even if you were nearby, you would have struggled to follow. But the quietest, shortest exchanges are not necessarily the least significant.

In the kitchen, Surinder and Jim alone.
    Jim (whispering): 'Is he all right? He looked a bit off.'
    Surinder: 'Don't worry about him. He's always a bit off.'
    Jim: 'As long as it wasn't something I said.'
    Surinder: 'Really, there is no problem.'

Jim (a hand on her arm): 'It's nice to see you again, after so long, Sue.'

Surinder (pulling away): '. . .'

Jim: 'I came back to the shop a few weeks after we met. But there was no sign of you. Just your brother.'

Surinder: 'He's not my brother. He works for the family. My father died.'

Jim: 'Oh. I'm so sorry.' (Averting eyes) 'I wanted a patch in London, but when Wolverhampton came up, I thought I'd take it.' (Pause) 'I was wondering if I could take you to d-dinner one day?'

Surinder (blushing): 'I'm not really allowed to go out in the evenings.'

Jim: 'Could I take you to lunch then?'

Surinder: 'I'm at *school* at lunchtime.'

Jim (boldly): 'Breakfast?'

Surinder (firmly): 'I'm not allowed to see boys at *any* time of day.'

Jim: 'So which school are you at anyway?'

Surinder (whispering): 'I don't think I should tell you.'

Jim: 'Don't worry, I'll work it out.'

Meanwhile, in the shopfront, Tanvir is serving a customer, Mrs Bains is cleaning the floor where O'Connor slipped and Kamaljit has to step over a rivulet of foam as she walks towards the counter.

Kamaljit (to Tanvir): 'So?'

Tanvir (to the customer, brightly, in English): 'Thank you very much, gentleman. Hope you're enjoying the weather.'

Customer (reaching for a wet umbrella): 'Hardly.'

Kamaljit (to Tanvir): 'And?'

Tanvir: 'What?'

Kamaljit: 'You said I was needed?'

Tanvir: 'Did I?' (Straightens boxes on the counter) 'Oh yes.

The moment has passed. I'm sorry for dragging you away
from that gora.' (Bitterly) 'You sounded like you were
having such fun.'

Kamaljit (glancing at her mother): 'What?'

Tanvir (still straightening the boxes): 'You heard what I said.'

Kamaljit (whispering): 'I was just doing what my mother
asked me to do. You should be ashamed of yourself for
thinking anything else. *Ashamed.*'

It may seem rather out of character that Mrs Bains did not over-
hear any of this, and that she did not suspect anything was awry
in the months that followed. After all, she watched her daughters
like a hawk, was aware of their movements, the slightest alteration
in their respective moods. But she had for months now been
distracted by the task of running the shop and the all-consuming
search for sons-in-law.

The response had been overwhelming, with photographs of
prospective husbands arriving from as far afield as India and
America, and the number of men exceeding more than two dozen.
The girls were young, after all, and attractive, and had British
passports. However, Mrs Bains was surprised to discover that she
enjoyed no part of the matrimonial process. Marrying off her
daughters should have been the pinnacle of a lifetime's work, the
satisfying conclusion of nearly two decades of nurturing and
development, but she came to loathe the formal arranged-marriage
tea parties which marked Sunday afternoons even more than
Tanvir, who would thrash around the shop for the duration.

It did not sit easily with her to be succinct, or servile with
strangers. She hated the cold physical evaluation of Kamaljit and
Surinder, as they made brief appearances to serve tea – a process
which, along with the awkward chit-chat, made her feel like a
pimp. She lacked the ability to let people down gently or take
criticism. The sheer amount of choice, meanwhile, stoked her

indecision. In the first three months of the search she rejected men for failings including: not being educated enough (for Surinder); being too educated (for Kamaljit); being of 'too pukka' a complexion – i.e. too dark (for Surinder); having a limp; having a squiffy eye.

Though when it came to Surinder, some men could not take a hint or even no for an answer. If Mrs Bains said her daughter wanted to work, they would suddenly see the appeal of a career wife. If she said Surinder did not want to live with in-laws, they would suggest moving out. Two of the men who declined Kamaljit expressed an interest in Surinder instead. One of Surinder's rejects appeared in the shop every day for a week afterwards, mooning about the magazine stand in the hope of catching a glimpse of his beloved. In turn, the only outright rejection Surinder received was on the grounds that 'my son is looking for a simple girl', the insinuation being that Surinder was complicated and troublesome, which in the arranged-marriage market was one of the worst things you could say about a girl. Mrs Bains did not take the feedback well.

'What do they mean, "not simple"?' ranted Mrs Bains at Mr Dhanda, who had turned up uninvited at Sunday lunchtime, and was hanging around the kitchen as Mrs Bains turned out paronthas. 'They cook, they go to the temple, they work hard. No one, I tell you, *no one*, is more simple than my daughters.' She brushed a square of rolled-out dough with ghee, and thrust it on to the thava. 'But then if by simple they mean "mentally subnormal" like that boy, then it's true.' The edges of the parontha snapped and crackled. 'It is true my daughters are not mentally subnormal. I tell you, that boy couldn't even look me in the eye. Let alone his future wife. His own mother, the fiteh moon, had to tell him when to pick up a samosa, when to try some barfi. Then they say he is training to be a doctor. Leh. That boy, I tell you, is the one who needs medical attention.'

With the parontha lightly cooked, she brushed some more butter on it, browned it all over and slapped it on to a plate. Dhanda took it, without asking, and, not even waiting for it to cool down, tore off a corner, dipped it into some achar and wolfed it down. A bolt of irritation shot through Mrs Bains. Dhanda's offer to buy the shop had been filed away and forgotten, along with all the other things she found too difficult to confront, but she had nevertheless, since Mr Bains' passing, struggled to establish the boundaries of a relationship with her husband's old friend. His unsolicited advice was hectoring, his omnipresence intrusive. And as she began to make some more dough for the extra paronthas she would now, inevitably, have to churn out, this feeling intensified.

'Of course, you might be looking too far,' said Dhanda, speaking with his mouth full, pouring himself some tea.

Mrs Bains: 'Huh?'

He repeated himself, making half-lidded eye contact, and in between pouring the tea from cup to saucer to cool it down, and slurping noisily from the rim, he added casually, 'What I mean, of course, Mataji, is that if you are looking for a Jat with a shop, someone with a British passport, of good character, and someone who Mr Bains would have approved of, maybe you do not need to look so far.'

Mrs Bains was so distracted by the appellation – it was the first time he had ever called her 'mataji', mother; he normally called her 'pehnji', sister – and so perturbed by what he seemed to be saying, that she asked him for clarification. 'What do you mean?'

'Well, the age gap between dear Mr Bains, God bless his soul, and your good self was not all that different to the age gap between, say . . . Surinder and I.'

In that moment, the floor seemed to tilt. Feeling sick, Mrs Bains put both hands on the worktop to steady herself, and then felt a wave of grief for her dead husband. This would never have happened if he were still around. Then, a pang of anger towards him: this would never have happened if he hadn't been so indulgent of this narcissistic, impudent man.

There was, academically, nothing wrong in what Dhanda was suggesting. The rules, when arranging a marriage, were that you must not marry within four gotras of your family, or within your village. And Dhanda was right about the age gap between Mr and Mrs Bains. But she had been a widow, had not been in a position to resist the overtures of any man, whereas her daughters were far from desperate. Moreover, Dhanda's proposition exposed as a fiction the idea he had long propounded that he was Mr Bains' brother and an uncle to her daughters. The girls called him 'chacha', for God's sake – the appellation for one's father's younger brother. Mrs Bains was shocked, and registering her expression, Mr Dhanda glanced at his watch, which he kept fastened upside down on his left wrist, mumbled something about an urgent appointment and slipped away.

On his departure, Mrs Bains did what she always did in an emergency: she shut the living-room door, picked up the telephone and called her sister in Southall for advice. The voice on the other end of the phone was scandalised. She gasped at the right moments, and despite having been vocal in her complaints about Mr Dhanda in the past, resisted saying 'I told you so.' But having digested all the details, she surprised her sister by launching into a tirade that made Mrs Bains' own monologues seem like playful asides.

This, ultimately, was all Mrs Bains' fault, she pronounced. She had petted her daughters too long, allowed Surinder in particular to be spoiled by education; God knew what ideas were swishing about in that unnaturally pretty head of hers. She had never known a girl to read so many books. Had never known a girl to read *newspapers* in the way Surinder did. It was not normal. She had been influenced too much by the West. Mrs Bains had been too lax, had lost focus since Mr Bains had died, the girls were running rings around her. She herself had married off two daughters and a son within the space of a year, and yet in the many months that had passed since Mr Bains had died, Mrs Bains had not even *set up* one girl. All mothers were proud, of course, considered their daughters too good for most men, but people were beginning to talk. Maybe watching too many Bollywood films had given her strange ideas about 'liking' and 'happiness' when all that mattered was 'suitability' and 'duty'. Frankly, it was time that Mrs Bains stopped faffing about.

The lecture was painful to endure but she accepted the criticism that came her way, conceding every point. She had been lax and proud. Running a shop and finding two husbands was probably too much for one woman, and maybe fear of loneliness was making her delay the painful moment she lost her daughters. It was so hard, she sobbed. So hard. This was the reason it was better to have boys than girls, she lamented. They weren't better. But you didn't lose boys to another family through marriage.

The phone call ended with a series of instructions. First, Mrs Bains should not reveal to anyone what Dhanda had suggested. It was important not to alienate or humiliate the man: he was respected in the community, you needed friends in this godforsaken country, and Lord knows what damage he could cause the izzat of the girls if provoked. Second, it was essential the girls be married off quickly. To aid this, Surinder should be sent to her aunt in Southall as soon as her exams were over. Her aunt would not only knock some sense into the girl, with the back of her hand if necessary, she would also find her a husband, freeing Mrs Bains to concentrate on Kamaljit. Finally, Mrs Bains must not ever mention any of this to anyone – not to any relatives, any customers. No one. Especially her daughters.

Mrs Bains followed her sister's advice to the letter, clinging on to the plan as if her life depended on it. She knew Surinder would resist being sent to Southall, even without her realising the full nature of the plan. She had spent one summer there a few years earlier and had complained of being treated like a slave by her aunt, who had made her work fourteen-hour days in their shop. But it all went smoothly. Like clockwork. Except for one thing. When discussing Dhanda's request on the phone that Sunday afternoon, Mrs Bains had failed, not for the first time, to keep her voice down, and Surinder, reading upstairs, had overheard some of what had been said.

In the event, Mrs Bains didn't inform her daughter about her confinement to Southall for months. But she needn't have been so careful: seemingly distracted by the task of studying for her exams, Surinder accepted the news without fuss. And when the time came for her to depart one hot morning in June, the day after her final A-level paper, the surprise was that no one was more upset than Mrs Bains. She couldn't even glance at her daughter's packed suitcases without tears filling her eyes. Life, it seemed to her, was just one long painful lesson in learning to let go. When Surinder had finished packing, she would have endured the pain of childbirth ten times over to be spared the torture of sending her daughter away.

The van, which had been driven to near destruction some years earlier by the General Post Office, and had suffered further years of abuse and vandalism under the ownership of the Bains, seemed to find the mile-long journey to the station with Surinder in the back as much of a strain as Mrs Bains. It emitted an explosion on being started by Tanvir, and once it droned into life, the floor rattled and the transmission whined. Throughout, Mrs Bains, in tumult, complained about the roadworks that seemed to perpetually afflict Wolverhampton.

'Leh, what they doing now? New ring road, schming road. How many family shops and churches have been destroyed to build this? What godforsaken country is this that bulldozes the dead, for roads? And what kind of people leave bodies to rot in the soil? It's disgusting.'

There was little solace to be found at the new high-level train station, given that it, like the roads, and the town centre, which had been torn up to make space for new shopping centres, had been rebuilt in the name of progress, and in the process had been robbed of anything resembling comfort. The ticket hall was a featureless concrete box, and passengers on platforms were exposed to the elements, the idea of a 'roof' having been dismissed as a design remnant of the past. The three of them stood perspiring in the sun with the two suitcases Mr Bains had used when he emigrated to England, Mrs Bains attempting to conceal her emotional turmoil with incessant advice.

'Your massi will be waiting for you at the station. If you don't see her, wait at the end of the platform and she will find you. Make sure you call us as soon as you leave for Southall. Make sure you offer to pay for the petrol – if she doesn't take the money, leave some on their mantelpiece. Always cover your head when your masur is in the room. Remember, they are more traditional than us. You will not be able to flounce about like you do at home, OK? Make sure you always use 'ji' with your cousins when they visit. If there are any visitors, make sure to give up your bed and offer to sleep on the floor. Don't sit around reading books in your room. Do not address your uncle unless he speaks first. Keep your head covered in his presence, do not laugh loudly, nor run anywhere, and don't start eating until your masur has finished. And for god's sake stay out of the sun or you will turn into a blackie like your sister.'

Surinder, who had barely spoken that morning, rolled her eyes and said, evenly, 'I know, Mum.'

Mrs Bains broke down.

'Don't cry, Mum.' The more hysterical her mother grew, the calmer Surinder appeared.

'You will always be a child to me, putt.'

She kissed and hugged her daughter, even as Surinder stiffened. 'I know you are a good girl. I just want you to be happy. You know that, don't you?'

Her daughter looked so beautiful. No wonder men lost their senses around her. And just when it felt like things could not get any more emotional, Tanvir sneezed. A big, snotty, no-hands sneeze. Mrs Bains would have been no less horrified if he had just thrown himself on to the newly electrified track. Of all the superstitions she lived by, the one she held on to most fervently, even more intensely than physicists held on to Newton's laws of motion, was the belief that it was bad luck to sneeze on embarking on a journey or new initiative. For a moment, all three of them froze in shock on the station platform.

Neither Tanvir or Surinder seemed to know how Mrs Bains would react. In the event, she made a unilateral decision to reach for her daughter's suitcases and announced they would have to go back to the shop, come back another time. There were plenty of trains, she would pay whatever was necessary to send Surinder later, the risk simply wasn't worth taking. Tanvir and Surinder had to chase her down the platform and spend a considerable amount of time persuading her to change her mind, to remind her that the effects of a sneeze could be counteracted if the person waited a few minutes – the train was still fifteen minutes away – and if all the parties in question ate something sugary. Thank God they ran a sweet shop. Thank God Tanvir always carried mints.

Fearing another scene, Tanvir managed to get Mrs Bains to leave the platform with five minutes to go, and he helped Surinder on to the train alone, while Mrs Bains sat in the van crying. She was still crying when, on the way back home, after they had descended a hill and the van had misfired two or three times, Tanvir came to a standstill at a set of traffic lights, cleared his throat and made an announcement. 'There's something I'd like to discuss with you, bibiji.'

Mrs Bains was too shattered by the morning's events to digest what Tanvir had said.

The van set off again and soon they were speeding down a new smooth section of the ring road – though speeding was a relative thing in this vehicle: it could, in theory, reach 77mph, and the speedometer wound round to indicate 90mph whenever Tanvir ventured near the accelerator, but it was difficult to imagine it hitting such numbers even if driven off a cliff. Eventually they slowed down again, the van emitted a farting noise, and he continued, staring intensely at another red light, 'In short.' Yellow. 'With all due respect, bibiji.' Green. 'I would like to marry Kamaljit.'

It was too close a day to sit in the van for more than a few moments when stationary, but having parked up outside the shop, Mrs Bains was still sitting in it alone fifteen minutes later. No matter how hard she thought, she couldn't make sense of what had just happened.

Whereas Dhanda's request had resulted in shock and dismay, Tanvir's had just produced incomprehension. She had grabbed the sides of her seat and stared at the petrol gauge, almost expecting it to provide some sort of direction or guidance, when the fact was that it didn't even provide a clue about the contents of the petrol tank, having been stuck on 'empty' for years. Her response, when she finally did manage one, amounted to nothing more than: 'You want to marry my daughter?'

'Hahnji.'

A silence ballooned between them. After a while, Tanvir broke it, inserting, tersely, in a tone she had never heard him speak before, 'Perhaps you think we are not well suited?'

Of course they weren't well suited! Tanvir was indispensable in the shop, loyal, as reliable as gravity, and Mr Bains' death had meant that he was more or less running the place, but he was also a Chamar, whereas the Bains were Jats, and Jats could no more marry Chamars than one of the road cones that were whizzing past. The fact was that in India someone from a scheduled caste like Tanvir would not be allowed to draw water from the same well as Jat Sikhs like the Bains; at school, Jat children would have to give away or throw away their food if he had touched it; some Jats would feel the need to clean their clothes with soap if he so much as touched them; in England, on the factory floor, some Jats would not take water from the same tap from where someone of Tanvir's caste had drunk, and there were even some customers at Bains Stores who refused to take change or produce from Tanvir directly, asking for it to be put on the counter to avoid direct contact.

Mrs Bains had protested on his behalf when this happened, but she ranted and raved about lots of things, and besides, the rules that dictated behaviour in a shop did not alter the ancient and eternal differences between the castes. She could still remember how at village feasts Chamar families were obliged to eat separately. In India, he would not have been allowed into the family kitchen, being regarded as ritually unclean. Why, she could remember how his grandfather, like many of his generation, would have to warn others of his arrival to avoid tension or trouble. In the Punjab, Tanvir would have risked being locked up, beaten up or thrown down a well just for thinking such a thought about a Jat girl. Even in England, if they got married, they would be ostracised by the community. Surinder's marriage prospects would be ruined by association, the family would face disdain at social gatherings, and close relations would stop visiting. It would be a calamity, a disgrace, even worse than Dhanda marrying Surinder, and Mrs Bains' extended silence said as much. All she could manage by the time they finally pulled up in front of the shop, Tanvir braking sharply, was: 'Kamaljit is too young for you.'

Mrs Bains didn't know why she said this, perhaps it was what she wished she had said to Dhanda that time but had failed to, maybe she was just babbling, but Tanvir wasted no time demolishing the argument. 'Kamaljit is twenty. She is older than Surinder, who you are also marrying off. I am twenty-nine. And before you say it, some of the men who have come to see her have been older than me.'

Tanvir continued his well-rehearsed argument. He had served the family dutifully and without complaint for many years. Furthermore, he had read through the Holy Book with Kamaljit, and they had found nothing objecting to intercaste marriage. The Gurus if anything said it was wrong to discriminate along the lines of caste, that all men and women were equal in the eyes of God. Besides, in England people of all colour and creeds were equal before the law. He and Kamaljit cared for one another deeply, a lesser man would have eloped but he respected the Bains; and if in spite of all this she would not allow their marriage, he would respect her decision, leave the shop that very evening and spend the remainder of his days alone and celibate.

'Right.' Mrs Bain breathed in and out deeply. 'So, you actually mean this?'

'Yes.'

He said this in English.

'You're actually serious?'

'Yes.'

'And you have discussed this with Kamaljit? My daughter?'

'Yes.' Impatience had crept into his tone. '*Your daughter*, Kamaljit.'

And with that he got out of the van, slammed the door behind him and, having checked the lock on his side of the car twice, walked into the shop and up to his room.

Sitting in the van, nothing became clearer. Surinder was the one inclined to flights of fantasy. Tanvir, meanwhile, was as solid as a rock. This was the man who every morning had to wash his hands a certain number of times before starting work. Who had to touch objects a certain number of times before exiting a room, who had the mickey taken out of him by the newspaper boys for doing his mental arithmetic aloud ('Ten pence minus three pence means seven pence back to you'). The idea of the pair of them embarking on some kind of illicit romance was unimaginable. And all that Mrs Bains managed to conclude after what turned into half an hour of deliberation was that Tanvir had gone mad under the stress of his work. A holiday would have to be arranged. Kamaljit would have to be exiled to Southall – she had sent the wrong daughter down south. But before that, she would have to call her sister for advice. And before that, she would have to get into the living room without crossing her daughter.

The feeling was mutual, because when Mrs Bains did finally get out of the van and walked into the shop, Kamaljit, who had been minding the counter, fled upstairs. Mrs Bains was then prevented from calling her sister by an influx of customers. She struggled with the chit-chat and the change, and when she finally got the chance to call, shaking so much that she struggled to dial the number, she was told that her sister had not yet returned from picking up Surinder at Euston.

She tried every ten minutes thereafter, but it was hours before she finally got through. And she had only begun rushing through the story when her sister emitted a sob. She was grateful for the sympathy; she had been fighting the urge to sob herself, the whole thing somehow feeling much worse because there was no one else to blame – she was the one who had suggested hiring Tanvir. But she hadn't actually got to the point yet. She resumed her story only to be interrupted by a howl.

'What's wrong, pehnji? Has something happened?'

Her sister cried out again. A deep, guttural howl.

'Hai rubba. Has there been an accident?'

It was worse than an accident. Surinder had not turned up at Euston train station as arranged. Instead, a stranger, a black man in a suit, had approached the aunt with an envelope. Inside was a note, written in English and Punjabi. It read:

I will not be coming to Southall. I am not going back to Wolverhampton. I know about Dhanda's proposal. I am getting married to Jim O'Connor, the salesman. I love him. Please do not look for me, or try to contact me, and please do not worry about me. I have taken my wedding jewellery.

Surinder

It's a bitterly cold Sunday evening in November and I'm sitting in a German 4x4 with 3,000 miles on the clock, tinted windows that do not, as the law states, allow at least 75 per cent of light through the windscreen, and heated front seats which, when switched on without your knowledge, make you feel like you are slowly soiling yourself. The satellite navigation system identifies the location as a suburb of Birmingham, while the 1,000W stereo blasts out a bhangra track in which the vocalist pleads for his beloved to remove her veil so that he can admire her beautiful cat-like face.

Ranjit and I are on a 'mission'. Not one of his usual kind, i.e. popping to the cash and carry, or picking up a bucket of chicken from KFC, but an actual real-life mission — worthy if not of Steven Seagal or Bruce Lee, then at least of a detective played by David Jason in a prime-time ITV drama. We are staking out a house which may or may not be the home of my long-lost aunt Surinder, and my uncle Jim, both of whom I hadn't realised, until a few weeks earlier, existed.

The journey has been a challenge. If Ranjit wasn't distracted by the task of lighting up a spliff, or enraging fellow motorists by reacting to traffic signals with the kind of lethargy most people reserve for filling out tax returns, he was fretting in his paranoid dope-addled way about being followed by 'the Feds'. Though just establishing my uncle and aunt's names, and where they lived, had been even more arduous. After casually informing me of

Surinder's existence, and being subjected to a barrage of questions, Ranjit had vaguely alluded to my aunt marrying a gora, before suddenly complaining of feeling unwell and heading home. He then became as unobtainable and uncontactable as he had previously been obtainable and contactable.

The sudden sheepishness was no surprise. The first rule of chuglia is: don't get caught trading in chuglia. Being branded a gossip in the village that is Bulberhampton, or being accused of interfering in another family's private affairs, is the only thing worse than not hearing the gossip in the first place. Also, as far as scandal goes, a Punjabi woman eloping with a white bloke in 1970 was pretty scandalous. I understood why he might have immediately regretted mentioning it and I also understood why my parents might have hushed it up. More than forty years later, I still lacked the courage to bring up the subject with my mother. But I couldn't leave it alone, and when Ranjit didn't respond, I popped over to Buy Express anyway, to see if his father might be more helpful.

As with his son, conversing with Mr Dhanda was far from a straightforward affair. His English was excellent, so much so that it made me realise that, as with human civilisation at large, one generation of a family does not necessarily build on the achievements of another. But a lifetime of barking orders, whether as a shop owner or as a local politician, combined with age and decades of obesity which made even getting up a challenge, had turned him into more of a projector than a listener. He sat at the back of the shop, sometimes in a wheelchair, sometimes on a chair, and shouted at his staff, his customers, his wife, children and grandchildren. Visiting him invariably required being subjected to lectures about Wolverhampton racial politics; accounts of Punjabi political bodies which always seemed to be disbanded after the outbreak of infighting among the leaders; reminiscences about my grandfather; and an account of his own family history, which like all Punjabi family histories seemed to involve a grandmother who was reputedly a hundred years old, a cousin called Happy whose life unfurled in distinctly unhappy fashion, and endless impenetrable violent disputes over farmland in India, which might have been triggered by anything from a murderous betrayal to a misjudged glance at someone's wife.

This time, when I did finally get an opportunity to explain the purpose of my visit, tentatively enquiring whether he could tell me anything about the youngest of Mr Bains' daughters, he acted as if he hadn't heard; being a little deaf can be a useful thing. Instead, he launched into a lengthy account of the activities of the General Secretary of the Council of Khalistan, who in 1975 was apparently imprisoned for thirty days in Pentonville prison for riding his motorcycle while wearing his turban, in order to protest against the law as it stood.

'1975?' I inserted. 'Interesting. MY AUNT SURINDER WOULD HAVE LEFT WOLVERHAMPTON BY 1975. Do you remember anything about Surinder, babaji?'

'The problem was that Section 32 of the Road Traffic Act 1972 said it was compulsory to wear a helmet.'

I sighed.

'Did you know that in the 1974 General Election, an activist called Baldev Chahal stood as a candidate in Southall on the issue?'

God knows what this had to do with anything. Mercifully, I was saved from much more by a customer who came up and asked where he could find the Weetabix.

'Second aisle, top shelf, at the end,' responded Mr Dhanda quickly, suddenly recovering the facility to hear. Before he could get started on another lecture, I got down on my knees, right in front of his chair, uncomfortably close to the diabetic boil on his bare foot, and shouted out loud, something I had seen Ranjit do when he really needed his father to respond. 'I KNOW THAT MY BABA HAD TWO DAUGHTERS, MY MOTHER KAMALJIT, BUT ALSO A YOUNGER DAUGHTER CALLED SURINDER. YES,

SURINDER. DO YOU REMEMBER HER? YOU MUST DO. I THOUGHT SHE HAD PASSED AWAY, BUT SHE MIGHT BE ALIVE. DO YOU RECALL WHO SHE MARRIED? DO YOU KNOW WHEN SHE LEFT WOLVERHAMPTON?'

He could no more ignore me than a pedestrian could ignore an HGV hurtling towards him on a zebra crossing. And it seemed as if he would have preferred to face one. A look of infinite exhaustion passed over his prehistoric face, his tiny eyes withdrew even further into his head, and his stringy neck suddenly seemed to strain under the weight of his large, lopsided white turban. I remembered something my father would say: 'Never trust a man with a turban but no beard.' Eventually, he waved his hand dismissively and said, 'Listen, the past is the past, some things, best left.'

I laughed. 'Look, I really need to speak to her if she's still around.' I added, 'My mother is alone now, apart from me. She needs all the help she can get. I think Mr Bains, my grandfather, would have wanted his two daughters to know one another, to help each other in old age. Don't you think?' I made a cynical attempt to push his buttons. 'In the way he was looked after by you. Families should be together. Ranjit mentioned that she had married a gora.' There was a time I hated the *g* word, it was as bad as the *n* and *p* words. I had been so cross when I heard my mother using the term in relation to Freya once, but nowadays it tripped easily off my tongue. 'Do you remember anything about him? His name? Where he was from? What he looked like?'

'Um.' He suddenly sounded about twenty years older. 'I think the man, that man, if memory serves, he was someone who visited the shop.'

'A customer, you mean?'

'No, no.'

'Someone from the council?'

'A rep.'

'A rep? For who?'

'A sweet company.'

'Do you remember which one?' I mentioned the two big outfits.

'No.'

'His name?'

'Cornell, Connell, something like that.'

'Do you remember his first name?'

'No.'

'Do you remember where he lived?'

'Never met him.'

Clearly, 'Cornell, Connell, something like that' was not much to go on. But the conversation was proving exhausting. I figured there couldn't be many Surinder Cornells or Connells around, and it looked like it was all Mr Dhanda was going to give me, anyway. So I thanked him for his time and left him alone, and back at Bains Stores I gave up avoiding mindless chit-chat with customers by pretending to be on the phone and instead avoided chit-chat by searching for my aunt on the internet.

However, after a fortnight there was nothing to show for my efforts but an email account jammed with spam from the social networks I had joined and messages from a handful of Cornells/Connells telling me they had no idea who I was looking for. I was considering a return to Dhanda when there was a sudden, accidental breakthrough. I was visited by a sales rep from a confectionery company and mentioned the problems I was having locating a former employee called Cornell/Connell. She informed me there was an association for former sales reps, so I got in touch with them. At the mention Cornell/Connell, the person in question guessed who I might be on about and, seemingly oblivious to the Data Protection Laws, and the right of individuals to privacy, she sent me the last known address of Jim O'Connor, which turned out to be a forty-five-minute drive from where my mother lived.

You might have thought from the elation I felt on getting this information, the first time I think I had felt anything resembling joy since my father's death, that I'd got my father back. And, looking back, my excitement was rather disproportionate. After all, it's not as if I grew up deprived of aunties. From the youngest age, as the result of growing up in a shop, I have been surrounded by aunties who pet me, aunties who compare me favourably/ unfavourably to their own children, aunties for whom I am obliged to perform menial tasks purely because I am told they are aunties, aunties who are black, aunties who are white, aunties who are my aunties because they come from the same Indian village as my parents, aunties who still pinch my cheeks and chuck my chin in my thirties, aunties who claim to have nursed my grandfather, aunties I am scared of, aunties I fancy, aunties in India I don't recognise but who I am nevertheless obliged to talk to in bad Punjabi for at least five minutes when my mum makes me call them up for her on Skype.

But an actual, real-life biological aunt – that was different. Surinder. A blood relative. The importance of her role as an aunt emphasised by the specific title – 'massi' – she got as a result of being my mother's sister. Someone to consult about my mother's future. Someone who knew my parents when they were young. I suppose, in a small way, I *was* getting my father back: Surinder-massi would be able to tell me things I had never known about him. Though after I had shared the news of my discovery with Ranjit, who finally picked up the phone, accounting for his absence by citing flu, and after I had taken him up on his suggestion that we drive out to Birmingham to 'check out' the house, this sense of purpose started to flag rather.

The suburb had looked green enough on an internet map, and according to the satnav we were surrounded by parkland. But the shopping trollies strewn across front gardens and the groups of youths drinking high-strength lager in doorways told a different

147

story. It didn't help that it was raining and it was dark and we were sitting in a car which, with diagonally stitched leather upholstery, and plush, two-tone cognac/cedar natural leather interior was the vehicular equivalent of Blenheim Palace. But I doubt it would have looked any better from the windscreen of my father's dilapidated van. As for the house, it might have once been a reasonably attractive 1930s semi, if they hadn't done one of the worst things you can do to such a property, by installing UPVC frames in the massive bay windows. Meanwhile, the front garden had been paved over, to make space for a battered old Rover.

I found myself ethnically profiling the house, examining it for signs of Indian residence (property being another of the defining things about my people). The preoccupation with wealth and the idea of living as an extended family, with grandparents looking after children, and brothers sharing responsibility for parents, seems to have translated into an obsession with buying houses. I remember Ranjit expressing bemusement that I hadn't bought a flat when I was still a student, and my ex may have been just twenty-six, still resident with her parents, but she nevertheless owned a flat in Earls Court which she rented out for profit. However there was nothing obviously Asian about this house. No shoe rack in the porch, no gold door handles. Moreover, it looked like council housing, and I knew no Sikhs who lived in local authority property, or who drove a *Rover*, for that matter. I struggled to imagine Surinder living in it.

This doubt gradually morphed into anxiety. Why had I come? I could hardly suddenly present myself to Surinder as the offspring of the family she had disowned decades earlier, without giving some kind of notice, without having prepared myself for it, and without consulting my mother. Though Ranjit's response to my concern, when I vocalised it, was predictable – 'Leaaaave it, yeah?' It's the thing he says most often. What he meant was: 'Have a smoke.' And while I normally declined the offer, this time, because I didn't know what else to do, because I actually needed to chill out, I took a drag. Then another. And then: *Jesus*. It turns out that either spliff or my metabolism have altered significantly since I last smoked because I suddenly feel like I'm on *crack*, not weed.

Before I know it I'm saying the words 'dude' and 'whoah', I'm asking 'What is this shit?' and he is telling me 'skunk', and I am addressing Ranjit as 'Jay', allowing him to address me as 'A', and the bhangra track on the stereo is making complete sense, even though the singer seems to be talking about how the shawl belonging to his beloved matches the colour of his turban.

'Turn it up, Jay,' I say.

He turns it up.

'What they singing about?'

'It's one of the all-time classics, man.'

'What they singing about?'

He provides a running translation. Apparently, the vocalist is telling us about how he threw some kind of flower at his beloved's cheek, and it left a bruise on it, which spread like black eyeliner, because she is so fair, and the sight of this, in turn, left the black bees speechless, as if a snake, or some kind of reptile, had stung their tongues. To be honest, I struggle to follow the translation, the metaphor is puzzling, I can imagine a snake being stung by a bee, but can't imagine a *bee* being stung by a *snake*, but the beat is mesmerising and I turn it up some more and nod meaningfully, sensing a connection to my culture, feeling like I am watching myself in the third person (if that makes sense), like I am in a silent movie, with sound (if that makes sense), and suddenly, everything, from my father's death, to my mother's predicament, to my floundering relationship with Freya, seems clearer, the answers to all my problems sitting behind the white UPVC front door.

'Hey, Jay, shall we go and say hiii?'

'What?'

'Let's say hiii.'

'To who?'

'The people in the . . .' I momentarily lose my train of thought. 'The house people.'

'Yeah, man,' responds Ranjit. 'Let's go and say hiiiiii. Check them out, innit.'

Getting out of the car and to the front door takes an eternity: the fact that I can't unbuckle my seat belt sparks a giggling fit; the fact that Ranjit leaves the engine running sparks another. The sight of a Phil Collins CD on the passenger seat of the Rover has us both bent over in hilarity for three or maybe four minutes. All the while, every bit of me is tingling and when Ranjit presses the doorbell, and it emits the chimes of Big Ben, time seems to slow down between one bong and the next, and when the door is finally opened by a young man, of about eighteen, sporting a baseball cap, barely making eye contact and grunting 'Yeah?', I experience an intensification in my symptoms, everything feeling dark and yet bright at the same time (if that makes sense), like I am dreaming and yet I know that I am not (if that makes sense), and in that moment it becomes obvious why I am here, why I have been sent, why this was the right thing to do, what has been propelling me on this journey: my loneliness.

You see, if you're Asian, people expect you to have a big family. 'You probably have lots of brothers and sisters,' people say. Or 'I don't have a big family, like you.' But unlike Jay's enormous brood, there has never been more than three of us. My father's family, almost entirely in India, hardly represented at his funeral; my mother's family in Southall, a cold and self-absorbed bunch. Never anyone to play with, measure myself against. No brothers to bear down on bullies, no sisters to tie a rakhri around my wrist in August, no reason to complain afterwards about the colour running from my wrist on to my brand-new white shirt. But now, finally, a cousin, a young brother to call me paji, if not to play with, because actually we might be too old for that, then someone at least to take to the pub, hang out with, and I am imagining taking him out for a drink, introducing him to drink and skunk, wonderful skunk, when I hear Ranjit speaking in an English accent that sounds like it has been lifted from a Merchant Ivory movie, or most probably from a character in a Chuck Norris vehicle.

'Hello, we're from Her Majesty's Revenue and Customs.' He licks a finger and smooths it over his eyebrows. 'I'm Frank, and this is Andy here. Could we speak to James O'Connor Esquire?'

The youth glances at us with the kind of scepticism and disdain that two stoned men with a combined age of more than seventy frankly deserve, takes a few steps backwards and kicks the door behind him in the hallway. 'Oi, fatso! You got visitors.' As he slinks away, I sober up enough to ask Ranjit, 'Frank?' And 'Inland Revenue?' I kick him in the shins. 'Do we look like tax men?' He's in a hoodie and Nike Air Force Ones, while I am in a jumper and jeans and Converse. 'And why would two tax men be visiting on a Sunday evening?'

'Leeeave it, yeah?' he responds, now, for some reason in a Jamaican accent. He sways on the spot. 'It's gonna be aiiight.'

The shock of Ranjit's idiocy, and my cousin's disrespectful tone to his parents, has the effect, if not of sobering me up, then at least providing enough focus so that by the time 'Fatso' appears at the door, round and heavy, completely bald, teeth so yellow that I make a mental note to whiten my own, I make an attempt to take control of the situation.

'Hi,' I say quickly, before Ranjit has a chance to say anything stupid. I glance at him anyway, in part to discourage him from interrupting, in part just to check that I have actually said this word out loud rather than just thought it. Then, taking in Jim's face, with its creases and crevasses, his enormous belly, too big even to laugh off as a pregnancy, I continue, 'We're from the local council.' A pause. 'Yes, we're from the council. Just doing a quick check of who lives in certain properties . . . for reasons of . . . council tax.' My intonation, for no particular reason, rises at the end of my sentence. 'According to our records . . .' I suddenly feel the absence of a pen or notepad in my hands – something, anything, to make me look more official, less of a waster. 'According to our records we've got one . . . James O'Connor, age sixty-three, at this address.'

God knows how much time passes before he speaks, everything has slowed down, but the gap is long enough for me to become suddenly aware of my hands and experience another moment of clarity, albeit a less exhilarating one, about why I am here. I'm here because of Freya. Our relationship is strained, we are drifting apart, but in the good old days when I was still trying to get my mother to like her, the one thing I longed for more than anything else was a successful interracial Sikh couple I could point at and use as an illustration of what was possible. I can see now my excitement at finding my uncle and aunt was in large part about finding a precedent. But the sight of this man has made me doubt how useful an example he would have been.

Eventually, he replies, 'Yes.'

Phew. I am not sure what I felt more relieved by: the fact that he hasn't seen through our lame identity fraud, or the fact that I have actually found my uncle.

'Yes!' I exclaim, before immediately apologising for yelping. 'Sorry. And your wife . . . ?' My heartbeat quickens and I peer into the hallway, hoping, I guess, to see some photographs or other evidence of matrimony.

'What about her?'

'We have her down as aged . . .' I've worked out the dates. '. . . fifty-nine?'

'Fifty-nine?!' He laughs like he has just heard the funniest joke in the world, or been at some of the skunk soaring through my bloodstream. Ranjit starts laughing too, as Jim shouts behind him, 'She will absolutely LOVE to hear that. Michelle! Some blokes out here have a question for you!'

They say that with marijuana you tend to notice things you've never noticed before, that it makes your senses more acute, but in my case the drug seems to be having the opposite effect. Having somehow overlooked the fact that the boy, my 'cousin', doesn't look remotely Indian, I somehow manage to overlook the name 'Michelle', and brace myself to see my aunt walking down the hallway. But the penny finally drops when the woman who appears is in her forties, Chinese, and visibly not my aunt.

Jim – if that's who is, to be honest I am no longer sure – continues, with an arm around his wife, 'These young men have a question for you.' Laughing. 'Go on. Ask her.'

I feel a sudden and overwhelming urge to lie down on the floor and sleep for a very long time. This intensifies when Ranjit turns to me and whispers, 'He's got jungle fever.' And then: 'He's of the Asian persuasion, innit.' But I also know I have to carry on, to find a non-degrading exit or at least a way out that doesn't involve us getting arrested. I find the energy to continue from somewhere. 'We just needed to check your age, madam. For our records.'

'I'm sorry, but who are you with?'

Dammit, Michelle is sober. 'The council.' Suddenly, my mouth feels as if it is full of cotton wool. 'Birmingham Metropolitan Council.'

'You mean Birmingham *City* Council?' Busted. 'Can I see some ID?'

Ranjit, to my mortification, opens his mouth. 'Of course, madam,' he says, now seemingly mimicking a BBC newsreader. 'I'll just get it from the company vehicle.'

There is no way he is going to leave me there alone. 'I'll give you a hand, *Frank*.'

We turn on our heels, breaking into a run, and make the least discreet, least competent getaway in history: the stereo blasting out a thousand watts of bhangra as soon as we get going, the 460bhp engine almost blowing birds out of the trees, a bright yellow car with an orange Khalistan flag flying out the back window and a private number plate identifying us as JAT 14, and turning the wrong way into the cul-de-sac before having to turn past the house again.

I can't, I'm afraid, account for what happened next in great detail. I think I may have taken another drag of another cigarette to calm my nerves. Or perhaps running to the car made the chemicals warping my brain have a deeper effect. But both of us were so stoned that despite travelling in a car with 3D satellite navigation and surround-view and night vision with pedestrian recognition, we got completely lost. I remember getting out of the car at a series of roundabouts, each one looking exactly like the one before – with a sign pointing out the A38 and the M6, and a branch of McDonald's standing temptingly on a corner nearby. There probably isn't anywhere that is particularly good to get lost when you're totally wasted, but Spaghetti Junction must surely be among the worst.

Nevertheless, we somehow managed to make our way into Birmingham city centre, and ended up in a dimly lit bar playing a mixture of hip hop and bhangra, and serving a selection of lethally potent cocktails. I remember Ranjit taking off his wedding ring and ordering champagne at our table. I remember being surrounded by a phalanx of Asian girls, some of them half our age, all of whom seemed to know Ranjit well. And God, if weed has changed since I was a youth, so have Asian women in the Midlands. They were unrecognisable from the ones I recalled from my youth, who would only meet in libraries in case they were seen with a boy.

The first one I talked to asked me what kind of girls I liked, to which I, in avoidance, asked, 'What kind of boys do you like?' She replied, 'Men in glasses,' before, ironically, removing mine and sticking her tongue down my throat. I managed to extricate myself, only to end up in conversation with a friend of hers who stroked the biceps I had developed since taking up weights on Ranjit's advice, wanted to know if I had a girlfriend, and when I said that I had, asked, 'Does she let you fuck her up the arse? Because I would.'

I was, despite my utter inebriation, scandalised. To think that just a few decades ago, these girls' grandmothers or mothers were in the Punjab, and if they so much as exchanged a glance with a member of the opposite sex, let alone made signs at a boy from the balcony of their house, would face being married off into oblivion.

The next thing I remember is being in Ranjit's penthouse flat in the city centre and gawping at the terrible art on his walls: massive Jack Vettriano repro prints hung like installations. The door knobs were gold, the furniture was white, and the table on which he produced two lines of coke, two lines of ketamine and a line of MDMA was made of glass. We snorted one each. I'm not sure who ended up with what, but Ranjit disappeared into a bedroom with one of the three 'friends' he had bought back, another curled up and fell asleep on the sofa, while the third removed her underwear and determinedly undid my jeans.

My remorse, afterwards, was instant, but perhaps not all that deep because after I had taken a shower, to get rid of the smell and the guilt, still buzzing on everything I had smoked and snorted over the course of the evening, the girl who had been asleep joined me in the bathroom and, to use one of Ranjit's favourite expressions, 'put it in her mouth'.

I'm not sure how I got home. Maybe I got a cab back. But the next thing I recall is standing outside the shop, my eyes red, my mouth dry, feeling an urge to listen to Pink Floyd on a loop, and bemoaning the fact that fast food outlets close so early in the West Midlands. At some point I must have recalled I ran a corner shop, as I remember eating a microwaveable burger at the counter – one of the items, along with much of the medication shelf, that my father would stock via the local pound store, buying ten or twenty at a time for a pound each and flogging them for £1.59.

The cheeseburger tasted amazing; it may as well have been something served at The Fat Duck as far as I was concerned. So much so that I put a second into the microwave before I'd finished the first. And then I remember freezing in horror as I heard Mum coming down the stairs. I'm not sure what I was most worried about: Mum seeing that I had eaten beef, her seeing me stoned (she had never even seen me drunk), or picking up on the fact that I had been smoking. In my confusion I grabbed the air freshener Mum kept behind the till and sprayed it all over myself. And then I hid, switching off the light, trying to conceal myself between the chiller and the freezer.

I might have got away with it if the microwave hadn't pinged when she peered in. She switched on the light to find me slumped on the floor against a wall, shielding the remains of my cheeseburger as if protecting a prized haul from bandits.

'What are you doing?' she asked.

A long pause. 'What time is it?' I slurred back.

'Half four.'

Shit. Morning already. 'I'm tying my shoelaces,' I added by way of explanation.

'What's that you're eating?' She sniffed the air.

'A veggie . . . burger,' I lied.

'And what's that on your shirt?'

I looked down and there were patches of red lipstick all down the front. I blinked. 'Just some ketchup.'

The Edwardian dining room, with its crystal mouldings and Boucheresque murals, was designed to dazzle. But Surinder was more taken by details regular diners would have considered banal: tablecloths starched and ironed to cardboard stiffness; people scooping soup from bowls in smooth, outward movements, sipping from the sides of spoons. On the table next to her, a lady was wiping her plate with a piece of bread, which itself was on the end of a fork, while straight opposite, a man was eating a banana with a knife and fork. White people would, it seems, do anything not to touch their food with their hands.

Then there was the menu she had been given to examine while Jim visited the bathroom. She guessed, with her schoolgirl French, that 'carré d'agneau Sarladaise' might be a duck salad of some variety, and that 'apéritifs maison' were the house drinks. But what was the difference between 'les hors d'oeuvres' and 'les entrées'? What on earth was 'croustade de langoustines'? And as for 'tête de veau' − she knew it translated as either 'new head' or 'head of eyes' or 'head of a cow'. But the idea of anyone dining on any of these things made her giggle, just as she had giggled when Jim had proposed dinner with the question, 'Cantonese or Polynesian?'

She had suggested he decide: whatever he wanted was fine with her. In the end he had picked this fashionable French place on the edge of Soho, once apparently the haunt of Whistler, a famous painter whose work she pretended to be familiar with, and staffed by waiters who spoke English in Parisian accents so thick that

157

when one slid towards Surinder as if on wheels and asked if she wanted a drink, she responded, 'I'm sorry, I don't speak French,' before adding, 'Je ne parle pas le français.'

He repeated himself slowly and gravely. 'Non . . . non . . . can I get zee laydee a dreeenk?'

'Oh, I'm sorry.' She blushed and glanced in the direction of the bathroom into which Jim had disappeared. 'I think I will wait for my fiancé.'

The waiter withdrew, walking backwards for his first few steps, bowing slightly, unaware that being able to utter the exotic word 'fiancé', a word with no apparent counterpart in Punjabi, gave Surinder more of a thrill than any of his fine wines would have done.

She took a deep breath and, alone for the first time in London, tried to digest the events that had led her to this table. Jim turning up at school one home time in his car, offering her a lift home. Jim turning up a week later even though he had been firmly rebuffed, suggesting he take her to visit the perfume counter at Beatties. A month later, he was still at it: driving along as she walked home, pleading for a moment or two of her time. She was flattered and touched, but, more than anything else, terrified. She knew of just one Sikh girl who had 'married out', and her family had cut her off completely – when her mother talked of her children, she referred to three, not four children. It was worse than if the daughter had died: it was like she had never been born. The girl herself had been cut off by all her relations and friends; no one would have her around in case she influenced children and others. She was a leper. And she had only married out of her caste. A gora? People had been killed for less.

But Dhanda's request changed everything. The desperados and losers she had to meet on Sunday afternoons were one thing – but that fat creepy old man? It was sickening. Horrifying. And when Jim reappeared and suggested lunch that week, she accepted his invitation, surprising him with her sudden acquiescence. There followed another visit to the cafe. Then a meeting in the Central Library. A kiss on the village green in Tettenhall. An afternoon in the back row of the Odeon when she should have been at school. Then, in quick succession, a tearful confession to Jim about her family's plans; Jim's horror and suggestion that they elope to London; her insistence that she could not elope without getting married first; Jim's assurance that they would marry as soon as they arrived in the south; an engagement ring in the form of an elastic band; her mother's convenient suggestion that she spend the summer in Southall; and then, the journey to London.

On the train, Surinder didn't have time to look out of the window, to watch the cooling towers and gasometers give way to green countryside, any more than Tanvir seemed to have time to wave goodbye. She bolted into the toilet as soon as the train pulled away and began the task of applying make-up, squeezing a pea-sized amount of foundation on to the back of her hand, as she had seen her mother do before weddings, dabbing it all over her face like a cream, applying black eyeliner, flicking it out at the corners.

It was harder than it looked and her concentration kept on being interrupted by passengers knocking on the door, like her sister had kept rapping on the bathroom door the night before, as she had washed her hair with lemon shampoo and rinsed it with water and vinegar. She had brought her mother's sewing scissors along to cut her hair, but in the end she didn't have the nerve, worrying that the results would be worse than what she had, and instead just rearranged it in a manner that her mother would have regarded as vulgar.

She had spent days and nights fretting about the details of her elopement, worrying about the arrangements, about whether Jim would actually turn up on time in Coventry to meet her, and almost having a cardiac arrest when it looked like her mother would not let her get on the train. But in the event she was the one who nearly missed the stop. An Asian man of Tanvir's age, who had kept trying to catch her eye, helped her off the train, and she saw Jim padding anxiously up and down at the other end of the platform. But she didn't dare wave at him until the man had withdrawn back into the carriage. Jim eventually spotted her and ran to greet her – smart in a blue-striped suit, a white cotton shirt, a cotton cravat. He kissed her on the lips, right there, in front of everyone, tasting of strawberries, and a little bit of the beer he had been drinking in the pub as he waited. Surinder stiffening as he did so, keeping her eyes open, scanning the area for spies.

Jim caught her and launched into a version of the speech he had made dozens of times before. He reminded her that she was eighteen now, an adult, and could therefore do what she wanted, that legally speaking her family could not drag her back. She knew he was right, and understood that a reliable friend of his was going to hand over the letter they had written together to her aunt in Euston, that her family would have no reason to call the authorities. But she just couldn't relax, and in Jim's car she slumped down in her seat as low as possible, hoping, like a bank robber, to avoid detection.

However, a few hours later, sitting on a pavement table outside a Soho wine bar, having dropped off her belongings at a luxury hotel in Mayfair, allowing Jim's fingers to linger in her mouth as he fed her French fries, the paranoia began to subside. The anonymity of London, its sheer size, soothed her. In Wolverhampton a white man would never have been able to sit outside with his Indian girlfriend: the National Front would have got to them, if the Sikhs didn't get there first. However, here no one seemed to care. She felt invisible among the crowds of black men 'shooting crap' on the pavement and office workers on the way to work.

There was also the dizzying, paradoxical familiarity of it all. The capital was new to her and she was beginning to realise that her family's references to Southall as 'London' were ludicrous. But she recognised the black taxi cabs and red buses and shops from films and TV shows and magazines, while the plaques on the walls of houses alerted her, reassuringly, to the former residences of Henry James, Mary Shelley and other authors she had read. Then: the startling diversity. Everyone she saw seemed to look different, had their own way of dressing, and the variety of it all made her feel less self-conscious about her unfashionable long hair, her skin colour, her home-made dress.

Nevertheless, Surinder leapt at Jim's suggestion, in Carnaby Street, that they pop into a boutique to look at new clothes. She had planned her elopement primarily in the form of outfits, and had made several dresses for the weekend, under the pretence of producing outfits for Mr Dhanda, telling herself as she sewed fringe and appliqué flowers on to her creations that making your own dresses was better than buying them, because they were truly expressive of your own feelings and taste, and fitted more closely. But when the opportunity came, Jim pushing a tenner into her closed fist, she took it.

He had hung around as she tried things on, a pair of flared trousers, followed by a small rib sweater with short sleeves, proffering opinions and suggesting alternative items. However, his ideas – a bikini, a near-backless, fire-engine red swimsuit – were too much for a girl who had not worn jeans in public before; for a girl, moreover, who knew all too well that this was the season of the floor-length skirt and the midi, which looked best without an inch of leg showing. And when he suggested he leave her to it, while he did some shopping of his own, and they meet up later in the wine bar opposite, she was touched by his consideration.

The truth was that she had given up on Jim endless times. There was, for instance, the moment when Mrs Flanagan had noticed her grades were slipping, had called her in and said, 'I hope I haven't made a mistake with you, young girl.' Then Jim's relentless efforts to get her into bed, even hiring a hotel in Ironbridge one afternoon for the purpose. But now she was beginning to feel the rightness of her decision. All her life she had been trained to put her husband first, and taught the importance of duty. But she had swapped it all for a man who cared about her feelings, who put *her* first.

She met Jim at the wine bar after an hour with a bag containing a pair of peach trousers and some Wrangler jeans. She had also bought a brown and tangerine Madras cotton lace-up dress that she had loved so much that she had packed up her home creation and walked out of the shop in it. Jim, who was on to his second glass of wine, praised her for her choices and raved at how pretty she looked in her new dress. This gushing was constant with Jim. He complimented her almost as much as he touched her, for her eyes and skin, for her thick, luxuriant hair. She appreciated it, though it was odd being admired for the darkness of her skin when aunties normally went on about how fair she was, and she found it difficult to gush in return. Once, sitting in his car in a country lane, he had asked what it was that she liked about him, and all she had managed was 'I like your hair.' He had laughed and said, 'You might as well admire me for my shoes.' Turns out she did actually admire him for his shoes – he had excellent dress sense. But he didn't understand. It was not that she didn't consider him beautiful, or admire him. It was just that the things she loved about him would have sounded silly uttered out loud. His quiet walk, for instance. The way he called her 'Sue'. How, when he got stuck on a word, he would sometimes repeat it, slowing down and prolonging the first sound until he got it out. Besides, she was afflicted by her mother's superstitious notion that by praising something, you curse it by attracting 'nazar', the evil eye. To admire something was to put it at risk.

But sitting there, as he stroked the legs she had spent half an hour shaving, and almost as long cleaning up after to ensure there was no incriminating evidence in the bathroom, this time she was the one who kissed Jim in public, in front of everyone. Something flashed in his eyes, and he suggested they return to the hotel to drop off the shopping, and so he could get changed before dinner. But when they got back, he had other ideas. For months she had resisted him, not letting his tongue explore when they kissed, and pushing his hands away when they ranged too far. But this time she did not fight his kisses, or his right hand when he unclasped her bra. She found herself moaning softly, letting him unlace the front of her dress. But she stopped herself going further when he began to undo his belt.

'Let's wait,' she whispered.

'Why?' he implored.

'I just want to wait.'

'For what?'

She whispered into his ear. 'Until we're married.'

'But we're getting married tomorrow, Sue.'

'Exactly. Just one . . .' A kiss. 'More.' Another kiss. 'Day.'

Jim whined, but acquiesced. He disappeared into the bathroom, and when she next saw him he was wearing his new purchases: a safari suit in beige linen, with short sleeves and a matching belt. They were set off with a silk scarf and a smart set of black sunglasses. She cooed. And she was impressed all over again when she saw him returning from the restaurant bathroom, still wearing them. She was fortunate, she told herself, to be with someone like Jim. He had said the same about her when they were walking down the street. And maybe, she thought, this was the secret of a good marriage: both people feeling like they were the lucky one.

There was a jolt of electricity in her arm as Jim sat next to her. He ordered a gin and tonic and asked Surinder if this was her first French meal. She admitted it was, omitting to mention that it was her first ever restaurant meal, the first time she had come across warmed plates, the first time she had seen people eating mussels, the first time she had worn make-up in public. He unfolded his napkin and placed it across his lap, and Surinder copied him.

'Decided what you fancy?'

'I'm not sure I understand the menu,' she confessed, coyly. 'Could you order for me?'

'Let me have a look.' He removed his sunglasses, placed them on the table, and squinted at the text. 'Maybe you fancy the snails? Or perhaps the deep-fried frogs' legs?'

Surinder looked horrified. 'Just teasing.' He squeezed her thigh. 'I'll get you something simple. A classic.' He returned to the menu and continued, as if to himself, 'Some people say the food is as good in London as in Paris now. But I'm not so sure.'

'Oh. Have you been to Paris?'

'Bien sur. Places like Lasserre, where a dinner might cost £6 or £7 a head, still has no match in London in terms of quality. But in the intermediate £4 range, standards in London have improved.'

She was, in part, impressed, being reminded of a line from *Tess of the d'Urbervilles* that had appeared in an exam question the day before: 'My life looks as if it had been wasted for want of chances! When I see what you know, what you have read, and seen, and thought, I feel what a nothing I am!' But at the same time she was stunned at the thought of anyone spending so much on one meal. In Wolverhampton, there were large families who spent less than £4 on their weekly groceries.

'Don't worry,' interjected Jim. 'I'll be earning that in an hour now that I'm in London.'

He stroked her forearm, told her for the fifth or sixth time that evening that she was the prettiest girl in the room, remarked, 'The truth is, you can't go wrong in a French restaurant if you start with charcuterie and finish with cheese,' and then at a speed which made Surinder feel dizzy, clicked his fingers, pointed out a few things on the menu to the waiter, ordered a bottle of wine, asked to be moved to a table with a better view, and, as they were seated elsewhere, joked that the waiter's accent was so French that he probably came from Guildford.

Surinder laughed, another lump of her anxiety having been chipped away, and sitting on what was a platform overlooking the whole restaurant she was overcome by a feeling of modernity. Here they were, an Irish man and an Indian woman, dining in a French restaurant in London, dressed in fashions that would be acceptable in Monte Carlo or New York. It was the start of a brand-new decade which would see the beginning of communication by extrasensory perception, the development of tomatoes with no pips, and her free to devour every opportunity that came her way. And she got an opportunity to do so when the food and drink arrived.

Her first ever gulp of red wine did not go down well: it tasted of cough medicine. She didn't know how Jim could stomach so much of it. But the platter of cured meats was a delight. Nervous apprehension had suppressed her appetite for days, if not weeks. That morning she had not even managed a quarter of the parontha her mother had cooked, leading to an inevitable lecture on how she wasn't to waste food at her aunt's house in Southall. But she motored through the sausages and salt pork ham, reminding herself to hold the knife and fork the correct way round. Soon she was out-eating Jim, dispensing with every last crumb on the platter before washing it down with another, more successful swig of wine. 'That was delicious,' she remarked with satisfied finality.

'But there's more to come!'

'Oh.' She blushed, gathering she had made yet another faux pas.

'The *main* course!' Jim squeezed her arm and drained his glass of wine. 'Clue's in the name! Don't worry. Portions are never that large here. And I ain't got you snails.'

A platter of snails might not actually have been as daunting as what did turn up: steak. Greyish on the outside and red in the middle, with a sliver of vegetables on the side. There was no rational reason why a slice of beef should have felt like such a challenge. In the preceding twenty-four hours Surinder had stolen jewellery from her parents, sampled booze, tried on a bikini for Jim's amusement, kissed a white man in public and walked around the streets of London with her bare legs showing. Besides, while there were strict Sikhs who avoided all meat, there were also some very serious bearded, turbanned sword-wielding Sikhs who freely partook of all kinds of flesh, including beef, the theological position being ambiguous.

Still, the dish felt like the biggest obstacle she had faced that day. Not least, there was the practical challenge of consuming the meat. How are you meant to eat steak? Should you cut it in half before proceeding to devour each half? Or should you go from the end, progressing through the steak until you reach the core? Also, was it acceptable to ask for ketchup? Or would that be the beef equivalent of putting salt and pepper over your food before you had even tried it, a faux pas she had once made with him at lunch in the Midlands. In the end, she made a timid compromise, sprinkling salt on one end of the slab of meat and taking a tiny bite. She swallowed it whole. And managed to get the next bit down with it barely touching her teeth or tongue. By the third bite she was masticating fully, albeit joylessly.

'This is fabulous,' said Jim, speaking with his mouth half full, hacking at his fish course. 'How's the steak?'

Surinder struggled to swallow.

'Oh G-God, you don't eat beef, do you? I completely forgot. Are you all right? Shall I get something else?' He raised his hand as if about to beckon a waiter. Surinder patted it down.

'Don't worry,' she said, coughing. 'It's fine.'

'You sure?'

'Seriously. It tastes . . . good.'

'Really?' Jim leaned over to pour himself another drink. The waiter, seeing him do so, rushed to intervene. 'Then again, it's not, strictly speaking, the first time you have had beef.' A mouthful of booze. 'You know that pâté you just had?'

For some reason, the realisation that she had inadvertently eaten beef made her feel more ill than the beef she was actually eating. She put down her cutlery and risked another sip of wine, one unfamiliar taste concealing another. Meanwhile, Jim gestured at the view they enjoyed of the restaurant. 'So then, my love, have you spotted any famous faces? This place is meant to be *packed* with them.'

Surinder sat up and peered across the restaurant. It consisted of two large interconnected rooms. The one they were sitting in was dominated by a zinc bar, at which there were standing a line of well-dressed young women, in the company of a middle-aged man with an ostentatious moustache, all of them laughing along at some remark he had just made. Next to them, a small dancefloor, on the edge of which a three-piece band were swaying along happily to jazz. No sign of any celebrities.

Jim continued. 'Do you know who those women are at the bar?' He tapped the side of his long thin nose. 'Hookers.' He whispered into Surinder's ear. 'Prostitutes. You don't see that many on the pavements nowadays since the law was changed; girls have gone indoors, out of the rain. They call themselves hostesses. Not all of them take men back home, but most will if the payment offered is high enough.'

Surinder stiffened as Jim continued, regaling her with some of the oldest tricks of the oldest of trades. Leaving aside the fact that she was not used to talking during meals, having been brought up to believe that conversation was disrespectful to the food, Jim's predilection for such talk had been one of her reservations about him. She hadn't liked it when he had pointed out that the Blue Ball on the corner of Piper's Row in Wolverhampton was used as a base for ladies of the night. She had bristled when, walking through Soho that afternoon, he had observed that some of the prostitutes working there were as old as seventy-five. She knew he considered her prudish and innocent, that he saw himself as a man of the world, and this was just one of his ways of educating her. But there were things she just didn't want to know.

'Don't believe me?'

'Jim, I just don't want to talk about it.' She offset the sternness of her tone by stroking the back of his neck, but Jim took this as encouragement.

'Any doubt whether a girl does or does not can usually be settled with a pound note slipped to a waiter or a barman. They usually take a cut of the full sum. Look. I'll show you.'

Before Surinder had a chance to stop him, Jim was shouting across the room for the attention of the waiter, slipping a pound note into his jacket pocket. It was at this point Surinder realised he had already polished off their bottle of wine, on top of all the drink he had knocked back during the day. The fear that he might be drunk grew when the waiter removed the pound note from his pocket and, before striding off, thrust it into Jim's wine glass.

Jim laughed and shrugged. 'Turns out it's the owner. That's his wife and friends. Her birthday apparently.' He licked his knife and then raised his empty glass at the revellers. 'Can't win them all, eh?' He stroked Surinder's inner thigh. 'Anyway, got room for cheese? The cheeseboard is as good as it gets in London, though it is wasted, I tell you, on English palates. But maybe the lady fancies a dance first?'

Surinder really didn't want to dance. But Jim stood up, bellowed an order for more drinks and she followed him, timidly, on to the dancefloor, where the feeling of being watched, of wanting to shrink away, returned. To her mortification, Jim broke into some dramatic Northern Soul moves. She stood by, doing an embarrassed version of the gidda she did at weddings, while an elderly white couple shuffled a foxtrot next to them and the bassist in the band winked at her lasciviously. Mercifully, Jim suggested returning to the table at the end of the song.

'The drinks have come,' he slurred, sweating through his new shirt, stumbling back to their table.

The drinks hadn't come. Nor the cheese. Instead, on the table, a small tin plate with a bill placed on it. Jim pointed out the mistake to a passing waiter, but before they or any other customers realised what was happening, before anyone had a chance to object or bemoan the declining standards of Soho, the young couple were being thrown out of the restaurant, the entire manoeuvre accomplished with such elegance and grace that watching the scene unfold you would have thought they were being taken upstairs for a drink with the proprietor or a tour of the kitchen.

Outside, Surinder felt sick and disorientated, as if she had just had a near miss on the motorway. She leant against a lamppost, and as her eyes slowly became accustomed to the dark, she made out a nearby doorway marked out with the word 'model', and a man, at the end of the street, blowing a perfect smoke ring into the air. The streets were unrecognisable from a few hours earlier, transformed by a rain shower and the descending night. Jim had been pushed to the ground by a doorman. He got up and started pummelling the rear door with his fists.

'Did you s-s-see that?' he spluttered, covered in a number of scratches and cuts which couldn't really be explained by the neatness of what had just happened. For some reason, there was even a grass stain on his shirt. 'They took £10 out of my pocket. And no change! The fucking fuckers have robbed me.' He switched to kicking the door with his snakeskin loafers. 'My sunglasses are still on the table. They have nicked my fucking sunglasses.'

Surinder felt cold on her bare arms. The rear of the restaurant bore no resemblance to the grand front entrance, backing as it did upon a street so narrow that it was almost an alleyway. It was lined with bins, and she could make out a solitary newspaper seller nearby, who, in a cubicle about five square feet, had on display a panoply of international publications – *Nuit et Jour*, *Il Popolo d'Italia* – she had never seen in her shop.

The thought of home provoked her nausea and revived the fear she had struggled to repress for weeks, of being caught by her family, having her face blackened and being dragged along Victoria Road by her hair. But then, something in her – pride, an instinct to survive – switched on, and she repressed the thought. Whatever happened, she decided that she would never, could never, return.

'Calm down, Jim,' she found herself saying, in a tone she had not used with him or anyone else before. 'Destroying your new shoes isn't going to help.'

Jim paused, momentarily taken aback. He continued to appear perplexed as Surinder took her turn to embark upon a lecture. She told him that she would call the restaurant from the hotel and tell them they had lost some property and collect it in the morning. He should remember what he had told her earlier: that he would soon be earning enough to purchase endless pairs of sunglasses. In the meantime, they should go back to the hotel, get some rest. Tomorrow was a big day, their wedding day, and he had clearly had too much to drink.

Surinder stood stock-still. For a moment or two, as he swayed on the spot, it seemed as if Jim might take her advice. But then he stepped back, pushed Surinder away and said, 'Do you know how much those sunglasses cost?' He wiped his nose with the back of his jacket sleeve and gave a two-fingered salute to a curious passer-by. 'You can go back to the f-fucking hotel.' Steadying himself, he added, 'As for the wedding, there isn't going to be one, you silly bitch.'

And with that he shot off, zigzagging down the alleyway, ping-ponging along the pavement, as if he were walking through a meteorite shower that only he could see, staggering and tripping along the way.

Alone in the dark, Surinder felt as if she were falling down the deepest and darkest of wells. She threw up, wine and beef coming up in waves, the booze staining the pavement like blood. Slumped on the floor, she half remembered another line from that Hardy book. It went something like: 'It was from her lips that came the murmur of unspeakable despair'. She had been confused by it when she had read it, not being able to comprehend how a sound could be 'unspeakable'. But now she understood. She had grown up, as the result of melodramatic Hindi movies and hysterical funeral rituals, believing that desolation was raucous. But it turned out you could actually lose yourself quite silently, as if it were nothing.

I know some people so dread the agony of a break-up that they will do anything to avoid it, up to and including spending the rest of their days with someone they don't love or, in some cases, don't even like. But not me. In fact, I would say I have a *talent* for splitting up, the agony of the process being almost always outweighed, in my experience, by the exhilaration of freedom and the titillation of sexual possibility. And for me, before Freya at least, it really was a process, in that it almost always took place after a certain amount of time (usually three months), and almost always at the same place (Pizza Express).

Friends have in the past described the choice of venue as callous, but the fact is that there is no such thing as a *good* place to end a relationship. If you took someone to Le Gavroche to dump them, you'd be accused of cruelty for choosing somewhere so nice to do something so nasty. Let's face it, you're never going to be the good guy. So you may as well go somewhere cheap. Though Pizza Express has advantages besides economy. Quick, attentive service, useful for when the shit hits the fan. A certain guaranteed level of busyness, which lowers the risk of a scene. The name – 'Ex-press' – acting as a subconscious primer for the task at hand. Also, there is always at least one diner who is already eating alone and crying, so no one is going to stick out.

And this is why, the weekend after that night out in Birmingham with Ranjit, a few days after sitting in a STD clinic, trying to avoid eye contact with other patients in the waiting room, dying of shame when the doctor called out my name in full, I tried to google a branch of Pizza Express in Wolverhampton. Though I should have guessed that the woman who had finally broken my pattern of three-month relationships would also play havoc with these rituals of termination. Everything went wrong.

There turns out to be no branch of Pizza Express in my home town, so we ended up in Pizza Hut in a retail park on the outskirts of the city. And it turns out Pizza Hut is good for nothing, not even pizza. The Fanta that I ordered tasted like booze, while Freya's booze tasted like Fanta. The service was lethargic and hostile. My usual restaurant trick of trying to guess what Freya might order (I would basically point out the thing I least wanted on the menu) failed because *everything on the menu looked like the thing I least wanted to eat*. Also, Freya looked so lovely, was so cheerful, lunging for a French kiss underneath a sign at the salad counter announcing 'Please use tongues', that when it came to the crunch, I floundered.

Apparently, it's not unusual for adulterers to be afflicted by contradictory feelings. Straying can paradoxically make you appreciate what you have at home. But for me, these conventional paradoxes were intermingled with a maelstrom of other contradictions. I felt guilty, but at the same time I couldn't help feeling my actions were a symptom of a deeper relationship malaise for which Freya bore some responsibility. I wanted to confess and come clean, but at the same time I couldn't see the point. (It was not like I had been in touch with the girls since. Or even Ranjit, for that matter.) The desire to leave the shop and return to my life in London was more intense than ever, and had become even more so after a bunch of kids ran into the shop, stole £200 worth of goods in a raid, and the police didn't come to take a statement for almost a whole week afterwards. But at the same time I was less sure than ever how to get Mum out of the store. I missed Freya, looked forward to seeing her, but at the same time our weekly meetings were increasingly awkward and we were bickering, with Freya complaining endlessly that I 'never talked'. I was grateful that she had stuck with me, but at the same time the old anxieties about our cultural incompatibility were still there. It was all utterly paralysing.

In the end, as we waited for our food, I went to the bathroom to give myself a pep talk. I stood before the red basins, looked into the red-framed mirror and, making eye contact with myself, went through a speech I had mentally run through tens of times before.

It's time to call time on things. The problem, ultimately, is that she is white and I am brown and while I used to think our love could bridge the racial divide, I'm not sure any more. She fell in love with Arjan the metropolitan graphic designer, but I am now Arjan the provincial shopkeeper, and while she clearly expects to get her old boyfriend back, I don't think I can separate the latter from the former. Moreover, I don't want to separate the latter from the former. I used to think race didn't matter, but my father's death has made me realise that I need to maintain my link to my past, that I need a narrative connection between who I am and who I was. I used to think that Asian men who dated English girls and then went on to marry Asian women were cowards, men who didn't have the courage of their convictions, who caved under social pressure and emotional blackmail, but now I can see that they usually give in because it is impossible. Because, no matter how many books she reads, she will never really understand what it means to be Asian. She won't understand the intense sense of duty and responsibility I feel towards my mum. She won't ever have the experience of someone despising her for her colour. Conversely, she will never know the pleasure of being alone in a room full of white people and for a stranger to come up and make you feel instantly at ease with just one word – 'Kiddha?' – or have the simultaneously infuriating and comforting experience of a car hire firm calling to say they have discovered several Tupperware boxes of curry, which your mother has squirrelled away for you despite your insistence that you

*don't need to take any food back to London. And what about our
unborn children? If we have kids, what will they be like? If they
come out white, like interracial children do sometimes, I will walk
around the park with strangers thinking I have kidnapped them. If
they look like me, then they will have the burden of appearing Indian,
but without actually being so. Because let's face it, when it comes to
marriage, one family always wins, and it is obviously going to be her
family. They have the numbers and the cash, and my children will
grow up white, if they ever see my mother they will not be able to
communicate with her, if anyone ever gives them racial grief, they
will not be able to make sense of it, their dislocation reflected in a
grandfather who, on some level, resents them for being half-breeds.
And while she and I can put up with her old man's bigotry now,
apologise for it even, I am pretty sure that I won't stand for it when
it comes to a child.*

The speech went on. And would have gone on even longer had
a Pizza Hut worker not emerged from the toilet cubicles he had
been cleaning. He had heard me muttering. We exchanged an
awkward glance in the mirror and I pretended my hands needed
washing. As I did so, I imagined Freya's reaction. She would cry,
of course. Maybe ask if there was someone else. But I would stick
to my guns. Not mention the girls. Move on. Come on, I told
myself. Let's do it.

However, this sense of resolution evaporated as soon as I
returned to our table. When the food arrived – a 'Shrimply
Delicious' pizza which looked neither shrimpy nor delicious, and
Freya's 'Virtuous Veg' option, which, being covered in a layer of
grease, really didn't look very virtuous at all – we both laughed.
Freya began eating anyway, and I was reminded of another thing
I loved about her – unlike so many of my previous girlfriends,
she was not funny about food, forever fasting on a juice diet, her
appetite an echo of her lust for life. And then, out of nowhere,
she said, 'I've got something to tell you.'

My heart skipped a beat, and I began perspiring. Out of nowhere, an alternative speech popped into my mind, something about the mind-bending, character-crushing nature of drugs and diminished responsibility. *Have you tried skunk lately? Ketamine is a horse tranquiliser, for God's sake!* But I would not need to use it. Freya put her hand on my arm and announced, in an apologetic tone, 'I've found your aunt.' I succumbed to a coughing fit. 'Are you cross?'

I wasn't cross. Just surprised. And relieved. And disappointed. And, as often seemed to be the case lately, bewildered. The fact was that I had barely even thought about my aunt since *that* night. Except to accept that my expectations of family reunions were unrealistic, being, as they were, based almost entirely on denouements in Disney movies, scenes from Shakespearean comedies and episodes of *Surprise, Surprise*, the TV show in which Cilla Black reunited tearful, invariably cheerful members of the public with long-lost loved ones, often in the chirpy presence of Bob Carolgees, famous for his ventriloquist act with Spit the Dog.

Seeing Jim, if it was Jim, and I didn't really know or really care any more, made me realise that if you are the one doing the searching, the long-lost relative may not be the person you expect or want them to be. Also, if you are the one who has become estranged from your family, you may not want to be found. And the plain fact that Surinder Bains had done such a good job of disappearing suggested that she did not want to be.

However, maybe because Freya was more thorough than me, was not assisted by a maniacal skunk-addled Punjabi, she had found her. Though her key breakthrough was perhaps even less cinematic than mine had been with Jim. Apparently she had typed the words 'Surinder Bains' into an internet search engine, some kind of logarithm prompted the search engine to ask 'Did you mean Sue Baines?', and she was directed to an article in a regional trade magazine. She opened her handbag and handed it over. 'I know you didn't ask, but I just couldn't help myself.'

The Valley Country Hotel, which aims to be Surrey's number-one four-star hotel, has appointed Sue Baines as General Manager. Her appointment to the 132-bedroom hotel that boasts one of the region's largest conference facilities reflects the hotel's determination to firmly position itself as the number-one choice for leisure and conference guests.

Baines, who previously ran The Orchard in Rye, and assumes responsibility for over 80 staff and conferencing space for up to 387 delegates, said of her appointment: 'The Valley Country Hotel is a hidden gem that has established a great reputation for service. During the last two years the hotel has renovated all its guest rooms and pavilion. I want to build on that. We can definitely improve when it comes to corporate bookings and weddings.'

To be frank, this small article wouldn't have detained me for a second. I saw my hypothetical aunt, even after reading it, in terms of my mother, and could no more imagine her as a high-flying businesswoman than I could imagine my mother at a drum-and-bass gig. But Freya was nothing if not meticulous in her research. She had looked up the electoral register for the hotel in Rye and, sure enough, found that one of the permanent residents was one 'Surinder Bains'.

I could tell she was excited from the sheer amount of stationery she had invested in the search: there were highlighted photocopies, the relevant sections emphasised with arrows on Post-it notes. I could vaguely recall once feeling such excitement myself, but was disorientated by the direction lunch had taken. I didn't know what to say. Then, from among her documents, Freya produced a printout from the hotel website, advertising a £60-a-head five-course Christmas lunch. It announced: 'Leave the cooking to us this Christmas and enjoy world-class food and service with Christmas Day lunch at the Valley Country Hotel.'

'Shall we go?' she asked.

Christmas? I hadn't thought that far. Needless to say, when I did, I had mixed feelings about the idea. On the one hand, neither my mum nor I were going to feel particularly celebratory, with Dad gone, and with Christmas being when Freya and I had once planned to wed. But on the other hand, we were supposed to have been split up by then. Could I walk around with the guilt another whole month? Pretend that night in Birmingham had never happened? I had no idea.

'You don't want to spend Christmas with your family?' I asked.

'What, with my father complaining about the food he doesn't help with and my brother molesting his teenage girlfriend?'

'Ha.' I stared at my pizza. What would we be like in a month's time? 'We would just be going to look, right? A recce?'

'Just to look.'

'We don't have to talk to her, even if she is there?'

'Absolutely not. Doubt she will be there anyway. I mean, who works on Christmas Day?'

My father didn't work on Christmas Day. And he would bang on all year about how much he was looking forward to the one time of year the shop was closed. 'Can't wait until Crimbo,' he would remark whenever anything went wrong, or if he felt particularly exhausted. But on the day itself, he would invariably be up at 4.30 a.m. as usual, and if someone rang on the door to ask for emergency supplies, he wouldn't be able to resist serving them. Long hours, seven days a week, were the reason my grandfather, my father and thousands like them did well. My father disliked even leaving the shop to go to the loo, arguing that people always expected to be greeted with a smiling face if they popped in for some milk, emphasising how small shops relied on repeat trade. But Christmas highlighted the fact that all-day shopkeeping had made him dysfunctional.

It also revealed his fundamental lack of frivolity. I remember once coming home from infant school bearing a present given to me by 'Father Christmas', which prompted my actual father to take me to his study and present me with the *Encyclopaedia Britannica* entry for Santa, and an accompanying lecture. My mother, who still talks of 'Christmas Father', attempted to provide comfort, but she has never really been a ray of festive cheer either. And, true to form, she announced, before I had to make any excuse, that she planned to spend the whole day at the temple.

The weekend was more fun than most of our Midlands assignations. Freya came up to help in the shop on Christmas Eve, which turned out to be unexpectedly entertaining given the surprising number of people who came in to buy emergency presents. My mum was uncharacteristically pleasant to Freya. And we dropped her off at the temple before heading to Surrey at ten on Christmas Day morning, spending the journey working out what signal I would employ if I wanted to leave, and wondering out loud what the lunch might be like.

It was our first Christmas Day away from home for both of us and we decided it would most likely be a small affair, that the revellers would include a spattering of French people (apparently, in France the big day for celebrating Christmas isn't the 25th but the 24th) and professionals who had to work alone away from home on Christmas Day (radio DJs, BBC continuity announcers, tow-truck drivers, priests, etc.). I think the image, for me at least, was built around a Jamie Oliver Christmas cookery special. But as we stood in the middle of the 'intimate pre-lunch bucks fizz reception', in the 'country-house hotel', we realised we were wrong.

For a start, it was hardly intimate: there must have been more than a hundred people in the overheated room, ranging from one to a hundred years in age. A peek through the net curtains covering the floor-to-ceiling glass doors revealed no sign of actual 'country' or 'valley'. The room itself felt more civic centre than country-house hotel, it being a large 1980s brick extension attached to a Georgian mansion. As for the bucks fizz, well, it was one part flat supermarket champagne to three parts Del Monte fruit juice, served in a plastic flute by a waitress who didn't seem to realise that she could make life a lot easier for herself by pouring champagne down the side of the glass, rather than straight into it.

'I feel like I have gatecrashed a registry wedding,' whispered Freya under her breath.

'I feel like I have gatecrashed a funeral,' I replied.

'An unfriendly funeral. Where everyone has fallen out over the will.'

'Anyway, happy Christmas.' I sipped the bucks fizz, attempted to chink my flute against hers, and laughed when the plastic made no sound.

'Happy Christmas,' said Freya, leaning over for a kiss. 'The man from Del Monte say "yes".'

Several young children ran around us, playing with new toys, presumably presents, and highlighting another thing we had been wrong about: the preponderance of solo diners. Most people had come in large family groups. The only two couples were Freya and I, and an elderly couple, who looked like they had a combined age of more than 200. She was in a wheelchair and plugged in via tubes to canisters of what was presumably oxygen. He was pushing her along, but seemed barely capable of the task, given his own frailty.

'Bit, um, white, isn't it?' said Freya, who had tied her hair into two bunches with tinsel for the occasion.

'A day in Wolverhampton and you develop racial Tourette's,' I said, unable to resist making the point.

She conceded. 'Touché.'

Like so many provincial hotels out of season, the Valley Country Hotel seemed to be staffed entirely by schoolgirls, presumably from a nearby town, who for the occasion were dressed in short skirts trimmed with tinsel and fur. One of them came up to us with a tray piled high with Christmas crackers. We pulled at the ends of one and the contents – a plastic comb, a joke – spilled on to the brown carpet. Freya read out the joke.

'What would happen if cows could fly?'

'Oh God, I hate jokes.'

'That is so you – "I hate jokes".'

'What?'

'Cheer up, for God's sake.'

My essential joylessness was one of her most frequent complaints – next to disapproval at the weightlifting, which had taken me up a jacket size. I mounted a defence. 'It's the difference between, say, seeing something acted out badly at the theatre and someone describing something amusing they saw in the street. I just prefer natural wit.'

'As I was saying,' continued Freya, who liked the theatre. 'What would happen if cows could fly?'

'Let me guess. They would fly to the Milky Way?'

'No. Actually, you would get a pat on the head.'

I groaned, she pulled a face, and in the pause that followed we noticed the elderly couple struggling with their cracker. They had managed to get hold of their respective ends, but she didn't have the strength to hold on to hers. In the end he pulled both ends himself, and when another comb and joke fell on to the floor, Freya retrieved it and read out the joke for the benefit of the couple.

'What do you call a bunch of ducks in a box?'

'Um.' Like me, he seemed to approach Christmas cracker jokes like crossword puzzles. 'A box of quackers?'

'Yes! How did you know that?'

'I hate jokes,' he laughed.

'See,' I interjected at Freya. 'Not just me.'

We got chatting. It turned out the couple had lived in a village near the hotel their whole lives, though it was more or less a town now. He was a retired engineer and they had been coming here for decades, from back when the main house had belonged to a local aristocrat who used to open it up once a year for a ball. Two of their three children had got married here, and they had spent eight of their last Christmas Days at the hotel.

'It's hard to cook at my age,' said the wife. To be honest, it seemed hard at her age for her even to speak, and to breathe. 'And we've been coming here for ever. Must be nearly seventy years!'

'That's amazing,' said Freya. 'Congratulations. And we hear the hotel is under new management.'

'Oh, yes, she's a lovely lady. Mrs Barnes.'

'I thought it was Banares,' her husband corrected. 'Glamorous lady. From Spain, I believe.'

I laughed to myself. I had recently watched an internet video entitled 'Shit Punjabi Girls Say' where one of the lines, along with 'Mum, I'm at the library' had been, 'People sometimes think I'm Spanish.'

And then — whoah — there she was.

I think some Asians will understand when I say I sensed my aunt was in the room before I even looked up. We have an almost supernatural ability to seek each other out, this ethnic version of Gaydar enabling us to sense where all the Asians are in a particular crowd in an instant, and allowing us to work out where a person may be from, how rich they are, their caste, religion and marital status, from the briefest glance. This was one of the reasons I had decided that my aunt should be left alone. If she had managed to disappear despite this, then she must have *really* wanted to disappear.

When I dared risk a more direct glance, what I saw left me breathless. It was not just that my aunt looked like my mum, though she did, in her eyes, nose, chin and lips. But she resembled my mother if my mother had been Photoshopped. There was no sign of grey in her short hair, whereas my mother's hair was almost completely grey and had never been cut. Meanwhile, her skin was clear, her teeth looked whitened, she didn't need spectacles, and she was thin, ridiculously thin. From the angle I was looking at her, you would have thought she was in her late forties. And her complexion was such that, yes, she might have been Latin.

Freya, who had spotted that I had spotted her, seemed no less stunned. She nodded along as Mary and Harry continued talking, but her eyes were fixed on Surinder, whose clothes also couldn't have been more different from my mother's pastel-coloured salwar kameezes. She was wearing a blue suit, a tight white blouse with a certain amount of cleavage showing, and a pencil skirt revealing calves that suggested hours of gym work. When Freya finally extracted herself and managed to speak, she said, 'She's had work done.'

'Maybe.' I remembered something Ranjit had said about the appeal of Asian women. 'Black don't crack, innit.' Surinder appeared to be going over some kind of list with a male colleague who couldn't have been over twenty, but who nevertheless seemed ancient compared to the remainder of the staff.

At this point, the room began to spin. Literally. The sliding partition that divided us from the main dining room was pushed away, maybe at Surinder's instigation, and a dining room was suddenly revealed, with rows and circles of tables marked out with signs declaring 'CLARKE' and 'MURRAY'. From where I was standing I spotted a small table in the middle of the grand arrangement marked 'BANGA', and in the background I could hear Mud playing 'Lonely This Christmas'. My aunt hurried past us, not making even momentary eye contact as she did so. The last time I had wanted to eat this little, we had been in Pizza Hut.

'Think I might have left the van unlocked,' I said, employing the exit signal we had agreed upon.

'Can't imagine anyone breaking into it here,' replied Freya in a monotone.

'No.' I wobbled my reindeer antlers in her direction. 'I mean, I might, you know, *have left the van unlocked.*'

'Oh, right. You sure?'

'*Yes.*'

A squeeze of the hand. 'Don't you think we should have a chat?'

'Who's to say she wants to talk to us?'

'But . . . we have come all this way.'

'I thought we had an agreement.'

'I know, I know, but . . .' Her big brown eyes. 'It's Christmas Day. Aren't you curious?'

I was curious, but also terrified. I needed, to use some of the phrases Freya's self-help authors would have used, to 'withdraw' and 'process'. I felt tense. And I would have gone right then if Freya hadn't been there, if the alternative wasn't taking her for a Christmas lunch at a motorway branch of McDonald's.

'Look,' offered Freya. 'How about this. We stay for a couple of courses, make an attempt to talk to her, we don't have to say who we are, just congratulate her on her hotel, on the meal or something, and then we go home. At least that way, when you write to her, she knows who you are.'

I sighed. '*If* I write to her.'

'Yes, *if*.'

'OK. But promise me it won't go beyond that.'

'Promise.' I grabbed her champagne flute and emptied its anaemic contents into my mouth. 'At least we know we won't be getting scurvy soon.'

The fact of the hotel's refurbishment was most evident in the reception area, though the sophistication of the overall effect of the spotlights and artfully discarded copies of *Country Life* was rather undermined by a brass plaque above the main desk. It celebrated the opening of the extension by a married government minister who subsequently, if memory serves, had to resign for performing a sexual act in public with a rent boy.

Freya approached the teenager manning the desk. 'Hello.' A bright smile. 'We're here for the Christmas lunch. Which was absolutely lovely, by the way.' A lie. 'I was wondering if we could have a quick word with the manager.'

The receptionist looked startled. Clearly, having to converse with customers was not something she had bargained for that afternoon. 'I'm afraid the manageress is not available today,' she blushed. 'It's Christmas Day.'

Freya continued. 'Oh, we thought we saw her earlier.' She leant against me. 'We're not looking to complain. It's just that my boyfriend . . .' An arm through mine. '. . . just proposed to me. And we were wondering if we could ask the manager about the possibility of booking our wedding reception.'

I could have been sick all over the brand-new cream rug we were standing on. What the fuck did she think she was doing? This wasn't a game. But it turned out that Freya simply knew what would work.

'Congratulations,' simpered the girl behind the desk. 'I'll just see if the manageress is available.'

I began remonstrating to Freya as soon as she left, but before I managed to articulate a fraction of my fury, there was my aunt, striding towards us, bearing a bottle of champagne and a teddy bear with the hotel's name emblazoned upon it. Maybe those *Surprise, Surprise* fantasies weren't so unrealistic after all.

'What wonderful news.' She spoke English without a hint of an Indian or Wolverhampton accent. 'A Christmas engagement. Just *wonderful*.'

'Thank you,' said Freya, flushing, I hoped, at least a little out of embarrassment. 'And would the hotel be available in the summer?'

'Absolutely! I hear you're here for lunch. But I would love to arrange a tour of our new wedding pavilion before you go.'

'Oh, that's OK. We just wanted to say hello. Make contact. And maybe leave our details?'

'Let me take a note.'

The child receptionist handed over a stack of Post-it notes.

'My name is Freya Tunstall. And my fiancé's name – his name is Arjan Banga. That's A.R.J.A.N. and Banga, as in the son of Tanvir Singh Banga. And Kamaljit Kaur Bains.'

Freya said this very quickly, and if there was a hint of recognition on Surinder's face, I didn't spot it. 'I see,' she said after writing down the name in full. 'Well, if you have a minute or two, maybe you had better come and talk to me about your *wedding* in my office.'

Walking into the manager's office was like stepping off a film set and into the parking lot which housed it. The budget for the refurbishment clearly hadn't extended this far. Wires webbed the walls and the floor. Behind her desk you could see that someone had made a desultory attempt to clear up a spillage but given up halfway through and left a pile of napkins on a shelf. And it was only after Surinder had apologised for the untidiness – 'I'm of the view that one trip to clean ten coffee cups is much more efficient than ten trips to clean one' – and shouted 'Jessie!' that we noticed a small dog among the detritus.

Freya immediately grabbed the beast, a small black-and-tan Cavalier King Charles spaniel, and began cooing over him. Her inability to walk past a cat or dog without petting them was something I usually found charming, but at this moment it added to my simmering resentment, for it meant the awkwardness of the explanation fell to me. This was typical of Freya, I seethed: starting something and then leaving me to pick up the pieces.

'We were actually supposed to get married this week,' I mumbled. 'We were engaged.' It was too complicated. 'I'm sorry for surprising you like this, it probably wasn't what you were expecting on Christmas Day.'

Surinder didn't respond. Instead she did something I could never imagine my mother doing. She took off her jacket, opened the door behind her desk, which revealed a small roof terrace, pulled out an ashtray from her desk drawer, a packet of cigarettes from her handbag and, after offering us a couple, lit a fag.

'Hope you don't mind.'

'Not at all.'

She took two deep drags, making sure to blow the smoke behind her. I noticed that the rest of the office was littered with empty cups, stuffed promotional toys and a dirty gym towel. If it is true that a cluttered office is a sign of a cluttered mind, then Surinder was on the verge of a mental breakdown. Blowing the smoke away from the smoke detector, which I noticed had been taped over anyway, she said, 'So, Kamaljit and Tanvir got together in the end?'

She said 'Kamaljit' in the English way, closer to 'camel' than 'kumul'. And she asked the question without a hint of the gushing we'd got when she thought we were customers. Was she happy about it? Had it come as a surprise? No idea. The tone reminded me of a friend of mine who when presented with a young child would always say, flatly, 'Oh, it's a baby,' before handing it back.

I gave her the basic facts. The year of my parents' marriage.

The year of my birth. The details of their shopkeeping. My only-child status. Where I went to university. And then, the facts of my father's death.

'Oh, I'm sorry,' she said, stubbing out her cigarette, reapplying lipstick, smudging it with a tissue, only to pull out another cigarette and start smoking again.

'And how is your grandmother?'

'Bibi?'

'Mataji. Mrs Bains.'

'I called her Bibi. I'm afraid she passed away. I was about four. Must have been around 1980. I'm sorry.'

She bit her thumbnail. Her BlackBerry rang. She glanced impatiently at the screen, diverted the call to voicemail and set it to silent. There followed a barrage of questions. How is your mother? What kind of cancer? What stage? What happened to your father? Did Kamaljit know we had come? Throughout, her BlackBerry vibrating plaintively.

I guess this was something else I hadn't expected about reunions: the sheer amount of interrogation. You think the meeting will involve an exchange of information and revelation, but the whole thing reminded me of taking Mum to an appointment with her oncologist, a doctor firing question after question from the other side of a desk. I had a million questions of my own. Did she have children? What happened with Jim? Was that a keyring for a Porsche on her desk? But I didn't get a chance to ask a thing. And then there was a knock on the door. She stubbed out her cigarette and, waving away the smoke like a guilty teenager, snapped, 'Come in.'

It was the boy she'd been bossing around in the dining room.

'Sorry to interrupt, Mrs B, but you're needed in the kitchen.'

'Not something you can deal with?'

'Afraid, it's the chef.'

'And?' Impatience in her tone.

'It's Terry.'

'Oh, for fuck's sake,' she muttered under her breath. Swearing was something else I couldn't imagine my mother doing. She turned to us and in a headmistressy tone added, 'I'm sorry about this. I will be right back. Please do wait.'

As soon as she left, Freya put down the dog, went behind Surinder's desk and examined the label inside Surinder's blazer. 'I knew it. Yves Saint Laurent.'

It struck me as a moronic thing to focus on. Freya returned to her seat.

'What do you make of her then?'

'Cold,' I replied. 'She seems cold.'

'Really?' She sounded disappointed.

'Did you see how her tone switched the moment she realised we weren't customers? Also, it felt like a job interview. I almost expected her to ask me what I would consider my main weakness.' The dog sniffed at my trousers. I tapped him away.

'You're being harsh. This must be a shock to her. She has just found out that her mother has died, that her sister has cancer, that she has a brother-in-law and that he is dead.'

'Yeah,' I responded dismissively. 'But she hasn't even offered us any tea.'

Looking back, this was a strange thing to say. If anything I found the Punjabi obsession with plying visitors with food and drink annoying. I guess what I was trying to convey was that Surinder didn't strike me as being like my family. Overbearing hospitality is, after all, one of the defining features of our community life. It is impossible to visit a stranger's house without the whole family being dragged down to welcome you, small children being sent into the garden to pick olives. Spreading your fingers out over an already full plate of food is our equivalent of the handshake. But my aunt had just sat there having a fag. I was beginning to understand why my parents might have decided to

189

have nothing to do with her, and when Freya responded by saying 'You sound like your mother,' I lashed out.

'I wouldn't expect you to understand. This is my family, real life, not *The Muppet's* fucking *Christmas Carol*.'

Freya's eyes brimmed with tears. We were right back to the moment with the leaflet for the sheltered housing. But instead of making me feel apologetic, they exacerbated my irritation. She had dragged me into an awkward situation I hadn't wanted to get into, ignored my reservations and was now trying to make *me* feel bad.

'Do you want to go then?' asked Freya, sadly.

'Yes. I want to go.'

I grabbed a piece of letterheaded paper from Surinder's desk, on which my aunt had written our names in spidery handwriting, and scrawled my email and telephone number with a short note: 'Drop me a line if you want to.' I left it under her laptop. Then we left.

On the way back, I seethed, didn't say a word until we got on the motorway. Then, staring out at the empty road, I made the speech I had intended to make all those weeks earlier at Pizza Hut. It all came out fluently, including a full confession about what had happened that night with Ranjit. And actually, *this* is the best way to end something, on the road, not in a restaurant. Lack of eye contact makes it easier to be frank. And when you have finished, done the brutal deed, you can drop the person off, as I did with Freya at her parents', and literally move on.

When I got back home, there was an email on my computer. The subject line was empty but it said:

Dearest Kamaljit

Your son and his fiancée came to see me today. They are a wonderful couple. I wish I had had more time to talk to them, but it has been hectic at work today. I'm so sorry about Tanvir. Looking back now, I can see that he always loved you, and it is a sign of my self-absorption that I didn't notice at the time. I'm so sorry you have not been well. I do not know if you wish to be in touch, but if there's anything I can help with, please just ask.

Yours, Surinder.

I printed it out and handed over the note to my mother, with a translation, struggling with the words for 'loved' and 'self-absorption'. She was quiet for a long while, but eventually she spoke.

'So you and Freya are getting married now?'

Not everyone envied Tanvir when, within a week of Surinder's elopement, a day of being married to Kamaljit, and hours of Mrs Bains' tear-strewn departure to her sister's in Southall, he found himself running Bains Stores. Even by the standards of the gloom that permanently besets the institution of the British small shop, independent retail was besieged in the 1970s, what with everything from the introduction of VAT to decimalisation and mounting competition from supermarkets. Meanwhile, it says something about Blakenfields that the biggest event of the decade was the demolition of a major chemical factory, and barely a week passed without someone writing in the newspapers that 'something had to be done for the Great British shopkeeper'.

But when Tanvir came across these reports – and he became a voracious reader of the newspapers and magazines he stocked in increasing quantities – he did not fret. Running a shop was a relentless challenge, and he had, admittedly, despaired the first time he pushed a trolley down supermarket aisles the width of coffins, gawping at stacks of baked beans priced twopence cheaper than what he could offer, presenting an avocado pear to his wife as if it were a Martian meteorite. But the panic subsided.

It slowly became apparent to Tanvir that supermarkets were not immune to the challenges faced by small shops. Housewives did not, like the press seemed to assume, examine the US Department of Agriculture world commodity forecasts once a week to keep track of price changes, and the fact was that the small shop had many advantages over the supermarket. It could generally ignore controls on opening hours: in practice, you were unlikely to be prosecuted for opening late and on Sunday. Small shops didn't have the burden of employing security guards: you are less likely to steal from someone you know. They had the advantage of convenience: if you found yourself short of milk for breakfast one evening, you were not going to go all the way to the supermarket. Also, when confronted with the complexities of retail, the small-shop owner had more options open to him than the supermarket manager. He could work longer, and could, if necessary, delay paying labour (himself) to balance the books.

Moreover, it turned out that Tanvir had a real talent for retail management. He was organised (to the point of being irritating), he did not waste time engaging in long conversations with members of the public or with 'trade bods' (to the point of rudeness). He also had a great memory (essential when prices changed so often) and a feeling for the market. Not long after taking over the shop, there had, for instance, been a newspaper report that there was a shortage of bog rolls in parts of the Far East and Europe. Tanvir bought a large volume of stock, stacking so many boxes in so many nooks and crannies that it became, ironically, impossible to shut the door of the indoor toilet and bathroom that he had persuaded the landlord to allow him to install. He had done a brisk trade for months afterwards, selling them in packs of half a dozen, years before the invention of the multipack. He had also spotted a sugar shortage at an early stage and devoted time and effort to finding loose supplies and then packing it himself into individual bags. This enterprise had been less successful, if you offset the profits against the cost of the mouse infestation that subsequently plagued the shop. But it was another illustration of the indefatigability of Tanvir's entrepreneurial spirit.

Though if you had asked Tanvir for the secret of his success, he would have had the humility to acknowledge luck. He realised he had been fortunate to have been plucked out by Mr Bains, who had given him the kind of apprenticeship that British grocers stopped offering in the nineteenth century. He had also been fortunate to have been forced to abandon counter service in the first week of ownership. It was done out of necessity: with two people suddenly running a shop that had been staffed by four, they simply couldn't afford to spend all day pulling things off shelves and out of cabinets. But it turned out to be the right thing to do. The older folk got used to it, and pilferage didn't turn out to be a problem.

In a way, even the emergence of supermarkets turned out to be a blessing in the end, for it brought home the importance of diversifying. Tanvir realised he had to sell as large a range of produce as possible. So, as well as expanding the number of newspapers and magazines, the shop started offering stationery, bacon, knitting wool and haberdashery. Housewares, toys, cosmetics, flowers, greetings cards and light bulbs. Sanitary towels, hair sprays, false eyelashes, boxes of tissues. It went well. Turnover increased and he had plans to boost it further by installing a cigarette vending machine outside the shop, setting up a travel concession to arrange taxis or coaches for day trips, and, if his wife permitted it, the piping of music through the store, which, he had read, had the effect of relaxing customers, who may then be inclined to buy more.

Which brings us to Tanvir's greatest piece of luck: Kamaljit. He adored his wife for a great many reasons. The way she had planted and tended scores of rose bushes in the back garden, transforming a patch of concrete into something glorious. How she decorated the house and put a candle on the table when they ate dinner together. It still stunned him that this unobtainable girl, whom he had so adored from afar, now massaged *his* feet when he was tired, kissed *him* good morning and good night. And she never ceased to surprise him, whether it was getting him flowers on his birthdays – a woman buying *him* flowers, how about that – or proffering opinions on which clothes did and did not suit him.

But the quality he most admired in Kamaljit was patience, something he knew he didn't have enough of. Take the time when Stan the roofer popped into the shop one Friday afternoon, revealed he had forgotten to pick up some butter and cheese from the supermarket, and asked for some on tick. Tanvir was incensed at the man's nerve, wanted to throw him out for the cheek, but Kamaljit took over and gave Stan what he wanted. And sure enough she was proved right in the end. The next week Stan paid off his debt and spent £5 in the shop.

Kamaljit had a way with people. She also had a way with him. He knew he could be uptight, had overheard the newspaper boys mimic and mock him often enough. But Kamaljit never criticised him for the way he sometimes gave people extra money in change to avoid saying the number nine out loud, how when brushing his teeth he had to spend ten seconds on each individual tooth. If anything she indulged what he liked to see as meticulousness, becoming as methodical as he was. She got up half an hour before him every day to make sure there was a cup of tea waiting for him when he came down. She made sure to cook saag on Wednesdays, mince keema on Fridays and what they called English 'dinner' every Saturday: chicken and mash sloshing in pints of watery gravy. She also wilfully succumbed to a daily routine as rigid as that of a school day. They would serve customers together during the morning and evening rush, but otherwise Kamaljit would work in the mornings, Tanvir in the afternoons, Kamaljit doing housework and Tanvir doing admin or going to the cash and carry while away from the counter. Then, late in the evening, as Kamaljit cooked, caught a bit of telly, dealt with any late customers, Tanvir would kick back in his favourite place, his study.

The study hadn't been part of Tanvir's grand improvement plans, which had, among other things, seen the removal of the hatch from which newspapers had been sold in the mornings and which had given the customers an excuse not to come into the shop, and the excising of a partition that had shortened the depth of the shop by about twelve feet. If he had had any intentions for what had been his bedroom when he started lodging with the Bains, it was to turn it into a nursery. However, years of having sex month after month at predetermined times, of Kamaljit raising her legs against a wall and staying in position for up to an hour afterwards, had produced no child. Gradually, without acknowledging it to Kamaljit, or even to himself, he had begun to make the space his own. First, a wood-topped Alma Series 8100 desk, bought from a nearby estate agent, when it was closing down. Then, a glass fibre and polyester chair, and a set of plastic stools which stacked into one another and could be used as occasional tables. Finally, his pride and joy, a complete set of the *Encyclopaedia Britannica*.

Like everything else in his life, the study was highly organised. All the piles of newspapers and magazines had been stacked according to date, his books – *The Great Train Robbery* by Michael Crichton, *The Dead Zone* by Stephen King – were arranged alphabetically on the shelves, and the stationery on his desk arranged symmetrically and in lines. The only disruption came in the form of the occasional boxes of stock scattered over the floor and the shelves.

As you might expect, he had a routine for what he did when he came up each evening. He would pour himself a slug of whisky from the bottle he kept concealed from Kamaljit in his filing cabinet, sit down at his desk and tally up the day's takings, move to his armchair with a copy of the dictionary and commit a single new word to memory, read an entry in the *Encyclopaedia Britannica* and then, reclining in the armchair, make his way through the evening paper, starting with the back page (not out of interest, just to have something to say to customers), and flicking through the classifieds for bargains and business opportunities before making his way through the main news section.

And it was when he was going through this ritual one November evening in 1975 – having memorised the word 'pulchritudinous' from the *Collins English Dictionary*; scanned an entry in the *Encyclopaedia Britannica* on the Karankawa, an extinct group of Native American people; and read about how the national final of the Bus Driver of the Year contest, which had been held in Wolverhampton for the first time last year, would not be held there again – that he was stopped in his tracks by a headline declaring, 'Migrants want their culture taught at school.'

The article continued:

An immigrant organisation has demanded the inclusion of Asian and West Indian cultural activities in Wolverhampton school programmes. The local branch of the Punjabi Workers' Alliance said it was 'alarmed at the programmed murder of Asian and West Indian cultures in Wolverhampton schools'.

Mr Patwant Dhanda, chairman of the PWA, announced his intention of starting a hunger strike outside the Wolverhampton Town Hall in support of eight demands, including the teaching of minority languages in schools, the replacement of imperial history with black and Asian history, the promotion of black teachers, and a ban on National Front supporters working in education.

It was only after Tanvir had got to the words 'National Front' that he noticed the steel tumbler in his hand had become deformed. That man Dhanda was insufferable. There was no escaping the fat sod. Just a month after Tanvir had married Kamaljit, Dhanda had taken a bride fifteen years his junior, the extravagant wedding ceremony highlighting the meagreness of Tanvir's own. Just a few weeks after Mrs Bains had departed for Southall in distress, preferring to live with her sister than her own daughter, Dhanda had decided to convert his drapery store into a grocery shop, informing Kamaljit (he always spoke to her rather than Tanvir) after the fact that he would remain true to the non-compete agreement he had struck with his great friend and mentor, Mr Bains. Then, in the five years that Tanvir and Kamaljit had failed to conceive, Dhanda had fathered no fewer than three children: two daughters and, most recently, a son.

None of these things had bothered him, in themselves. It was true that the number of guests at his wedding had not exceeded a few dozen, and that at the wedding Mrs Bains had heartily embraced the convention for the mother of a daughter to cry through proceedings. But being married to Kamaljit was prize enough. Meanwhile, Dhanda had, in ostentatiously and sanctimoniously honouring the non-compete arrangement in memory of Mr Bains, chosen to focus on Asian supplies, which was, as far as Tanvir saw it, a laughable strategy. The retail sector was in flux, what with the challenge of rising costs, complex red tape, a weak economy, endless stoppages due to industrial disputes, a sharp increase in unemployment, chronic inflation and food shortages. But it was obvious that Asians would eat less and less food from the subcontinent as they integrated. With the arrival of frozen food and ready meals, the trend was towards convenience food, not towards Indian dishes that took half a day to cook.

As for Dhanda's children, well, the truth was that Tanvir rather liked life as it was. It was nice not to have to share Kamaljit. But it did sometimes grate on Tanvir that his wife was bothered by Mrs Dhanda's fecundity, her desperation for a child evident in her ever-increasing superstitiousness and religiosity. And he resented

Dhanda's grocery venture for the same reason he resented this plan of his to mount a hunger strike. The man was, like the Sikhs who were opening separate temples for different castes around Blakenfields, in defiance of the founding principles of their religion, trying to recreate the Punjab in Britain, complete with its repressions and divisions between Jat and Chamar.

There had been a time when he had gone along with it all. But he was young then, trying to impress Kamaljit, and he only kept the turban and beard now because he thought he looked better in them. In reality he was agnostic, flirting with atheism, and sometimes he even found himself agreeing with the opposition. At least, he had shared the anxieties of Enoch Powell when he objected to Britain taking in tens of thousands of Ugandan Asian refugees when dictator General Idi Amin expelled 80,000 from the African country. Why should hard-working men like him subsidise these people? And when more recently Powell's replacement, Conservative MP Nick Budgen, had caused consternation in the Asian community for remarking that 'when the Asian girls reach the age of sixteen or seventeen, Dad trots off to India or Pakistan and sells her to the highest bidder', he did not identify with the outrage. After all, had that not almost happened with his wife and her sister?

As for Dhanda's idea of teaching Indian culture in English schools, he saw through it straight away. Having lost half the Punjab during Partition, and failed to create an independent Sikh state after Partition, Punjabi Jats like Dhanda were trying to make up for it in England. It was infuriating and Tanvir felt so incensed that, after refilling his misshapen tumbler, allowing himself one more drink than he would normally permit himself on a Thursday, moved to his desk, grabbed some writing paper from the top drawer and, with his Parker fountain pen, began writing a letter to the editor.

Dear Sir,

Your pulchritudinous publication bears witness to the fact that colour prejudice is a fact of life in Britain. Just last week you reported a judge in a Birmingham Crown Court saying 'Roughing up of coloureds is almost a hobby in some parts of the Black Country.' More recently, we have read about Nellie Jones, Labour councillor and school governor of St Luke's infant school, accusing other governors and the vicar of attempting to keep Indian and Pakistani kids out of school.

Tanvir stopped, reread his words and wondered if he should start again. That day's letters pages featured missives on a vast array of subjects, from asking for house lights to be turned down during symphony concerts at the civic hall to benefits ('When I was a child every unemployed man was given the task of clearing roads and pavements after a bad blizzard. Why is this not done today?'). But the thing they all had in common was personal stories. Maybe he should tell his own tale. He started again.

Dear Sir,

Your pulchritudinous publication bears witness to the fact that colour prejudice is a fact of life in Britain. And as someone who runs a shop in Blakenfields, I have to live the reality of racialism. Rare is the week that passes without my wife and I being threatened or abused for our colour.

However, when the PWA talks about introducing Indian studies in schools, does it also want to preach to young minds the bigotry of the caste system? A system where, for centuries, high-caste Hindus and Sikhs in India have not only discriminated against but inhumanely treated their brothers whom they call scheduled-caste or untouchables.

I know that last week you reported a judge in a Birmingham Crown Court saying 'Roughing up of coloureds is almost a hobby in some parts of the Black Country.' We have also had reports on how there have been five assaults on Indians in Wolverhampton pubs in just one week.

But these stories are fairy tales compared to the stories the Indian press carries about people being raped, killed, beaten and robbed as a result of their caste. The fact is that in India, someone of my caste could only escape their position if they joined the army, or became a priest, or were a talented singer or wrestler. But here I have built a thriving business and can consider myself an Englishman equal to any other. I feel liberated, and as far as I'm concerned the Indian culture that the PWA wants to preach should go the way of the Karankawa.

Yours sincerely,

Tanvir Banga

Proprietor, Bains Stores

He reread the letter, changed 'Proprietor' to 'Director' and, satisfied with its content, took another swig of whisky and imagined the look on Dhanda's face when it was printed. No doubt he would respond in some way via the PWA, raise the issue at the temple run by Jats, where he was a member of the committee, and find a way of informing Tanvir's mother-in-law, who seemed to have rebonded with him over their shared loathing of Tanvir. In turn, she would find a way of letting Kamaljit know her feelings.

But it was time he stood up to them both. Over the years he had tried everything he could to win over Mrs Bains, abandoning his bedroom whenever she visited so she could relive the days when she was queen of the castle, trying not to take offence when she mentioned Surinder's elopement in the same breath as his marriage, as if they were on the same moral plane. But it was to no avail. She was determined to treat his introduction to the Bains family as a calamity, never gave him the benefit of the doubt and tended to make the worst possible interpretation of his actions, even taking offence when he put up a shop sign which kept her late husband's name, seeing it as an attempt to cover up his caste. Sometimes she became tearful at the very sight of him. Frankly, he should have done something like this years ago. If he could have, he would have taken advantage of the newspaper's dictation service right then, which allowed readers to phone in their letters. But the line closed at half five. So, instead, he folded the letter and sought an envelope to put it into. And it was only when he was about to seal it that he thought of a possible obstacle. Kamaljit.

She was a supportive wife, but had weaknesses. She was fearful of confrontation, indulgent of Dhanda, claiming that in the absence of her mother and sister he was the closest thing she had to family, romanticising his relationship to her late father. She also longed, to Tanvir's intense frustration, for her mother's approval, and couldn't always be relied on to be on his side when it came to anything to do with religion. They rarely argued, but when they did, the trigger invariably had a spiritual aspect. They had fallen out when a guru she had consulted about her failure to conceive had suggested they fast, hammer a nail into the corner of every single room, and bathe in milk once a week. She had objected on moral grounds to Tanvir's introduction into the shop of men's magazines, fought his plan to sell booze, and even complained, on occasion, about the sale of meat products.

Tanvir had won the argument with the porn, arguing tenuously that if he could deal with flogging sanitary towels to female customers, she could serve men's magazines, which happened to offer excellent profit margins. He had won the argument on serving meat too. But he had conceded on booze. Marriage, after all, was about compromise. Communication. Women were a mystery to him, but he understood, from the women's magazines he occasionally flicked through, about the importance of talking things through. And with that in mind, he emptied his tumbler, brushed his teeth in the bathroom downstairs to remove any signs that he had been drinking, and went to tell his wife about his planned response to Dhanda's hunger strike.

He didn't find her, as expected, in the kitchen – though he saw from the frying pan on the hob that she was making samosas. He didn't discover her in the living room either, though he could tell from the neatly rolled-out dough and the saucepan of spiced mashed potatoes on the coffee table that she was probably planning to fill the samosas in here, doubtless in front of *Coronation Street*. She was in the shopfront, cleaning the counter.

Walking in, he saw that she had her hair tied up, in a way that he liked, and was struck as ever by his wife's prettiness; she was such an attractive girl, much more interestingly so than her sister. He was struck also, despite its familiarity, by the smartness of the shopfront. It had been transformed by the introduction of strip lighting, and the installation of a brand-new glass panelled door with an aluminium surround to allow for a full view through to the interior. The thought that there would soon be a booster fan above the entrance to greet customers on extra-cold days distracted him momentarily from his mission. But then, standing opposite his wife, on the customer's side of the counter, he got back to it.

'Did you see this?' he asked, waving the newspaper in her direction.

It was a rhetorical question. The only thing Kamaljit read was prayer books. The newspapers they sold were no different to her from packets of crisps. He had failed to get her interested in improving her English, in the same way he had failed to persuade her to wear English clothes. So he translated it for her, repeating the particularly annoying bits for emphasis.

'Oh, yes,' Kamaljit replied evenly in Punjabi. 'He told me about that. About time someone did something. Some of these Indian kids nowadays, I tell you, barely a word of Punjabi, they may as well be goras.' She finished wiping the counter and turned on her heels. 'Can you give me a hand filling the samosas, ji? Won't take long.'

Tanvir followed her back into the living room as she took a seat in front of *Coronation Street*. He didn't understand how his wife could refuse to speak English and yet be so addicted to soap operas like these. It was not a serious show like, say, *The Six Million Dollar Man*. He resumed his case as she set up an assembly line, passing him cones of pastry into which he was required to spoon the filling.

'But pray, what is the point of teaching Punjabi?' he asked, rubbing some yoghurt into the edges of a filled samosa. 'It is hardly an international financial language.' He sealed it up. 'These kids should be learning about the country they are actually living in now.'

'Hmm,' preferred Kamaljit, distracted by Hilda Ogden. 'They may be in England but they will never be English.' A glance at her husband. 'Don't fill them up too much, ji.' She reopened his creation, took some filling out, and resealed it. 'This much, or they will burst in the pan.'

Tanvir continued with his protest, even though he suspected Kamaljit was only half listening. 'Don't you think hunger strikes make us look stupid? Why can't he just debate like a normal person? One of the great things about living in England is free speech. You don't hear about English politicians threatening to starve themselves or set themselves on fire.' His wife laughed at something on screen. 'Also, can you see him actually doing it? The longest that man has gone without food is three minutes. You could sustain a small town on his body fat for a week. We all know what this is actually about. His ego.'

'Is it?' Kamaljit asked distractedly.

'Yes! He just wants to make sure no other castes or religions get ideas above their station. That the Jat Sikhs remain in charge.'

'I'm sure he doesn't, ji.'

As the credits started rolling, Kamaljit, humming along to the theme tune, got up and took the tray of filled samosas into the kitchen. Tanvir followed her, maintaining his lecture as she turned on the hob, tested the oil – throwing a small cube of stale bread into it – and when satisfied, thrust three of the samosas into the pan.

'I see your point, ji,' she said eventually. 'But, you know, I would like my child to grow up knowing about his religion and culture.'

Tanvir, only half hearing his wife, felt a stab of irritation towards her. He had never liked Surinder, she was arrogant, without morals, it transpired. But this was the one respect in which he wished Kamaljit would mimic her sister. She was always too happy to go along with the established view.

'So this culture is worth teaching even if it dictates that some of us are second-class citizens?'

'Like I said,' answered his wife, pushing the samosas around in the oil, checking they were being cooked evenly. 'I want *my child* to know about Indian culture.'

Missing the emphasis, Tanvir's annoyance intensified. He was almost as irritated as the time Kamaljit started making puris, just so that she could offer them to pigeons in the park, having heard such acts could induce fertility. 'Even if this culture treats everyone else like second-class citizens?' He was raising his voice.

Kamaljit had to repeat herself another time before the penny dropped.

'What did you say?'

Tanvir had not been completely unobservant. He had noticed that his wife had been unwell recently, distracted, attending the doctor's twice in a week, going back to bed after the morning rush, when he needed her most. But he had put it down to the postcard with the London postmark she had received from her sister. He didn't know what was worse when it came to Surinder, contact or no contact. When they heard nothing, Kamaljit imagined the worst, panicking that every visiting policeman was coming with news that her sister had been found dead in a ditch. But then contact seemed to destroy her too.

However, there was a more surprising explanation.

'Give me your hand,' said his wife. She took one of the pods she had been shelling that afternoon, and there was a sharp snap as she popped a single pea into his palm. 'This, apparently, is the size of our baby right now.'

It was not just the news that came as a shock to Tanvir, but his own response to it. Tanvir had, over the years, convinced himself that he didn't want a child. He had grown tired of conversations with doctors about retrograde ejaculation and hypsospadias, found depositing semen specimens in clean jars in laboratories humiliating, not to mention questions about the state of his testes and the kind of underwear he wore. But suddenly he found himself crying and laughing at the same time, lifting his wife up and kissing her.

When the shop bell rang indicating a customer, he ran out and insisted Mrs Hill take her breakfast cereal for free, and a bagful of sweets with it, for it was traditional in Indian culture to hand out food on receiving good news. He locked up as soon as she departed, shutting up early for the first time in his life, took his wife upstairs and made love to her.

It was not until the following morning, after Kamaljit had rung her mother to tell her the good news, walking back from the Jat temple his wife had insisted he visit to give thanks, that he remembered the letter. He couldn't recall the words he had written or even the intensity of the anger he had felt when he read the article. But he decided to post it anyway. He wasn't sure what caste his child would be when it was born, given that it was the product of a Chamar and a Jat. There was an argument to be made that it might be Khatri, of mercantile class, which was nothing to be ashamed of, given it was the caste of the ten Sikh Gurus.

But he didn't want his child's life to be blighted by the notion of caste at all. No, his son or daughter would not have that contracting feeling in their chest when a Jat spat the word 'Chamar' at them. His child would grow up British. He was sure of it. Just as he was sure of the continuing success of his shop, the failure of Dhanda's enterprise, and that he himself would prove to be the most devoted of fathers to his child.

The only positive thing about the aftermath of my break-up with Freya was that I no longer felt confused. It became clear almost immediately that I had made a mistake. I realised it when she put our shared flat on the market and her best friend got in touch to tell me I would have to continue contributing to the mortgage until it was sold. It became evident again when Freya changed her telephone number, blocked my emails and calls. Yet again when our friends started to choose between us, which, because I was now in Wolverhampton, meant they mainly chose Freya, including my best mate Matt, who, before deleting me on Facebook, sent me a message telling me that he always thought I was a cunt, and now there was finally proof.

The whole thing felt like I had just endured an amputation. Even when I wasn't thinking about what had happened (and I was rarely not thinking about it) the pain was never absent. The worst thing about it? The amputation was entirely self-inflicted. I had wilfully removed a limb. And the knowledge that I had done so pushed me into the deepest depression I have ever endured. I lost interest in food, the ability to concentrate, read and sleep. I also gave up weights to go back to running, sometimes twice a day, which in Wolverhampton meant having the *Rocky* theme tune sung at me sarcastically every 800 yards, and being offered a lift home every mile or two.

Mum wasn't in great shape either. She had reacted to the news of her sister's re-emergence with a bout of illness, succumbing to a flu-like bug which had her in bed for four days. Though, somehow, amid this gloom, the sisters began corresponding, my mother dictating the messages to me in Punjabi, me translating the messages into English and sending them to Surinder from my laptop, Surinder replying in English on her BlackBerry, and then me reading the response out to my mother in a mixture of Punjabi and English.

It was like the twenty-first-century revolution in communication had never happened. And actually, the content of the messages made me feel like large parts of the twentieth century had not happened, given that they were packed almost entirely with banal information about their respective working days and Jessie's health, and inconsequential anecdotes about customers. The exchanges reminded me of eavesdropping on children in the shop: however intense their conversation, it almost invariably turned out that they were discussing little of any consequence.

It wasn't long before I tired of my role, tired as I was by everything, and suggested they meet, and all I can say about what followed is that I now realise what it must be like negotiating an international climate change treaty. Each sister had a different objection to whatever time or place I suggested. Surinder's excuses included: Jessie got sick in cars, her Porsche was in the garage, the hotel was busy in the build-up to New Year's Eve. My mother said that long journeys sparked migraines and the shop was too busy. The shop was never busy.

I wasn't sure what all this reticence was about. But I had other things to concern me – not least being skint and finding some work, even if it was of the freelance variety, and even if it involved working between London and the Midlands. So I put my foot down, named the time and place: lunch at a swish cafe in Tettenhall, on New Year's Day. It was going to be quiet enough for us to be able to close the shop at lunchtime, and the New Year's Eve madness in the hotel would be over. Meanwhile, Tettenhall, where I went to school, was perfect: familiar enough for my mother, in that it was a district of Wolverhampton, and yet posh enough for a resident of Surrey not to experience culture shock. Neutral ground.

No mention had been made about Surinder visiting the shop, let alone staying overnight, but my mother's reaction was as energetic as her initial response had been enervated. She launched into a frenzy of cleaning and preparation: the curtain between the shop and the house was washed and rehung; the crystal glasses – given to us by the old owners of the garage next door, which I used to think was a mark of their warmth, but which I now realised was a consequence of all the Esso points they had collected as a result of their high petrol consumption – were put on display; the sofa bed in my father's study was pulled out and prepared; the smell of Mum's cooking filled the house.

It all made me nervous. Leaving aside the way the day had ended, my festive meeting with Surinder had hardly been a success, and she had seemed tetchy and reserved over email. I didn't want my mother to be disappointed, and my fears were realised when I sent Surinder a text, double-checking, that all was in place for her arrival in Wolverhampton on New Year's Day, and she replied, 'Yah, shd be. I hope. ;)'

I'm not sure what was most annoying. The vagueness of 'shd be' and 'I hope' (passive aggressive), or the smiley (people over the age of twenty should never use emoticons). What was wrong with her? She didn't seem like the kind of person who tolerated flakiness herself. I texted a firm and grammatically coherent response.

'I'm sensing you're not sure about coming up. I don't want my mother to be let down. So if you don't fancy it, I will understand and will try to explain it to her, but do let me know as soon as possible.'

Massi: 'It's not that I'm not keen, it's more a case of dealing with what the day brings.'

Me: 'I understand, you're busy, but please let me know for sure by six tonight.'

Massi: 'Sure.'

Sure? When did English people start saying 'sure'? What was wrong with 'OK' or 'yes'? But then, at precisely 6 p.m., beep, beep. 'I will be there. Train tickets booked.'

And then at midnight: 'Your mother is lucky to have a son who cares so much xx.'

The second time I saw my aunt, striding down platform three of Wolverhampton train station on New Year's Day, was, I think, more startling than the first. I had been sitting in the coffee shop for a while, wincing as people within earshot referred to 'lattes' as 'lartays' and 'macchiatos' as 'mojitos', being hung up on by Freya's father, when Surinder appeared, sporting a pair of sunglasses, even though there was no sign of sunshine, and high-heeled boots, though the frost was making it difficult to walk even in trainers. She was wearing a black fitted turtleneck, tight black jeans, two layers of necklaces, and a thick woollen coat the exact shade of Jessie, who was camouflaged under her arm. She stood out a mile.

To my surprise, she then offered up her cheek to be kissed. Jerking my head indecisively, I planted a kiss meant for a cheek on her ear. Apart from the occasional bear hug, we're not the most physically expressive of families. I have no memory of my parents ever kissing in my presence, or even touching one another. The awkwardness continued as she lit up a fag outside the station, right in front of a line of disapproving Punjabi taxi drivers. She kept her sunglasses on the whole time, barely said a word as we got into the van. I resolved, as we pulled away, that I wouldn't be the one who caved in first. But I caved in first.

'So,' I coughed. 'Welcome back to Her Majesty's royal city of Wolverhampton.'

'A city now, is it?'

'Since 2000.'

She peered over the top of her sunglasses. 'Doesn't look much different.' She glanced to her left. 'What's that?'

'That' was Wolverhampton's £22.5-million bus station, the most ambitious infrastructure project the city had seen in years, the pride of the city. As with so many Wolverhampton developments, it didn't look quite finished, and was still obscured by hoardings, the city being most at ease when it resembles a building site.

'What did Thatcher say about people who still got the bus again?' She continued before I recalled the quote, something about how a man who, beyond the age of twenty-six, finds himself on a bus can count himself a failure, 'The problem with Birmingham is that it is always trying to be the city of the future. The problem with Wolverhampton is that it is always trying to be Birmingham.'

With someone else, at another time, I might have been amused. I can see there is something intrinsically funny about the sound of the word 'Wolverhampton', something undeniably grim about the view of the city as you arrive by train. I had laughed along when the Lonely Planet guide had branded it the fifth worst city on the globe, alongside El Salvador and Detroit, half smirked when Freya's father had asked if the riots had caused any 'improvements'. But having already made me feel Punjabi at the taxi stand, Surinder's sneering now managed the impossible by also making me a defensive Wulfrunian. It meant making several traffic violations, but I found myself attempting to find a scenic route through town. We drove past the handsome, Gothic, Grade II building that housed Barclays Bank, past the stunning art gallery and the statue of Prince Albert, inaugurated by Queen Victoria herself and seemingly in a different position every time I visited. I may even have found myself pointing out the site of England's first automatic traffic lights.

However, it was a futile gesture. Wolverhampton looked as grim as I felt. No fewer than one in four of the shops had closed down, their boarded-up fronts pasted with posters designed by the council to create the illusion of activity. The banks that had turned into flash bars in the 1990s, when Wolverhampton briefly became an attractive nightspot, were now empty, making me nostalgic for the days when we could complain about the banks turning into bars. Even an undertaker's and associated stonemason had closed since I'd last looked.

I realised during the drive that Surinder and I had something in common: we'd both left town at a time when it was on the up. In 1970 there was a glimmer of hope after decades of industrial decline, with the Queens Arcade, a central shopping street, having been demolished to make way for two modern shopping centres, and large areas being cleared in anticipation of the building of the ring road. In the 1990s, when I left for university, the town was once again thought to be coming out of years of industrial decline, with the polytechnic having gained its university status, the arrival of a new racecourse, the refurbishment of the football ground, and so on. But both transformations had turned out to be false dawns.

Surinder's silence acknowledged as much. The only remark she uttered on the way to Tettenhall came as we passed a once-grand department store. 'If you wanted to impress a girl you took her to the perfume counter at Beatties.'

The next time she spoke was in the car park at the back of the cafe.

'Time for a quick one?' she asked, pulling out a box of fags.

'Yes,' I replied, pretending to be relaxed, praying that this would not be how my mother saw her sister for the first time in more than forty years. Standing there, watching her smoke, I was reminded of driving my old mate Matt (who was now literally an old mate) to his wedding as his best man. There was the same feeling of bringing two people together. The anxiety that something might go wrong. The sense of occasion, everyone stiff in new clothes, the desire to smoke, to paper over nerves with mindless chit-chat, which this time seemed to mainly involve regaling my aunt with tales of Tettenhall, a suburb so posh that the older residents continued to state their county of abode as 'Staffordshire' rather than the West Midlands.

'Actually, I know it quite well,' said Surinder.

'Oh.'

'Will I recognise her?' she asked.

'Mum? She'll be the Indian one.'

Surinder looked down the twee village high street, a slice of the Home Counties in the West Midlands. 'I see what you mean.'

'Want me to come in with you?'

'Of course, darling. Of course.'

She cleared her throat, and, putting her arm through mine, I went from feeling like a best man to feeling like the father of a bride.

The cafe was even busier than it had been an hour earlier, when I had dropped Mum off. The young waitresses could be heard arguing with the kitchen about absent orders. The queue of customers was threatening to snake out of the front door. In the middle of it all, my mother, taking up a table for four, showing no interest in the magazines that had been laid on for her perusal; the coffee I'd bought her, judging from the pristine latte art that still graced the foam, untouched. Peering over her glasses, she caught our eye as soon as we walked in, and I held my breath as I waited for the first words to be uttered.

'Did your train arrive on time?' Mum asked, in Punjabi.

'Hahnji,' replied Surinder. She spoke the following sentence in English, albeit with an Indian accent. 'Reduced Sunday service today. Engineering work.'

'*Hai. Hai,*' tutted Mum. 'And tickets are so expensive nowadays, hunna.'

214

Then, apropos of nothing, Surinder, still sporting her sunglasses, lifted up her dog and said, 'Ah Jessie hai.'

'Ah,' said Mum, awkwardly. She disliked dogs but found it in herself to shake his paw. 'Kiddha, Jessie Singh.'

The exchange came to a halt. It was not clear at this stage whether English or Punjabi was going to be the dominant language, and standing opposite each other, the contrast between the sisters made my heart go out to my mother. She looked so tired next to Surinder – and it wasn't just because of the viral illness she had just endured. Thousands of hours of shop work, her chemo, all of it was suddenly visible in her face and stoop. Her hair used to be lush and glistening as a child, I wanted to touch it all the time, but now it was reduced to a sad rat's tail.

In the end the deadlock was broken by a small child on a nearby table. He sneezed. Loudly and violently. As a father castigated his offspring for lack of manners, a flash of anxiety ran across my mother's face and she said, 'Oh, we'd better stay here, for now.'

Surinder removed her sunglasses, revealing that her mascara had smudged.

'Oh, pehnji,' she proffered in fluent Punjabi. 'You're exactly how I remember you.'

The two sisters stood embracing each other in the middle of the cafe, blocking customers from coming in and going out. A white woman in the queue tutted, I thought how nice it would have been to tell Freya about the meeting, and, having apologetically ordered another latte and a couple of random expensive items on the menu, I grabbed the dog and took it for a walk.

King Charles spaniels are meant to be, by temperament, easygoing. Highly affectionate, apparently. But Jessie Singh wasn't. Once parted from his owner, if he wasn't barking or whining, he was snapping at old ladies and young children who wanted to pet him, jumping at strangers who had no interest in petting him, starting fights with passing dogs, and, more than anything else, crapping everywhere. I've never been good with animals, and it turns out I am even less proficient at dealing with their faeces. Every time Jessie soiled a path or lawn, I disowned him, walking determinedly ahead, pretending he wasn't mine. But it transpires letting a dog crap on a village green is one of the worst things you can do in Tettenhall. The owner of a border collie saw me shirking my responsibility and shouted, 'PICK IT UP!' when I attempted to walk away. 'PICK IT UP!' they continued as I ran on and Jessie followed. 'PICK IT UP. PICK IT UP! PICK UP YOUR DOG'S SHIT!'

I returned to the cafe sooner than expected, sweating slightly, and didn't object too forcefully when my mother, visibly more relaxed in Surinder's company, though still not having touched any of the food or drink I'd bought, suggested leaving.

'Let's get out of here,' she said, gesturing at the cafe, which she kept on referring to as 'the coffee'. 'I'll feed you both some proper food, not this gora rabbit feed.'

If my aunt hesitated it was only for a moment – it would have been easier to deny a toddler an ice cream on a sunny day. In the car park, as we realised there was one seat too few in the van, we had one of those stand-offs that punctuate Punjabi family life – Mum offering to get in the back, Surinder offering to get in the back, me calling a local taxi firm, which, employing Muslims, refused to take the dog.

In the end, Surinder surprised us with an unexpected solution: it was decided that I would get in the back with Jessie, while Surinder drove us to the shop. In the driving seat, her sunglasses replaced by red-rimmed designer spectacles, soaring through Wolverhampton at a pace that betrayed her as a one-time Londoner, she was transformed, as chatty as she had previously been taciturn.

'Remember, pehnji, when they began changing the livery of

the buses?' she asked as she pulled up behind a blue bus. 'When I left, they were just beginning to appear blue and cream.' The precision of her Punjabi took me by surprise. She spoke like a native. I'd not yet accepted, I suppose, that she was a native.

'Oh God, yes,' Mum laughed. 'People thought Wolverhampton was being invaded by Birmingham.'

'You remember the cafe that used to stand there?'

'The Italian one?'

'Yes. The Milano.'

'Always wanted to go there.'

'You didn't?'

'Mataji would have taken her rolling pin and beaten me to death.' She turned to look at her sister. 'And, what, you did?'

I caught a mischievous glance in the rear-view mirror. She laughed, and then, distracted by the sight of a branch of the State Bank of India, gasped. 'My God, right in the middle of town. Who would have thought. The Asians really have taken over, haven't they?'

I saw an opportunity to defend Wolverhampton. 'Actually,' I shouted above the din of my aunt crunching the gears, 'Jaguar Land Rover are building a big new engine plant in the north of the town. And they're an Indian company now. You could say that the Indians who took the jobs are now creating the jobs.'

Surinder slowed down for some red lights. 'Look at *that*. Exactly the same as it was.'

From the back I couldn't see what she was referring to. All I could make out was an unmodernised townhouse, near the centre of town, whose only defining feature was that it was maintained a little better than the houses around it.

'You don't remember that house, pehnji?' asked Surinder.

'No,' said Mum.

'That's where Enoch Powell lived.'

My mother barely blinked, but I was taken aback. So this was the constituency home that Powell was living in when he had complained of living 'within the proverbial stone's throw of streets which went black'. The constituency home to which the post office assigned a van to make a special run several times a day following his 'Rivers of Blood' speech, so deluged was he with postal expressions of support. The house where, despite the raised temperature, a guard posted around the clock to protect him from retaliatory attacks, Powell found time to garden and read political biographies aloud in bed to his wife each night. In short, one of the most significant houses in the city, and yet it was not marked with a plaque and I had walked past it a thousand times on the way to and from school without realising its significance. It was opposite a care home that I knew was run by a Housing Association providing supported housing to 'South Asian women' suffering from mental ill health.

'I wonder what Powell would have made of that,' I remarked. The lights changed and Surinder pulled away. 'Not much, to be honest,' she replied in a mixture of Punjabi and English. 'Do you think he was racist? I mean, he said things which were racist in modern terms. But his point that many immigrants didn't want to integrate? Just take a look around.'

My aunt was, I think, referring to one of several new temples we were driving past, which seemed to sprout up every time members of an executive committee fell out. And the slight needled. My faith was a wavering thing, but I'd recently, in my distress, been finding solace in visits to the gurdwara. Also I had never heard an Asian defend Powell before. My father began voting Tory in the 1980s – though that was, I suspect, because Dhanda had become a Labour councillor. For most people of my generation, Powell was simply a byword for racism.

However, my mother didn't seem to share my discomfort. 'Jes,' she responded, attempting some English. 'Bulberhampton full of bloody Iraqi now.'

I was pretty sure this wasn't what my aunt had meant. But we were saved from any further extrapolation by Jessie Singh, who marked the return of his owner to Blakenfields after an absence of more than forty years by vomiting all over the back of the van and her nephew's Levi's.

Surinder was so mortified by Jessie, and so preoccupied with the task of cleaning up his mess, and, I guess, Blakenfields had changed so much, that I don't think she realised that we had asked her to pull into the car park of Dhanda's superstore until she was approached by Mr Dhanda himself.

'Sas ri akal, Surinder Kaur,' he croaked. He wasn't in his wheel-chair, was instead leaning against Ranjit, who I had been avoiding for weeks and who by way of acknowledgement of what he would have called my 'skankery' sucked his teeth. His father, clean-shaven and sporting a large blue turban, continued in Punjabi, 'Today is a blessed day. Your father would have been so happy to see you two sisters together again. I am so glad that I have lived to see this. So glad. What a blessed day.'

There was a long pause and I wondered for a moment if Surinder had not recognised him. She'd obviously seen him — it was impossible, given his girth, not to notice him. I remained uncertain as Surinder, tissues still in her hand, enquired, 'What happened to the tower block?'

Dhanda, determined not to be ignored, or oblivious to the fact that he was being ignored, cleared his throat and answered, 'You know you're no longer young when you're outliving buildings you saw being put up.'

'That is Dhanda's shop?' resumed Surinder, as if Dhanda wasn't there. 'The whole of it?'

'Yes, well, God has been kind to us,' said Dhanda. He peered at Surinder's face through his filmy eyes. Looked her up and down in a way that reminded me of his son. 'It looks like God has been kind to you. You're looking very . . . healthy. Very healthy, Surinder. And that is the thing that matters most. Good family. Good health. Good health for your family.'

At this point Dhanda held out his hand as if to bless Surinder, and as my aunt, towering over him, failed to bow her head in response, and then walked off, claiming she had a call to make, any doubt over whether my aunt was deliberately ignoring him dissipated. As a teenager, I had hated this obligation to bow down before elders, not least because it meant I couldn't fetch a can of Coke from the chiller, or get to the bus stop without my carefully sculpted bouffant being messed up. But I would have no more dared to decline such a blessing than swear at my own mother. It was, without question, a diss. A palpable diss. And Ranjit acknowledged it as such when he sucked his teeth again and, spotting that I had a small dog under one arm and Surinder's handbag in another, added, 'Suits you, bro.'

Dhanda retreated slowly, waddling, leaning against Ranjit. My mother took my arm, and it took us a minute or two to catch up with Surinder, my mother's stride a fraction of the length of her sister's.

When we got to the shop, Surinder was standing on the pavement opposite. She looked wan. She pointed out an art deco portrait of a woman in the window of the hairdresser's next door, concealed behind a poster advertising cut-price wigs and etched on a glass-panelled door. It was the same as it had been in 1970. Then she pulled out a silk scarf from her handbag. It may have been made by Hermès, but it was also white, the makeshift chuni reminding me that for my aunt this visit was as much a wake as it was a reunion.

The first thing my mother did when she got into the shop was disappear into the kitchen to prepare food. There wasn't a single occasion, it seemed, from Diwali to family reunions, that my mother wouldn't miss by standing slaving over her gas stove. I found it almost as irritating as Surinder failing to offer any food or drink at all on Christmas Day.

But my aunt didn't seem to mind. It gave her an opportunity to walk around the house and reminisce, every nook and cranny evoking a memory. Her tearfulness came as a surprise, as did her tactility, and made me wonder if her coldness on Christmas Day had been shock, and her terseness after being picked up at the station a result of nerves. By the time my mother started bringing in the food, bowls of curry and sabzi, the salty smell of butter rising from a mound of freshly cooked rotis, she was overwhelmed.

'Is it too spicy for you?' asked my mother.

'No,' replied Surinder, tears running down her face. 'No, not at all. It's just . . . it tastes exactly . . . exactly how . . .'

She didn't need to finish the sentence. The thought of Mrs Bains set my mother off. I left them alone for the second time that day, to spend a little more time with Jessie Singh, who had been locked in my father's study upstairs, and to check for only the fifty-third time that day whether Freya had replied to any texts or emails. I missed her more that day than even before.

When I returned, my mother had the old family photograph albums out. I assumed they were poring over old pictures of my dad and my grandparents, those stilted old portraits from India where everyone was always in their best clothes, and the developer had adjusted the exposure so that everyone appeared paler than they were. But to my mortification my mother was showing my aunt pictures of *me*. Me at my graduation. Me in something that looked like a dress in 1978.

It was embarrassing in part because I couldn't imagine my aunt possibly being interested. But also because the pictures were a cringe-making reminder of the fact that, while we may not have taken many holidays, and our Christmases were far from festive, I was a hideously spoilt child. The Holy Book had been opened at random a few days after my birth, as tradition dictates, the first letter in the left corner dictating my name would begin with the first letter of the English alphabet. But even this was not enough for my lovestruck parents. I was given the nickname 'Rajah', translating as 'king'. I was stationed in a cot behind the counter and anyone who passed was subjected to tales about my advanced achievements, whether it was a word I'd learnt to utter, or a particularly successful bowel movement. From the very youngest age my mother hired pundits and palm readers who, knowing which side their bread was buttered, regaled her with tales of my glittering future.

'He is such a good boy,' beamed my aunt, seemingly interested in my tedious biography. 'And Freya is such a nice girl.'

My mum smiled a tight smile. A knife through my heart. 'Ah, well, we broke up.'

'Oh no, when did this happen?' My aunt looked almost as upset as I felt. 'I thought you were engaged?'

'We were. It's a long story, Massi. I'll tell you another day'

My mother corrected me. 'It's Massi-ji.' Then she started cleaning up. It would, after all, have been a calamity to leave the dishes for a few hours, or, for that matter, actually to use the dishwasher that I had installed. Surinder sidled up to me after Mum left the living room.

'Now tell me, how is your mother? Healthwise?'

'Good. She has been in remission for a while now.'

'Should she be *really* working in the shop? Why doesn't she retire?'

This was another long story, but one worth telling. I told Surinder about my father's dedication to the shop. About my mother's refusal to give it up. That I had gradually come to the conclusion that the shop, as nightmarish as it was to run, gave Mum a sense of meaning and purpose. Obviously, the days when Bains Stores played a central role in the community were long gone. People didn't pop in to use the phone when the callbox outside was broken; didn't ask us to call midwives or ambulances, pass on messages, or come in to have knives sharpened. Even the days I dimly recalled when the police would come round to ask if someone's spending habits had changed were over. But the thing that had made it hardest to get Mum out of the shop was that I could see she got something from the regular auntie conferences, the brief conversations she had with customers about the rising price of carrots, or the laugh they had when she asked for their ID in broken English, though they were over sixty.

'But *you* can't want to stay here,' said Surinder. 'I looked you up on the internet. Your pictures, amazing.' I blushed with genuine embarrassment. I'd not thought about painting for months, let alone done any. 'Why doesn't she move in with you in London?'

'Why?' It was one of those questions so big, like 'Why does God allow war?', that it was impossible to know where to begin. I wasn't even sure I would have a place in London soon. In the event I proffered one of the least significant reasons: 'London wouldn't suit her.' I squinted into the bare bulb lighting the room, and finished the orange juice which had been poured into one of the Esso crystal wine glasses. 'You know what, I am coming to the view that she might be OK if I spend part of the week here. With Ranjit helping out occasionally.'

'The *Dhandas*?' There was a flash of something in her eyes. Meanwhile, the door behind her opened. It was Mum returning with another mound of food, a tray of sticky jalebis and soft gulab jaman.

'Hai rubba, pehnji,' protested Surinder, laughing. 'We've only just eaten!'

'Hush. You should never measure when it comes to food.'

'Mataji would always say that,' my aunt informed me.

Mum put the tray down, came back with some tea, and then moved towards the bottom drawer of the display cabinet that stood against the back wall of the room. 'Look, I've got something to show you.'

She produced a dusty old box, the kind my father would file receipts in. But this did not belong to my father – it was hers. Sitting down, she opened it, revealing a bunch of papers, cuttings, postcards and letters. I would pore over them for hours in the weeks that followed, and discover all kinds of things, from letters my grandfather wrote to my grandmother, postcards Surinder wrote to my mother, letters my father wrote to the local paper, and one, in return, from Dhanda taking issue with something he wrote ('Mr Bains mentions the caste system in relation to the Sikhs. He is factually mistaken. We Sikhs do not observe the caste system. Yours sincerely, P.D.'). The idea that my mother would collect written material at all, given her determined disinterest in literature, came as a surprise. But sometimes it is people who don't read who have the most respect for the written word. And this evening she had something specific to show her sister.

'I thought it was time you got your A-level results,' she said, producing a newspaper cutting that had been laminated in plastic.

Surinder yelped at the sight of them. Biology: A. English: A. History: B.

'They printed all your school's results in the paper,' said Mum. 'Tanvir cut them out.'

'I can't believe you kept them.' She covered her mouth with her silk scarf, then raised it higher as Mum produced a thin scrapbook containing a selection of magazine cuttings and posters that my aunt had compiled as a youth.

'Oh my! The Monkees!! I can't believe you kept all this.'

My mum continued delicately. 'I kept them because they reminded me of you. But also for Mataji. When she visited, she would always want to take a look.' Tears again. Her voice dropped an octave. 'I don't know if this is the time to talk about this, but I have waited years. I know you think that Mataji wanted to marry you off to Dhanda. But she was against the idea. That's why she sent you to Southall. And you know, I don't think Dhanda really meant his proposal. He was still grieving for dediji, and I think it came out of that. He is not a bad person. He and his family have been a source of strength to me over the years, and to us, since Tanvir died. Haven't they, Arjan?'

I weighed up the evidence, trying not to look startled by the revelation for the sake of my aunt. On the one hand Ranjit had, in a roundabout way, caused my split with Freya and totally ruined my life. On the other, he had led me, in a roundabout way, to my aunt. 'If it wasn't for Ranjit, I would not have found you,' I conceded. 'It was because of him that I met Jim.'

'You met Jim?' asked my aunt, her voice unsteady.

'I think so. To be honest, I'm not sure it was really him. It was a man in Birmingham who answered to his name and seemed to be the right age.'

She asked for a physical description.

'Yeah, was probably him.' She looked pale. Produced her BlackBerry, scrolled through the messages.

My mother continued. 'What happened with him, Surinder?' she asked. 'You know, there are lots of people who are divorced nowadays. People remarry all the time. You don't need to feel ashamed.'

I cringed at my mother's choice of words. Even when trying to sound modern and liberal, she used vocabulary from 1950s Punjab. Surinder, who had been looking increasingly pained, said she needed to make a quick call, and disappeared into the backyard. Alone with Mum, I castigated her for taking things too far too soon, Massi was clearly not ready to go over everything, and sure enough when my aunt returned, red-eyed, smelling of cigarettes, she announced she had to go home. 'The last direct train is at seven,' she said, in an official tone.

Mum looked crestfallen. 'You're not staying?' She stood up. 'I've got your room ready.'

'Oh, pehnji, I'd love to, but it was hard enough getting time off today. And I've got to take Jessie to the vet tomorrow. I promise to be back soon.'

'When?'

'Very soon.' She began putting on her coat.

'I'll drive you to the station,' I offered.

'It's no problem. I've ordered a taxi. It will be here in a few minutes.'

I don't think I had ever seen Mum look so happy and so sad within such a short space of time. She took straight to bed after her sister left, where she would again remain for days. As for me, well, I checked my phone and saw that I'd received a message from Freya's best friend. It said: 'Offer received on flat. Please pick up your things within next fortnight. Anything you leave will be thrown out.' The gloom that had been encircling our home re-descended, and this time it felt like it would claim us entirely.

Brixton Hill Medical Practice had expanded rapidly since 1970, taking on new partners, growing its list of patients and substantially increasing turnover. Not that you would have guessed it from walking around the surgery six years later. The five doctors had 8,500 patients on their lists, but employed just two receptionists between them. And while conventional wisdom dictated that your average doctor's waiting room should allocate one chair per 100–200 patients on the books, the ratio at BHMP was stuck at around one per 400.

Leaning against a wall, Surinder tried to distract herself from the aches which had brought her to the doctor's for the second time in a month by taking an interest in her surroundings. A bare, wooden floor, which should have been carpeted to reduce noise. Announcements on the noticeboard: a list of immunisation schedules, and the outlining of consulting hours which seemed to have been set according to some obscure local tradition dating back to the nineteenth century.

But when she still hadn't been called through after half an hour, she stepped across the desultory children's play area consisting of a small table and plastic chair and, heading towards the reception desk, did something she hadn't done in years. She picked up a magazine. There had been a time when she had read for comfort. It had made her feel less alone. But nowadays the perspective provided by the written word just made her feel worse about her place in the scheme of things. The first article she came across, a letter to an agony aunt in a women's magazine that had lost its cover and was greasy from overuse, illustrated why.

Q. Dear Sarah. I have been with my husband for eight years now, and he is kind and supportive. But I hate being married. Sometimes I feel so unhappy and useless I want to sleep for ever. I seem to live in a velvet-lined prison. What should I do? Annie.

A velvet-lined prison? Surinder *dreamt* of such a prison. Marriage, in her case, was a cold, unlit, cockroach-infested cell with a bare concrete floor. Jim had turned out to be a drunk. And a seducer. The glint he had in his eye during their first day in London was not romantic love, but excitement about booze and what he might get in bed. When he realised he wasn't going to have his way, that Surinder was not going to salve his conscience by returning home, he had agreed to marry her. But she lamented daily, sometimes hourly, that she had badgered him into doing so.

Tanvir was right. He had been forever warning her about salesmen. 'If a rep appears who you've never met before, you should never pay him cash, unless he brings in produce and offers a receipt . . . Don't fall for their off-the-cuff claims, they will say anything for a sale.' And this was the thing: Jim had, more than anything else, turned out to be a salesman. The promise of marriage hadn't been his only fib. He wasn't, it turned out, Irish, except distantly: he had grown up in Essex and put on the accent as part of his sales patter. Central London was just as foreign to him as it was to her aunt in Southall, his knowledge of metropolitan life coming from newspapers and magazines. The job in London was a fiction: it turned out he had failed what had been a trial in the West Midlands, and was now reduced to the role of casual labourer, working in dairies and factories. The poems he had sent to her during their courtship were copied from books.

His enthusiasm for Hardy was fake, his opinions taken from the comments on the back of paperback editions. And she wouldn't have been surprised if even the story about being set upon in Wolverhampton was made up too, a trick designed to re-enter her life.

Surinder accepted these revelations, when they came, with equanimity. No one had forced her to elope with Jim. He had exploited her naivety and her family were pushing her into marriage, but that was the culture she had been born into. Looking back she wasn't even really sure how keen her mother would have been on Dhanda's proposal, and in her heart of hearts she always knew something wasn't right about Jim. What was that line again? *Ignorance is as structured as knowledge.* She knew now that she had chosen not to know certain things. She had been disturbed by Dhanda's expression of interest, and incensed, panicking, she had taken a gamble on the only available alternative, blocking out any reservations she might have felt. Her elopement was a mistake, a disaster, but it was her disaster, a situation of her own making. There was no way of going back to Wolverhampton. She had done the worst thing a Sikh girl could do, and in the early days of marriage she had tried to make the best of it.

She didn't complain when Jim drank. Didn't deny him sexual satisfaction. When he failed to find regular employment, she got two jobs to support them, working in a supermarket during the day and as a waitress in a Spanish restaurant in the evenings. However, it is one thing to accept that your husband is a drunk and a liar. But another to conceal your disdain at him being so. She found him lazy and self-pitying, and couldn't hide the fact. For his part, Jim found Surinder impatient and condescending, and couldn't pretend that he didn't do so. They brought out the worst in each other. And six years into it, though Jim sometimes still found himself seeking her approval – both had largely given up trying. No subject was too insignificant to fight about. Mistakes were pounced upon, never forgiven. Neither of them had a sense of humour when it came to each other. In Surinder's case, her husband suspected she had no sense of humour at all. They communicated almost entirely through threats and name-calling. And when Surinder glanced at the agony aunt's reply, she cringed at the platitudes about 'commitment' and 'patience', and began drafting an alternative reply in her head.

'*Dear Annie*,' she began. '*Young people sometimes think they know what is meant when they hear that marriage is hard. They imagine there will be times when they will not feel so close to their spouse, times when they won't be carried to bed at night or brought breakfast in bed. But the reality is more brutal. Sometimes you will actively despise your partner. Married life is not only marked by occasional bouts of antagonism, but also by sustained enmity. The person who was once the centre of your world can become the person you least want to spend time with. The mere reference to the fact that he is your husband will cause you embarrassment . . .*'

Surinder was still drafting this letter, thinking about how, if Jim died, she would probably have to peel onions to make herself cry, when she was snapped out of her reverie by the sight of the receptionist running out of the office, separated from the waiting room only by way of a glass partition, with a bucket. The young woman stopped abruptly in front of a toddler, who promptly vomited into it. Doctors' receptionists probably developed a sixth sense for such things, but it was still impressive to see.

However, admiration quickly gave way to enervation when the child was taken into the consultation room that she had been assigned, delaying her appointment still further. In the time the other doctors had seen four or five patients each, her doctor had seen two. She put down her magazine, picked up another, opened it at random and was confronted with a headline pronouncing, 'How to spot if your husband is being unfaithful'. The list of 'giveaway signs' didn't do much for her nausea.

'Angry, critical and even at times cruel.' Tick.

'Constant put-downs and little to no patience.' Tick.

'Expresses a "my way or the highway" type of attitude during arguments.' Tick.

She felt her throat tightening. Despite everything, Surinder would not have tolerated infidelity. But then, amid the dread, a reassuring thought: wasn't she as guilty of many of these cited crimes too? She had never been unfaithful, wouldn't have known where to find the time for it, but she was 'angry, critical and even at times cruel'. She subjected Jim to 'constant put-downs' and had 'little to no patience.' She never 'consulted' her 'partner about purchases'. And she often expressed a '"my way or the highway" type of attitude' towards her husband. Plainly, the author of the article did not understand marriage.

Indeed, Jim and Surinder had casually committed most of these cited offences between them just the previous evening, during one of their regular flare-ups. Surinder had come back from her day job at the supermarket and was on the mattress on the floor she used to avoid sharing a bed with Jim, trying to sleep off the headache and fever that had been bothering her, before heading off to La Tasca, when her husband had turned up and, unsteady on his feet from a day of drinking, bellowed, 'I need to l-l-lend some money.'

Surinder turned around so that her back was to him. 'You mean borrow.'

'What?'

'You mean, you want to *borrow* some money.'

'Look, we are married. You are meant to listen to me.'

Surinder snorted at the irony of his choice of words. Throughout her childhood her mother had brought her up to respect her future husband, to always succumb to his decisions and desires, and now the man who had inspired her to reject that life was appealing to those values.

'What's so funny?'

'There's some food in the cupboard,' she sighed, placing a pillow over her head to block out the light and his voice. But she could still hear him through it.

'Call that food?!'

Jim had a point. Surinder was at this time living almost entirely on packets of Complan, milk powder supposedly fortified with all the vitamins and salts you needed for good health. It was sold in packets at the chemist in Brixton High Street. When she grew tired of the taste, she would mix the powder with fruit squash. If she tired of that, she would drink eggs, raw and beaten up in milk.

She told herself this was because they didn't have a fridge in their bedsit. But in truth it was the logical conclusion of her avoidance of any kind of flavour or seasoning or spice, the slightest whiff of which could remind her of home and send her spiralling into a calamitous depression. She also bought it for the same reason she sometimes visited the local church for warmth: thrift had become a habit. In Bains Stores, one of her mother's most frequent complaints was that Surinder was extravagant, that she didn't, as the saying went, 'know the difference between a penny and a pound'. But economy was yet another area of life on which she had come over to her mother's view. Married life is hard. Reading magazines and books puts silly ideas into your head. Thrift is more worthwhile than extravagance, because it requires effort and thought.

Surinder cleared her sore, aching throat and summoned the energy to respond. 'If it's not good enough for you, James, you could always get a job and use the extravagant wages to dine in Soho.'

Jim, enraged, pulled the pillow from Surinder's face and thrust a copy of the *Mirror* into her face. 'Do you know what it's like out there?' The headline pronounced, '1,430,369, IT'S GOING TO GET WORSE'. Underneath, a smaller one elaborated, 'Foot's warning as jobless total hits new peak'.

He wouldn't have dared to have been physically forceful if Surinder had been well. His one attempt to bully her physically had resulted in a broken plant pot and a visit to Casualty.

'There is work, if you want it enough.' She curled her lip.

Jim dropkicked the pillow across the room, sending a cloud of dust floating down from the battered, polka-dot lampshade. 'I know you have money. Where do you fucking keep it?'

He began rifling through Surinder's possessions. Seeing it was time to get ready for work, Surinder sat up and lit a cigarette. Breathing in deeply, feeling the smoke clearing out her throat and sinuses, she appraised Jim with the detachment of a parent enduring a toddler's tantrum. His hair was another of his lies: underneath the dye it was a mousey brown, and now thinning, in that awkward phase between full-headedness and baldness when it develops a life of its own. There were signs of wrinkles near his eyes, hairs growing out of his nostrils and ears. And he was no longer a dandy. He had pawned off the best of his shoes and clothes, which wouldn't have fitted him any more anyway, and was now rarely out of the same pair of jeans and knee-length boots, even though they seemed to cause him visible physical discomfort.

It wouldn't take him long to get through all of Surinder's things. She had over time reduced her belongings, just as she had cut back her diet and could fit everything she owned in a single suitcase. And he wouldn't find any money. She put everything she earned into a Barclays Bank account. The account book was kept in a bank safety-deposit box, along with her wedding jewellery. And the key for the safety box was accessed by the showing of a passport, which she always kept on her person.

The security measures were necessary not only because Jim was not to be trusted when it came to money, but also because he was right about Surinder hoarding cash. It's amazing how much you can save when you have no social life, take no holidays, work two jobs, live in a bedsit, and when you manage a portfolio of ten flats and bedsits for your slum landlord on the side.

Sometimes Surinder felt that Mr Grant had been the only good thing that had happened to her since arriving in London. Not that he had looked like good news when they met. A West Indian in his sixties, almost as wide as he was tall, with an overbearing third wife and a brood of children, he charged an exorbitant rent for a single damp basement room in Brixton with a shared bathroom and WC; specialised in renting out to the poor, the unmarried, others who couldn't finance their own homes; and offered her reduced rent in exchange for sex on the second occasion that they met.

His self-ascribed nickname, meanwhile, was 'Enoch', on the confused grounds that he (a) opposed race relations legislation that made it illegal to discriminate when it came to letting out property ('It is my right to decide if I no want my house to be stink up with goat curry'), and (b) Powell had said, 'In this country in fifteen or twenty years' time the black man will have the whip hand over the white man.' ('Now there is a brother who understands black power.')

Grant's brutal tenant management methods, meanwhile, seemed to be a subconscious response to the chaos of his home life, involving, as they did, dumping cooked potatoes on floors, leaving dead rats in beds, sprinkling itching powder on bedding, removing slates from the roof, taking up carpets, cutting down washing lines, putting snakes in bathrooms and, his favourite tactic, standing for hours outside windows and staring at the tenant when they were alone.

But times were changing, and when the amendments to the Rent Act were introduced to legislate against greedy and incompetent landlords, and families found they automatically had security of tenure provided they paid the rent, Grant found himself facing a tribunal and turned to Surinder for advice. No one was more surprised by this request than Surinder, given that she and Jim had been among the tenants he had, until recently, been trying to remove, kicking their door whenever he passed it and persuading all the children in the building to do likewise. But it turned out not to be a request based on friendship or trust or any such conventional human emotion. He had spotted, during one of his illegal inspections of Surinder and Jim's living quarters, some of Surinder's old books from Wolverhampton, and not being good with paperwork, and not knowing anyone who was, he assumed she could help.

Surinder could. Having been trained at Bains Stores in the art of filling out forms for the illiterate and, at times, criminal, she slipped into the role, wrote letters, made calls and, in exchange for a month's rent, got Grant off the hook. It was the easiest money she had ever made, and after it was over she decided to take advantage of Grant's disproportionate gratitude by offering her services as an agent. She had heard there were small businesses that found tenants for landlords. She knew lots of people looking for rooms through work, and offered to start finding reliable tenants for Mr Grant in exchange for discounted rent.

She made her case carefully and fluently, pointing out that if he had better, more reliable tenants, he would have fewer rent reviews and, in turn, an easier life. She made sure that the arguments were backed up with examples and, where possible, numbers. It was a presentation, in fact, worthy of a professional estate agent. If professional estate agents made presentations in corridors, that was, and if the proposed client wasn't drinking lager throughout and gawping at your breasts as you spoke. Grant refused outright. Furiously so. Banging his fist against the wall in the corridor he conducted most of his meetings in, displacing loose plaster with every thump.

Surinder admonished herself as he did so. What had she been thinking? He was never going to agree to something so *rational*.

This, after all, was a man who co-owned an unlicensed drinking club on the Railton Road, and yet complained incessantly about the traffic and litter caused by other unlicensed drinking clubs near his digs, who professed to loathe the police ('They bust a case in your arse for just walking down the street') and yet, when there had recently been riots in Notting Hill as the result of the arbitrary harassment and arrests of young black attendees, he had decided he would never rent to the blacks again ('Ain't no white man not paid me rent on time.') He was an idiot.

But it turned out that Grant was cross not about her suggestion; he was infuriated because he had something else in mind for Surinder. He didn't want her to find him tenants, but she could manage his whole property portfolio for him, if she so desired. He had been left shaken by his brush with the law. The brave new world of responsible landlording with the drafting of contracts and furniture inventories was not for him, and if she could take over the whole thing in exchange for a percentage fee, he could extricate himself from his nightmare family and professional obligations and one day move back to Jamaica, where he would sit around on the beach 'raising pussy' and living off the proceeds.

'I don't wanna spend me twilight years dealing with tenants making rab 'bout towel rails. Enuff is enuff. Time I reap the rewards for the toil I put into this godforsaken country. It's yours if you want.'

Surinder wanted it. Soon, when she wasn't stacking shelves in the supermarket or being sexually harassed in the restaurant, she was checking references and fixtures and fittings, writing contracts, returning deposits (less any charges), putting adverts in papers. And making, as Jim suspected, a shed-load of money.

'I know that fat bastard gives you cash,' shouted Jim, resuming his rant. 'How often do you have to fuck him for it? Are you sending it to your family?'

Most of Jim's insults washed over her like small talk about the weather – she had heard it all before. But the comment about her family riled. It was astonishing to her that Jim still seemed to have no appreciation of the sacrifice she had made to marry him. Did he really not understand that there was no way she could ever contact her family again? And, more importantly, did he really not understand how proud she was?

Pride, after all, was the defining characteristic of her people, dearer to the average Punjabi than life itself. It was what made Sikhs good soldiers, the thing that made them susceptible to vendettas and family disputes that rumbled on for decades; it was why her father had lived in a house with fifteen other men, surviving on baked beans, while he worked in a foundry to save up enough to set up his shop, when it would have been easier to return home; why Mr Jolly really would have, if necessary, gone through with his threat to set fire to himself in the road directly outside Wolverhampton Town Hall 'in the mid darkness with only four or five companions' if Wolverhampton Transport Department hadn't conceded on the point of the turban.

But Surinder knew better than to express her annoyance. It would give Jim too much satisfaction. Instead, she got up and got ready for work, applying make-up, smoothing her hair, which she had for the last year worn short, jaw-length and streaked, cutting her own fringe every two weeks, and getting changed into the tight white polyester blouse and tight black cotton skirt that amounted to her uniform. She had asked to be allowed to wear trousers instead, with the unisex, long-sleeved tunic that the waitresses in the Italian restaurant opposite wore. But her manager wouldn't permit it, and as she put on her shoes, she wondered whether he had also deliberately ordered her uniform one size too small. Once ready, she lit a cigarette, took a drag, smiled at Jim and remarked, 'The thing about you, Jim, is that you really are quite thick.'

Jim was, for some reason, standing in the middle of the room clutching a saucepan. 'Right. That's it. I want a d-d-divorce.'

'Very well,' she agreed quickly between puffs. 'You can have one. Please. I would love a *d-d-divorce*. Get your lawyer to write to me.'

Jim's stammer had once seemed charming. But this was another thing about marriage: it could turn the vulnerability that once enticed you into a fair target. Jim fled from the bedsit, slamming the door behind him. The whole episode had bothered Surinder no more than if she had mislaid a dessert spoon. Doubtless Jim would return in a day or two, and they would go through the whole thing all over again.

The pain and the fever had worsened by the following morning and Surinder, to the astonishment of her colleagues at the super-market, tarnished her immaculate attendance record by taking the morning off to go to the doctor. Her appointment was at 11 a.m. but it was gone midday by the time she was called in. However, the relief of finally getting to see a doctor was momentary. For on opening the door, it transpired that the GP she had been assigned was the worst thing possible. He was Indian.

Since coming to London, Surinder had avoided all things Asian. If anyone spoke Punjabi or Hindi to her, she would profess not to understand. No 'Hare Krishnas', as Grant referred to people of her background, got a chance at a room. If anyone asked where she was from, and people seemed to ask where she was from fifteen times a day, she would say she was half Spanish, answering any follow-up questions with the back story of one of her restau-rant colleagues, a 23-year-old graduate from the Universidad Autónoma de Madrid, whose estranged father had been an airline pilot, and whose mother lived in Streatham.

There had been moments of weakness, such as the time she visited Tooting in a fit of homesickness, knowing it to be home to a sizeable Punjabi community. But there was no pleasure in the nostalgia. She felt self-conscious with her short hair, was convinced the aunties could smell cigarettes on her, and lacked the courage to enter the temple in her Western clothes. In the end, she went into an Indian grocery shop and, almost choking on the aromas of methi and mirch, bought some pomegranates and the ingredients for chapattis. Back in the bedsit, she put herself through the ritual she had once resented at home, mixing the dough, turning it out on to a lightly floured board, kneading it until it became smooth and elastic. She didn't have a thava – just an English frying pan. Her first effort fell apart as it cooked. She did better with practice, but consuming the fruits of her labour with baked beans merely highlighted the gap between her efforts and the memory.

That evening she had penned a postcard to her sister, even though Kamaljit was, for all she knew, no longer living in Wolverhampton, or even in England. There was nothing therapeutic in the writing; it just made her feel even more lonely. The act of sending it simply made her finally appreciate the futility of dwelling on her past, and she had since become expert at shutting things out, so practised at lying that she almost believed her fictions herself. And as she took a seat in the doctor's consulting room, still warm from the preceding visitor, and as the doctor wrote up the notes for the previous patient – appendicitis, it turned out – she planned how she would lie if he called her 'pehnji' or, after that Indian yes/no head roll, enquired about which part of India her parents came from.

In the event, she needn't have worried. He spoke the kind of English that was only spoken by the upper classes and the graduates of private schools in India, and barely looked up from his notes when he did so. 'You're being treated for a urinary infection, I see,' he remarked by way of introduction. 'Dr Barker gave you amoxicillin. Any good?'

Surinder breathed out in relief. Clearly he was the kind of doctor more interested in disease than people.

'No. I'm feeling quite a lot worse.'

'Did he examine you? Do any swabs?'

'No.'

'Treated you blind,' he said to himself, making a note. 'Could you describe your symptoms?'

Surinder didn't know where to begin. But focusing on the books on the shelf behind the doctor's head – *The National Formulary*, *Prescriber's Journal* – she tried. Unfortunately, the more information she provided, the more questions there were. What kind of pain was it? Was there vaginal bleeding between periods? She answered as fully as she could bring herself to, but then, to her dismay, Dr Chaudhari, peering at her through his spectacles, asked, 'Married, it says here. Is there pain during intercourse?'

Oh God. Maybe it would have been better if they had acknowledged their shared ethnicity after all. At least, her Indian family doctor in Wolverhampton would never have been so direct. How on earth could she possibly explain her sex life to a complete stranger when she couldn't face acknowledging it to herself? In the beginning, it had seemed to be about frequency for Jim, rather than quality or length. But it had been the first thing to go, as their marriage floundered. In the preceding year they had slept together just once. She was at the time having one of her periodic attempts to make things, if not work, then tolerable. She had decided that she would have one more shot at being a wife. So when Jim went on at tedious length about something utterly inconsequential, she resisted the urge to say, 'You're making a big deal out of things for no reason.' She tried not to wince when he spoke in clichés ('That's life . . . you have to break a few eggs'), tried not to roll her eyes when he returned every story and situation to himself ('That reminds me of the time . . .'). Jim had responded in kind, if not quite complimenting her, then telling her about the efforts he was making to find a job and to drink less. But it was going to bed with him that brought home the hopelessness of her efforts. When he touched her, her instinctive reaction was to lash out. Sleeping with almost anyone else would have been preferable. She knew that she could not go through it again.

Surinder had taken in most of the surgery – the flat-topped desk, the examination couch – before answering. 'It might be painful,' she said vaguely, unable to use a personal pronoun.

The doctor glanced at her directly for the first time, with the hint of a raised eyebrow. He wrote down something which Surinder couldn't decipher. Then he put both hands on his desk, looked at her directly and said, 'Right. You have a choice. I could do a swab of the cervix here today. We have a female chaperone. Or I could refer you to a clinic.'

Surinder glanced at the examination table, the trolley containing plastic gloves, imagined the shame of sliding off her pants, lying down on the table, her feet in the air, the doctor squirting gel on his glove-clad fingers, and opted for the clinic.

'I'll get my receptionist to write up a referring letter,' continued the doctor. 'It will be ready by four this afternoon. But we are open until six.' He slid back on his chair and rose. 'I'd get to the clinic early – long queues in the day. Plenty of fluids in the mean-time.' He opened the door. 'And rest.'

Surinder took the doctor's advice and didn't go to work that day. Instead, she slept, rising at half five to check that a departing tenant had left his single room at the top of the mansion block in good order. A large part of being a landlord, or a surrogate land-lord, involved preparing rooms as people arrived and left. And this tenant, an overly polite Kenyan student with a job in the centre of town, had, as she expected, left his room in pristine condition. The plain red fitted carpet was as new. The hessian curtains had been cleaned. Even the Hoover had been serviced and the mop head replaced.

She felt a wave of warmth for the boy. He was reliable and clean – the perfect tenant – and also utterly beautiful. A face unlike any other she had seen, different from every angle you viewed it, and eyelashes longer than she had ever seen on any man. Letting out to single black men was something else Grant was wrong about: the ones she had chosen had turned out to be much less trouble than the couples and families.

Walking around the room, looking out of the window at a patch of urban greenery, she found herself envying the next tenant of the flat. It was so quiet and peaceful upstairs compared to her basement bedsit, and as she desired it, she wondered whether her main mistake in life had been confusing desire for romance with desire for solitude. She had replaced the clamour on Victoria Road – children cowering as their mothers admonished them, her mother yelling at the top of her voice – with a marriage of bickering and strife, when what she had really needed was peace and quiet. It was not something most Indians could conceive, but maybe solitude was the key to contentment.

Little did she know that in a few hours' time, she would have it. On collecting her referring letter from the doctors, she would move her meagre belongings from the room she shared with Jim, have the locks changed and throw her husband's bits and pieces into a bag, which, in turn, would be left out on the street. You see, on opening Dr Chaudhari's referring letter, she realised there was one sign that *Cosmopolitan* magazine had missed out in its article on 'How to spot if your husband is being unfaithful': when you find yourself being sent to a VD clinic.

Ranjit, ultimately, proved right about another thing: my aunt. The idea of finding Surinder so that she might free me from my retail obligations worked out better than either of us could have imagined. By February she was spending every weekend in the shop, pitching in behind the counter. And by spring of the New Year, she had taken early retirement and moved in, insisting as she did so that I return to London to find work. The whole thing happened at the speed of light. It felt like a miracle. But if it passed without a single expression of delight or joy, it was because it was prompted by the most painful of developments.

The illness that my mother had succumbed to over Christmas, and again when Surinder departed suddenly on New Year's Day, was not, as I had assumed at the time, psychosomatic. She turned up for her annual check-up in the first week of January, and a key biomarker in her blood was elevated. There followed a CT scan, and an appointment with an oncologist at which she was informed that the cancer was back in her spleen and in the lining of her diaphragm.

My mother took the news with her habitual what-will-be-will-be, chaloo-koi-gaal-nahi composure. She continued working in the shop, and embraced the consultant's suggestion that she needn't embark upon treatment until she felt worse. She didn't even allow me to shut up shop to accompany her to appointments, instead taking up the hospital's offer of a translator. The only real change was a slight increase in her praying and a minor uptick in the religiosity of the conferences she had with her auntie friends in the shop every other day.

I guess I should have been philosophical too — I had been through it before and was aware the cancer might come back. But knowing is not the same thing as accepting, and the return of the disease made me appreciate how much my father had protected me the first time round, how great Freya had been throughout, and I missed them both almost as intensely as I worried about my mother. I descended further into depression, went from running all the time and not being able to sleep at all, to sleeping as much as I could, going to bed early and snoozing in the middle of the day, like a Punjabi farmer during the height of summer. In the shop, the most common remark from customers went from being 'Are you open?' to 'Cheer up, it might never happen.' But the thing is: it had. And it says something about the hopelessness of that time that it didn't even occur to me to inform my aunt about Mum's news until several days afterwards.

I texted her one afternoon, during the quiet period in the shop between lunch and the end of school. She rang back minutes later, as I was serving a customer, then called again and again until I finally picked up — tears in her voice, a barrage of questions — and drove up to see us that very evening. She stayed the night, even though she had not planned to do so, leaving in the same clothes she had arrived in, asking me to make an emergency visit to a chemist for some contact lens solution. She returned the following weekend, with a wheelie suitcase this time, spending two nights in the shop. She accompanied Mum to her next appointment, insisted on arranging for a second opinion with a private doctor, despite my mother's protestations about expense. Looked into clinical trials. Went down to a three-day week at the hotel, to help out more meaningfully at Bains Stores. Then, as Mum finally began a course of chemotherapy, Surinder, without really discussing her plan, only remarking on the way to her leaving do that she had never really enjoyed working for someone else, took early retirement and moved into the house, taking over my father's former study, and trading her Porsche in for a BMW estate which Mum could manoeuvre in and out of with more ease.

It seems odd, looking back, that I accepted her return so uninquisitively. But I think I did so in part because she was only doing what I had done, and in part because she was a Punjabi woman, and the defining characteristic of Punjabi women, after all, is self-sacrifice. Also, analysing it would have been like questioning a pools' win. It was all just too useful to fret about; with Massi, right from the beginning, without me even explaining my situation, refusing to countenance the idea of me working in the shop for more than a few hours, insisting she could manage with Mum, more often than not adding, 'Just get back to that lovely girlfriend of yours.'

Not that my mum's news had suddenly brought Freya and I back together. But it did bring about a cessation in hostilities. She let me keep my things in our flat until the sale finally went through. And while she rebuffed any notion of getting back together, she suggested we do our breaking up via a counsellor. There was a time when any kind of couples' therapy would have brought me out in hives, and the idea of having marriage guidance to break-up a prospective marriage struck me as odd, to say the least. But I read on the relevant website that some people had couples' therapy when they weren't in a relationship at all, and I was grateful, to be honest, for any kind of contact, for even a glimmer of hope.

A new routine developed. In the week, I travelled to London for freelance work; Freya would let me know when she wasn't around and I would then use the flat. But otherwise I would either commute from Wolverhampton or work from home, toiling in my bedroom above the shop, except when my aunt and mother were visiting hospital, when I would man the counter. On Saturday mornings I would travel to Nuneaton, where Freya and I would sit for an hour in the front room of a 'culturally sensitive' mixed-race mother of three and talk about what had gone wrong. Then, after hugging awkwardly on the pavement outside, I would return to the Midlands to help my aunt and mum with shopkeeping duties for the remainder of the weekend.

It was a surreal time, life felt like it had simultaneously come to a standstill and was galloping on at an uncontrollable pace, though the weirdest aspect of it all was watching my aunt go through a version of what I had been through, being hit as if by a brick by the tedium of Black Country retail. Except she had a rather more proactive approach to it all than me, managing to transform the shop in just her first day of involvement by getting rid of the hectoring signs in the window – 'Only 2 School Kids at a Time', 'CCTV in Operation', etc. – having the window shutters fixed, and dumping the pile of £4.99 shirts at the back of the shop, unwanted gifts from Indian weddings, which Dad flogged to the men who would turn up in ripped clothes at 5 a.m. on Saturday mornings.

The changes became more pronounced when Surinder moved in. She altered the way the newspapers were displayed, moving the piles we stocked on the counter on to a modern newspaper stand, arguing that the front pages increased the likelihood of impulse sales. She began stocking sandwiches in the chiller cabinet, pointing out that with Britons spending £5 billion on them every year, it was daft not to. Every time I came back from London, something was different, whether it was Surinder delisting the slowest-selling 10 per cent of the confectionery and crisps ranges, or putting the best-selling products in the best positions, or introducing a rack of greetings cards, or replacing the pizza and out-of-date oven chips in the ice-cream freezer with actual ice cream.

All this energy was, I think, mainly the result of her natural entrepreneurialism. She didn't enjoy talking about herself, would try to change the subject if you enquired, but I slowly managed to piece together the basic elements of her business biography. She had, apparently, been given a chance to buy the mansion block she had been managing in South London in 1980. She took the opportunity, purchasing it using her savings and a series of loans, and buying the flats next door during the '80s property boom, before getting planning permission to convert the whole thing into a hotel. It was successful for some time: she specialised for several years in catering for the homeless, getting paid a premium from the local authority to house them. But there were financial difficulties during the recession of the 1990s, the banks repossessed some of her portfolio and she ended up taking a break from running a business to study for an executive MBA.

Which brings me to the other thing that drove her: her intellectual belief in independent retail. As she was keen on pointing out, if the small shop was done for, then why were Turkish families and supermarkets getting into the convenience-store trade? Why did the Dhandas own three Audis and a portfolio of nineteen rental properties? The fact was that small shops were not dead, but small shops that didn't adapt to the marketplace were dead. It was clear that if she was going to be stuck in Bains Stores, she was going to make sure it was successful. In her first two months, she managed to double turnover. And, amazingly, she did this while shortening opening hours. Bains Stores now opened between 7 a.m. and 6 p.m., cutting two hours off the start and the end of the day. And, in a truly remarkable development, on Sundays we shut at lunchtime, so that we could go for walks together in the English countryside.

These jaunts felt no less spectacular for having been originally conceived as something significantly more ambitious. If memory serves, it all began during one of Surinder's first weekends back. It was about nine on a Saturday evening, I had endured a shattering counselling session earlier that day in which Freya had admitted to sleeping with her Canadian ex over the New Year, and the three of us were sitting together in the living room, in worlds of our own.

I was vacantly scouring the web on a laptop, wondering if it was too early to go to bed. My aunt had just written a letter to the local paper expressing dismay at the failure of the council to build the much-heralded estate of eco-homes opposite the shop, and was now reading the *Financial Times*, lounging about in a T-shirt and tracksuit bottoms. My mother, sitting opposite us, in an armchair, her hair unplaited, enveloped in shawls, was watching a TV show on an Asian satellite channel hosted by a bearded yogi who seemed to be suggesting that consuming turmeric could prevent the common cold, or that he could cure AIDS with Ayurvedic drugs that were conveniently sold through his online store. To be honest, I wasn't really listening.

'You know,' began Massi, her legs crossed. 'There's no reason you should stay here. You could sell up and retire.'

'He's right about turmeric,' said my mother in my direction. 'My gums stopped bleeding when I started taking it. You should have it in milk once a day — you're always sniffling.'

My aunt tried again. 'You know, pehnji, we could always sell up and go travelling.'

The expression on my mother's face reminded me of one I had confronted a few weeks earlier, when I had tried to explain the couples' therapy Freya and I had embarked upon. The fact was that my mother had no talent for leisure in the way that we, as a family, had no talent for Christmas. As a child, I remember nagging my parents into a day trip, having claimed, fraudulently, that my complete ignorance of the sea was holding me back at school. They had a conference, and one Sunday we headed off, after the newspapers had been delivered, to Rhyl. It wasn't a success: after a three-hour journey during which I threw up twice in the back of my father's VW van, my mother produced a five-course Indian meal amid a crowd of sunbathing locals. I nearly died of cringe, and after just forty-five minutes it was time to head home.

'And go where?' said Mum eventually, her voice dripping with disbelief.

'I don't know,' said my aunt. A pause. 'New York?'

If Massi sounded uncertain it was because she was. The idea of America was clearly inspired by the picture of the Empire State Building emblazoned on her newspaper. A workaholic, she had travelled as little as my mother.

'I have no interest in going abroad,' pronounced Mum, with an air of finality.

'What about the Punjab then?' offered my aunt, uncrossing her legs and sitting up to make her case. Her hair, blow-dried, smoothed down and flicked up at the ends, belied the fact that she had just returned from the gym. 'Neither of us have visited India since we were children. The doctor says it would be good for you to be out and about. Don't you think it would be fun?'

The use of the English word 'fun' was a strategic error. Mum didn't do fun. Even buying birthday presents for her was a nightmare: she didn't want chocolates, gave anything she didn't need away to the temple, rarely shopped for clothes and would complain bitterly if she thought money was being 'wasted'. I knew what was coming.

'I have appointments to keep,' declared Mum. 'The shop to consider. We can't afford it.'

At this point, my aunt took the remote from the arm of my mother's chair, turned down the volume and made a rare biographical admission. Watching her, I could see she was uncomfortable going over it, and she made no eye contact while she spoke, instead glancing at the newspaper on her lap – she was always reading, whether it was a book, messages on her phone, or some magazine or paper – but she pointed out that she had taken gold jewellery from her mother when she had left home. She had justified the theft to herself at the time on the grounds that it was something that would have come to her anyway in the event of marriage. But in the years that followed, the guilt of taking it had gnawed away at her. She should have returned it when she started making money but had instead used the proceeds to help buy the building that became her hotel. It could be argued it was the ultimate source of her not inconsiderable savings, and she now wanted to make amends, to return the investment, and spending the money on her sister seemed an apt way of doing so.

There was a lengthy pause as Mum digested the argument. There is a Punjabi tradition with presents, that when you first receive them, you refuse them, and then, if the giver persists, you say in mitigation, 'Oh, that's too much, please halve it.' But in this case, Mum didn't even want half.

'I would never in a million years waste our father's hard-earned money on such nonsense,' she protested. 'To think how he worked all those years in the shop, the goras giving him hell, no wife or children or family around to bring him roti at the end of a long day, just to make money that his daughters would eventually waste swanning around foreign hotels, eating steak sandwiches in swimming pools for breakfast.' I have no idea where Mum got this image from, but it was clearly in her view something that decadent white people did on holiday. 'I wouldn't be able to live with myself.' She had not just taken the moral high ground, but once on it, she had taken a hot-air balloon flight.

Surinder withdrew meekly – 'Whatever you think best, pehnji' – hurt, but trying not to show it. My aunt had a natural air of authority. She had a way of asking for things, of ending her sentences, which made people instinctively obey her. This was the reason she had made inroads into the £4,000 of newspaper debts that my father and I had accumulated, why the pilferage and vandalism that had afflicted Bains Stores since my return, had ceased. Not only were local ruffians wary of her, the police almost always responded when she called. However, my mother was the one person immune to her charm.

I assumed that was the end of the holiday idea. But it turned out Surinder didn't give up. She kept on at Mum, emphasising the health benefits of getting out of the shop, suggesting a break in England when Mum objected to travelling abroad, introducing the concept of a day trip when Mum objected to a week away, and eventually, Mum made a concession. After a while, walks in the country became as much a part of Bains Stores' weekly routine as trips to the cash and carry.

There were many astonishing things about these jaunts, not least how we looked: my mother, the shorter and stouter of the two ladies, dressed in a shapeless pastel salwar kameez, wearing chappals with thermal socks; my aunt, stately, in a Barbour jacket and fashion trainers completely unsuitable for cross-country trekking, almost always on her phone, her hair underneath a silk scarf; me, clutching a travel-sick spaniel wrapped like a sausage roll in a duvet.

Then there was the unique way we tackled the walks. Mum, who struggled with the concept of 'views', objected to the countryside on the grounds that 'there is nowhere to sit down' and had no interest in the nature or the history around us, would often stop at random points, insisting we continue and pick her up on the way back, and if she ever saw a corner shop, she would insist on popping in to have a look at the produce and compare the prices with those at home. Meanwhile, my aunt would combine a need to keep up a brisk pace with an insistence on sticking to clean footpaths, which in practice usually meant walking around the gardens of stately homes in circles, slightly ahead or behind me, taking a call or checking for a mobile phone signal, breaking off occasionally to chase after Jessie, who was in the habit of disappearing into bushes and flower beds.

The phone thing was constant. I know it is a cliché to wonder out loud why shopkeepers are always on the phone – but in the case of my aunt, I really did wonder. Who on earth was she talking to, given she had given up her job and there was no sign of any close friends? And one afternoon, while encircling the grounds of yet another stately home in Staffordshire, feeling not unlike Albert Speer, Hitler's chief architect, who famously passed time in Spandau prison pacing out a circular course, I dared to ask.

'Just a friend,' she replied, shoving her phone into her Mulberry handbag and increasing her already considerable pace.

'A boy . . . friend?'

Silence. I had never met anyone who could combine such warmth with such awkwardness.

'That was Vivek.' I was almost jogging now to keep up with her.

'Ah, Indian. I see.'

Massi was bought some time by Jessie, who had scampered into some rhododendrons, causing walkers around to exclaim in dismay. My aunt, passing her handbag to me, ran after him. 'Jessie! Come back!' She returned with the dog under her arm, ignoring the tutting around us. 'This dog. A nightmare, aren't you?' She kissed him – something my mother hated seeing her do – and returned to the subject. 'Anything else you want to know?'

I ignored the mockery in her tone. 'How long have you been seeing each other?'

'Oh, on and off, about ten years.' She was almost mumbling.

'Wow. And you haven't even mentioned him before. Can we meet him?'

'Absolutely not,' she snapped.

'Why?'

'Because it's not going anywhere.'

'Is he not marriage material?'

'No. Well, yes, he is. In the sense that he is married already.'

'Ah.' I blinked. Tried to pretend I wasn't surprised. 'Will he leave his wife?'

'Wants to. Hence the drama on the phone. But to be honest, I know I'm not really cut out for marriage.' She brushed some dirt off Jessie. 'Anyway, this is depressing. What about you, Arjan? When are you going to give us something to celebrate?'

'Massi. You're turning into my mother.'

I'm not sure why I said this. The truth was that my mum never nagged me about marrying Freya; all she really wanted to know was when we would finally call it a day. Maybe what I meant was that Surinder shared a certain relentlessness with her sister.

Surinder continued, regardless. 'Freya is such a lovely girl.'

'I know she is. She is great, but . . .'

We had by this stage done six laps of the courtyard. And as I began updating my aunt on couples' counselling, still carrying my aunt's handbag, I made a break for it – veering off the gravel path on to a lawn, walking towards the obelisk which towered over the southern part of the estate. I told my aunt, unsteady in her trainers and slowed down by the task of carrying the dog, that there had been some progress. Freya and I both liked our counsellor and, sitting in her front room, surrounded by pictures of her happy mixed-race children, she seemed like someone whose advice was worth taking. We missed one another. Our therapist had remarked upon how comfortable we were in each other's company, for a couple who were breaking up. Some of the exercises we were set afterwards, such as having to 'discuss how sex was regarded in your family', were inadvertently entertaining. But others, such as the half-hour we had to spend listening, without interruption, to each other talk about our relationship, were less so. It turned out that Freya couldn't forgive me for my infidelity, I was finding it difficult to forgive her for sleeping with her ex, and, if I was honest, many of the issues about cultural incompatibility remained.

'So let me get this,' my aunt summarised. 'You fell in love with someone, got engaged, lived with her happily, your dad dies and you suddenly decide it might be better to marry a complete stranger because they just happen to be Sikh?'

'When you put it like that, it sounds . . .' I searched for the word, slightly out of breath. '. . . mad, I realise, but isn't it just easier to be with someone of your own background? I mean, look at Ranjit.'

'*Ranjit?*' She came to a standstill. The pupils in her eyes contracted. 'Are you serious?'

I made the case for arranged marriages, emphasising the advantage of basing a relationship on something other than passion, having a whole family interested in keeping a relationship going. When I saw my case was having no effect, I added, 'She left someone to go out with me, what's to stop her leaving me in turn?'

'So now you want a virgin bride?'

'That's not what I meant.' I sighed. 'Look what happened to you and Jim then.'

'There's no comparison between Jim and me, and you and Freya.' We started walking uphill again. 'It was a different time, and I hardly knew him before I got married.'

'I just think I might have a better life if I ended up with someone my mother connected with.'

'Arjan, you do realise that your mother won't like anyone you marry? You are her only son. No one will be good enough. If you marry an Indian girl it will just give her more of an opportunity to fixate.'

There was some truth to this. I had not once dared to introduce an Asian girlfriend to my mother, anxious about the politics which might ensue. I paused and thought about what she had just said. 'What I can't believe is that you, of all people, are making the case for romance.'

'Romance?' She was speed-walking. 'I'm talking about kindness and compassion. That's what I saw in Freya on Christmas Day. And you know what, marriage is a strange idea, it's a lottery, it can often turn out to be a mistake, but it's a mistake everyone should make once and it's the best environment to raise kids. Just get back together with Freya and have some babies, for God's sake.'

This was the thing that Massi said most often. The subtext was clear: having children was, in her view, the only thing that mattered. And it was the one thing she hadn't done.

I groaned. '*Massi.*'

We had by this point reached the obelisk. From our vantage point we could see the grand Georgian mansion at the centre of the estate, which like every other Georgian mansion in the Midlands claimed to have once provided a hiding place for Charles II. To one side, we could make out the knot garden in which Mum was sitting on a bench, admiring the flowers. The chemotherapy wasn't affecting her as badly as it had done the first time, which was encouraging. But she still looked small and frail.

'I really don't know why your mother insists on wearing those sandals,' said my aunt. 'She must be freezing. And that paste henna from India which turns her temples red. And what's with the patterns? I know as a widow she would never wear vivid colours but everyone knows patterns are best avoided at our age. She won't listen to anything I say.'

Surinder's words made me remember how I used to watch Mum get ready for the temple on Sunday mornings, smothering my face in Oil of Ulay as she smothered her own, spraying a little perfume on my wrist as she perfumed hers, Mum stopping me from using her lipsticks as crayons. But she had given up on make-up at some point.

I read out the plaque at the bottom of the obelisk which commemorated the man who had built the house, apparently an important example of its style of architecture. Over tea I had learned about how he had never finished his work, instead living a reckless life of drinking and gambling.

Surinder absorbed the information. 'In my experience, the thing that most people regret at the end of their lives is that they listened to other people too much.' She placed the dog down, fastened him to a leash. 'It is important to live the life you want to lead, not the one you think your mother wants you to.'

'But you could say that things would have worked out better for you if you *had* listened to other people a little more.'

She laughed, put her arm through mine. 'Fair point.' We were walking downhill now, across the lawn, back to Mum. 'I suppose you could say that.'

Our drive back home was, as ever, totally unlike the few family road trips I recalled from my youth. My father was an anxious driver. He would hog the middle lane, driving fixedly at 54mph because he had worked out this was the speed at which the van was at its most economical, not permitting the radio or excessive conversation in case it distracted him. In contrast, when my aunt drove on the motorway in her BMW – and she always insisted on driving – she would do so either at 77mph (arguing you were unlikely to be stopped if you were within 10 per cent of the speed limit) or at 99mph (she claimed, rather unconvincingly, that you got banned only if you tipped into three figures). There would always be music in the background. And she was one of those people fond of 'lively debate' to make time pass. In forty-five minutes she challenged my mother on everything, from her view of the monarchy to her increasingly fanatical vegetarianism.

'So you don't eat meat?'

'No.'

'And you don't touch food that has been cooked by someone who has cooked meat?'

'No.'

'And you won't be in the same room as people eating meat?'

'Sometimes.'

'But I see you wear leather shoes.'

'It is important to be practical.'

'You know the Gurus hunted animals and the Sikh code of conduct allows you to eat meat, as long as it isn't halal?'

Mum grimaced, sank into her leather seat and pretended to sleep. And it was at this moment, more than three months into Surinder's return, that I accepted a painful fact: the two sisters' relationship was not as straightforward as my relationship with my aunt. For me, Surinder's return was an unmitigated joy. She had not only transformed my life in practical ways, and loved me unconditionally, but also changed my relationship with Mum. Communication between us had always been restricted by my bad Punjabi, and our respective awkwardness, but suddenly I found that if there was something difficult I wanted to say, I could ask my aunt to say it on my behalf; she was always there to provide a sensitive translation.

But while on the face of it the sisters were a tight unit – going to the temple together, liaising about the cash and carry – and while in the shop it was all 'pehnji' and 'hahnji' and 'Could I get you a cup of tea?', their dealings were more fractious. My aunt's devotion to my mother was total, but when it came to religion, Surinder just couldn't help but express her doubt and objections, even though we both knew that Mum took solace in her faith. Mum, for her part, was at times actively antagonistic. She baulked at many of my aunt's plans for the shop, in particular anything that might compromise the decades-old non-compete arrangement with Dhanda's. She objected to my aunt's plan to buy a touchscreen till, because she feared she would not be able to use it, objected to any changes which might have involved the removal of anything that my father had installed – the microwave, for instance, or the rusty unused baskets behind the front door. And out of earshot of her sister, and on the phone to me, and sometimes even directly to Surinder, Mum found no shortage of things to complain about, whether it was wearing skirts that came above the knee ('Leh, a woman of her age'); watching endless DVD box sets late into the night, keeping her awake; 'wasting' money by dragging her off to restaurants in places like Ludlow when you could eat better for a fraction of the price at home; not eating the food she cooked at home because it wasn't apparently 'healthy enough'; 'always' yomping off to the gym or hair salon when not working; leaving her bedroom a mess; drinking occasionally at Singhfellows; smoking; indulging her messy dog; reading all the time; or being disrespectful to Dhanda, not even covering her head when he visited the shop.

Unfortunately, Surinder's response to her sister's disapproval would usually involve physically withdrawing and doing something – having a fag, going for a drink at Singhfellows, taking the dog for a walk – that would irritate Mum yet further. I identified with the urge. Sometimes she just had to be alone. But occasionally the tension would become so intolerable that I would have to intervene. Such as the time that Surinder made the mistake of having a cigarette in front of the shop instead of in the back garden, and inspired a despairing rant from Mum about how she was 'bringing shame upon the family'.

Surinder conceded immediately. 'It's a disgusting habit and I should have given up years ago,' she said. We were at the cash and carry and I was pushing a giant orange flatbed trolley down the giant orange aisles. My aunt tackled these trips in the same way she walked around National Trust properties: as if someone would die if she dropped below a pace of 4mph. 'I will try to give up. Again.' She placed a box of Crunchies – £14.99 for forty-eight bars – on to the trolley, taking time to pat Jessie, who was lounging across a box of beans. 'But God knows why she gets so upset when she has been selling fags her whole life. Come to that, what I don't get is why we sell cigarettes at all.'

It was inevitable, I suppose, that my aunt's efforts to modernise the shop would eventually hit a wall. I remember my mother once remarking inexplicably that the shop was cursed because it had a 'wide front and narrow back and was overlooking a T-junction'. It turns out she was voicing an inverse version of a peculiar old superstition which asserts that dwellings that are narrow at the front and wide at the back are 'cow-faced houses' and lucky. But she had a point in a way, in that the structure of the shop was against us. Bains Stores was mid-terrace and, unlike Dhanda's Buy Express, which had been surrounded by vacant lots of land, there was no room for the business to expand, even if there had been a reason or incentive to do so. Moreover, Bains Stores just faced too many obstacles, not least reliance on newspaper and tobacco sales. A large part of the shop's turnover was tied up in cigarettes, but the profit margin was tiny — we basically acted as an unpaid tax collector. A ban on tobacco displays was on the cards. Also, smuggling was killing the business. A 25g pouch of Golden Virginia was sold for £8.25 in the shop, but my aunt had recently discovered Singhfellows was flogging it illegally for as little as £5. Which explained where Ranjit got his supplies.

Massi, incongruous in a wrap dress and Ferragamo shoes before an enormous stack of value-brand bog roll, continued. 'So let me get this straight. Because of some vague, unwritten arrangement between my father and Dhanda, which no one really remembers being made, and no one ever discusses, they get to sell booze and Indian food, and everything else we weren't selling in 1971, and we get, what, fags? Newspapers? Two dying trades. I mean, everyone sells everything now.' For some reason she gestured at dog food on our trolley. 'The car wash next door sells water and sweets. Tesco's sells Indian food. And have you visited Buy Express recently?'

'You visited Dhanda's shop?' I complained.

'I may have popped in yesterday,' she confessed diffidently, before striding off in the direction of the soft drinks. Suddenly the trolley felt twice as heavy, and as I struggled to catch up, I imagined what would happen next: Mr Dhanda would complain to Mum, Mum would be on at me again, and Ranjit, who was aggrieved that I had stopped seeing him, would send me a succession of aggressive texts.

When I pulled up, my aunt was using the web browser on her phone to check whether a twenty-four-pack of Lucozade Energy was cheaper at a rival cash and carry. This was one of many reasons why she was a better retailer than me. I would never have bothered, had basically given up even visiting cash and carries when I realised you could make orders online. Surinder resumed her defence.

'Look, the Dhandas visit us all the time, so why can't I pop into theirs?' She gestured at the crate; it turned out to be fifty pence cheaper here. 'Shall we take two?' She checked the best-before date, then returned to the topic. 'I went because I needed some saag. Your mum is teaching me to cook. And I couldn't help noticing while I was there that while they might not sell fags and newspapers, they sell *Stardust* and *Asiana*. Who decided Asian magazines weren't part of the agreement, eh? When was it decided? Did your dad ever mention it?'

The only thing I could recall on the theme was an argument my parents had when I was a teenager after Amy Wilson had come in and asked if she could take some chapattis for her family tea. 'Six chapattis for the kids and one for the dog' was the phrase she had used. Mum had sent her to Dhanda's, who sold Indian food – enraging my father. He couldn't see why they couldn't start catering for such demand. Though I remembered it mainly as a comic incident. 'Six chapattis for the kids and one for the dog' became a catchphrase in the shop for a while. But then, like all children, I was blind to the tensions between my parents, their arguments about the shop merging into the noise of arguments about religion and parenting and everything else.

Massi headed towards the checkout. Racially, the wholesale trade was a reversal of the retail trade: all the customers were Asian, the staff white. We began scanning our purchases. Boxes of Kellogg's Nutri-Grain, followed by Sun Valley oat bars, a case of Pringles, a box of Liquorice Allsorts, twenty to thirty outers of cigarettes. The total came to about £1,650, and as my aunt paid, she said, 'I just don't understand why your mother is so insistent on observing this so-called agreement. But you know what, I think your father was thinking about changing things. I've got something in the car I want to show you. Found it the other day when I was going through his files.'

My heart sank. My aunt had been coming up with all sorts of strange theories since she had started going through my father's historical accounts, wondering out loud the week before, for instance, whether he had been taking cash out of the business. 'Did he have any gambling debts?' she had enquired, making me roar with laughter. My father was so careful with money that he didn't even buy lottery tickets.

In the car, I took the document and saw nothing of any interest. It was just a leaflet entitled 'Do I need a licence?' and seemed to be about the process of applying for an alcohol licence.

'It's an information leaflet, Massi,' I said, holding on to my seat and clutching Jessie as my aunt tackled a series of roundabouts at speed, boxes of Lucozade crashing about in the back of the car.

'Take a closer look.'

I tried. Someone had underlined various sentences. But then my father underlined everything he read – the paper, books. So what?

'He was thinking about applying for a licence, Arjan,' said my

261

aunt. 'Look.' She pointed at something, taking her eyes off the road and a hand off the steering wheel. 'He has underlined the bit that says, "Any Interested Party or Responsible Authority can make a representation against a new Premises Licence application." I reckon he was thinking about asking the Dhandas if they would object. It's a good idea. I mean I'm sure your mum will get better, but whatever happens, we need to think about selling the shop, and when we do that, we will get a better price for it as a going concern with an alcohol licence.' She overtook a van at illegal speed. 'We could just go ahead and apply, but it might make it easier in terms of, you know, village politics if you ask Ranjit if they would object. Could you?'

I murmured vague assent. To be honest, I was only half listening. The way Surinder drove made me travel-sick. And turning the document around, I had seen that my father had made some notes on the back, which included the word 'Dhanda'. Though it was not the name that had floored me. Rather, it was his painfully neat handwriting, which reminded me of the encouraging notes he would send me at university. The encouraging notes which stopped coming when I switched from medicine to art and broke his heart.

I remember walking into Blakenfields Infants for the first time and finding I was already a celebrity, known across the school as 'the boy in the sweet shop', an object of widespread, if not universal, envy. I also remember struggling with the logic. Spoilt for choice, I had never really developed a taste for chocolate or boiled sweets, preferring instead savoury foods like pakoras, which my mother made on special occasions and which Ranjit's dad sold in his store.

Along with this admiration came a degree of fear. My father was notorious for enforcing discipline in the shop. If you came in with a tenner he'd make sure to mention it to your folks when he saw them next. If you were caught pilfering any stock he'd drag you by the ear through Blakenfields, all the way home. God knows what would happen if I had tried that in 2012, but I still met customers who told me that they were warned to behave as children with the threat of being taken to 'Mr Bains' if they didn't.

Did my father frighten me? No. He was, admittedly, not as gushing as my mother, who incessantly had prayers said for my welfare, and worried obsessively about my diet, so much so that I became totally neurotic about food, eating little more than chips, pakoras and what I called 'yellow dal' with chapattis for most of my youth. But my dad was more awkward than anything. For him, fatherhood seemed to be mainly about setting rules and boundaries. He was forever lecturing, assigning exercises, making me pay for anything I broke out of my pocket money, even if it was a jar of Branston pickle in the shop. This was annoying. But never scary.

It helped, I suppose, that I grew up knowing that, despite the discipline, my father's life revolved around me. At least, when by 1980 he had saved enough to put a deposit down on a three-bedroom semi-detached in a (relatively) bucolic suburb of Wolverhampton, he did so because 'Arjan will need more space when he grows up.' When we singularly failed to spend any time in it, because it was always easier to sleep above the shop at the end of a long day, he rented it out, arguing that 'Arjan is happier in the shop' (which I was). It also helped that I knew he adored my mother. As the saying goes, the best thing a father can do for his children is to love their mother.

In short, I was a happy child, at home and at school, whether I was playing with empty bread crates with Ranjit, or running up and down Victoria Road with an army of other kids, completely oblivious to the fact that the foundations of the shop in which I lived this happy life were slowly eroding. What was behind this decay? Well, if you had asked my father to explain, I have no doubt that he would have cited the macroeconomic factors that are conventionally thought to have undermined the small British shop in the 1980s. Out-of-town shopping had become a trend, with the Merry Hill Shopping Centre in Dudley, at the time one of the biggest malls in Europe, becoming a prime attraction in the West Midlands. Retail parks began to be located, catastrophically, just outside the ring road, ensuring there was no need for residents to go anywhere near the town centre. The collapse of traditional industry had left Wolverhampton with one of the highest rates of long term unemployment in Britain.

But I actually think it was other things, closer to home, that really did for Bains Stores. Things such as the demolition of the last major steelworks in the area, in a controlled explosion, which is another of my clearest childhood memories, everyone gathering to watch it from a nearby park, cooing in amazement, unaware we were witnessing one more stake being driven through the heart of our community, and the creation of a large waste ground where people would dump old cars and take drugs.

Also, it didn't help that many of the Asians who lived in the area had become affluent and began moving out to the suburbs. They returned regularly to visit one of the two temples on the road, their choice depending on their caste, and to buy Asian produce from Dhanda's, which by the mid 1980s was running a fresh grocery section, a post office, an Indian catering business, and functioning as the base for Dhanda's work as a Labour councillor, his campaign to get support for the teaching of Indian languages in schools on Saturday mornings and his chairmanship of the committee running the ever-expanding Jat temple. But these customers felt little need to pop into Bains Stores.

The fact was that my father had been proved wrong about the appetite among Asians for Asian culture. Not that this became evident quickly. The decline in trade was not extreme. After all, there are always days in any shop's life when takings drop for no apparent reason, when a proprietor wonders if some event or holiday has taken everyone out of town. But in the 1980s, these days occurred more and more often. And though it feels like an act of vandalism upon my happy childhood memories to remember such things, there were all sorts of other warning signs, from the increasing number of household items kept behind the counter which might prove handy in the event of attack, to the deepening ominousness of the nicknames we gave customers. In my early youth, the characters I recall were people like 'Hamboy', the kid who was sent every three days to buy half a pound of ham, and 'Flash Gordon', a glamorous single bloke who would do all his weekly shopping in one go with a £10 note – so much money that my mum would have to get change from the safe in the living room. But by the late 1980s the regulars were people like 'Nails' (a man who appeared to have a phobia of washing his hands) and 'Pashab' (a more directly abusive phrase translating as 'urine').

I remember my mother once casually asking a customer about the whereabouts of her son, only to be told that he had gone down for two years in Featherstone for rape. And somewhere along the line the entrepreneurialism that had led my father to start offering a bike repair service, and then become an agent for coach tours, turned into penny-pinching and paranoia. Pretty much the only capital investment he made in the shop in the 1980s was an under-floor safe. When the till broke, it remained unfixed for years, and Dad never replaced the pricing gun – meaning labels had to be written by hand, a task I was occasionally burdened with.

I think I was quite old, however, ten or eleven, before I finally realised that the Dhandas' were doing much better than us. Until that point, if Ranjit got a bike, I got a bike. If anything, I was the one who felt envied: Ranjit was the one forever asking *me* for sweets and magazines. But then Mr Dhanda bought a brand-new Mercedes S-class saloon. It was silver and cool and Ranjit nicked the keys so that we could sit in it in the garage. As we did so, he explained casually that the reason his family had so much more money was that they were Jats, who were the strongest of the Sikhs, and we were Chamars, who were by tradition servants. This was also the reason, he added, why he was stronger and taller than me.

It was only kids' talk, and I guess he was just repeating things his father had said, but I was upset and I remember my mother's attempt at consolation: she wiped away my tears and told me that she was Jat, which therefore made me one too. There was no attempt to challenge the gist of Ranjit's argument, Mum adding only that I mustn't under any circumstances tell my father what Ranjit had said.

Nevertheless, regardless of all this, my father decided in 1987 that I was going to benefit from a private school education. His only son was not going to be educated at the nearby comprehensive along with the likes of Ranjit and the other local ruffians who spent their afternoons skiving and smoking. I was going to do more than run a shop. I would grow up to be a doctor or a lawyer. To achieve this I was going to attend the local independent grammar school.

It was an insane plan: I wanted to go to Westfields like Ranjit and the rest of my friends. We absolutely could not afford the fees. But my father was insistent, saying he would sell the house we had never lived in to pay for it. And in the build-up to the entrance examination he became excited in a way I hadn't see him get excited before. He devoured the prospectus with the kind of enthusiasm most middle-aged men reserve for checking out Harley-Davidson catalogues. He dragged me along to the Open Day, where to my mortification he tried to engage the history teacher on the topic of Henry VIII, who had just been the subject of a recent BBC TV series. Conversely, I had never seen him look so depressed when I scuppered his ambitions by deliberately failing the entrance exam.

However, he would not give up on his dream. He found another private day school, this one in Tettenhall, which had the advantage of being cheaper and not offering places by academic selection. We were called in for a family interview, and my father celebrated my entry as if he had just sired another son, even making a rare trip to Dhanda's shop to brag and to buy twenty boxes of Indian sweets, which he gave away to customers in celebration.

As for me, I succumbed to gloom. I don't think any child looked forward to starting senior school in the '80s. Such was the bleakness and popularity of *Grange Hill* that we all grew up expecting to encounter sadistic teachers and children addicted to heroin. But I had the additional problem of Ranjit winding me up with scare stories about Tettenhall Royal. He warned that I would have to wear a top hat to school, that I faced having to pray in Latin and being beaten with a crook-handled cane for talking in class. It would not be long, he prophesised, before I would be cleaning my arse without using water like a gora, and bathing in my own filth.

My parents sought to ease my anxiety, but did so in characteristically ineffectual fashion – my mother embarking upon a programme of lengthy prayers, insisting I accompany her to the temple; my father spewing hectoring advice at every opportunity. *Behave in a way that won't get you noticed too quickly. Tell your new schoolmates a joke.* You would have thought, from the way he banged on, that he had spent seven years at Eton, not two years in a dusty-floored village school in the Punjab so poor that it couldn't afford tables. Maybe this is where my loathing of jokes came from.

My parents watched me as I walked stiffly towards the bus stop in my regulation black single-breasted jacket, black pullover and long, charcoal-grey trousers (cloth material – not denim or corduroy), clutching an outsized leather briefcase as I did so. Both of them were waiting anxiously for news of my day when I returned at half five. I told them all about the school buildings, which seemed enormous at the time, and the teachers whose names seemed to determine their roles and personalities: the idiosyncratic Mr Strange for French, a frail Mrs Gaunt for Physics. But when it came to describing my classmates, I had nothing specific to say. So poleaxed was I by the poshness of my classmates that I had not talked to a soul.

There is something self-perpetuating about silence. Once you become known as the quiet kid, the prospect of actually speaking threatens to become an event, which makes you retreat further, and the whole thing becomes self-fulfilling. I became cocooned in silence. It took more than a fortnight to find someone I could call a friend at school: good old Matt Metcalfe. Though I suspect he responded because he was the only other boy who got the same bus as me to school and because I was a marginally better alternative to staring into space. He lived on a farm outside Wolverhampton, which required getting a bus through Blakenfields, was an exceptionally small child, afflicted with a disastrous bowl-shaped haircut (his mother's handiwork) and had absolutely no sense of personal space. When he spoke, he would get right in your face and witter non-stop on his subject of choice, which was usually his Commodore 64.

A result of this enthusiasm, which was less infectious than relentless, was that I persuaded my parents to buy me one, arguing that I needed 'a computer' for my work, though I don't think a minute of actual useful study has ever been conducted on a Commodore 64. By this point I had worked out that I could almost always get my way if I framed things in terms of my education. In my first year at Tettenhall Royal I got my father to buy a video recorder, arguing I needed it to study BBC Shakespeare adaptations, when I actually used it to record *Doctor Who*. I also got my parents to give me exclusive use of the living room at weekends to 'concentrate on homework', when I was actually using the space to kick back and play marathon games of *Frogger*. However, this honeymoon would come to an abrupt end with my first school report.

Tettenhall Royal had a combined letter and number grading system then, whereby for each subject you were given a letter indicating your effort, going from A to E, and a number, indicating your attainment, going from 1 to 5. So the worst grade you could possibly get was E5: zero effort and zero attainment. The best, A1: maximum effort, maximum attainment. My highest grade was B1, in Art. The remainder, however, were a dismal bunch of C4s and C3s and one D5 (in Physics). Though the thing that annoyed my father most was not my lowly attainment, but that when he attended parents' evening, putting on his best suit and best turban for the occasion, a couple of the teachers struggled to recall who I was.

'How can you be the only Indian boy in class and yet your teachers don't know who you are?' He flicked through my school report. 'What do you actually do when you get to school? Do you even speak when you get there?'

'You told me not to draw attention to myself,' I mumbled.

'That was advice for the first day! Not for the whole year!'

Mum intervened. 'But look at his Art, *ji*. B1. Did you see his picture of a flower?'

'We sold our house, we work ninety hours a week, so that our son can *paint pictures*?'

My bottom lip trembled. 'I never wanted to go in the first place.'

'WHAT DID YOU SAY?' My father lifted his hand, as if to hit me. I knew it was mere theatre – my mother would not have stood for it, he was unlike Dhanda's father, who was known to throw his wife and Ranjit around the house. But I cowered anyway. 'WHAT DID YOU SAY?'

My mother positioned herself between us. My father threw the school report into the bin, ignoring the front slip that demanded a signature of receipt, and stormed off to his study. He didn't speak to me for a week afterwards, giving me my first taste of the silent treatment which would characterise our relationship for life. His disappointment in me was tangible, a physical presence in the shop, so palpable that you could have put it in a jar and served it out like a quarter-pound of bonbons.

It caused me considerable pain, but it still didn't provide me with the necessary motivation to do better at school. I was stuck in a rut. But an unexpected opportunity arose to change things in my second year when, standing in a corner of a classroom with Matt Metcalfe one morning break, listening to him talk on his pet subject (developing his own compiled programming language for his Commodore), while trying to turn the conversation to my pet subject (*Eddie Kidd's Jump Challenge*), we were approached by Warren Nelson.

Nelson was the captain of the rugby team, who was dropped off each day in a Morgan sports car by his father, a local restaurant owner, and, to me, Nelson was the scariest boy in my year. Just his appearance was enough to render us both mute.

'Hey, Banga, you live in a newsagent, right?'

I tensed up. The thing I got teased for most was my surname. But I got almost as much grief for living in a shop. 'Why can't Indians play football? Cos each time they get to the corner, they open a shop.' 'What do you call a Paki without a corner shop? Doctor.' Etc. On the rare occasion I spoke up in class, some wag would more often than not remark, 'Could I have a bag with that?' But knowing that attack was the best form of defence, I squeaked, 'Fuck off.'

Nelson got me into a headlock.

'Listen, shithead. Can you get me some fags?'

'What?' I was in more pain than the time he had thrown a spitball at my head before class registration – a clump of surprisingly dense paper he had chewed and steeped in saliva.

'Fags. You know, Embassy. Benson & Hedges.'

He let me go, and I fell to the floor. 'You know those things in little packets that your parents flog?'

I gawped back in fear and blank incomprehension. In my innocence, I genuinely did not understand what he was on about. My mother had brought me up to believe that smoking was the worst thing you could do, and I was so prudish that I could no more imagine Nelson with a cigarette than I could imagine Matt Metcalfe seducing Heather Locklear.

'Think about it, Mr Singh-a-ding-a-ling.' He stamped on my foot. 'Might even pay ya.'

I thought about it. Did nothing. Probably would have continued to do nothing if Ranjit hadn't made a version of the same request

271

more than a year later. You see, in the absence of any other friends, I was hanging around with Ranjit a great deal by this time. Which is not to suggest that we didn't play together as young kids – I remember cutting a hole in a hedgerow at the back of my shop with Ranjit, making it into a den and calling it the 'Hedge Club'. We were, despite my father's and Mr Dhanda's seeming inability to be in the same room together (when you run a shop, there is always an excuse not to appear at social occasions), always standing next to each other in birthday photographs. But as teens we were inseparable.

We both had mountain bikes and would ride for tens of miles – into Dudley, around abandoned quarries, to his relatives, to gawp at the properties that his family already owned in significant quantities. He would get me to do his homework, calling me professor as I did so, would play me Bobby Brown albums and the concluding scenes of various Bruce Lee and Chuck Norris films, and, more than anything else, we would play marathon games of *Street Fighter II*. If memory serves, I would always play Chun Li, a female fighter, who, while not as powerful as the others, was the quickest, and he would play Dhalsim, an Indian character whose fighting style was based on yoga. He would often give me a head start, not attacking me for the first ten or fifteen seconds, but would still always win, using a series of special combo moves like 'yoga fire' and 'yoga teleport' to obliterate me time after time.

I guess it was a sign of how keen I was to retain his affection that I carried on playing despite defeat. And it was another sign that when he asked me to get him some fags from our shop, I found myself casually suggesting to my parents one evening that I do my homework at the counter so that they could have dinner together, in front of *Neighbours* and *Home and Away*. 'Doesn't really matter where I do my homework, really,' I croaked in my breaking voice. 'The shop is never busy anyway.'

My parents seemed chuffed. The offer of helping in the shop

fulfilled my mother's fantasy of a caring son, who would look after her in old age, while I think my father simply liked the idea of customers encountering his studious son sitting at the counter in his visibly posh school uniform. Almost all the photographs of us from that time have me standing next to my father in Tettenhall Royal garb. As for security, my dad had by this stage installed a buzzer underneath the counter which set off an alarm in the house in case of trouble, so it was safe enough. And soon after Dad had given me a pep talk – his view, when it came to pilferage, was that you should view any man below the age of twenty-one, or anyone who made eye contact, with deep suspicion – I removed a packet of twenty-five Royals from the display behind me and put £2.25 in the till so that my meticulous father would not notice anything.

The following day I gave most of the fags to Ranjit at face value. I only kept five as an afterthought for Nelson, and was stunned when he gave me £2 for them. From then on it was just too much temptation to resist. I became a teenage rebel. Nevertheless, as far as rebellion goes, mine was pretty timid. I didn't sell cigarettes to anyone other than Nelson and his closest friends, though I could have sold five packets a day. I didn't take more than three packets a week. I always put the correct money back in the till. I transported the contraband in my leather brief-case, making use of the combination lock. I never smoked a cigarette myself. I didn't let the money I was making go to my head, my only indulgence being the occasional computer game, which my parents never monitored anyway. For me the real prize was not the cash, but a modicum of social acceptance. Not to suggest that the popular kids suddenly befriended me – they still called me 'Sootie' – but they didn't mind me hanging around so much. I was pathetically grateful.

It was during this time I learnt something important about the English upper middle classes. I had, until then, had them down as morons. And they were, what with their fondness for Chinese burns and, mid-chat, kicking each other in the shins. But on closer inspection it became evident that this idiocy did not preclude hard work. They were under just as much pressure to justify the investment of their parents' fees, it was only that they made sure it didn't look like they were trying, a phenomenon I have since realised is more commonly known as 'effortless superiority', accomplishing amazing feats, seemingly with ease, and without any desire for approval.

Or, to put it another way, their goal at school was the grade E1 – zero effort, maximum achievement. And while this went against the immigrant family's need to repeatedly recount their story of struggle, and against my people's inability to self-deprecate (even when referring to himself as a buffoon, the Punjabi will come across as boastful), for some reason I found this goal more inspiring than the aim of getting A1s.

Not that my father was impressed.

'What this?' he asked, glaring at a string of C2s, C1s, and once even a D1 (English).

'English. I was top of the class.'

'D?'

'I know, but I came top.'

'It says here, "It is a shame he feels a need to disrupt class."' What have you been doing?'

Well, among other things, I had orchestrated a game which involved my classmates asking our teacher the meaning of any word of four syllables or more, and I had participated in something called 'The Wailing Wall', whereby ten of us stood in the corridor before lessons wailing at the top of our voices, to replicate The Wailing Wall in Israel. But I wasn't going to tell Dad that.

'You wanted me to do well, to be noticed, and now you still complain.'

I genuinely thought my father would have preferred me getting an A4. That was Bains Stores all over. Maximum effort, minimal achievement. And he descended into one of his habitual silences after this report. But by then I didn't care. I was taller than him, was supplying some of the girls at the school opposite with fags, and was dating the Indian daughter of a local factory owner who went there. Though when I say 'dating', I actually mean 'sitting and holding hands in the Central Library, out of view of everyone'. Nevertheless, this boosted my credibility further, and when Nelson started including me in conversations about girls, and asked, 'So does your papa sell porn mags?', I was struck by an idea which would increase my influence further.

Filching porn mags was never going to be as easy as fags. For the right person Dad would put the mag inside a newspaper, but if he saw anyone lingering, or anyone underage trying to sneak a peak, he would shout, 'This is not a library!' and have them out of the shop in seconds. Ranjit had been on at me to get him some porn for years and I didn't dare countenance the possibility. As for my mother, she dreaded having anything to do with the magazines, complaining that she thought some men got a sexual kick out of being served by an auntie. Between them my parents watched the mags like hawks, would spot a sold or missing copy instantly, and getting one would require the nous and diligence and planning of a bank job.

This, as it happens, was exactly the manner in which I devised my plan. It involved Matt, who was mooching around like an abandoned lover and eager to regain my friendship. The basic idea was this: he would pop into the shop while I was at the counter, take a porn mag, rush to the nearby library, photocopy a few of the juiciest pages, and then be back within the hour, putting the mag back in position before anyone had noticed its absence.

The way I saw it, Matt was trustworthy and motivated by the offer of friendship, if not by his fee of ten pence a photocopy. I would sell the photocopies only to people I knew – for fifty pence a shot. My parents were hopelessly addicted to *Neighbours* and *Home and Away* and almost never came into the shop during that hour. However, unbeknownst to me, Matt Metcalfe, a boy who I thought was more interested in coding than pictures of dumpy middle-aged women exposing their labia awkwardly to camera, was making extra copies of *Men Only* for his own sordid gratification. His mother discovered his stash of murky black-and-white porn, he confessed, she informed the school, and I was suspended for a week.

I try, in general, not to recall the incident because the whole thing was so mortifying, but when I do, the main thing I remember is my father's terrible silence. I didn't hear him utter a word as the headmaster discussed my case with him in private. He said nothing in the van as he took me home, on a Thursday lunchtime. In fact, his first utterance on the subject didn't come for a full eight hours after he had received a phone call about it. I was standing in the dining room, with my head bowed, when his first words came. They weren't extensive.

'So then?'

I waited for an extrapolation. But none came. It wasn't words that my father used as weapons, but the silences between them.

Eventually, I spoke. It was a surprise to discover that I had a great deal to say. I told him about the cigarettes. I told him about Warren Nelson. I revealed my profit margins, the games I had bought. I told him about the brands of cigarettes my classmates preferred, the pass code for my combination lock for my briefcase, and speculated at length upon the notion of effortless superiority, citing the Elizabethan poet Sir Philip Sidney as probably the original example, his feats including improvising a poem in French on his deathbed (which he had set to music and which was sung back to him by a minstrel while he died).

I did this not from guilt, or from a desire to confess, but because anything was better than acknowledging the sexual element of my crime. However, when I stopped, hoping for my father to launch into a bitter speech about duty, about how much money of his was being wasted in the time I was suspended from school, he didn't play ball.

'So, thief *and* pervert.'

I could have died.

My mother interrupted: 'Have you been smoking?'

'No!'

'Are you taking drugs?'

'What? God, Mum, *no*.'

'Are you going around with white girls?'

This came out of nowhere. Until this I didn't even realise that such a thing would be forbidden. My parents were liberal. They had fallen in love, for God's sake. My father wore a turban but was a borderline atheist, and I had never been pressured to have long hair. Mum produced a prayer book out of nowhere.

'Put your hand on this and swear that you have never smoked or taken drugs or have a girlfriend.'

This was insane. But I was grateful, in a way, for the distraction and intending to indulge her when my father grabbed the prayer book.

'Stop this nonsense,' he barked. 'If you hadn't spoilt him so much, if you weren't so obsessed with mumbo-jumbo, he wouldn't have turned out like this.' My mother wept. 'As for *you*,' he said to me, 'you disgust me. I'm ashamed that you are my son. *Ashamed*.'

With that he sent me upstairs, without food, which I think was intended as much a punishment on my mother as me.

I don't think my relationship with my father ever fully recovered from the awkwardness of the episode. Though my mother was more forgiving. She smuggled a tray of food into my room that night, some chapattis with yellow dal, and watched me eat as she explained my father's reasoning.

'Your dad says you have a choice,' she said as she stroked my hair. I normally hated it when she petted me, but this time I didn't withdraw. 'You can stay on at Tettenhall or go to Ranjit's school. If you stay, the condition is that you get nothing less than an A1 or B1 in any subject. And you have to do the sciences for A level. Have a think about it, putt. And you mustn't hate your father. Everything he does, he does for you. *Everything*.'

I thought about it, and decided to stay.

The thing I recall most vividly about that Sunday is the brightness. I had been spending so much time indoors, whether it was with Mum in hospital, or working at my computer in the shop, that I had missed the start of summer. But travelling to Wolverhampton after my first Saturday evening in London in many months, it was impossible not to notice the sunshine. It redeemed everything it shone upon, even the post-industrial sprawl of the Black Country visible from the train window, making me appreciate, for the first time, what W. H. Auden may have meant when he wrote, 'Dearer than Scafell Pike my heart has stamped on/ The view from Birmingham to Wolverhampton.'

Though this cheerfulness didn't survive the return to Bains Stores. The counter unmanned, my aunt was eating a salad alone in the living room, while my mother ate sabzi, separately, in the kitchen. Of course, this is how shopkeeping families often dine: the need to serve customers means you rarely sit down together, and consequently have little sense of yourselves as a social unit. But the tension was palpable and, sure enough, it turned out that the sisters had had yet another argument, the culprit sitting innocently at my aunt's feet.

'Jessie has been a very naughty boy, haven't you, Jessie,' whispered my aunt at the dog. 'Very naughty waughty.' She hung a lettuce leaf before his mouth and he snuffled it up. She looked up at me and provided an explanation. 'Weed in your mother's bedroom.' There was a hint of humour in her voice – the dog could do no wrong in her eyes – but I failed to see the funny side. Jessie had in recent weeks literally become Mum's pet hate. She hated him for the way he smelled, how he barked at customers and how he tried to copulate with everything, even if it was a hundred times his own size. Massi defended the beast passionately in return, and the whole thing had made me appreciate why dog ownership might be so low among Indians. The essential appeal of dogs seems to be that they are relentlessly loyal and proffer extremes of emotion: they are either very pleased that you are taking them for a walk, or hugely disappointed that you are not. But given the neediness and emotional hysteria of the average Asian extended family, that's the last thing we need. 'Don't worry about your mum,' added my aunt. 'She will calm down. It's just the drugs. They make her testy. Anyway, want some lunch?'

I didn't. I had had a sandwich on the train, and had also arranged to meet Ranjit in Singhfellows, to talk about my aunt's hope of applying for an alcohol licence, three weeks after she had suggested me doing so. The delay had been mostly my fault – Ranjit not being someone you want to deal with when you're feeling vulnerable. Also, I had wanted to clear the idea of meeting Ranjit with Freya first: with our counselling at a sensitive stage, I didn't want to do anything to rock the boat. But, needless to say, on the day itself our failure to meet on time was down to Ranjit.

The wait gave me more time than I needed to take in the atmosphere. The air was thick with the stench of the previous evening's burps and fried chicken, and the bright sunshine that wasn't absorbed by the unswept black wooden floorboards served only to highlight the boxes of rat poison that had been laid since I last visited. There was a smattering of half-pissed male wedding guests standing around the bar, skiving from various religious ceremonies down the road. Meanwhile, the jukebox regaled punters with a tale in which a Jat had got drunk after drinking a bottle of whisky, and, with a machete on his shoulder, was going around threatening anyone who passed.

I had, to kill time, grabbed a bunch of newspapers on the way out from the shop, but they also had the effect of killing the remainder of my morale. The nationals seemed packed with stories about Asian men being prosecuted for various sex crimes, in England and in India, while the local rag painted a depressing picture of the economy. It used to be said the paper's motto was 'If it don't bleed, it don't lead'. The news editors enjoyed nothing more than a grisly motorway pile-up or murder. But the obsession with guts and gore had seemingly been replaced with a morbid obsession with the decline of Wolverhampton retail. 'Riot-hit city businesses are still paying the price,' proclaimed one headline. 'Wolverhampton's struggling high street named among the worst in the country yet again for empty shops,' added another.

The stories made me wonder if there was any point meeting Ranjit: even with an alcohol licence, Bains Stores seemed doomed. What hope could there ever have been for a business set up in a part of Britain called the Black Country, and in an area of the Black Country known as 'Blakenfields', a name that in itself alludes to the ominous Old English for 'dark'? And then, because there was nothing else to do, I started watching the Bollywood movie which was unravelling melodramatically on a flat-screen TV opposite me.

Watching these films was the one thing, besides the walks, that my aunt, my mother and I had found that we could do together. Though while my mother watched them for sincere enjoyment – she actually liked the lip-synching, the mindless dancing of lovers around trees – my aunt and I took more ironic delight in following the tales of star-crossed lovers and conniving villains enduring convenient coincidences and crashing dramatic reversals of fortune.

The worse they were, the happier we were, and in this respect, this one, called *No Smoking*, looked like a classic. My Hindi was ropey, and it was hard to catch everything with the bhangra blasting out nearby, but the character development seemed worthy of an episode of *The Gummi Bears*. The actors would have struggled to convey the concept of pain if smacked with a cricket bat, and the plot was insane, involving as it did a chain-smoker who checks into an 'alternative' rehab clinic to get over his addiction to fags and is subjected to a series of increasingly bizarre punishments whenever he gives in to his vice.

With nothing else to do, I texted the basic details of the plot to my aunt, who seemed in need of cheering up.

Text: 'Punishment one: having someone you love almost killed after they are locked in a room containing all the cigarette smoke you have smoked in your life.'

Text: 'Punishment two: the severing of a finger.'

Text: 'Punishment three: death of a loved one.'

She texted back, 'Have these people never heard of Nicorette patches?'

I laughed. Then I texted Ranjit, asking where the hell he was – he was nearly a hour late. He eventually responded, calling me a 'dickless khota', blaming his delay on the wedding ceremony he was attending and claiming he was just around the corner ('Linkage soon'). Preparing to wait yet further, I went for a wee.

They say you can learn a lot about a drinking establishment from its bathroom facilities, and Singhfellows is a classic illustration, what with the mess, the lack of bacterial hand wash, and the 'humorous' sign on the urinal cistern labelled 'beer recycler'. That lunchtime the bathroom was in a particularly dire state, the smashed-in toilet doors not fully closing or opening, the blue pull towel unreplaced seemingly in weeks. Just getting to the urinal required negotiating an ocean of fag ends and piss.

Then, having made it to the steel trough, there was something even more off-putting: the sudden appearance of Ranjit, in wedding guest regalia. He was dressed in a tailored suit made for him on Jermyn Street – not for reasons of taste or style, but because he could never get anything off-the-peg to fit over his outsized biceps and triceps. He had smothered himself in about a litre of CK One, which had the advantage, at least, of momentarily masking the ambient stench of urine and damp. But on entering he did the worst thing any man can do in a public toilet: he stood at the urinal right next to me, when there were several empty ones further away. Then, having started peeing, he did the second worst thing any man can do in a public loo: he looked directly at me and tried to start a conversation.

'So whaa gwarn, Arjy-Phaji?' I could tell that he was stoned and possibly a bit pissed. 'What's you wanna chats about then?'

How typical of Ranjit. You arrange to have a serious conversation, and he arrives, ninety minutes late, pissed, at a urinal. He continued despite my visible discomfort and inability to pee.

'Why so shook? Scared by what I might see? Or by what I might not see, innit?' He snorted with laughter. Waved his penis in my direction.

'Oh, for fuck's sake, Ranjit.' I zipped up.

'D'aint have a problem getting your dhanda out for those two gundies in Brum. Hope you wore a hat.'

This was also typical Ranjit: he would find the thing you least wanted to talk about and bang on about it mercilessly. Crimson with embarrassment, I turned into the toilet cubicle behind us. Ranjit continued talking, shouting out, as I held the door shut behind me with my right heel.

'Saw your auntie here again, man, other night,' he slurred. 'With that waste dog. She's everywhere I go, man. I'm in the car park and she's there in her van. I'm on road and she's bunning a fag outside your shop. I come here to escape aunties and there she is.'

I sighed. Ranjit had joined my mother's campaign to stop her visiting Singhfellows, adopting her hatred of the dog in doing so, his objections coming mainly in the form of late-night texts.

Text: 'Why is your auntie in my local, bruv? People go there to cotch, ya get me?'

Text: 'Have a word with your auntie, man. It's embarrassing.'

Text: 'Serious, bruv, get your massi and her waste dog to go cotch somewhere else, innit.'

As it happens, I had brought up the subject with my aunt two days earlier, over the phone. I was spending a day freelancing at an office in Soho and she listened patiently, but it was obvious from the tone of her response that she had no intention of acquiescing, as she had with the fags. Instead, she explained that she disliked Singhfellows, for most of the reasons I did, and had no active desire to go there. But Mum didn't allow alcohol in the house, she didn't drink and drive, and sometimes, after eleven-hour days in the shop, Mum being difficult, having given up fags after decades of smoking, she needed to escape for a drink. Take the edge off things. Be alone. Singhfellows was simply the nearest option.

'Besides,' she continued, in a tone she normally reserved for sales reps visiting the shop. 'I don't know if you've noticed, Arjan, but I'm quite old now, and I can remember when that place was a working man's club and had a colour bar. In 1968, a day after that speech, I remember that its 4,000 members voted unanimously to keep coloured immigrants out of the club "under any pretext, either as members, visitors, or visiting artists". Unanimously. Four thousand people. Apparently, one member, just *one* member, proposed a debate on the possibility of at least allowing coloured artists into the club, by which I presume they meant a black stripper or something, but even this was too much. They couldn't find a single seconder. Not one.' She broke off to serve a customer. '*My eyes.*' She groaned, explained a customer had turned up in his boxers. 'You wouldn't even walk around your house like that.

284

And Doritos before 9 a.m. For *breakfast*. The people round here.' The sound of the till being shut. 'What was I saying? Oh yes. Of course, it's wonderful that kind of racism is a thing of the past, that this place is run by Indians now, but what was the point of the fight, that struggle, if we just replace one form of bigotry with another? If we go from banning blacks to banning women? So if it's all very well with you, and your mum, and his highness, Maharaja Ranjit Singh, I will continue to go there occasionally.'

The speech had impressed me. Though, to be honest, the full effect, when I repeated elements of it to Ranjit, was rather undermined by the acoustics of my cubicle and the sound of Ranjit urinating thunderously, like a horse, throughout. When I got to the line 'What's the point of replacing one form of bigotry with another?', Ranjit responded with: 'Big-o – what? Can't you speak fucking English?' I could hear he was washing his hands. 'You realise there are Muslims who come in here, and for them dogs are haram. The landlord is losing bare business because of your aunt.'

'Dude. *Alcohol* is haram. If they're Muslim enough to drink then they are Muslim enough to deal with a dog.'

Ranjit began drying his hands under the drier. 'THE POINT OF DESI PUBS IS JUST TO GIVE PEOPLE A SHOT OF PUNJABI CULTURE, INNIT,' he shouted above the whirring. 'LIKE THEM IRISH MIGHT GO TO O'NEILLS JUST FOR A BIT OF NOSTALGIA. 'SIDES, WEREN'T LONG AGO WHEN GYALS WEREN'T ALLOWED IN *GORA* PAKORA PUBS.'

Irritation at Ranjit's misogyny intermingled with annoyance at his myopism. There were, officially, fewer than half a million of us in Britain, there were more Christians than Sikhs even in India. We didn't matter as much as he thought we did. 'YEAH, BUT WE DON'T LIVE IN 1934,' I shouted back.

It was at this point, as a way of changing the subject, as a result of just wanting to get my conversation with Ranjit over with as quickly as possible, I found myself bellowing, 'ANYWAY, DID MY DAD EVER MENTION ANYTHING ABOUT APPLYING FOR AN ALCOHOL LICENCE? MY MASSI RECKONS HE WAS GOING TO APPLY AND WE WERE WONDERING IF YOU WOULD OBJECT IF WE WENT AHEAD. I KNOW WE HAVEN'T COMPETED FOR YEARS BUT WITH MUM BEING SICK AND EVERYTHING WE HAVE GOT TO THINK ABOUT THE FUTURE OF THE BUSINESS SELLING IT ON AND SO FORTH, AND EVERYONE SELLS EVERYTHING NOW.'

The hand-dryer went silent. I assumed, when I heard footsteps, that Ranjit hadn't heard what I had said and had returned to the lounge. Perhaps, for the first time in our lives, Ranjit and I might have an adult conversation. I flushed the loo, relieved to be able to wash my hands in peace. The exchange had been typical not only of Ranjit, I bemoaned, but of Wolverhampton too. It was a village. An Indian village. You never really had any privacy or peace, even on the bog.

But as I turned around and pulled open the door, Ranjit was standing in front of me, his arms crossed, blocking my exit and asking, 'Why?'

'Why what?'

'Why are you asking me about a booze licence?' He pronounced 'ask' as 'axe'.

'Well . . .' There was a slight pause, during which I noticed that Ranjit had a new tattoo – of a dagger, on his neck, just below the scar he had received following an assault in his shop. I felt a little short of air. 'I am asking because . . . my aunt reckons . . . he was thinking about applying for one.'

He uncrossed his arms, stepped towards me. Ranjit was not as tall as me, but up close, his chest puffed up cartoonishly, his eyes half shut, it still felt like he was towering over me. 'You know what your problem is? Same as your pops. He didn't know his place in the world, ya get me.'

My instinctive response was to laugh, figuring this was a joke or another line from one of his idiotic martial-arts movies. But judging from the fact that he then grabbed me by the lapels of my blazer, remarked, 'Once a Chamar, always a Chamar,' and headbutted me, it was neither.

The first thing I saw when I came to was an empty milk bottle. The next thing: a bog brush, which had been discarded on the floor. Then, a grey bin, the kind reserved for sanitary towels, and a toilet, plumbed in via a hosepipe coming through the window. Ranjit was sitting on it, without his jacket, doing the one thing he did most in his life: rolling a spliff.

'Feeling at home?' he asked, without even peering down at me. 'You should. This is what your people have been doing for centuries, innit. Crawling around in da shit.'

This wasn't, strictly, accurate. I wasn't crawling, I was lying on the floor, on my back, with my shoes and jacket missing, one sock removed and my shirt hanging out of my trousers. Also, the Chamars were not toilet sweepers by tradition: my father's caste were leather workers. He was thinking of another scheduled caste. But I wasn't capable of speaking, and was rather distracted by (a) a searing pain across my skull; (b) the unfamiliarity of my surroundings; and (c) the question of why the hell Ranjit had suddenly gone postal.

Ranjit continued. 'You want to know why playas come to desi pubs?' Having put the roach into his joint, he rolled it between his thumbs and index fingers. 'Cos they have pride in their culture, innit. Pride, not suttin' you have experience of, I guess, being a cold-ass li'l Chamar.'

I had by this point managed to sit up and had pushed myself up against a wall. The tiles felt cold against my back, and cool liquid, which I assumed was snot, but turned out to be blood, trickled down my face. Slowly, I got my bearings. The bhangra playing in the distance suggested we were still in Singhfellows, while the view from the small window revealed that we were at the back of the pub. We must, I worked out, be in the disabled loo, near the banqueting suite, which I had always assumed was locked. Meanwhile, the unfamiliar look in Ranjit's eyes provided, if not an explanation, then at least a hypothesis: he had finally lost his mind.

Just a couple of his cigarettes had sent me around the bend that night in Birmingham, and he had been smoking at least three a day for two decades. Let's face it, some kind of psychotic break-down was always on the cards with Ranjit. Clearly, a compulsory detention order and some time in a mental ward beckoned. But until I found a way of alerting the men in white coats, I figured the best thing to do was to keep him talking. Fortunately, Ranjit often got chatty between his second and third cigarette of the day.

'It may not seem like much to you yo, but do you know how fuck hard Punjabis have fought through history to have some space of their own?' He lit his spliff and took a drag. 'First it was those motherfucking goras, who divided the Punjab in two, giving half to the fucking Muslims, and the other half to the fucking Hindus, leaving nothing – not a thang – to the Sikhs. Then it was dat sali kuti Indira Gandhi, who refused to give the Sikhs their own Khalistan and had thousands murdered just for suggesting it. And now in Ingerland, it is khotas like you and your aunt, who won't let us be. Do you have any idea of what we Sikhs went through during Partition, just trying to get some space of our own?'

I did. But, as you would with a crazed vagrant on the street, I let him rave on. 'Let me ejucalate you about yo' history, Mr Pataka. The Muslims went around the villages of my father disembowel-ling pregnant hoes. They slammed bare babies heads against brick walls. They cut off bare breasts and noses of other hoes and stuck metal rods up their pussies. They hanged Sikhs by their hair from trees. There were so many bodies to feast on that the vultures couldn't fly, they got so fat. That's what the goras did for us. These are the playas you're marryin' into. You. Get. Me.'

Again, this wasn't actually true. Freya and I were still tiptoeing around one another. The previous evening she had, for the first time, let me use her new flat for work while she wasn't there, but all my things had been put into storage and she had responded to my request to see Ranjit with 'Why should I care?' We were far from engaged. But I picked him up on something else. 'You know,' I began tentatively, talking like someone who was recovering from a dental procedure. 'The Sikhs and Hindus were as bad to the Muslims.'

'And where did you learn that, professor? In one of your gora books? At your battyboy school?'

He was almost shouting now. And as he did so I spotted a way out of the ludicrous situation: a red cord, the kind installed for the disabled to get help in emergencies, which people who shouldn't be using disabled loos habitually mistake for a light switch. It was tied up in a knot, but I managed to leap up and reach it, grabbing the white handles fixed on the walls as I did so, in one smooth movement.

But then. Nothing.

'Nice try, biatch.' Ranjit laughed like a Bollywood villain. He had not flinched as I had thrown myself across the room. 'You should know that nuffink in this pub works proper.'

He stood up, opposite me, and, taking a final drag of his cigarette, blew smoke directly in my face. I pushed him away, surprised for a moment to find his torso was soft to the touch; he looked like he was carved of iron, but was of flesh after all. 'What's wrong with you, you crazy fuck? Weed has made you deranged.'

He prodded me with a finger. 'That where you wrong.' He

removed his tie and broke into a rendition of 'I Can See Clearly'. 'How the fuck 'bout we make a go of this, battyboy?' He rolled up his sleeves. 'Like old times. *Street Fighter II*.' Hands behind his back. 'I'll give you a head start. Go on, motherfucker, hit me first.'

Now, maybe my brief foray into street fighting during the riots had boosted my confidence, or maybe I thought a slap would snap Ranjit out of his psychotic episode, because I called his bluff, took up his insane invitation and hit him. Hard. I'm not claiming it was a supercombo move worthy of Chun Li. But it was pretty 'fierce', as the *Street Fighter II* manual would have put it. Ranjit's head snapped back, and a flash of blood spattered out of his large nose down his starched white shirt. He stepped back, put a hand to his lip, and there was a hiatus as we both digested what had happened. His eventual reaction, when it finally came, was, like everything that afternoon, a surprise.

'Oh *teri*,' he remarked, looking down at his shirt. 'What the fuck are you doing? I've got a fucking wedding party to go to.'

I laughed nervously. He kneed me in my groin. As I doubled over, he punched me on the side of my head. Looking up at him from the floor, my ears ringing, my stubble rubbing against the tiles, with no ideas to hand, I made a pathetic attempt to buy some time.

'Hey, Ranjit,' I coughed. 'Tell me, what is this bhangra song about?'

I didn't, in truth, think he would engage me, but he actually smiled and answered.

'Good question, Chamar boy.' He listened and then sang along. '*Either I will die today/ Or crush someone. Cos when I get tired/ I whack heads open.*' He sucked his teeth. 'Quite expressive, bhangra, wouldn't you say? Better than that tutty Coldplay shit you're always listening to.'

He bent over, lifted my head up with the gentleness of a masseuse positioning a pillow for a client. Then he smashed it against the floor.

When I came to the next time, I did so to the sound of running water and a hand-dryer blasting out hot air. I could open only one eye, and that eye only a fraction, but when I finally managed it, I could make out that Ranjit had washed his shirt clean of blood and was drying it.

I may have passed out again, for the next thing I recall is Ranjit sitting on the loo once more, with another cigarette. He was still topless, his shirt hanging on a radiator. Ranjit had washed his face, the only sign of having been punched two small breaks in his upper lip. But this didn't seem to hamper his desire to talk.

'You and yo' ejucation, Mr Banga,' he resumed, when he sensed movement. 'You and your fucking auntie think you're mo' better than everyone else because you have books. And your big lyrics and dat shit. But you ever think 'bout how your Chamar father paid for your ejucation?'

My head and body, wracked with the conflicting effects of pain and sleep, succumbed to the latter. I closed my eye. Ranjit bent down, grabbed my face and forced me to look up at him.

'Who do you think paid for your private schooling, Pataka?'

'He sold the house,' I mumbled, my mouth having gone dry. 'My father sold the house.'

He let me go and laughed. 'Let me guess, you weren't too dope at maths. You know how much he got for that house? How much scrilla he was making in the shop? Take a guess who made up for Daddy's shortfall in the school fees, eh?'

Shortfall? Since when did Ranjit use words like 'shortfall'? The sudden improvement in his English was as surreal as the violent turn in events.

'What?'

'We paid your school fees.'

I didn't want to hear this. 'Fuck off.'

He laughed. 'My pops. Paid. Your. School. Fees. And. For. Your. Time. At. Uni. Ya get me?'

It was ironic, I suppose, that in that moment, lying on a bathroom floor, I felt an intense need to go to the toilet. I didn't want to accept what I was hearing, wanted to dismiss it all as the nonsensical rambling of a disturbed man. But it made sense, in a perverted way. It explained why my father could never seriously bring himself to compete with the Dhandas. Why my mother was so sycophantic towards them. Why my aunt thought money was regularly going missing from my father's accounts. God, it even explained why he was so devastated when I dropped out of my medicine to study design. My legs went cold.

'Course, my father was aiight about the dosh. That's how the fuck tha oldies hit dat shizzle up dem days. Help out a brother, innit. And know what, was worth it, just as an investment. Wiped out the competition, innit. My old fella was even rappin' 'bout ending the payments, cancelling out the loan.'

If I wasn't already on the floor, I would have laid down on it anyway, to lament my existence. 'Don't worry, I will pay you back,' I grunted. 'However much it is. My aunt will pay you back.' I thought of her wedding jewellery. 'She has the money.'

'You think this is about money? This is not about chedda, you wasteman. My little shit-sweeper friend.' He placed the tip of his shoe on my right hand and increased the pressure as he continued. 'This is about izzat, 'bout the fact that after decades of our generosity and support, yo' daddy decides to repay our asses by sayin' he wants to compete. Calls me up, says he wants to talk. Just like you. Wants to start pushin booze fo' realz. Asks if I would object to his ass applyin fo' a licence.' The pain across my hand was now making me weep. 'Guess what, I had bare objections.'

At this point Ranjit released my hand and walked around the room, as if he was stretching his legs before a run. In agony, I put my hand between my legs, and through the corner of my one open eye I saw him pick up the plastic bin next to the toilet, empty the contents on the floor – a load of tissues – and pull out the plastic orange bag that lined it.

'You know what's so sick about shops? Always plastic bags about.' He flicked the bag in the air so that it inflated. 'And you know what's so sick about plastic bags? They don't leave a single mark on the body. Though helps when someone like your Chamar dad has heart probz anyway.'

For a moment, I froze. And it could only have been a moment. But I lived it more intensely than any moment I had lived before. The preceding year suddenly made sense, as I realised that this was why Ranjit had been so keen to 'help' me get my mum out of the shop. At the same time I sensed my future and knew I wanted to live it. I had told myself several times in the preceding months that I didn't want to carry on, that I was holding on only for my mother. But it wasn't true. Somehow, aided by adrenalin and anger, I got up, and with my one good hand grabbed the plastic bag from Ranjit's chunky hands, tugging at it until it ripped in two.

Then I went at him with everything I had: wild kicks and slaps and swings and tugs of the hair. It was the computer game equivalent of pressing all the buttons on the keypad at once and hoping for the best. But the best was not what I achieved. The pain and the dizziness returned and soon I was on the floor, Ranjit having absorbed my blows with the indifference of a punchbag.

Bored, finally, of toying around, he pushed his kara down his wrist and on to his knuckles and punched me in the head. He followed it with a kick in the gut, not even blinking at the vomit and blood that spurted across the floor. Then, as I whimpered, he picked up the largest remnant of the plastic bag from the floor and stretched it taut. I remember his face seemed eerily calm through the orange plastic: it was not twisted or contorted. Then, thinking I didn't want this to be the last thing I saw, I switched my blurred focus to the one attractive thing in the room, a bleach bottle decorated with a picture of a meadow.

He knelt down. And I imagined it happening: the world going orange, and then red, my chest tightening as it did so. But then something fantastically banal occurred: the door opened slightly.

God. He hadn't locked it.

Ranjit stood stock still. And, perhaps sensing movement in the room, so did the person on the other side. Ranjit coughed and, putting on his best English accent, shouted, 'Excuse me!' It was a rather good impression of polite outrage, and seemed to have the desired effect when the voice on the other side responded with, 'So sorry, this toilet isn't usually occupied,' and began closing the door. But then Ranjit undermined his work with, 'I'm having a fucking shit.'

The door stopped closing. A voice in the corridor responded with, 'Well, do you know, there's no women's toilet in this godforsaken establishment,' and then a small dog darted through the opening, walked up to the vomit and blood which was plastered like a child's painting across the floor, and started lapping it up.

Jessie.

Confusion ensued. For some reason I cried out the dog's name, instead of my aunt's. She nevertheless pushed open the door, and instead of yelping out at the bloody scene, she stood on the spot and announced to no one in particular that she had 'come in for a drink, Kamaljit has been driving me around the bend'.

Ranjit responded to the bizarre declaration by producing some hand cream from his trouser pocket. He smothered his fists with it and then uttered some unexpected ramblings of his own.

'Kiddha, bhua-ji,' he said, torn briefly between the urge to commit homicide and respect his elders.

Looking at them, you would have thought they were extended

family members becoming reacquainted in the foyer of a temple at a wedding. I may as well have not been there. Ranjit did eventually lunge at my aunt, but it was almost an afterthought. I tripped him up as he did so, and he fell, like an oak tree, to the floor.

A frosty morning in the West Midlands and two groups of people stand blinking in the courtyard of a gurdwara, unsteady from the effects of an early start and two nights of drinking neat Scotch. The men, as tradition dictates, are dressed in lounge suits, some with ties, some without, their heads covered with hankies in the style of Italian politicians on holiday. The women, as tradition dictates, are decked out in suits and saris of blue and green and pink — anything but bridal red. The whole thing, as is customary, is running ninety minutes behind schedule.

However, the trained eye will spot this is not your conventional Indian wedding. The congregation, for one thing, amounts to fewer than a hundred — minuscule by the standards of these things. Not all the couples have divided along lines of sex, with some men and women leaning against each other as they look on, a few even holding hands. And after the guests have bowed at the conclusion of the opening prayers, touched the ground or knelt upon it, according to their religiosity or physical dexterity, the groom's side has only one person to offer for the milni.

She appears again and again as the families are formally introduced to one another, to exchange gifts, hang garlands, posing for photographs with the mother, the father, the aunt and the uncle of the bride.

'Is that her?' whispers a voice from the bride's side.

'You think she's had work done?' answers his partner.

'I reckon.' A peer around. 'Where's the bride then?'

The bride is in a chamber indoors, mehndi patterns meandering around her hands and arms, fighting a losing battle with a make-up artist insisting on gallons of foundation and eye liner. She is still fighting as the congregation wander into the langar hall, to eat samosas and sip overly sweet tea.

The tables are arranged in long, parallel lines, the traditional divide between the sexes defied once again, the groom standing in the middle, resplendent in an embroidered sherwani and red turban. People keep remarking on how elegant he looks, but he has rarely been more uncomfortable. The beard is scratchy. The turban makes it difficult to hear what anyone is saying. He is, frankly, regretting the decision to go along with fashion, was wary about it from the start.

But then he had decided there was more to turbans than Sikhism, just as there was more to Sikhism than turbans, and it felt right on the morning of his wedding day to stand in his father's study, stretching the material in front of the mirror in his wardrobe, pinching one end with his teeth, as his father used to, having several goes at wrapping it around his head until it was perfectly symmetrical. He got it straight then, but it feels lopsided now, while the whiteness of his sherwani is courting disaster with so much tea being sloshed around so carelessly.

Of course, the tradition at this stage is for the family of the bride to serve the family of the groom, the barat having usually travelled some distance to the bride's local temple. But in another break with custom, the temple in fact not even being the groom's family's place of worship, the organisers have embraced the fashion for employing Eastern European waiters.

The guests eat and drink standing up, only the elderly or the disabled being permitted seats, the religious occasionally casti-gating the black-jacketed staff for not covering their heads, groups of Asian men discussing their hangovers, the white women remarking on how Asian women age so well, a gaggle of white men wondering out loud why everyone they are introduced to is called Jas.

'Where's the bride then?' asks a voice on the groom's side between samosas.

Not long to go before she appears. But first the guests must remove their shoes and enter the darbar hall, kneeling respectfully before the Holy Book and paying a donation before sitting down – the elderly, knowing how these things work, taking the prized positions against walls, the women creaking into position on the left, the men on the right, everyone remembering or being reminded not to point their feet at the Holy Book.

The groom takes a seat at the altar, placing his sword in front of him, and with the Kirtani Jatha singing on stage, a Sewadar waves a chaur made of yak hair over the Holy Book, the shape and texture of it matching his beard. Eventually, the bride is ushered in by helpers, dressed in a bright red traditional lehenga and gold-embroidered shawl, dripping in gold jewellery commissioned by the groom's aunt.

It is customary at this point for the congregation to comment on the bride's fairness and suitability, for the couple not to look at each other, and for her to appear downcast – a wedding, for a bride, being a sombre occasion when she is separated from her family and cast into the clutches of an unfamiliar and probably hostile extended family. But brides don't get much fairer than this, and so many tears have been shed lately that no one minds when the groom steals a glance, and the bride smiles in return.

The Kirtani Jatha stops playing. The bride's parents and, in the groom's case, the aunt, are asked to stand while a prayer is said invoking blessings for the proposed marriage. The bride's father places one end of a saffron-colored palla in the groom's hand – the palla symbolising the couple being joined to each other and God – passing it over the shoulder and placing the other end in the bride's hand. The ragis sing a hymn and the bride and groom begin walking around the Holy Book four times, each circuit symbolising a different stage of love and married life, the groom leading in a clockwise direction and the bride, holding the scarf, following as nearly as possible in step.

Throughout, those who have experienced it a thousand times before check their mobile phones, the mother of the bride, in a salwar kameez, and the father of the bride, in a fitted sherwani of his own, weep — in part because they are moved, and this has been as much of a journey for them as for their daughter, and in part because they have no feeling below their waists, not having sat cross-legged on the floor of a hall since primary school.

'What are they saying?' asks a voice on the groom's side.

'Dunno, it's in Sanskrit or something, innit,' comes the response. 'How much longer you reckon?'

The enquiry is met with a philosophical shrug. The fact is that this chap, Jas, who is playing a marathon game of *Tetris* on his phone, knows, but the key to surviving a Sikh wedding, like surviving an actual marathon, or war, is not to dwell on the length. To ask 'How long?' is to risk facing the enervating realisation that there are hours and hours to go, and in this case the congregation still faces, among other things: the customary singing of the six stanzas of the Anand Sahib; another Ardas; a vaak (a random reading of a verse from Guru Granth Sahib); the serving of Karah Parshad; the sagaan, when the parents of the bride and groom, followed by every member of the congregation, bless the newly wedded with money, posing awkwardly for staged photos as they do so; not to mention the ritual where the bridesmaids hide the groom's shoes and force him to pay a ransom, in this case more than £500.

Be grateful, though, that there will be no speech at the end of the ceremony. The groom has paid bribes, made threats and emphasised the difficulty he has in sitting cross-legged as a result of his recent injuries, in order to excise the customary rambling talk at the end of the ceremony, in which a self-important member of the temple committee, oblivious to the yawning and visible boredom of his audience, subjects the congregation to a diatribe about the declining religiosity and morality of the Sikh youth, and/or the political situation in the Punjab.

In the groom's experience, this speech is often the straw that breaks the camel's back; the thing that can make three hours feel like six, or six like twelve. Besides, when everyone moves from the temple to the working man's club down the road, he plans to defy tradition by making a speech of his own.

He has learnt it by heart, though there is a copy in his trouser pocket in case nerves get the better of him and he knows better than to wait for the audience to be quiet, for this is a Punjabi crowd and Punjabis are physiologically incapable of being quiet. Instead, he will grab a mic plugged into a PA system, and will shout over the din, beginning conventionally, by Western standards, thanking the family of the bride for paying for the wedding, for sticking by him during the last year. Then he will thank the guests, for their donations during the sagaan, which will be passed on to the hospice which cared for his mother during her final days.

He worries that the thought of his mother will make his voice crack – and while it is traditional for the brides to weep at Indian weddings, it is not for men. So if it's difficult, he will skip the next bit about how he thinks it was the revelations and the trial that did for her, rather than her illness, will not say it was some consolation that she was surrounded by such kindness in her final days, and instead move on to addressing his bride, telling her, though it is not a very Punjabi thing to do, that she looks beautiful, that he loves her more every day, that he will make it his mission in life to make her happy.

Then his aunt. His beautiful, remarkable aunt, who, sitting across the table, was the one, he will say, who persuaded him to have an Indian wedding. He was of the view that Indian weddings are too sad, even without the groom being orphaned. And the last thing he wanted after the media circus was any attention. It was not something his parents would have enjoyed either. Throughout the preparations he could imagine his mother complaining that a display would just attract the evil eye, his father worrying out loud about the expense. Besides, he was aware of teams of religious fanatics who went around disrupting mixed weddings, their argument being that it is 'hypocritical' for a bride or groom to go through a ceremony when they do not truly believe in the Sikh faith, even though one of the defining things about Sikhism is that it is an open, liberal religion, one of the few faiths of the world to acknowledge that other religions may offer a valid way of reaching God.

Frankly he wanted to get married quietly, a civil ceremony somewhere anonymous, with no risk of people barricading themselves inside gurdwaras to prevent ceremonies taking place. He had had enough of encountering bigotry, of being on display, but it was his aunt who made him realise that for too long love had been a source of shame in his family, that too many weddings had been conducted in secret, love being treated as a cause for regret. Therefore this: a big fat traditional Indian wedding, the couple being driven across Wolverhampton in his mate Matt Metcalfe's incredibly naff red Rolls-Royce Phantom (you can take the boy out of Wolverhampton, but . . .).

However, these things are relative, and we all know that beneath the surface this Indian wedding is not that big and fat at all. For, look, there are Skodas and cut-price Fords, of all things, scattered among the lines of shiny German limousines in the car park. The women will be permitted to drink during the party, as well as the men. The first dance will not be to a bhangra track with creepy allusions to the sexiness of sister-in-laws, but to something soppy by an indie band. And though Amy Wilson, her sari blouse the wrong way round, so that the cups are on the back, will drink too much and get lairy, there will not be, as is traditional, a fight in the car park.

Moreover, at the end of it all, the couple will not be heading off on honeymoon. Instead, tomorrow morning they will, with their aunt, open the family shop one final time, selling what they can, giving away the rest, emptying it out before it is taken over by new owners, who plan to convert it into a tanning salon. Then, for old time's sake, Surinder Bains will make lunch. Saag and roti, as she had been taught to make by her sister, who had, in turn, been taught by their mother.

They will wash the food down with full-fat milk, dip the chapattis in achar, go over the wedding and maybe start thinking about the future. Freya wants to give up banking for academia. Surinder would like to set up a business in London – something completely new. As for Arjan, both his aunt and his wife think he should become an artist, but he disagrees, has accepted he doesn't have the passion or the talent. But he does have half an idea about setting up some kind of gallery in London. Something specialising in Indian art, catering for all the South Asians out there with more money than taste.

His aunt likes the thought, wonders if she could perhaps run some sort of cafe or deli or even a shop alongside. Though it would have to be one of the poncy kinds that wouldn't last a minute in Blakenfields. A place where brown paper and string was used for wrapping produce. Where fresh bread was flogged over a marble counter, and where customers could rely on being served by someone who knew their name and would, on occasion, let them buy something on tick.

ACKNOWLEDGEMENTS

This book is based on *The Old Wives' Tale*, a novel originally published in 1908. I have, among other things, shoplifted characters and elements of plot, and though I cannot credit Arnold Bennett enough, I owe as much to Lottie Moggach, who introduced me to his work and helped develop the idea of a remix. Friends don't come much more generous or kind.

When it came to researching the post-war political history of Wolverhampton, Frank Reeves' *Race and Borough Politics* and David Beetham's *Transport and Turbans* proved indispensable, while Ned Williams' works of local history provided an eloquent guide to the changing geography of my home town.

All quotes from newspapers and magazines are taken or adapted from contemporaneous publications, while the occasional paragraph may have previously appeared in draft form under my byline, with a feature about working in a Black Country newsagent for *The Times Magazine* providing a starting point for my research into shop life.

My editor Jason Arthur worked hard to help shape this book, and my brilliant agent Sarah Chalfant ensured I had the thing writers require most: time. I am indebted, in addition, to Lucy Kellaway and Mona Arshi for their critical guidance, and to Amandeep Madra and Nikesh Shukla for help with cultural references.

My gratitude also to all those who helped with research and advice, including: Nikita Amin, Aman Aneja, Graham Archard,

Perjit Aujla, Adam Bannister, Harjit Beghal, Sandeep Bhabra, Kuljeet Chahal, Aryn Clark, Katie Cooper, Celia Duncan, Dean Edwards, Lucy Ellison, Sarah Foden, Paddy Gill, Lachlan Goudie, Pamela Gupta, James Harding, Anoushka Healy, Nicola Jeal, Viney Jung, Jaskaran Kaur, Urmee Khan, Jamie Klinger, Lucy Kroll, Nirmalya Kumar, Chris Morgan, Mary Mount, Amarjit Nakhwal, Manjinder Nakhwal, Mark Payne, David Radburn, Sami Rahman, Robin Roberts, James Rothwell, Sarvjit Sra, Amit Sunsoa, Daniel Wainwright, Anna-Sophia Watts, and the staff at Wolverhampton Archives.